The Road To Glory

The Road
To Glory

Blayne Cooper
and
T. Novan

Renaissance Alliance Publishing, Inc.
Nederland, Texas

ISBN 1-930928-27-0

First Printing 2002

9 8 7 6 5 4 3 2 1

Cover design by Mary D. Brooks
Back cover artwork by Lúcia A. de Nóbrega

Published by:

Renaissance Alliance Publishing, Inc.
PMB 238, 8691 9th Avenue
Port Arthur, Texas 77642-8025

Find us on the World Wide Web at
http://www.rapbooks.biz

Printed in the United States of America

ACKNOWLEDGEMENTS

To A. E. Carpenter, Medora MacDougall, and RS Corliss—
your assistance was invaluable. To the friends who read
parts of this story and offered sage advice, criticisms, and
compliments—we love you. Day, your editing made this a
better book.

— Blayne Cooper
and T. Novan

DEDICATIONS

This book is dedicated to those precious few among us who refuse to take part in the maddening quest for a single, earth-shattered, once in a lifetime, love—but find it anyway. Lucky bums.

— Blayne Cooper

To the victims, families and heroes of September 11, 2001, may God bless. We will never forget.

Taylor: I love you.

RT, LL, ROC, as always thank you for sharing your gifts.

— T. Novan

Chapter
1

The stars twinkled overhead as Leigh Matthews barreled down I-90 at a constant speed of seventy miles per hour. Despite the fact that it was nearly summer, the cool evening air had forced her to flip on her heater at the last mile marker. It had been a long day of driving and, worst of all, it would start all over again—she glanced at her dashboard board clock—in less than six hours.

"What the—" Leigh mumbled as an unexpected Day-Glo detour sign directed her off the interstate and onto a lonely county road. It was paved and well-marked, but wasn't as straight as the highway had been. Leigh reduced her speed to fifty-five. What little traffic there had been moments before thinned out to nothing, leaving the young woman alone with only the night and her radio for company.

As her truck's cab grew warmer and warmer, Leigh's eyelids grew heavier and her breathing, slower and deeper. She pushed shaggy blonde bangs off her forehead and leaned forward to fiddle with the radio.

"Sinners, repent!"

Leigh jumped.

"Let Jeeeeeesus into your heart!" the speakers blared.

"Aw, Christ. Is it *really* necessary to take all the fun out of being a sinner?" Leigh rolled her eyes, carefully steered around an enormous, unidentified hunk of roadkill, and changed the radio station—somehow managing to do all three things at the same time. She hated A.M. radio, especially in the middle of the night and *most* especially in the middle of nowhere. Leigh had already listened to all of her books on tape, and her much-loved CDs held no allure at this late hour. She stifled a yawn and made a slow turn onto another road as another detour sign directed. *Why hadn't anyone mentioned this detour?*

Leigh blearily glanced down at her silent CB radio. Disgusted, she'd flipped it off earlier when she couldn't stomach another second of hearing how Big Bubby Bumboski had conned his portly, and clearly stupid, wife into believing he had an emergency run that would take him the better part of a week. Half the state knew he was going to meet his girlfriend and their two sons. Bubby had gone on and on about how proud he was of the oldest boy. It seems Little Big Bubby had made parole just in time for the visit.

The second turn had sent her into an area even more desolate than the first, and Leigh fuzzily began to wonder if she'd somehow gotten lost. Her breaths began to lengthen again, and her head began to droop. Her eyes fluttered closed...just for a second.

Leigh's head snapped up. Her eyes popped open at the sound of gravel under her wheels. Instinctively, she slammed on her brakes, kicking up a cloud of dust as the massive truck skidded to a halt along the side of the road. *Good thing I'm riding bobtail.* It would have taken three times the distance to stop with a full rig. Shakily, she clicked off the ignition and was enveloped in stony silence.

Leigh blinked dazedly, her heart pounding a mile a minute, adrenaline coursing through her veins. "Damn." *I fell asleep on the road? I haven't done that since I started driving!* She gazed out the large windshield at her surroundings. It was pitch black...almost. Leigh squinted bloodshot, baby blues as she peered down the road. Off in the distance, she could see the faint glow of lights on a sign. "Thank you, God! A motel. I'm going to get a shower after all," she said to no one. Sure, talking to yourself was a clear sign of insanity. But then again, Leigh was pretty certain a truly insane person wouldn't give a shit. So why should she?

Leigh had grown up on the road with her dad and knew that no matter how desolate an area seemed, you usually weren't too far from one of the thousands of mom-and-pop motels that lined America's highways. They catered to truckers like herself and other weary, or just plain lost, travelers.

The young woman started up the engine again, and her cherry-red big rig rumbled to life, its high beams cutting through the darkness. Slowly, she pulled back onto the road, hearing the familiar sound of crunching gravel die away as her wheels found the pavement. By the time Leigh shifted from third to fourth gear, it was already time to slow down again. She snorted at the flickering sign that read "ritz's." "Looks like I found the Ritz in the middle of the boonies. Who knew?"

Leigh pulled alongside the small building and pushed open the cab door. She was immediately greeted by a loud chorus of chirping crickets and the smell of damp prairie grass. The wind tossed her hair as she jumped down onto the dirt parking lot. With every footstep, she could feel her dreams of a hot shower and a big bed going up in smoke.

She wanted to stamp her foot in disappointment, but somehow resisted the urge. A fit where no one could see it, after all, didn't serve much purpose. Instead, she hung her head and scrubbed her face tiredly as she approached the building. This was no hotel. It was a diner. And—from the look of the darkened windows and the dim outline of chairs propped up on the tables—a very closed diner.

With a slight growl, Leigh stalked back to the truck and climbed inside. She locked her door and then the passenger's side door. Behind the two front seats was the thin curtain that separated Leigh's workplace from her home. She kicked off her shoes, not caring where they ended up, and tugged off her lightweight denim shirt and bra.

A small but comfortable bed folded down from the back wall of the truck, and the tired woman flopped down gracelessly, not bothering to remove her blue jeans.

She was asleep before her head hit the pillow.

Leigh's eyes fluttered open, and she moaned softly. "Noooo, it can't be morning yet. Go away," she petulantly ordered the sun. But for some reason, the sunshine streaming through the windows rudely refused to obey her command. She slid on a clean shirt and grabbed the backpack that contained her toiletries.

Yawning, she riffled her fingers through her short, fair hair in a half-hearted attempt to make herself semi-presentable. But to be honest, right now she was more interested in finding a bathroom than looking pretty. Blonde or no, it wasn't like she was going to be confused with that insane Martha Stewart anyway. Nature was calling. Loudly. Using her hand to block the sun from her eyes, Leigh stared up at the large sign on top of the diner. The place was called "Fitz's" not "ritz's," the top half of the "F" being burnt out.

When Leigh's gaze dropped from the dilapidated sign, it landed squarely on a figure leaning back in a wooden chair, sitting in shadows outside the diner door. Her eyes widened slightly. The body was long and lean, dressed in beige cargo pants and a blue cotton shirt, its two booted feet propped up on a barrel. *Holy hot damn.* She tried not to stare, but abandoned that idea immediately since she really did want a good look at whoever this was.

Please be a woman, please be a woman, Leigh chanted inwardly. Another two strides, and even through the light cloud of smoke that swirled around the body, a head of thick, short auburn hair came clearly into view. Leigh's eyes dropped to the pale blue shirt, which was, she could see now, unbuttoned, with a crisp, white t-shirt underneath. Then...*cha-ching!* Bells that sounded remarkably like a cash register opening went off in her mind as she took in the vision of two well-shaped breasts and a slender neck. A tiny growl escaped her throat, and she strained to more clearly make out the features of the woman's face.

Leigh stopped abruptly when a harried-looking father, holding the hands of two small boys, scurried past her and into the diner. "Potty emergency," was all the man said by way of an apology.

The woman in the chair took another long drag off her cigarette before tossing the stub into a butt can that sat alongside her. Then she brought a frosty, glass Coke bottle to her mouth and took a healthy swig. "Ahhh..." she hummed, smacking her lips with almost sensual pleasure. *Nothin' like a little carbonation to burn away the mornin' fuzzies.* Her green eyes tracked Leigh with idle curiosity as the short woman approached. She snorted and dropped one foot from the barrel, using the toe of her boot to scratch the belly of the cat that sat on the porch below her feet. *Lordy, it seems they're lettin' runts truck nowadays.*

Flea, a coal-black cat, groaned, causing the woman to chuckle. "Thirsty? You've had a hard morning of doing absolutely nothing. I'm sure you've worked up a powerful thirst."

From her position sprawled out on her back, Flea merely opened her mouth. The green-eyed woman finally tore her eyes from the blonde and casually leaned over to pour her Coke directly into Flea's waiting mouth.

As Leigh stepped onto the diner's porch, her jaw sagged at the spectacle. She was so engrossed at the sight of the beautiful woman, not to mention the feline lapping up a continuous stream of Coca Cola, that she didn't even see the door in front of her swing open. Until it hit her right in the face.

"Jesus, Mary and Joseph!" The woman in the chair jumped to her feet just as Leigh was knocked backwards, landing on her bottom with a resounding thud. A cloud of fine dust kicked up around her, and she coughed weakly as her world spun.

A short, heavyset man, who looked to be pushing sixty, came barreling out of the diner and immediately dropped to Leigh's side. He swallowed nervously, patting her back gently as she coughed again and tried to fan away the dust with erratic hand movements. "Are you okay, miss?"

Leigh had one hand cupped over the eye that was throbbing with her every heartbeat. She could already feel it swelling shut. "I um...I think so." She looked intently at the man, her brow furrowing. "And do I need to tell it to your twin, too?"

He glanced at the empty space next to him where Leigh was pointing. "Oh boy. I'm so sorry." The man offered her his hand, helping her stand. "I'm Pete."

"Hi, Pete. I'm—" She momentarily faltered as the diner, not ten feet in front of her, began to blur. *I'm going to pass out?*

"Whoa there, miss." Pete, who was dressed in white pants, a blindingly white t-shirt and a green apron with "Fitz's" emblazoned across the chest, wrapped a supportive arm around Leigh. "We'd better go inside and get some ice on that eye. Breakfast is on the house." His gaze flickered over to the tall woman. "Fitz, were you just going to leave her here in the dirt?" he asked grumpily.

"Bu—"

"And I thought you were going to fix that burned out sign." Pete shook his head. "I should fire your—"

"I'm fine," Leigh cut in, trying to get a better look at this Fitz woman, but now her good eye was tearing so much she

couldn't see much of anything. "Really. I was just going to
take..." She paused and her mind worked silently as she tried to
rephrase what she was going to say. "Umm..."

Pete grunted knowingly and offered, "There's a washroom
inside. C'mon." He pulled open the door, and Leigh was immediately assaulted by the delicious smell of sizzling bacon and
coffee.

"Oh, damn, that smells good. But first things first." She
made a beeline for the bathroom, automatically heading for the
rear of the diner where she knew it would be, saying a small
prayer of thanks that the door wasn't locked.

Just before leaving, she scrubbed her face with icy water
and brushed her teeth with the toothbrush she kept in her backpack. Leigh glanced in the mirror and sighed ruefully. "Not
great." Once again, she ran her fingers through her hair. This
was as good as she was going to look without a shower and a full
night's sleep, and while sporting what was already promising to
become a black eye Muhammad Ali would be proud of.

*Oh, man, the guys at Rosie's are never gonna let me live this
down. I'd better come up with a hell of a story to go with it.
Getting banged in the face by the door while checking out the
local eye candy and some bizarro cat is definitely one they'd
believe; it's just not one I'm going to give them the satisfaction
of laughing at.* She cringed at the sliver of bloodshot blue barely
visible between her puffy eyelids. *And to think I thought that
saying about things only being fun until someone loses an eye
was a crock of shit. Wrong!*

Leigh rinsed her toothbrush again, put it back in its case,
and tossed it in her backpack. "Breakfast and coffee. That's the
ticket."

Her stomach rumbled as she bellied up to the counter and
perched on a padded stool that swiveled as she turned.

Pete chuckled. "Coffee. Over hard, side of hash browns,
bagel, and two meats?"

Leigh could only nod and groan—the man was a mind
reader. She was afraid that if she spoke, the drool that had been
pooling in her mouth at the aroma of a hot breakfast would spill
out onto the floor. She swallowed and looked around, taking in
the retro 1930s or 1940s décor—she wasn't sure which. It was
charming in a weird sort of way. "Where is this place?"

"Heaven, of course," a waitress from behind the counter
answered sassily. "Couldn't you tell by the parking lot? We

fixed all the pot holes."

Pete made a face. "Very funny, Mavis." With a stubby finger, he pointed to a booth that had just gone empty. "Don't you have dishes to bus?"

"Yeah, yeah." Mavis waved him off and poured another cup of coffee for a man at the counter.

Pete turned to Leigh. "Welcome to Fitz's. The woman out front was RJ Fitzgerald, but despite the place's name, it's my diner."

"He lost a bet and she made him change the name," Mavis piped up helpfully.

Pete narrowed his hazel eyes, his gaze burning a hole through the waitress. "Thank you so much, Mavis," he said through clenched teeth. "By the way, I have a feeling the grease trap is going to need cleaning today. And tomorrow."

Mavis blanched and scooted her skinny body toward the dirty booth. At least there she'd only be able to get into a little trouble.

Leigh watched Pete and Mavis with mild amusement. "I saw the sign with the name on it out front. I meant—where exactly is the diner? I hit an unexpected detour last night."

"Ah." Pete nodded. "We've been getting you folks all morning." He poured Leigh a cup of coffee and set down a small pitcher of fresh cream and a bowl of sugar. "The nearest town is about twenty miles due north."

Leigh didn't comment. She'd check the map in her truck later. She poured cream into her coffee until it was a pale beige, not bothering to stir the cloudy mixture.

She waited while Pete waved a goodbye to the man who'd run in moments before with the two little boys in tow. When the screen door slammed, he glanced down, seeing Leigh's expectant eyes. "Oh, sorry." Pete grinned. "You are sitting exactly twenty miles from Glory, South Dakota. Population—"

"Who cares!" a group of old men playing dominos at a center table sang out.

"The lady asked, you grumpy old goats!" Pete reprimanded, shaking his dishtowel at the crusty men.

Leigh chuckled behind the rim of her coffee cup. Too many years of being on the road with her father had brought her into a million of these places. Now that she was inside, it only took a second for her seasoned gaze to tell her that this was more than just a place for travelers to eat. This was, to a precious few, a second home. Regulars were family—if not by blood, then by friendship and caring.

Pete winced at the bright purple shiner that Leigh was now sprouting. "Let me get you something cold for that eye. Be right back," he mumbled as he headed into the kitchen.

Leigh turned around slightly when the creaking of the screen door announced someone's arrival.

RJ Fitzgerald strolled into the diner, the empty Coke bottle held loosely by her fingertips, the bottle swaying back and forth in time with her long stride. She slid behind the opposite end of the counter Leigh was sitting at, and put the bottle away in a crate of others just like it. The sound of glass hitting glass was barely audible over the constant clatter of clinking silverware. RJ picked up a thick, white ceramic coffee cup. Unconsciously twirling it on her index finger, she crossed to a hotplate holding several silver pots of freshly brewed java. RJ glanced over her shoulder at Leigh and flashed her a sympathetic grin. *That eye's gonna be swelled shut tighter than a Scotsman's wallet in no time. Poor lass.*

RJ shifted to face the trucker fully and, after pouring the coffee, braced her elbows on the white, coffee-stained Formica countertop. She sipped her coffee and when she was completely sure she had Leigh's undivided attention, which, in truth, she'd had from the moment she walked in the door, she pointed to her own eye and mouthed, "You okay?"

Leigh's fingertips grazed the bruised flesh on the side of her face. It was tender, but not excruciating; and she smiled back and nodded her head. *I'd be more okay if you were sitting in my lap naked. God, I love butch.*

RJ winked, and then turned so she could yell through the serving window to Pete, who was still fiddling with an ice pack.

"Just so you'll know, at this rate her eye will be healed and her grandchildren will be grown before you get that back out here," she tormented, stealing a piece of bacon off one of the plates a hefty black woman had slid forward through the service window for Mavis.

Leigh sucked in an appreciative breath. Now that her head wasn't spinning from the impact of the door, she could for the first time truly hear and appreciate the sweet Irish lilt that laced RJ's words.

"Fitz!" Mavis barked, automatically adding more bacon to the plate in her hands. If RJ had been anywhere near it, the wait-

ress knew the serving would come up short. "Take yourself outside and find something useful to do. Don't be in here causing
more trouble." Mavis' warning was delivered in such an
aggrieved, mothering tone that it caused the young couple in the
booth near the door to cover their mouths to hide their sniggers
at RJ's scolding.

"*More* trouble? I'd like to know what I did the first time."
RJ crossed her arms over her chest, obviously waiting for an
answer. "It's not like it was my fault that she got hit in the face
with the door."

"Fitz, out!" This time the order came from the group of
men playing dominoes.

RJ shot the rusty codgers a dirty look. "I'm going. I'm
going. I know when I'm not wanted." She pulled a soft cotton
cap from her back pocket and tugged it onto her head, her wavy,
collar-length locks sticking out in wild directions in the back.
"I'll just go out back and play with a very sharp ax."

She grabbed a pair of well-worn leather gloves from her
other back pocket and slipped one on. When she walked past
Leigh, she grinned and flashed the fairer woman a heart-stopping
smile. "Hope that eye feels better, miss. I'm sorry I can't stay
and chat, but as you can see, I'm being kicked outta here on my
arse."

Leigh couldn't help but laugh along with the other diner
patrons. She had never actually heard someone with such a
charming accent. She smiled at RJ, and the tall woman disappeared out the door.

Pete returned from the kitchen with an ice pack and a deli-
cious-smelling plate of food, which he slid in front of Leigh.
"There you go, young lady." He sheepishly gestured at Leigh's
face. "I really am sorry about that."

"It's okay." Leigh shrugged, her mind more on RJ than her
conversion with Pete. "These things happen."

RJ peeled off her shirt and tossed it onto a picnic table,
leaving her clad in a men's white, sleeveless undershirt. Her
pale, slightly freckled skin instantly warmed in the strong morning sun, and she sighed contentedly, rolling the shoulders that
were now free from any constriction. Then she moved to the old
stump where a long-handled ax was buried, and yanked it free.

Next, she picked up a one-foot maple round that needed to be split so it could be used to fire up the open-pit barbecue later in the week.

Forest-green eyes flicked up and stared at the diner. She could see inside through the open, back screen door, and had a perfect view of Leigh's left leg. To RJ, it seemed that the vibrant woman was having a good time, drinking her coffee and devouring her breakfast. *And so what if I can only see just a little bit of her leg and foot? It's a very expressive foot!*

Without looking, RJ drove the blade of the ax directly into the center of the round, chopping it neatly in half. Years of chopping wood had made it second nature, and she proceeded by rote, her mind wandering as she picked up one of the half-rounds and placed it back on the stump to be split again. Right now, her thoughts were wandering all over a certain petite, blue-eyed blonde trucker. Just like her hands were itching to do. RJ moaned. Loudly.

Flea shuffled around the side of the building and flopped down in the shade of a large tree. She yawned and began licking her paws as her piercing yellow eyes watched RJ chop wood. Flea was glad she wasn't human. *Too much work. Losers.*

RJ finally looked down at her four-legged companion and cocked her head to the side. "All right. I admit it. She's a nice looking dame. Too bad she's not—"

Before the woman could continue her conversation with the cat, Leigh came around the side of the building with her back-pack slung over her shoulder. She marched right up to RJ, allowing her eyes to sweep the length of the taller woman's lanky frame.

Leigh's admiration of RJ's body was so frank and unabashed that RJ actually felt her cheeks heat as she lifted her ax for another swing. *Lord! I don't feel this exposed in only my birthday suit!*

The blonde woman smiled, pleased at the sweet flush covering RJ's face. "Excuse me, but, umm, Pete said there was an actual shower around here somewhere that I could use?" Her tone was doubtful, though she had no real reason to mistrust Pete. He had given her a free breakfast, and in the great pecking order of life, that put him just below her dead father and above everyone else.

RJ completely missed the half-round and, instead, buried the blade into the stump on which the maple block was sitting.

She groaned inwardly, thinking she was lucky she hadn't cut off her foot. She pushed back her supreme embarrassment, outwardly projecting an air of total confidence and serenity. RJ jerked a thumb toward the ax and said casually, "I meant to do that."

Leigh glanced down at the ax that was embedded at an odd angle, nearly shaving off the outside edge of the stump. "I'm sure you did," she said seriously, all the while wrestling the smile from her face.

RJ pulled a white handkerchief out of what Leigh was beginning to suspect were bottomless back pockets and wiped her forehead.

"Shower?" Leigh reminded.

"Oh, yeah, right in there." RJ tilted her head toward the building next to the diner. "It's the old garage. You won't find anyone lurking about in there, unless it'd be George, working on that clunker automobile of his. And I don't think he's here today. But there's a full shower in the back and a rack of clean towels besides. Help yourself."

Leigh smiled and adjusted the pack on her shoulder. It was on the tip of her tongue to ask RJ on a date or to join her in the shower. One or the other. Hell, she'd never been shy around women, and her gaydar was pinging so loudly when it came to RJ she was surprised she could still see straight. So to speak. "Thanks. Will um—" Leigh paused when she spied an old rusted-out 1942 Ford pickup parked alongside the garage. She snorted as she took in the ill-kept machine, saying the first thing that popped into her mind. "What self-respecting soul would drive such a piece of shit?"

RJ looked at the black truck, her brow creasing. *Piece of shit?* She scratched her jaw. "I guess that person would be me. Seeing as how that's my truck."

Leigh's eyes widened. *Oh my God.* "Ahh..." She winced and tried to think of something nice to say about the dilapidated machine.

Leigh had no qualms about bullshitting the ladies. Hell, she'd learned at her daddy's knee. And his nickname wasn't "Tom Cat" for nothing. When he'd died two years ago and she'd gone from doing the family bookkeeping to driving the big rig herself, the trucking community had taken to calling her "Tom Cat" too, though usually not to her face.

But she never, ever, stretched the truth when it came to

trucks. Even itty bitty ones. A woman had to have some princi-
ples. "I'm sorry."

RJ put one hand on her hip, sensing Leigh's quandary. "Are
you sorry that it's my truck, or for insulting it so?"

Leigh bit her lower lip. "Yes."

RJ's eyebrows jumped. *She's a sassy enough thing, that's
for certain. But still, there's no denying she's got a great backside.* RJ pulled the ax free and straightened the half-round she'd
missed on her previous swing. She didn't bother to look at Leigh
as she said, "Shower's in the garage. Door's unlocked."

The tall woman's demeanor had definitely cooled, and
Leigh tried not to frown visibly. *Great. She's the sensitive type.*
Secretly, Leigh believed that if you weren't too sensitive to actually be caught riding in—or worse *driving*—a piece of shit, you
shouldn't get upset when people commented about it. True, the
truck *was* unfit to share the roads with decent, well-loved vehi-
cles, but it had been Leigh's experience that nobody really liked
to hear that. She gave a short nod and quickly began making her
way to the garage, muttering another apology under her breath as
she passed RJ.

And though it wasn't easy, at the same time Leigh catego-
rized RJ Fitzgerald in that ever-so-tiny compartment of her brain
she'd dedicated to "those that got away." Now she was heading
for a hot shower, and later—the peace and loneliness of the open
road.

Chapter
2

RJ stepped into Sam's barbershop. Flea had wrapped herself around RJ's shoulders and was using the tall woman as a cat taxi. When RJ shut the door behind her, she gave a little shrug and Flea jumped down, immediately finding the soft pillow in the corner of the shop that was reserved solely for her.

RJ removed her cap, stuffing it in her back pocket. She huffed to herself, noting that every pair of eyes in the shop had trained themselves on her. With a quick movement, she stuffed her aviator sunglasses into the front pocket of her shirt.

The brunette stared back at the small crowd of men. "What? Did I grow another head? If I did, I'm sure it'll be needing its hair cut, too." She settled down in the chair, kicking long legs out in front of her and giving an almost dirty look to Sammy, the barber.

"You know," Sammy started, even as he snapped the cape around her neck then ran a comb through RJ's thick hair, "you are a woman. It would be okay if you wanted to let this grow out."

RJ's hand immediately went to her head. Her hair was barely trimmed up off her ears and worn combed straight back. It was longer on top, her uneven, reddish-brown waves just grazing the bottom edge of her shirt collar in back. "I know I'm a woman, you silly bastard. I also know I like my hair just fine the way it is. It's easy to take care of this way. So just cut it and keep the commentary to yourself."

"Yes, ma'am," Sammy snorted, taking his scissors in hand. Much to RJ's mother's chagrin, he'd been cutting RJ's hair ever since Mildred, the owner of the local beauty salon, had refused to give RJ her preferred short cut when RJ was still in high school. They had the same argument every time she came in. He always waited until she called him a "silly bastard" before he started cutting her hair. It was his own half-hearted protest. He knew that some young women liked it short nowadays, though why was still a mystery to him.

A man whose face was still shiny and stinging from the aftershave that had been slapped on it sat alongside RJ. He turned the page of his magazine. "That little trucker at the diner had pretty blonde hair," Luke said, his eyes never leaving the magazine. "Still, my tastes have always run to longer style. Remember Rita Hayworth? Now that was some lovely hair."

"Remember?" Johnny replied incredulously. "Do I look senile to you?" He leaned against the table that held the shop's cash register. "But the trucker was a looker." Johnny gave RJ a shit-eating grin. "I'm thinking her hair was damn near the exact color of sweet corn in the summertime." He shrugged. "Short and shaggy-looking, but still feminine." The slim man strolled over to Luke, who was now chuckling and holding his magazine unnaturally high so as to cover his face. "She was a real looker, wasn't she, Fitz?"

"I didn't notice her hair." RJ shifted uncomfortably in her chair. *I should have known coming here today would be a mistake.*

A third man with a rotund belly and a half-smoked cigar hanging out of his mouth croaked from his spot at the checkerboard in the corner, "Of course not, you were too busy looking at her boobs."

"I was not!" RJ defended, almost coming out of the chair.

"Damn it, RJ, settle down before I scalp you bald!" Sammy ordered, pushing the woman back into the chair and resettling the cape around her shoulders.

"You're all nasty old goats, the lot of you." RJ's cheeks were flaming hot, and by the intensified laughter among the men, she knew they looked as flushed as they felt. "I don't know why I put up with you."

"Because this is the only barbershop in town, and if you didn't come in here you'd be forced to cut it yourself. Then you'd be in a real mess." Johnny grinned as he crossed over to the checkerboard and jumped several of his opponent's pieces. "King me, Charlie."

Charlie's eyes turned to slits, and he yanked his cigar from his mouth. "I'd like to king you, you cheatin' rat bas—"

Johnny tossed the magazine into the pile, then leaned over to the old-fashioned cooler where Sammy kept a stash of frosty root beers. "So, if you didn't notice her hair and you weren't looking at her marangas, what did you notice? Her butt?"

"It was shaped just right," Luke cooed dreamily, just to torment RJ further.

"Bunch of perverts. I can't count the years between you, and you were staring at her backside? Hey," RJ pointed at Johnny, "don't even think of opening that root beer unless you're prepared to share with Flea. She has feelings, too."

RJ's words proved prophetic, and the cat silently wandered over and flopped down in front of Johnny. She scratched her face with one slender paw before rolling onto her back and opening her mouth, waiting.

"You spoil her." Johnny pried the top off the bottle with the opener attached to the machine, careful not to let the bottle cap drop into Flea's gaping mouth.

"That's what she's here for, among other things—to keep me company, and so I can spoil her. You're just jealous."

"Bet she gets steak or liver two times a week, doesn't she?" Johnny drizzled a little of the fizzing liquid into the black cat's gulping mouth, then he took a long drink himself before wiping his lips on the back of his sleeve. He looked at his sleeve and smiled at the small stain. He was damn near positive he'd gotten it all out of his mustache in one try. His horoscope had been so right. Today was going to be a great day!

RJ tilted her head down, and Sammy snipped no more than a quarter of an inch off the back of her auburn locks. He gathered a little of RJ's hair in his hand, thinking she could wear it in a tiny ponytail if she had a mind to.

"Flea gets liver twice a week, steak twice a week, and chicken twice a week. On Fridays we all have fish." RJ's tone turned irritated. "We're Catholic, you know."

Luke sniggered. "You might be Catholic. I'm not sure Flea is."

"Doesn't matter. I eat fish, Flea eats fish. We're a team."

Sammy jabbed RJ in the shoulder with his finger. "So, tell us about the little blonde with the big red truck."

RJ tried to shrug, but Sammy held her shoulder firm, silently scolding her for the anticipated movement. "What's to tell? She came into the diner, got knocked senseless by the door; Pete fixed her breakfast, she took a shower in the garage; and then she left." *Her smile was brighter than the morning sunshine. And if she'd asked me for a tongue bath instead of a shower, I'd have been more than happy to oblige. But did she have to insult my truck so?* "Not too damn much, if you ask me."

Sammy cleared his throat and grinned at his friends in the shop. "What color were her eyes?"

"Blue," RJ responded automatically, sending the entire room into a fit of laughter.

Charlie nearly choked on his cigar.

"All right! That's it!" RJ bolted from the chair, ripping the cape from her neck. She tossed it into her empty chair, then pulled her cap from her pocket and jammed it onto her head. Digging in her pocket, she pulled out some money, which she pushed into Sammy's outstretched hand. "You're all just...just... Aww, hell! Come on, Flea!"

The snorts and knee-slapping laughter could be heard out onto the street as RJ and Flea beat a hasty exit. The cat let RJ get a few steps in front of her, and then, with a running start, she bounded up RJ's back and settled on her shoulder, sneezing when she inhaled a small cut hair that had worked its way under the barber's cape. RJ didn't even slow her stride.

"Silly sons-a-bit—" She stopped suddenly when she realized her grouching and her cussing were about to be overheard by Mrs. Amos. RJ smiled and tried to look properly contrite as she moved to the door of the grocer's shop and extended her arms. "Can I give you a hand with those, Mrs. Amos?" she inquired, pointing at the two large paper sacks at the older woman's feet. The elderly tended to use the old grocer downtown, while everybody else frequented the newer, bigger store on the edge of Glory.

Mrs. Amos, a contemporary of RJ's grandmother, pulled on her white gloves, buttoned the small pearl at the wrist, and adjusted her handbag on her arm. "That'd be very nice, Ruth Jean, thank you." She held out her arms and Flea happily jumped into them, purring when Mrs. Amos gave her belly a good scratching.

RJ winced at the use of her much-hated full name and muttered, "My pleasure, ma'am." The young woman knelt and scooped both bags into her arms, then prepared for what would no doubt be an excruciatingly slow walk back to Mrs. Amos' house.

"How's your mother, Ruth Jean?"

"She's fine, ma'am. Busy as always, puttering around the house. It's this week, I think, that she's planning on painting the dining room. She wants it done before Easter, you know."

"Of course. Your mother's Easter brunches are legendary. Mr. Amos and I are looking forward to it, as always."

"Hmm, yes, ma'am, that they are."

"So," Mrs. Amos primly adjusted her handbag again, her gait so short and slow that RJ began to wonder if they were moving at all. "Mavis mentioned that the diner was busy yesterday."

RJ groaned.

Flea laughed. Sort of. Hell, even *she* felt bad for RJ. Sort of.

Does everyone have to know my business? What a town of busy bodies. You'd think we'd gone out back and necked under that old tree. Not that that was a particularly *bad* idea, but it hadn't happened and wasn't likely to now that the young woman had moved on. RJ rolled her eyes, hoping Mrs. Amos wouldn't catch the gesture and rat her out to her mother. "Yes, ma'am. We had our share of folks that were just plain lost due to that detour."

"Mavis mentioned one young woman in particular."

Of course she did. Mavis is a gossipy fishwife if there ever was one. "She did, did she?" *Oh, yeah. The whole town was talking about the blonde. Leigh, wasn't that what she told Pete?* She hadn't caught a last name.

"Oh my, yes." Mrs. Amos nodded. "Mavis told me she was a pretty thing about your age, driving a big red truck, if you can imagine that."

"That she was."

"Pretty or driving a big red truck?"

"Both," RJ allowed begrudgingly.

"Did you speak with her?"

"Not all that much." RJ shifted the bags in her arms. *What did she buy? Bricks?* "I was busy. There were logs to be split."

"I see," she snipped. "You're always too busy taking care

of other things before yourself, aren't you, RJ? Looking out for other folks first, that's what you do. You know, you might want to look around you and see that it's okay to take care of yourself once in a while."

RJ sighed quietly. "Yes, ma'am." *God, my mother's been visiting with her too often.* "But you know that my parents raised me right."

"That they did, dear." Mrs. Amos patted RJ's hand as the women slowed even further so two little girls on bicycles could zoom across the sidewalk in front of them. "You've always been a delight, except for those wicked puberty years, of course."

RJ smiled insincerely.

"Occasionally you just have to take time for yourself. I'm sure this lady wouldn't mind." She stroked Flea lovingly, and RJ swore she saw the cat stick her tongue out at her.

"I'll remember, I'll remember. But sometimes it's easier said than done, Mrs. Amos." *It's not like Glory is chock full of eligible women who can't resist my significant charms, now is it?* "But if the chance should arise again, I'll certainly think on it." *Hell, even if the chance doesn't present itself again anytime soon, I'll be thinking about the blonde.*

"You do that, Ruth Jean."

After delivering Mrs. Amos and her shopping safely home, RJ headed over to the hardware store to pick up the paint that would be required to spruce up the dining room in her parents' house.

She looked down at her furry little companion. "This place is going to be just like the last, you know?"

Flea licked her lips. *More root beer?*

"Well," RJ huffed, placing her fists on her hips, "glad to know you're on my side in all of this, pal. You could stand to be just a little more supportive."

This time Flea ignored RJ completely. If there was one thing she couldn't stand it was a whiny human. Wasn't it nap time again?

At Flea's obvious snub, RJ said, "Thanks so much." Shaking her head, she entered the store.

As RJ came through the door, the woman behind the counter turned down the blaring radio and offered, "Good morning, RJ."

"Mornin', Mrs. Morgan. I've come to fetch the paint for my mother."

"I put it on your tab. It's all boxed up and ready for you."

Alice Morgan gestured with her chin. "Right there by the door. A gallon of robin's egg blue and a quart of trim paint. I imagine you'll be busy for a few days."

RJ smiled and nodded as she looked into the crate. She was grateful that it seemed that at least one person wasn't interested in what had happened at the diner yesterday.

Alice leaned forward and whispered loudly to RJ, "I also slipped that new red shirt I made for you into the box. You might want to wear it down to the diner next time you go. I'm betting the trucker would like you in a red shirt."

RJ's shoulders slumped. So much for that theory.

One end of Leigh's route started in South Dakota. It ran from Sioux Falls to Rapid City, to Buffalo, Wyoming, and then into Montana. From Billings she went to Helena and Missoula and ended in Seattle, Washington, before she turned around and drove back. Three ten-hour days of driving from end to end if Leigh didn't count traffic, construction, detours, poor weather, or the occasional need to pee. Then a half day in Seattle and Sioux Falls to load, unload and load her cargo again, and she was back on the road. It was a grueling, endless loop that Leigh ran for three weeks straight, then took a full week off.

It wasn't the type of run most people could handle on a continuous basis, but Leigh's clients paid premium rates for her reliable service, and she continued to push herself hard. In just under two years, she'd earned enough to pay off her father's truck, give a lump sum to both of his ex-wives, each of whom had a couple of children by her father, and put a tidy sum in a jar under the truck seat, besides. Hell, the kids were all sweet, even if her dad's ex-wives weren't, and Leigh figured they shouldn't have to suffer just because her father died with only enough life insurance to bury him. Nearly twenty years separated her from the oldest half-brother, and a part of her was sad that none of them would really know her or her father. Their moms had both remarried, and there wasn't any place in their lives for a sister they never knew anyway.

A few more years of trucking, and Leigh planned to sell her rig while it still held most of its value. She was bound and determined to get a normal life and do whatever it was non-trucking people did. She hoped it included more sex, and that hemorrhoids wouldn't be an occupational hazard-come-true.

She'd pulled away from the diner right after her shower, telling herself not to give in to temptation and take one long last look at the beauty chopping wood. She'd been completely unable to resist the impulse, of course. Leigh didn't have the willpower of a gnat. Since then she'd made good time and was already enjoying the quiet beauty of Montana.

"Breaker 1-9, this is Red Rooster looking for Tom— errr...Leigh." Rooster knew better than to call Leigh "Tom Cat" over the airwaves...at least, while he figured there was a chance she'd hear him. After all, he still hoped to have children some-day. "You out there, Leigh?" He hated breaking protocol by using her real name, but she left him little choice.

As she passed a slow-moving station wagon loaded with kids, she pushed the button on her radio that allowed for hands-free communication. "Hiya, Rooster. Let's take it down to Mon-day." That was the code her daddy used when he wanted to switch from the main channel, just to have a little more privacy. Monday was the second day of the week, so Leigh adjusted her radio frequency two channels down.

"Will do, Leigh. See you there."

Another few seconds and Rooster's voice filled her cab again. "Well, now, 'bout time you started listening to the radio again. I've been trying to get you since yesterday."

Leigh snorted. "If I sat around and listened to you boys all day, I'd be as full of shit as you are."

Rooster laughed. "Can't argue with that. Everything okay, though?" He'd been a longtime friend of her daddy's, and tried to check in on Leigh every once in a while. The man had given Leigh her first beer. Okay, she was nine years old at the time, but he only let her drink half. In his mind, he was practically her godfather.

"Everything's fine, Rooster." Leigh's eyes filled with unex-pected tears, and she wiped them away angrily. "You don't have to worry about me."

"I didn't say I was worried," the man lied. "I just asked how you were. I haven't seen hide nor hair of you in nearly two months."

"I've been busy."

"Driving? Leigh, we're all busy driving. That still doesn't explain why I haven't seen you."

"Rooster," Leigh drew out his name menacing, "I've been

busy." She enunciated each word so precisely that Rooster knew the subject was now officially closed.

But he couldn't help adding, "I'm going to stop at Rosie's tonight." Rooster didn't phrase it as a question, but he knew by the long silence on the other end of the radio that Leigh was thinking about it.

Leigh glanced at her odometer, then her watch. "I'll be there," she said finally, clicking off her radio before Rooster had a chance to reply.

It was nearly 8:00 p.m. when Leigh pulled into Rosie's Truck Stop. She could see Rooster's royal blue rig already parked alongside another dozen trucks, several of which she recognized. Leigh eased the truck into the long spaces designed for her type of vehicle. She hadn't been avoiding this place, just not going out of her way to stop.

Leigh unconsciously gripped the steering wheel a little tighter. *What the hell is wrong with me?* Last night her dreams had been filled with piercing green eyes. In fact, Leigh felt as though she'd been set on a low burn ever since she'd stopped at Fitz's Diner. Her knuckles turned white against the large steering wheel. *Time to do something about that,* she thought determinedly.

The short woman jumped out of the truck and marched through the door of Rosie's. In the back, waiting on a table, was a waitress in a tight pink outfit. She was a little older than Leigh, with long, light brown hair and healthy curves in all the right places. The waitress leaned over to reach for a glass, and Leigh's eyes opened a little wider. *Oh, yeah. Come to mama.* She took a step toward the woman, only to be held back by Rooster.

"Whoa there!" Rooster's gaze drifted toward the waitress, and he shook his head. "Time for that later." Leigh heard several sniggers from a table behind her and a mumbled "Tom Cat" or two. "Come join us."

Leigh wanted to shrug Rooster's large hand off her shoulder. But she didn't. Instead, she drew in a deep, calming breath and turned to face the enormous man. Rooster was six and a half feet of pure, unadulterated blubber. Even his chins had chins. He was as carrot-topped as Lucille Ball, hence his unimaginative nickname. "Hi, Rooster," Leigh said softly, suddenly feeling terribly guilty for not seeing the old family friend in the last couple of months.

"Wow!" He gently touched Leigh's swollen cheek. "I hope she was worth it."

"Very funny." *And I'm sure she would have been.*

"Hello, Leigh. Or is it Slugger, now?" Rooster smiled gently and wrapped his arm around her shoulders to guide her back to his table, where several other truckers who Leigh knew almost as well as she knew Rooster were sitting. "I see you haven't grown any," the big man teased. "I was holding out hope."

Leigh chuckled to herself. "Do you have any idea how old I am, Rooster?"

The man's brow creased deeply as he thought. He'd known her daddy forever. But Leigh was just a tiny thing—compact and strong, but short as hell. He thought harder. She had to be at least eighteen to drive Tom Cat's truck. Hmm... She'd been at it for a while now. "Nineteen?" he hazarded, hoping he was within a few years either way.

"Jesus, Rooster," Leigh snorted. "I'm going to be twenty-eight years old next month. I'm not going to grow any more."

"Twenty-eight?" Rooster blinked. *Damn.* He began to wonder if the things his wife said about beer were true. Were all his brain cells were really dissolving like Jell-O on a hotplate? "Okay, Ethel." he mumbled, crossing his heart. "Light beer for a week, so help me, God."

"Tom Cat!" a man at Rooster's table stupidly called out when Leigh pulled out a chair.

Without hesitation, Leigh smacked him in the back of the head, sending his baseball cap into his chili. "God dammit, To—"

Leigh's evil stare stopped him mid word.

"Leigh," he finished awkwardly, aware that Rooster was now laughing at him. "That was my Braves hat, after all!"

"And now you're down to a million minus one. Live with it. And don't even ask about my eye. I'm not telling, and that's final."

A round of whining moans met Leigh's pronouncement.

Leigh raised her hand, indicating she needed a waitress. A shiver chased down her spine when the bony woman with dishrag-limp gray hair and a gap between her front teeth you could drive a truck through—even Leigh's enormous truck—

waved back tiredly in acknowledgement.

"Did you have to call over the butt-ugly new waitress?" Rooster complained. He tossed his napkin on his plate, which held nothing but crumbs. "Now you've made me go and lose my appetite."

"What?" Leigh spread her hands open. "I'm hungry. Besides, nothing has ever made you lose your appetite. And she's not *that* ug—" Leigh stopped when the woman sidled up to the table.

"I'm Stephanie." The haggard, middle-aged woman pointed to her nametag for those too stupid to understand what she was saying. "Your waitress."

Leigh nodded slowly. "You're new here, right, Stephanie?"

"Hell, yes." She stuck her hand up her blouse and began adjusting her bra.

Leigh wondered why she bothered wearing one at all. Two strategically placed Band-Aids would have done the trick nicely.

Stephanie popped her gum. "Who would work in this place, serving these slobs, for any longer than they had to? The tips suck."

"Gee, I wonder why," Leigh deadpanned.

"'Cause these guys are cheap-asses," Stephanie answered, oblivious to Leigh's sarcasm. Seeming to suddenly tire of the most stimulating conversation she'd had all day, Stephanie droned, "What'll you have?" She pulled a pencil out from behind her ear and turned bored eyes to Leigh.

"Hamburger with the works, onion rings, and iced tea."

Stephanie nodded and popped her gum again before turning around.

When the waitress was out of earshot, Leigh leaned forward and looked at Black Jack, who was, unsurprisingly, a black man named Jack. "I guess there's finally a waitress at Rosie's you won't try to bed."

Black Jack suddenly sank lower in his chair.

"Oh, my God," Leigh whispered loudly, her face twisting into the expression she usually reserved for when she had to scrape roadkill from between the grates of her truck's grille. "You slept with her? That's just so...so..." She gestured wildly.

"Disgusting," Rooster offered helpfully.

"Duh."

Black Jack didn't have to ask Leigh to keep his little indiscretion from his wife. There was a code among truckers: what happened on the road, stayed on the road. Where it belonged. "I shouldn't have done it."

"No shit. And your wife is a good woman, Black Jack," she reminded pointedly. Sure, he chased the waitresses at the diner. But it wasn't like he'd actually caught one before. She'd thought of it as harmless fun. Until now.

Black Jack looked properly chastised.

"God, you guys are so gross," the blonde woman snorted. "And you wonder why I like women. *Single* women."

Rooster scratched his neck. "No, we don't, Leigh."

All the men nodded their agreement, causing Leigh's eyebrows to crawl up her forehead.

"We understand completely." Black Jack sat up a little straighter. "We like them, too. In fact—"

Leigh leaned over and clamped her hand over Black Jack's mouth. "Please don't tell me. I'm already having trouble sleeping. Nightmares won't help." The waitress who had caught Leigh's eye earlier strolled past Leigh's table, untying her apron, her hips swaying gently with every step.

The blonde smiled broadly. "Well, boys, it's been real." She leaned over and kissed Rooster on the cheek. "I'm not hungry." *At least not for burgers.* "You can have my dinner." Leigh tossed a ten-dollar bill on the table. "The change is for Stephanie," she warned the men before following the waitress out the front door.

Rooster pushed his plate out of the way in preparation for the arrival of Leigh's order. Good food should never go to waste.

"You still worried about Tom Cat?" Black Jack asked at the same time the diner door closed.

He hadn't talked to Leigh about her life or what was going on with her, but she seemed pretty much the same as always. Maybe a little tired looking, but trucking was a hard life. Nobody knew that better than Leigh. "Nope." Rooster unbuttoned the top button of his jeans. A man had to be comfortable. "I think Tom Cat is doing just fine."

"You ignored me."

"I did not."

"You did. And I should make you beg because of it."

A soft laugh. "You did make me beg."

"No, that was me."

Leigh yawned and snuggled back into damp sheets that felt cool against her overheated skin. Her chest was still heaving, and she consciously made an effort to slow her pounding heart. "Oh, yeah."

The naked woman half-sprawled across Leigh drew the very tip of her finger up from Leigh's belly button to the baby-soft valley between her breasts.

Leigh arched into the sensual touch despite herself. "Judith," she said softly, "you trying to kill me?" She reached up and grabbed Judith's hand, kissing each fingertip before laying it back on her belly. But no sooner had she let go of the hand, than it began to wander again.

"Stay tomorrow."

Leigh closed her eyes. "I can't. You know that."

"Can't, or won't?"

Leigh sighed heavily.

"Don't say it, don't say it. You've got a schedule to keep." Judith's fingernail grazed Leigh's nipple, earning her a soft growl as Leigh's desire began to flare again. "Why do I always let you do this?"

"The same reason I always let you do this," Leigh whispered as she began to softly kiss Judith's neck. "It feels great."

The waitress gasped and shifted herself until she was fully on top of Leigh and straddling one thigh. "There is that," she groaned when Leigh's hands found their way to her hips and she began to slide against the sweat-slicked skin. "Are..." She swallowed hard as her hips picked up a steady rhythm. "Are... God... Are you ever going to stay?"

Leigh's hands froze, and she looked up at Judith seriously. She was panting slightly. "Probably not."

Judith leaned down and kissed Leigh hard, her own body moving once again. "That's what I thought."

The next morning Judith woke up in an empty bed that smelled like Leigh and sex. On Leigh's pillow was a note. Her smile was bittersweet as she unfolded the small slip of paper. Leigh always left a note.

No matter what anybody says, the most delicious thing at Rosie's is NOT the hamburgers.   Take care, Judith.   I had a wonderful time.   Thank you.

   —Leigh

Judith chuckled and tucked the note into the drawer of her nightstand.   If she tried, she could almost hear the hum of Leigh's truck in the distance.

Chapter
3

"I'm not. I'm not!" Leigh tapped the steering wheel in an uneven, listless pattern. "I'm not getting sleepy." She shook her head from side to side and tried to focus on the road. She'd been driving through thunderstorms for hundreds of miles, and the rain had finally given way to one of the densest night fogs the trucker had ever seen. She'd encountered numerous wrecks along the way and knew better than to park her truck along the roadside—even with her fog lights on. Besides, she had miles to make up. *Thirty miles per hour is no way to drive 'cross country,* she thought glumly. It was the middle of the night, and Leigh was miserable.

She blinked rapidly, but the motion still didn't clear her vision completely. *God, even I have my limit.* "Need a place to stop." Sleepy blue eyes scanned the roadside. She was halfway between nowhere and the boonies. And yet...

"I think...yeah." Leigh nodded a little. "It can't be too far away." It wouldn't be on her map, she knew. She'd checked after driving away a few weeks ago. Apparently, Glory, South Dakota, was too small to warrant even a tiny dot. Leigh passed through this area every week on her route, and just about every time she drove by, she had considered pulling off the interstate and finding Fitz's diner. But the road construction was completed, and the detour was gone. And she realized that even if she wanted to find it, she really didn't know exactly where Fitz's was. Other than being twenty miles from Glory. Wherever that was.

Leigh sighed. There was more to it than that, and she knew it. Her last, albeit brief, conversation with RJ made her hesitant to return. They hadn't exactly argued, but still, it was awkward. Why, oh why, did she have to drive such a piece of shit? Leigh didn't even know what kind of car Judith drove. Had never even thought about it. Ignorance, she decided, truly was bliss.

Taking a chance, Leigh pulled off on the very next county road and headed north. She had to slow to no more than ten miles per hour when even her truck's powerful low beams weren't cutting through the dense curtain of hazy moisture. Another hour passed, and when she was certain she was good and lost, Leigh pulled onto a wide dirt road and drove only about fifty feet. She eased her truck to the side, killing her engine and lights, half-expecting to see the blinking "ritz's" sign in the distance. But she didn't.

Unbuckling the seat belt, she popped open her door and dropped down onto the wet ground. The air felt heavy against her skin and fine mist instantly enveloped her, dampening her hair and clothes. She pulled in a deep breath of fresh, moist air. "I'm totally lost," she moaned, her eyes scanning her surroundings. She saw nothing but mud, prairie grass, and fog. Leigh rubbed her temples and debated relieving herself outside. It wasn't like anyone was going to see her in this weather and at this time of night. But then she remembered the ticks that had attached themselves to her ass while she was squatting a few years before. Scowling, Leigh unconsciously rubbed her butt. Their removal was even more humiliating than their discovery. No, morning would be soon enough.

It was so dark, she didn't bother to close the curtains in the small living space of her cab. Instead, she stripped down to her panties and crawled into bed, pulling up the soft sheet. Her eyes fluttered shut and she exhaled deliberately. Her body relaxed immediately, and she tumbled into a deep, dreamless sleep.

The male squirrel wearily sat up and cracked open his beady black eyes. "*Where am I?*" He looked around the back of what appeared to be a moving truck. *Moving?* "I've been kidnapped!" he wailed piteously. "Stolen from Potter Park. Torn from the breast of my community in the prime of my life!" The rodent tried to bury his head in his arms as he sobbed. But sadly, his stubby appendages were too short. *Damn God and her sick sense of humor!*

"You have not been kidnapped, fool," his long-time mate hissed. "You went on an all-night bender and passed out drunk!" The larger squirrel kicked at the half-crushed beer can that the male was leaning against.

He only groaned, looking at the can. It was white with black letters that proclaimed, "Beer." *Generic beer?* When he pushed off the can, it rolled over and the back was revealed. "Suitable for human consumption." Oh, the misery! How low had he stooped?

The sound of a honking horn caused the female to reach up to cover her ears but, like her mate, she couldn't reach them without ducking her head awkwardly. She repeated her husband's virulent curse, not knowing the chain of events their simple words would set in motion.

RJ blew on the embers, igniting the tinder so the flames would grow and consume the larger sticks. Once she was satisfied the fire was doing all right without her, she stood and picked up her beer from the table. Taking a drink from the long neck bottle, she watched the fire grow. *I'm a firebug. It's a good thing those stories my mother told me about playing with matches weren't true.*

Flea stood up from her spot in the very center of the picnic table and gave a good cat stretch, her arms outstretched in front of her, purring all the while. Then she proceeded to dig her nails into the table; it was the perfect scratching post.

"Ruth Jean Fitzgerald! What is it that you think you're doin'?"

"Mother?" RJ whirled around, quickly putting the bottle behind her back and spilling most of it down her legs when she did. "Damn," she muttered as she tried to surreptitiously toss the bottle away. *Now I look as though I've pissed myself. I am twenty-seven years old. It's not fair!*

Flea smiled and plopped back, content to watch the show. She hated beer anyway, unless, of course, it was root beer.

Katherine Fitzgerald crossed to the picnic table, placing two large milkglass bowls down. RJ tried to look into the bowls, sure that they would be holding potato salad and coleslaw, both of which her mother made the very best of.

"Playin' with matches?" The stout woman waggled her finger at RJ. "You know that causes people to wet the bed."

"Mo—" RJ swallowed hard at the look on her mother's face. "Excuse me for interrupting, ma'am."

Katherine nodded and cleared her throat. "As I was saying...was that a beer you were drinkin' at this hour of the mornin'?" She leaned over and discreetly sniffed the air, making a face at the odor now wafting from her oldest daughter.

RJ sighed and nodded; there was no use in denying it. Besides she really did smell like a brewery now that she was wearing most of her drink. "Yes, Mother, it was."

Katie gave RJ her famous exasperated look. "I don't know what I'm going to do with you." She threw her hands in the air. "Your short hair, your drinkin' and smokin,' and don't think I haven't heard you cussin'."

"Mother..."

"There's not a respectable person who'd have a thing to do with a heathen such as yourself."

RJ sighed again. Normally she only got the lecture on Sundays, but with the town social being today, apparently Mother Fitzgerald felt the need to get it out of her system.

Flea sniffed and licked her lips, hoping Mrs. Fitzgerald remembered the olives in the potato salad. That was just the way she liked it. But either way, Katie was a good mother. She should have been a cat.

One by one, just about everyone in town began to arrive at Fitz's. It was going to be a lovely day. The grass was still a little damp, but the light spring breeze and warm sun had mostly taken care of that. The enormous outdoor grill was going strong and would cook enough food to last the entire day. Bright red and white checked cloths covered picnic tables that dotted the grassy area behind the diner.

"Hey, you!" a strong male voice boomed from behind RJ. She slowly turned to face a young man about her own age and height. He had a head of bright red hair, and his blue eyes were hidden behind a pair of sunglasses, but his smile was familiar. Liam Fitzgerald held up two long necks. "I'll trade you a beer for a smoke."

"Yeah, and if Mother is lurking about, I'll get the short end of her temper again, big brother. No thanks."

"Mother is in the diner with Mrs. Amos and some of them old hens. You're in the clear." He bumped shoulders with RJ. "Has your big brother ever led you astray before?"

"Do you really want me to answer that, you silly bastard?"

"Nah," he laughed. "No need." He jiggled sweating bottles invitingly, clinking them together. "So how about it?"

RJ snorted softly at her own lack of willpower and fished her Luckys out of her pants pocket. She tapped one from the pack and exchanged it for a beer. Taking a tiny box of matches from her pocket, she flicked her nail against a match tip, causing it to flare to life.

Liam bent and lit the cigarette, taking a deep drag as soon as he was able. He spat an errant piece of tobacco from the end of his tongue and took a seat on the picnic table, smoke swirling around his head. His bright blue eyes tilted skyward. "It's a beautiful day. Going to be good for the picnic." He waited a moment before saying, "I hope that Mary comes down today. It'd be a shame to miss her."

RJ's arched an eyebrow at her brother. "You be careful there, Liam. If Mother and Father find out you're trying to get your hooks into one of those O'Reilly girls, there'll be hell to pay." *And I would know.* She smirked inwardly, thinking of Mary's older sister. RJ stopped smirking, however, when she remembered that the pretty brunette had taken up with the postmaster, and they now had six kids.

"Are you gonna be telling on me, little Miss 'I wonder where the cute blonde trucker went to'?"

RJ choked on her beer and tried to hide the grin. But Liam was right. She hadn't been able to think about anything since. And even her stash of "special reading material" didn't touch the ache that had appeared along with Leigh. "No, of course not. I'm just saying be careful, that's all. I think Mary is a pretty girl." RJ shrugged. "She likes you well enough, I'm thinking."

"You know this to be fact, do you?" Liam perked up and looked over his shoulder to make sure no one was around and listening. "How would you have this information, Ruth Jean? Don't be holding out on me now." He suddenly sat up a little straighter as if the light bulb in his brain had just blinked on. "And just how well *do* you know Mary O'Reilly? Hmmm?"

Leigh opened her eyes slowly, blinking at the bright sunshine. She swung her feet over the side of the bed, and her bladder immediately protested the movement. "Oh, man. Bathroom now."

The trucker yawned and slid into the front seat with a little more urgency than usual. She automatically reached for her sunglasses and then seatbelt, wiggling a little as the cool strap covered her breast. She looked down and blinked stupidly, realizing she'd strapped herself into her front seat wearing only her panties. Leigh laughed, wondering just how many free truck washes she could score if she rode around like that. She unbuckled her seatbelt and glanced up to find...

"I'll be goddamned! I drove right by it last night in that fog."

Not five hundred feet down the road she'd turned off last night sat Fitz's diner. The "F" on the sign had been repaired. But the lights either weren't working or were not in use during the daylight.

Fitz's equals bathroom. Fitz's equals shower. Fitz's equals good, hot food. Fitz's equals buff, butch, beautiful woman chopping wood in skimpy undershirt with no bra on! Leigh's mind screamed. The young woman scrambled behind the curtain in her cab and tugged on a pair of faded blue jeans and a mint-green polo shirt. She tucked in the shirt and skipped the belt, wiggling her feet into a pair of comfortable, well-worn high top sneakers. Leigh ran her fingers through her hair and grabbed the bag that contained her toiletries, a fresh pair of panties and a bra.

She was sliding across the front seat to get out, when she suddenly stopped and began digging through her bag. When she found the antiperspirant, she made quick use of it before tucking it back into the sack. She'd already insulted RJ's truck; the last thing she needed to do was come walking back into the diner smelling rank.

Instead of driving to the diner, Leigh jogged the five hundred feet. It was beautiful out, and by the high position of the sun she could tell it was early afternoon. She'd slept for nearly ten hours, but felt worlds better for it.

The small parking lot was mostly full of old beaters, though she spotted a shiny new Taurus and a 1980s model Chevy Caprice near the diner door. As she got closer, she could see throngs of people milling in and about the diner. The air smelled like BBQ, and Leigh's stomach growled appreciatively. *It's a party. I wonder if she'll be there.*

When Leigh pushed open the diner door, the conversation in the small building ground to a halt. Even the song on the juke-box seemed to end at that very moment. Nearly every set of eyes in the place turned to Leigh and stared.

Leigh could feel her face growing hot. She looked over to Mavis helplessly. "Am...uh...am I interrupting something? I mean, are you guys closed? I didn't—"

"Oh, don't be silly. C'mon in. This is a little town party, but we're still open. See?" Mavis gestured toward a harried-looking family of travelers that brushed by Leigh on their way out the door.

With Mavis' warm smile, Leigh began to relax.

Then the chubby woman turned around and announced in a voice loud enough for everyone to hear, "It's just Leigh."

A collective "ahh..." rang out and then, as if by magic, the noise in the diner rose back to its usual level as silverware clanked and people laughed and talked as they ate their lunches or drank their coffee. The diner's patrons all went back to what they were doing before Leigh walked in. All except Katherine Fitzgerald.

"I don't mean to be rude, Mavis. But—"

"You know where it is."

Leigh nodded quickly and wove her way through the tables to the bathroom in the back of the diner.

Katherine sidled up to Mavis, and both women stared at the door through which Leigh had just passed. After a few moments, Katherine needlessly asked, "So that's the little thing that's got the town so abuzz?"

"She's the one caught *RJ's* eye," Mavis corrected.

Katherine crossed her arms over her ample bosom. "I don't like her."

"Katherine!"

"Well, I don't!"

"You've never even spoken to her. She seems like a nice enough girl."

Katherine chose to ignore Mavis' affirmation. "Does Ruth

Jean know she's back?"

Mavis snorted a little. "If she did, don't you think she'd be sniffing around in here instead of playing with the grill out back?"

Before Katherine had a chance to answer, RJ strode in from outside. She headed straight for the bathroom to get cleaned up, but before her hand hit the knob, the door opened and Leigh stepped out. She was carrying her backpack slung over her shoulder, and her hair was wet.

RJ's eyes widened. "Well..." She swallowed. "Hello."

Leigh felt a smile tugging at her lips at the sight of the tall woman. She was suddenly very glad she'd had time to brush her teeth and wash her hair in the small sink. "Hi." Her gaze drifted from deep green eyes down to RJ's leg, and she winced. "Looks like you didn't get here soon enough." Her face scrunched up into a smile; she could smell that it was beer, but wasn't above having a little fun.

RJ's shoulders slumped. She just couldn't seem to catch a break when it came to this woman. "You see, I spilled a beer and I was just going to try to get it off my pants." She grinned. "It's not what it looks like, really."

"It never is." Leigh peered down at RJ's leg again, shaking her head. When she looked back up, she couldn't help but notice Katherine Fitzgerald was staring at her with a look that could only be described as either intense dislike or severe constipation. Leigh was betting on the latter since they were standing in the ladies room doorway. "Who in the hell does that woman think she is?" Leigh mumbled, tilting her head toward Katherine. "She's giving me the creeps."

RJ bit down hard on her cheek to keep from laughing. She leaned over and whispered, "Why, that would be my own sainted mother, thank you very much. If you'd like to just get it over with and call my younger sister a whore, you will have insulted all the women in my life."

Leigh closed her eyes. "Oh, my God." First RJ's truck, now her mother. With her luck, she'd have slept with her sister, too; and she'd be one of the several women who had taken a scissors to her already limited wardrobe over the years. God, she hated when they did that. "I am so sorry," she said genuinely. "I always seem to be apologizing around you."

"It's all right. Really it is. There are days when she gives me the creeps, too." RJ gestured toward the back door. "Let's make a quick exit out the back."

Leigh nodded silently. She was more than willing to follow RJ out of the diner and away from the intense gray eyes that belonged to Katherine Fitzgerald.

Once they'd stepped out back, RJ clasped her hands together rather nervously. "Can I get you something to drink?"

Leigh looked at RJ's pants again and laughed. "No thanks. I think I'll help myself." She strode past RJ over to where there was a table holding a washtub full of iced drinks.

RJ decided to give up beer for the rest of the day. Now that Leigh was here, she wanted to keep her wits about her. She reached for a pitcher of lemonade and began pouring some into a paper cup. "So, what brings you back this way?"

Leigh dug a Pepsi out of the ice. She looked at the glass bottle for a second. *Where the hell did they get these?* "Well, I needed to stop last night, and I figured I was close to Fitz's." She shrugged one shoulder, grunting a little as she tried in vain to twist off the soda top. "Frankly, I can't believe I found the place. But here I am."

RJ watched her for a moment, then extended her hand for the bottle.

Leigh wordlessly passed it over and watched carefully as RJ lined the cap up against the edge of the table and gave it a hearty smack, taking the cap off in one swift motion.

RJ passed the bottle back, careful to hold it away from both their bodies as a little brownish foam erupted out the top. She took a seat next to Leigh on the bench. From behind her glass of lemonade, she offered quietly, "I'm glad you found your way back."

Leigh regarded her carefully for a moment. "Me, too. By the way, I don't think we've ever really been introduced." Leigh wiped the hand that was damp from her frosty Pepsi bottle on her jeans before holding it out. "I'm Leigh Matthews."

The brunette gently took Leigh's hand and gave it a firm squeeze. "RJ Fitzgerald, at your service, ma'am." *Boy, would I like to service you.*

Leigh smiled broadly and spent several long seconds imagining the many ways she'd be happy to let RJ service her. RJ still hadn't let go of her hand.

Flea snorted and jumped up from the table. There was only so much she could take before gagging out loud.

Leigh set down her Pepsi. "The pleasure is all mine, RJ."

She paused for just a second before her curiosity got the best of her. "Is it okay if I ask why your mother was glaring at me? Usually it takes somebody's parents at least a day to start to hate me."

She shrugged, clearly embarrassed. "It's a mother thing, you know. And um..." she cleared her throat softly, "I may have mentioned you a time or two. My mother's just a tad protective."

Leigh leaned forward, suddenly all ears. "Mentioned me?" *And you hardly look like the type who needs protecting.*

"Well, yeah. It's, ah," she cleared her throat gently, "not often that we get attractive blonde truckers through here." RJ glanced up at Leigh and held her gaze. "I may have mentioned that a time or two."

She thinks I'm attractive? A slow smile spread across Leigh's face. Looks like they'd each been thinking about the other. She could see that RJ was blushing, and she quickly said, "Don't worry about it. I'd say your mother's instincts are dead on. I'm basically trouble," she admitted freely. "Your mom just saved me the chore of having to do something incredibly stupid for her to dislike me. But, um...well, if we get to know each other, I guess you'll figure that out for yourself."

RJ's brows drew together, but she didn't press for more information. *What does that mean? From where I'm sitting, she doesn't seem like a stupid person.*

Blue eyes flickered around the crowd. "So, what sort of party am I crashing?" *And why am I still here? I've got to get back on the road if I'm going to make it to Sioux Falls on time.*

"There's nothing I'd like better than to get to know you, Leigh Matthews. And you're not really crashing a party. It's just a town cookout. We just use them as an excuse to cook and eat good food. They usually last all day and well into the evening. Can you stay for a bit? Or do you need to get back on the road?" RJ glanced in the direction of the road.

"Oh, no. I can stay," Leigh said, a little too quickly. Mentally, she kicked herself. *Lord, I'm so pitiful.*

"Good." RJ sat up a little straighter, proud of herself for having had the courage to ask her to stay. "It may not be the most exciting thin' you've done in a while, but there's always good food. So where are you headed next? Someone waiting on you at home?"

"No." Leigh shook her head, and her normally bright smile

was suddenly edged with sadness. "Nobody's waiting," she said quietly.

"Then it seems like I'm a very lucky person today." RJ raised a single eyebrow. "Would you like to take a walk with me?" She whirled around and shot a dirty look at every pair of eyes that were fixed on her and Leigh. "So folks will quit staring at us like we're doing something we shouldn't be doing." She said this just loud enough for everyone to hear.

Leigh jumped up from the table. "Sure." She wasn't anxious to explain to RJ, at least not at this very moment, that she'd sold her and her dad's small house nearly two years before, that she only maintained a post office box in Seattle, and that she lived in her truck. Even if it was a *really* nice truck.

As they moved away from most of the crowd, the blonde found herself with the urge to take RJ's hand as they walked. Instead, she stuffed her hands in her front pockets, keeping her eyes trained on the ground in front of her.

RJ walked slowly, turning around and walking backwards so she would always have Leigh in sight. "I'm sorry about that back there. They tend to be a bit nosy. We'll have more privacy back here. That way you won't feel like they're all talking about us, and they can feel free to do so. They're the biggest bunch of busybodies you've ever met, but they mean well." She grinned. "I swear to you, they're harmless enough."

"They're okay with thinking..." Leigh gestured awkwardly between them, "that there could be something between us. Sort of. Potentially?" *If I have anything to say about it.* She was used to stolen moments of privacy in bathrooms or cars or cheap motels with women who wouldn't want their affairs known, mainly because Leigh was a woman. It was a little disconcerting to think that the people at the picnic were watching them with curious eyes that still held no malice.

Leigh looked up at RJ, who was smiling as she walked. She didn't seem worried. Of course, it didn't escape Leigh that they were moving in the opposite direction of RJ's mother. The bright white smile intrigued Leigh, and she found herself wanting to know more about this woman. "So, what do you do for a living, RJ?"

"Oh, me?" RJ spread her arms wide open. "I'm a 'Jack of all trades, master of none' type. I do a little of everything. I'm what you might call a handyman." She grinned and wiggled her brows. "I like to work with my hands."

The shameless flirting wasn't lost on Leigh. In fact, the only thing unusual about the words was that she wasn't the one saying them.

"I also do a little bit a work for the town of Glory. City Council has made me a guide or Welcome Wagon of sorts."

"Welcome Wagon?"

RJ tilted her head down as she spoke. "Sure. When we get a new resident, I show them around, help them find a place to live, a job, that sort of thing."

"Sounds interesting." *You sound interesting. And you look good enough to eat. Pun intended.*

"I suppose." The light spring breeze tossed RJ's auburn locks, sending a tussle of hair—normally combed back over her forehead—nearly into her eyes. "It's not so much, really. Glory is a small town, and we don't get that many new folks. But I do my best."

Leigh opened her mouth to warn RJ that she was only two paces from walking right into a shed. But RJ spun around, threw open the door and growled loudly, "All right, you little monsters. Take your cigarette-smoking backsides outta there! I know every single one of your mothers, and your fathers besides." A small group of kids ranging from ten to twelve years old stared at RJ with round, guilty eyes, too stunned to even move.

RJ put her hands on her hip and glared at down at the little delinquents. "Move!"

Leigh laughed as a gaggle of boys and one tomboyish-girl scattered like roaches caught by the kitchen light, both she and RJ knowing instantly that the lone girl was leading the pack of troublemaking boys. "I can see that you're going to be a bad influence. You're taking me someplace where naughty things happen, aren't you, RJ?" she teased mischievously.

"Well, if you're twelve and you've just snitched a smoke from your father, and you've come out here to have it, I guess so." RJ licked her lips and leered at Leigh. "But if you're an adult and there are two of you of the same mind, could anything you decided to do really be considered naughty?"

"Absolutely not," Leigh said softly. She was definitely liking the direction of this conversation, and took a step closer to RJ. "And I never said there was anything wrong with naughty." She quirked a playful brow. "Naughty and I are intimately acquainted."

RJ laughed. *I'll just bet you are, lass.* "Well then, let's get comfortable, shall we?" RJ reached through the window of the shed just above the bench and pulled out a blanket. "Sometimes at night I come out here and look at the stars. I've found it's better if you don't get dirt in your shorts."

Leigh coughed a little on the stale smoke that still filled the shed.

RJ's face creased into a frown. "Not to worry, we're not staying in the delinquent hideout. C'mon." She grabbed Leigh's hand. "Would be nice to cloud watch, wouldn't it?" Without waiting for Leigh to answer, RJ snatched up the blanket and exited the shed, tugging Leigh behind her. She carefully spread out the blanket on a patch of grass beneath a large tree that stood alongside the small structure. The tree was on a slight hill, and the grass on top was almost completely dry, despite the storms of the day before. While they could still just barely hear the music from the party in the background, they were tucked well out of sight.

RJ let go of Leigh's hand and flopped down on the blanket, lacing her fingers behind her head and crossing her long legs at the ankle. She gazed up into the bright blue sky dotted with fluffy white clouds. After several seconds had passed and Leigh still hadn't joined her, RJ said, "Sit down, lass. Don't be pretending to be shy." The tall woman smothered a grin. "I have a feeling you're just about as shy as I am."

Leigh snorted to herself and joined RJ on the blanket, suddenly feeling like she'd just met her match. "Won't we get wet?" She could see the puddles all around them.

"Nah. We're on a high spot. Lay back and close your eyes."

Leigh looked at RJ hesitantly.

"C'mon. I haven't bitten anyone all morning. You're perfectly safe here." *For the time being.*

"Said the spider to the fly," Leigh mumbled.

"I heard that."

"Heard what?" Leigh's eyes went round and innocent.

RJ laughed, despite her attempt to keep a stern face. "Aren't you afraid of getting struck between the eyes with a bolt of lightning for telling such lies?"

Leigh scooted closer to RJ and lay down. "Oh, I'm sure I'll get a bolt in the kisser one of these days, but it won't be for telling lies."

"You're right." RJ rolled over and pinned Leigh to the ground by the arms. "It will probably be for the delinquents catching us doing—," she bent down and lightly kissed Leigh's neck, hearing a tiny gasp, "—this. And—" Another kiss. "This."

"Can't live forever," Leigh muttered happily.

"Tell me something interesting about yourself, Leigh Matthews."

Leigh's eyes fluttered closed, and she threaded her fingers into silky reddish-brown hair, tugging RJ's body closer. "Now?" she breathed. RJ's kisses felt as good as she'd imagined they would. Soon she'd be nothing more than a puddle.

"Now."

"I'm..." Leigh licked her lips and groaned. "Ooooo, that's nice. I'm not sure I know anything interesting." She tilted her jaw upward to give RJ better access to her tender throat.

"I'll be the judge of that."

"Why are you here?" the male squirrel groaned. He'd vowed never to be seen with her again.

The female squirrel put her hands on her hips and glared at the smaller squirrel. "You don't remember?"

"Ummm..."

"Never mind." She sat down next to the male on the crushed beer can. "It'll be quicker if I just tell you. We were doing the chicken dance—"

"On the fraternity hayride that was going on in the park. Right. Go on."

"I was there with that really cute gopher from behind the north bench."

"Slut."

"Sterile drunk."

"I'm not sterile!"

"You're right. I'm pregnant."

The squirrel fell backwards off the can. "Noooo!"

Just then the truck came to a stop and the driver got out, a thermos in hand.

"This is our chance," the male declared. "Come on!"

The squirrels jumped out of the truckbed, their tiny paws sinking slightly into the damp ground in front of Fitz's diner.

"Where are we?" the female wondered aloud.

"I don't know. Looks like a godforsaken wasteland to me, but I'm not going to discuss it in the parking lot." He was sure that chunk of squirrel he'd seen on the road a while back was his old high school sweetheart. Either that, or his boss. He couldn't be sure. Despite what they liked to say, they really did all look alike.

"Look." The male pointed. "A tree."

They both scampered around the diner, around the milling people, and over to a tall tree alongside a small shed. "Continue with your story," the male said.

"There's not much more to tell. Libations were flowing, and you fell off the wagon. Literally. Loser."

The male's eyes widened as the night's events came rushing back to him. The hay wagon had stopped alongside a pickup truck, and he'd seen his mate with that nasty gopher. In his rage, he began to shake, then fall. The last thing he remembered was yelling, "Die, bitch, die! I'm taking you with me!" as he pulled her over the edge with him. They had been on the very top of a tall stack of hay bales, and the pickup truck had been Japanese. He couldn't believe they'd survived.

The squirrels darted up the side of the tree, climbing high into its branches where they felt safe.

Panting, the male squirrel glanced down and saw a blanket with two female humans on it. The bigger human was suckling the smaller one. He cocked his head to the side. Wasn't she a little old for that? Wait. "Those humans look familiar."

The female followed her mate's line of vision. "The humans we spy on back home!"

"Not quite."

"The hair..."

She squinted. "The eyes..."

"Just a little different. But not much. Same builds. Same wonderful screen presence, no matter the location or genre." She rolled her eyes. "We all know what they're going to look like."

"Genetic mutations because of the inherent weakness of their race?"

"Or lazy writers."

The women below talked and kissed and talked a little more, until the talking turned into broken whispers and the kissing grew more and more fevered.

The female squirrel watched as her mate walked out to the edge of a rickety branch. She could see there were many dead and dry branches mixed in among the new buds, and as her mate began to jump up and down, the twigs fell on the women below.

"What the—"

Leigh's hand shot to her forehead when a good-sized piece of wood landed right on her head.

RJ was pelted in the back, causing her to interrupt her kissing.

Both women stood up and stared into the tree.

"What are you doing?" the female hissed. "Are you insane?"

"Bwahahahahahahaahahahah!" the male laughed hysterically, jumping even harder. "Come on, join in! They're only humans!"

Just then the branch beneath the male gave way, and he began to plummet to earth.

The female did at least have the decency to wave goodbye.

The male pawed the air and flapped his arms...but sadly, he was not a flying squirrel. So, he dropped like a stone. His landing, however, was buffered by RJ Fitzgerald's head.

"Jesus!" Leigh screamed when the rodent fell from the sky, and took a large step backwards, landing squarely atop RJ, who, of course, began to yell, curse and spin in circles, trying to pull the squirrel out of her hair.

Before RJ could extricate the squirrel, Flea appeared from out of nowhere and sprang into action. She bounded up from the ground and attached herself to RJ's head in an attempt to dislodge the frightened, flailing squirrel.

The female squirrel's eyes widened.

Leigh stepped forward to try to help, but there was nothing to be done. RJ lost her balance as soon as Flea pounced. The tall woman ended up tumbling down the hill, skidding to a stop in a large puddle of sun-warmed mud.

Leigh took off down the hill, sliding as she tried to make it to RJ in time. She'd seen the movie *The Birds* when she was a kid. Who knew what damage a squirrel could do?

Flea used lightning-fast paws to fling the squirrel away from one of her favorite humans. She wanted to pursue the furry beast, but decided to allow his escape in order to stay with her traumatized woman. Her high-maintenance kind had had to seek therapy over much less. Flea's golden eyes narrowed. She and the little squirrel would meet again. *Oh, yes* her mind purred. *We'll meet again.*

"God, are you okay?" Leigh knelt down, heedless of the grime, and pushed mud-soaked bangs out of RJ's eyes. She peered down at her with concerned eyes.

RJ panted and flicked mud from her hands, realizing now she must be a right mess. A muddy mess that smelled like warm, wet, stale beer. "I'm fine. My ego is in shreds, and I'm really sorry to expose you to all this, but I'm fine." She sighed and looked at herself. "I should probably go get cleaned up. I'm so sorry, Leigh."

Leigh looked at RJ regretfully. "I suppose so." The voices from the party had grown louder, and she suspected their respite from the crowd was just about over anyway. Leigh leaned in and kissed RJ lightly on the lips. "It's been an adventure, RJ. But, yes, you do need to get cleaned up. And I need to go anyway." She was a little surprised at how tempted she was to say she'd wait for RJ to shower and then hang around for the rest of the party, but the trucker tucked that thought away for future examination. Bracing her hands against her knees, she stood and reached out for RJ and said the only thing that she could think of at that moment. "I'll be back."

Chapter
4

RJ grumbled to herself as she reached out for a screwdriver that was just beyond her fingertips. The garage was dark except for a hanging light attached under the hood and another flipped on over her workbench. She needed to keep the throttle spring just so...

"Damn thin'!" The tool at her fingertips clattered to the concrete floor, causing another stream of four letter words to be launched into the air.

"What would your mother say?"

RJ jerked her head up at the sound of Leigh's voice, and collided with the underhood of the truck. Her hand unclenched with the impacting of her head, and the throttle spring made a dutiful "sproinging" noise as it flew across the room and bounced on the floor.

"Ow!" RJ rubbed the back of her head, glancing up sheepishly at Leigh, who didn't even try to smother her chuckles. "Very funny. And my mother would no doubt try to wash my mouth out with soap, if you have a burning need to know." The brunette grinned as she continued to rub the back of her head. Now this was a lovely surprise. Despite the near-continuous teasing she'd endured after coming back to the picnic covered in mud, she found herself thinking of Leigh often. Maybe even missing her. Still, it was due to Leigh that she was putting up

with two and a half tons of shit. She wanted a little revenge.
"But, hello to you, sexy. What brings you back this way?" RJ
took a few steps into the corner of the room and bent down to
retrieve the spring.

"Shower." Leigh jiggled the backpack that contained her
shower supplies and a clean change of clothes. "Pete said I
could use it again. I had dinner at the diner." She took a step
closer to RJ. Stepping in out of the shadows, she smiled. "I was
hoping you'd be there."

"My night off." She gestured to her truck. "I thought I'd
give Carole a tune up. Her carburetor needed to be adjusted.
She's not purring just right."

"Carole?" Leigh peered at the charcoal-black bucket of
rust. *Typhoid Mary would be a better name.*

RJ fetched the screwdriver and quickly attached the spring.
"Yeah, Carole." She spoke with her head in the engine. "My
grandmother named her Carole after the actress Carole Lombard.
My grandmother had a thing for short blondes, too." She
glanced up at Leigh and winked, surprised that in the dim light
she could see a faint blush working its way up Leigh's neck.

"So this was your grandmother's truck?" Interested, Leigh
joined RJ under the hood to see what she was doing. "And I'm
not that short."

RJ snorted as she made the adjustment to the carburetor.
"Five foot three and no more, or I'm not RJ Fitzgerald." Her
eyes dared Leigh to disagree. But by the narrowing of Leigh's
baby blues, RJ knew she couldn't. "And yes, this was my grandmother's truck. Saved for three long years and bought it brand-
spanking new before she went overseas in '42." She wiped her
hands on a rag. "And you are short, but you're cute, too. So
that's bound to count for something."

"Thanks." Leigh smiled wryly. "I think." Leigh retrieved a
wrench RJ was eyeing. "So, why keep something so..." she gestured vaguely, "so—"

RJ glared at her.

"—antique?" Leigh finished quickly.

RJ was quiet for so long that Leigh worried she'd hit
another sore spot. She was about to change the subject when
RJ's quiet voice breached the silence in the garage. "Because,"
the tall woman paused, "it's all I have...of hers, anyway.
It's...well, it's sort of a sad story, lass." RJ glanced at Leigh,
feeling unsure of what to say, but more in the mood to talk than

she'd been in quite some time. "It's probably nothing you'd want to hear about."

Leigh laid her hand on RJ's forearm and gently squeezed. "You're wrong," she said solemnly. She could feel the warmth of RJ's skin through the gray coveralls she wore and was momentarily distracted. She licked her lips. "I'd like to hear."

RJ nodded slowly as she finished removing the last spark plug. "All right." Another few moments and the plugs were replaced.

Leigh let her backpack slide to the floor as RJ clicked off the light above the workbench, casting them into gentle shadows.

RJ straightened to her full height and used her arms to hoist herself onto the bench, her long legs dangling freely over its edge. She patted the spot next to her, inviting Leigh to join her.

With a boldness that surprised even Leigh, she didn't join RJ on the workbench. Instead, she moved in front of RJ, standing so close that RJ had to spread her legs to accommodate Leigh's body. The blonde woman's hips brushed against RJ's calves, then inner thighs, as she came to rest nearly flush against the bench. She placed both palms flat against RJ's thighs and looked up into her eyes.

The unexpected closeness seemed so intimate, so intense, that it was arousing and disconcerting at the same time. RJ sucked in a surprised breath.

A slow smile edged its way onto Leigh's face, and she patted one of the thighs beneath her hand. "Go ahead."

RJ tentatively returned Leigh's smile. "My grandmother, for whom I'm named, by the way," she interjected, "delivered planes from base to base in the South Pacific. Where she was killed." *Jesus, Mary and Joseph! Nothing like starting at the end of a tale!* RJ looked away from Leigh.

With one hand, Leigh cupped RJ's chin and gently guided the brunette's attention back to her. For reasons Leigh didn't understand, what was supposed to be an interesting story about RJ's truck now seemed very important. To both women. "I never knew any of my grandparents," Leigh uttered quietly, hoping to put RJ at ease. She ran her thumb along RJ's jaw before removing her hand. "So it's nice that you at least have something from her. I didn't know women actually flew. I figured back then they were all nurses and secretaries and stuff like that."

"Well, most were. But there were a few who flew. They

didn't fly fighter planes in combat, but they ferried many of the planes to their final destination. Especially near the end of the war, when every available male pilot was attached to a fighter squadron in some way. Women also flew cargo planes, even at the most dangerous fronts. My grandmother was shot down by the Japanese during a mission to deliver a bomber."

"I'm sorry."

RJ's smile was bittersweet. "Well, it's hardly your fault, now, is it? Besides, it was a lifetime ago and certainly nothing to be brooding over now. At least not by me."

"So I guess you don't know what happened exactly. Just that she was shot down?"

"No. I know more of the tale from my mother. Two Japanese fighter planes took off one of her wings when she was about a minute away from her landing point." RJ made a twirling motion with her finger. "The plane spun in circles and dropped like a stone into the Pacific Ocean. She broke both her arms and cracked open her head on impact, but was alive."

Leigh's eyes went a little wide.

"Course, she was trapped in the plane, which instantly filled with water." RJ cocked her head to the side, green eyes luminous in the dim light fluttering closed. "It's not hard to imagine the burn of the salty water if you try."

"I..." Leigh wasn't sure what to say. Her heart began to beat a little bit faster. "I don't think I want to imagine that."

RJ opened her eyes. "Me neither." Oddly, she smiled. "Anyway, Grandmother's co-pilot and navigator, a chubby, red-haired crop duster from Iowa, fished her out from under the water when she was already about twenty feet down."

Leigh tried not to think about what it would be like to be buckled into a sinking plane, unable to move your arms to free yourself.

"The co-pilot got them both out and held on to my grandmother until they were rescued about an hour later." RJ shrugged. "I never knew her, of course. I just inherited the truck. My mother has always told me the stories, which were told to her by her grandmother, who looked after her after her mother was killed."

"Sounds like you've got something to be proud of, though."

RJ frowned. "Didn't you hear the story? She didn't deliver the plane. She was shot down."

Leigh blinked. "I heard the story. She died serving her

country."

"I suppose," RJ allowed. "Folks say she was a brave woman. Some of the folks in Glory knew her back then." She looked away again. "But I'm not so convinced she was all that brave. She wasn't much older than I am now. And I think that maybe, just maybe, there was a big part of her that was scared, especially when she knew her plane was going to crash and there was nothing she could do to stop it." RJ's eyes seemed to glaze. She'd told the story so many times, she knew it by heart, could feel what it was really like. "Crashing into the ocean. Knowing you can't get out. Being trapped, feeling the water dragging you under. Breathing it in and choking. Knowing you failed in your mission and watching the world go black all around you."

RJ stopped, realizing she had gotten completely away from Leigh. "I'm sorry." She smiled weakly. "Yeah, I've got something to be proud of."

Leigh had paled a little at RJ's vivid description. "You're quite a storyteller, RJ Fitzgerald."

RJ snorted a little. "So I've been told. Maybe I'm a'wasting my time in Glory and ought to head out to Hollywood, eh?"

"Maybe," Leigh whispered, feeling slightly ill.

"So what did you have for dinner? Shrimp?" RJ grinned, trying to lighten the mood. She certainly hadn't meant to cast such a dour mood over Leigh's visit.

"Umm..." Leigh blinked in confusion. *Is the story over? I guess so.* Leigh vowed she'd never again say another word about RJ's truck. She couldn't believe RJ was even talking to her now. "Soup," she said absently, completely missing the darker woman's barb. "That's what I had for dinner."

"Hmm, yeah, Mavis makes the soup here. It's some of the best." RJ clicked on the light above her head, causing Leigh to shield her eyes and squint. Leigh backed away, and RJ pushed herself off the tabletop. She reached under the hood and clicked off that light. "How long can you stay?"

Leigh shook her head a little, pushing RJ's gloomy story far from her mind. "The truck's parked alongside the garage. I'm here until morning."

"I'm finished here." RJ lowered the hood, letting it slam shut." She scratched her face, then wiped her hands on a rag. "Can I buy you a beer?" With her chin, RJ gestured to a beat-up old fridge in the corner. "Then maybe we can take a walk." She wiggled her eyebrows. "I know how much you like to take walks with me, and it's a beautiful night tonight—stars all twinkling and happy." *Like me with you.*

"Absolutely." Leigh grinned, then began to laugh softly. "Here." She took the rag out of RJ's hands and folded it in half. "You have a grease mustache." Without waiting for permission, she gently wiped RJ's lip and cheek.

RJ patiently allowed the fussing. "If you don't stop that, Leigh Matthews, you just might get kissed."

"In that case..." Leigh leaned over and wiped the other side of RJ's mouth. Raising her eyebrows, she waited.

RJ shook her head. What the hell was she getting into? She lifted her palms to Leigh's face and drew her close, kissing her soundly. It was gentle, but passionate, and went on for several minutes before RJ finally pulled back and whispered through labored breaths, "I warned you."

"Warn me again." Leigh whispered, a warm sensation starting in her belly and radiating outward.

"Count on it." RJ stepped back and unzipped the front of her coveralls, exposing her street clothes. "Ready for that walk?"

Leigh nodded. "Sure." She grasped RJ's hand and dropped her backpack in front of the bathroom as they walked past it.

RJ opened the door, and the sweet evening breeze instantly enveloped her. Gone was the scent of oil and car grease, replaced instead with the scent of the prairie and french fries from Fitz's. RJ drew in a deep breath. "Heavenly, don't you think?"

Leigh laughed and tucked a stray strand of pale hair behind her ear. "Yeah," she breathed quietly, glancing around. "It's not bad."

Flea trotted up to the women as they began a slow walk.

Leigh's grip on RJ's hand tightened.

RJ's eyes slid sideways. "What's wrong?"

"That cat is weird."

RJ burst out laughing. "I couldn't agree more. Flea is one of a kind."

Flea narrowed her eyes. Humans were a real pain in her ass sometimes. In one jump she was up on RJ's shoulder, where she gave RJ a playful smack to the head. Well, sort of playful.

Leigh let go of RJ's hand and backed away further. The thought of a cat named "Flea" on her shoulder made her itch all over.

As if reading her thoughts, Flea hissed at the shorter woman.

"Be nice," RJ scolded mildly. "For all she knows, it's true." She addressed Leigh honestly. "It's just a name. Flea doesn't really have fleas. I promise."

A single slender blonde eyebrow inched upward. "You're sure?"

"Would I hold her if she did?"

"If you would, that's as close as you're getting to me." She gazed pointedly at the distance between them.

Flea began nibbling RJ's hair as though there was something in there.

Leigh's jaw dropped.

"Thanks a lot, cat!" RJ pushed the feline from her shoulders. "Leigh—"

The trucker held up both her palms and tried her best not to smile. "Stay right where you are."

Ignoring her, RJ stepped closer and lowered her voice. "Leigh."

Leigh's eyebrows sprang up at the deep timbre. Instinctively, she began to move forward toward the voice. *Oooo... Wait. Fleas.* She stopped. "Sorry, RJ. But that sexy voice won't work on me." *Okay, it will. But you don't get to know that.*

Sexy? RJ smirked inwardly and took another step forward. "Leigh." In the same voice.

Leigh closed her eyes for a second, then shook her head quickly. "Nope." She turned on her heel and bolted across the park area behind the diner, disappearing into the waning light.

"Shit." RJ shot Flea a dirty look before chasing after her.

Flea watched the women in amusement as two voices raised in laughter drifted back to her on the gentle spring wind. They were playing cat and mouse.

And humans wondered why cats acted superior.

They walked and talked, trading slow kisses in the moonlight for what had to be close to two hours. Leigh was having a wonderful time, and not a single fiber of her being wanted it to be over yet.

By the time they made their way back to the garage, the

diner parking lot only had a few cars in it, and Leigh could see
Mavis serving coffee to one or two stragglers who, apparently,
weren't anxious to get back on the road. *Been there, done that,*
she thought sympathetically.

RJ pushed open the garage door, but didn't turn on a light.
Their eyes had adjusted to the starlight outside, and the shadowy
interior of the garage posed no problems. The windows allowed
a good dose of moonlight to spill into the large room.

Leigh took the lead, wordlessly tugging RJ's hand, pulling
the woman toward the bathroom that held the shower.

The tall woman smiled and the smoldering burn that had
been driving her to distraction all night burst into flame with the
realization of where she was being invited.

"Are you taking me someplace where naughty things happen, Leigh Matthews?" RJ asked, her face split into a huge grin.

Leigh stopped walking and turned around to face RJ, allowing their gazes to lock and the look on her face to speak for
itself.

RJ's heart began to beat double time. She had never seen a
look of such pure, unashamed lust shining in a woman's eyes.

Leigh began walking again. "Depends on what you mean by
'naughty,' RJ," she whispered softly. "I mean, it's not like I've
got enough whipped cream to cover you in it and lick it off or
anything."

Sweet Jesus. RJ felt her knees go weak. She vowed at that
very moment to check her jacket and make sure she had her keys
for the diner, because when Pete and Mavis left, she would be
visiting the icebox to find the stuff Pete put on the top of the
pies. RJ figured there was only one thing sweeter, and it was
already leading her to the shower.

Leigh turned around and began walking backwards through
the garage, which was so quiet she could hear every breath RJ
took. The tip of her tongue appeared, and she wet her lips very
slowly.

RJ groaned out loud. She couldn't tear her eyes away from
Leigh's mouth. "Ohhhh, yeah..." rumbled from her chest. "You
and naughty...intimately acquainted, I remember."

The smaller woman simply hooked her pinky around RJ's
and continued to tug her into the small room. "Would you like
me to show you just how intimately?" Leigh asked as they came
to a halt just inside the bathroom. Her right hand worked its way
slowly up the front of RJ's shirt, while her left hand closed the

bathroom door and threw the bolt. As the metal bar slid into place, Leigh's thumb barely passed over RJ's painfully hard nipple.

RJ bit her lower lip and whimpered. She leaned toward the touch that disappeared all too quickly. She wanted—needed—this so badly that she felt tears well in her eyes. Her lips were dry from her breathing, now coming in short pants. She quickly wet them.

A warm, firm body pressed up against RJ, pinning her to the cool tile wall. Her chin was nudged upward as soft lips began a gentle exploration of throat. "I want you so badly, I can barely stand it," Leigh whispered roughly, as her tongue and lips continued to caress and brand.

RJ's eyes fluttered shut when Leigh's hot tongue found, then slid over, her jugular vein, applying pressure in a sensitive spot that earned the trucker a long, languid moan. She could feel the tickle of Leigh's breath along the hypersensitive damp skin just claimed by the questing tongue. It sent shivers up and down RJ's spine, and she fought the urge to turn the tables and push Leigh up against the wall. To take her where she stood. But the thought was whisked away by Leigh's insistent movement.

Small but determined hands unbuttoned RJ's shirt, and before she knew it they were pushing it off broad shoulders, allowing the night air to brush against heated skin. Leigh grazed RJ's muscular bared back with her nails, driving the auburn-haired woman to distraction. "You're so damn beautiful," Leigh growled into RJ's ear, continuing to nip and kiss, unable to stop her hips from moving forward and making solid contact with the body she was enjoying.

Leigh moaned long and low as she felt RJ's hands slide under her shirt and brush across her belly and ribs.

"You're not so bad yourself," the tall woman offered, lowering her head to drop a trail of tiny kisses from Leigh's chin to her ear and down her neck.

The blonde woman drew in a ragged breath, content to let RJ take the lead for the moment. In fact, her body insisted. "We," a deep breath, "are really," a low moan, "bad for each other." Her last words were slightly muffled as her shirt was pulled over her head. *How the hell did that happen? Do I care?*

"Uh huh," RJ whispered, giving her head a tiny nod. "I barely know you."

"And I barely know you."

"Does that bother you?" RJ cupped Leigh's breasts, smiling at the gasp that rewarded her.

Intense, sky blue eyes shone like liquid silver in the near darkness. "Do I look bothered?" Leigh growled. Threading the fingers of one hand into RJ's thick hair, she pulled her into a heart-stopping kiss, the trucker's tongue plunging deeply into RJ's mouth. Both women moaned out their approval at the move as they feasted on each other's mouths.

RJ kicked off her boots, which took her socks with them. Her hands worked the clasp on Leigh's bra, unhooking it and then sliding it from her shoulders, where she let it drop to the floor—forgotten. "We are bad."

"Then—" Leigh backed away and sucked in an appreciative breath at the vision that she was currently unwrapping. Under the handsome exterior, RJ was all woman. Impatiently, she tugged on the button of RJ's trousers and nuzzled her chest, her mouth watering as it tasted sweet flesh. "Why does it feel so good?"

Leigh slid her hands around RJ's waist and into her pants and underwear, not stopping until both hands were full of a firm backside. She squeezed and RJ hissed out her pleasure, the sound causing a flood of warm blood to settle in Leigh's belly. The heated flesh under her fingers only made her want to feel, see, and kiss more. So she did. RJ didn't *just* feel good. *She feels incredible,* Leigh's mind whispered. *She's making me feel incredible.*

"Dunno, just does. God..." RJ's words trailed off, but they were fully and completely immersed in exploring each other, and neither of them seemed to notice.

RJ caught Leigh in another kiss while taking the time to lower the zipper on the smaller woman's jeans. Soon they were both nude and hungrily enjoying each other's mouths, their hands moving frantically over naked skin made damp by the intensity of the moment. Skin met skin and Leigh shuddered under the sensual onslaught as full breasts pressed tightly together. Even standing, their legs were tangled together.

It briefly occurred to Leigh that they weren't in the shower and, despite the fact that they were only a few feet away, they weren't going to make it. But this thought was quickly washed away when she felt RJ's mouth land on her nipple, sucking it greedily and taking most of her breast into an impossibly hot mouth. "Oh God!" She was grateful for the strong arms that held her as her knees buckled and she was leaned way back. Her hands immediately went into RJ's hair, holding the head firmly in place as she writhed under her lover's skillful tongue.

RJ's own nipples swelled and tightened in response to Leigh's body. She kept one strong arm wrapped around Leigh to keep her from falling, while her other hand snaked between them and worked its way down Leigh's trim body. RJ sighed with pleasure, enjoying touching this woman so intimately.

It had been too long since she'd done this. Too long since RJ had found a woman who seemed to enjoy it as much as she did. She was enthralled with the overwhelming sensation of it all. Leigh's skin felt like smooth silk, then liquid velvet as RJ's fingers slid through soft curly hair to where Leigh was all smoldering heat and passion. "You are so wet." She smiled at the barely audible gasp that came from Leigh, who shamelessly pushed harder into her body.

Goosebumps broke out along Leigh's arms when she felt RJ's hand drop to her thigh and slowly caress it. She shifted her leg slightly, opening herself to more of RJ's coaxing, purposeful caresses. Without being conscious of the movement, she wrapped her leg around RJ's thigh as her body mindlessly responded to the pleasure. Speech was not possible. Logical thought was long gone. Her world consisted of nothing more than what she was feeling at this very moment as she willingly gave control of her body to RJ.

The trucker's head dropped forward, her forehead resting on RJ's shoulder. Her fingers tightly gripped RJ's forearms as she held on for dear life, whimpering and moaning her enjoyment and encouragement. When the caresses picked up speed and intensity, she helped them along by moving her hips in unison with RJ.

Feeling the pressure build, Leigh began to shake. Her muscles tightened and quivered as a wave of sensation intensified to the breaking point and beyond. Leigh's body froze as a strong wave of sensation crashed over her, causing her to clamp down on RJ's arms and shoulders. She cried out, her entire body shaking, just before she lurched forward, propelled directly into a second, even stronger orgasm. She bit down on RJ's shoulder to keep from screaming.

"It's all right, Leigh," RJ crooned. The tall woman held her prize with one arm as she eased her hand from between Leigh's legs. Her own chest was heaving and sweat dripped into her eyes. She felt Leigh tremble and she wrapped her up tight, holding her close as she whispered, "Okay?"

The blonde nodded against RJ's chest, her eyes shut tightly, her blood still pulsing hotly through her veins. "Mmm hmm." It was the best she could do.

"Make it stop! I can't take any more!" the male squirrel moaned. After barely escaping his hair-raising encounter with Flea, he and his mate had built a temporary nest high in the rafters of the garage. But it seemed that no matter where they were, they were going to be subjected to those two humans. Didn't humans mate in beds? Or was that sheep? He couldn't remember.

Suddenly, the noise stopped, and a few seconds after that, the sound of the water in the garage's bathroom filled the garage, and the old pipes began to moan...just not as loudly as the two human females.

The female pulled two bits of napkin out of her ears. "Is it over yet?"

The male's eyes went round. "You had earplugs and you didn't share!"

She put her hand on her hips. "Did you share that french fry you found on the ground the other day?"

"Yes!"

"Oh, yeah."

"Bitch."

"How's your paw?" The female yanked hard on the bandage covering the male's injured hand.

"Ouch!"

"Better, I see." She sat back on her husky haunches and frowned. "We need to find a way home."

More moans were heard over the shower. The male covered his eyes. His sex life was ruined. Sure, glancing through those *National Geographics* in the dumpster was kinky and fun at first. But he really couldn't take this assault on his ears. Squirrels, while incredibly passionate, were undeniably quiet in their love making.

Then something occurred to him. He studied his mate carefully. "You're not really pregnant, are you?"

"Of course not."

The squirrel crossed himself, dizzy with relief. "Then why did you say you were?"

"Just to torture you."

"It worked."

"I know." The female shrugged. "Besides, I don't have to worry about pregnancy ever again."

The male blinked. The only thing his mate loved more than sex was Pringles. Thank God her ass finally got too fat to squirm its way into those cans. That was downright embarrassing. "So what makes you think you won't get pregnant?"

"I'm gay."

"Noooooo!" The male fell out of his nest, right into the back of RJ's pickup. He landed on his head.

His mate could see by the dazed, stupid, nearly stoned look on his face that he was fully conscious and had suffered no appreciable damage. Just her luck.

RJ opened the door to the bathroom, allowing a heavy cloud of steam to escape into the garage. She stopped dead in her tracks, causing Leigh to bump into her back.

Pete was sitting on her workbench, talking quietly to a scared-looking boy who appeared to be in his late teens.

She flipped on the light, and everyone squinted and covered their eyes for just a moment.

Pete patted the teen's thigh comfortingly and ambled over to RJ and Leigh. He quickly looked over both women and smirked at RJ, who blushed. Twinkling brown eyes swung around to Leigh. "I see RJ reminded you where the shower was."

Leigh fluffed her wet hair with the towel around her neck. "She was a gracious host." The short woman leaned forward and winked at Pete. "The shower was spectacular. Thanks, Pete."

This time it was Pete who blushed, causing RJ to laugh loudly. She was definitely getting to like Leigh.

"Well, if you should ever tire of beautiful, tall brunettes..."

"You'll know the lobotomy was successful."

Pete shook his head and chuckled. *My, my, Fitz. You're up to your eyeballs in trouble with this one.*

RJ reluctantly put an end to the play when she asked Pete, "Who's the lad?"

Leigh shot a quick look at the boy. He refused to meet her

gaze, instead finding something very interesting about his sneakers. *Oh boy.* She winced, hoping he was older than he looked,
and wondering just how long he and Pete had been waiting outside the bathroom. Leigh sighed, then gave a mental shrug.
Nothing to be done about it now. Besides, some things were
simply too good to keep quiet.

"I hate to intrude on you girls' productive evening," Pete's
eyes conveyed true regret, "but I'm afraid I'm in need of Fitz's
professional services."

Leigh looked blankly at RJ for a moment, then remembered
what the taller woman had told her. "Welcome Wagon?" *At this
hour? With this kid?*

"Ahh..." Pete nodded approvingly. "She told you then."
He patted RJ's back. "RJ is a great asset to Glory."

It was obvious that Leigh was still confused, so RJ broke in.
"Pete is a sort of mentor to troubled kids. He's got connections
everywhere, and when he finds one he really believes wants to
turn things around for himself or herself, he brings 'em here for
a fresh start." RJ shrugged. "They're sort of my specialty. Like
I said before, I help get 'em settled, find 'em places to live and
jobs."

Leigh nodded. There was a little town outside Sioux Falls
that had a few state-run halfway houses. They were in the news
often, and the town didn't appreciate their presence. Leigh
looked long and hard at the boy. He was wearing torn jeans and
a ragged t-shirt. His hair was blonde and greasy, and he looked
like he could use a good meal. His gray eyes were round and
slightly haunted. *Damn.* She lowered her voice and asked, "Is it
safe?" She looked into RJ's eyes, clearly worried.

"It's perfectly safe," RJ said immediately. "They just need
a bit of help getting started. And Pete here," she poked Pete's
belly, "is sometimes a little old for these boys to relate to."

"Hey!" Pete straightened indignantly. "I'm not that old."

"Course you're not," RJ lied and pushed Pete toward the
boy. "I need a minute."

Pete took a step back, but didn't leave them completely
alone.

RJ shot him an irritated look, but quickly focused on Leigh.
"Will you come back soon? This might take a while, and no
doubt you'd be sleeping long before I'm finished." She ran her
fingertips gently over Leigh's arm. "I'd truly hate to think we
wouldn't see each other again."

A genuine smiled eased its way across Leigh's face. She'd already calculated the number of days until her route would bring her by again. "You'll be seeing me again, RJ." Ignoring Pete and the boy, Leigh leaned forward and placed her palms high on RJ's chest. Rising to her tiptoes, she gently brushed her lips against RJ's, sighing softly as she pulled away. *That felt so nice.*

"It's settled then!" Pete boomed. "Don't wait too long, Leigh." Pete made his way back to the teenager with RJ following behind him. She glanced over her shoulder several times, watching as Leigh adjusted her backpack and exited the garage. "You could have picked a better time for business, Pete," RJ grumbled.

Pete snorted. "You know I don't 'pick' when they come. It's not like I can exactly predict these things. I didn't expect Tony until tomorrow." He shrugged thick shoulders. "But he showed up early."

RJ smiled reassuringly at the thin teen. He looked very lost and alone, and her heart immediately went out to him. She knew just the place for him. RJ had been in his shoes herself. It wasn't an easy time. "Hello." She extended her hand. "I'm RJ Fitzgerald."

The young man looked at her warily, but extended his hand. "I'm..." He swallowed nervously. "I'm Tony."

"Pleasure to meet you, Tony. Has Pete explained that I'll be driving you into Glory and getting you settled?"

Tony's eyes flicked to Pete, then RJ. Then he nodded slowly.

"Good, then. No sense in putting it off." She inclined her head slightly. "Ready?"

"I guess." Tony shrugged one shoulder and grabbed his denim jacket from the workbench.

RJ dug her keys out of the jacket that hung on a hook alongside the bench. She moved to the driver's seat of her old Ford and waited.

Pete stood in front of Tony, smiling kindly. The boy sucked in a surprised breath when Pete pulled him into a strong hug. "Don't look so glum, Tony," Pete said gently. "Your prayers were answered." He laughed. "Though it may not seem like it at the moment. You'll get that second chance you wanted so badly. RJ will see that you're settled and answer any questions about what you can expect. You'll be seeing me again soon."

Pete pulled back and gently wiped away a tear that was working its way down Tony's cheek.

The boy sniffed, embarrassed by his inability to control his emotions. One moment he was in jail with nothing to look forward to, and it seemed like the very next, Pete was offering to help him. All he had to do was ask.

"Go on." Pete winked and pushed Tony toward the pickup. "RJ Fitzgerald is one of the most impatient people I know."

Tony stuck one arm inside his jacket, but decided it was warm enough to go without, so he tucked it under his arm. He slid into the passenger seat as RJ pulled the choke and turned the key and Carole began purring like a kitten.

"Ahhh." A satisfied grin curled RJ's lips. She patted the dashboard lovingly. "Now that's more like it."

When Pete pulled up the garage door, the female squirrel, who had been watching the human exchange intently, made her decision. Her mate was huddled in the corner of the pickup truck, which now appeared to be leaving the garage. She couldn't stand by idly while he was whisked away by the iron death machine. Sure, there were times when they disagreed. But they were squirrel soulmates. And that meant they would stick together through thick and thin. Even if she was occasionally blinded by jealousy or fury...they were still mated, and she still loved him. At least that was the speech she was going to give a jury of her rodent peers should her mate ever expire under slightly suspicious circumstances. Not that she was planning that or anything, but it never hurt to be prepared.

With a bravery that made Chip and Dale look like the pathetic fairies that they really were—the female dove off the garage rafters, intent on seeing her mate through to the bitter end.

"Uff." She landed on him with a thud.

"I knew you wouldn't let me go alone!" the male cried against his wife's breast. "You're not really gay, are you?"

She stroked his fur tenderly. "Uh...of course not. That beaver supermodel was just a phase I was going through. I didn't enjoy it at all. After all those screaming orgasms, I got to thinking...once I regained consciousness, that is. I thought...I can't make a life with her. She's hardly messy at all. I would miss living with a sloth. And who would tell me my new pelt style doesn't make me look *nearly* so fat as the old one?"

"Not a female. They're not sensitive like us males."

"And she never fell asleep right after sex, ignoring me completely and forgetting about my need for stimulating conversation and intimacy. I can really only count on a male for that."

"Huh?" He glanced around, bored, then looked up at his mate. "You still talking to me?"

They'd been riding in silence for about fifteen minutes. Most of these boys were quiet, but they usually broke under the curiosity of what their new digs would be like. RJ cleared her throat. *Looks like I'm starting this conversation.* She focused on the dark road. "Smoke?"

"Sure," Tony answered eagerly.

Realizing she'd left her cigarettes in her jacket pocket back at the garage, she gestured to the dashboard. "Glove box. And get one for me, as well."

Tony obeyed, tapping out two cigarettes and quickly lighting them. He pulled in a deep lungful of smoke and muttered a small prayer of thanks, closing his eyes in pleasure.

RJ chuckled and took her cigarette from his nearly limp hand. "I know how you feel." She cracked a window. The twinkling lights of Glory were fast approaching. "Don't you have any questions for me? It's my job to answer them, you know."

Tony shrugged. "Not at the moment."

RJ could only nod. "Suit yourself then." The tall woman turned onto a smooth, paved road, then onto Main Street.

The teenager looked around, his eyes wide. He'd never seen a little town like this. "It's fucking Mayberry!"

"Where?"

Tony rolled his eyes. "Never mind."

RJ pulled up in front of a three-story house right across from the park in downtown Glory. "This is Mrs. Amos' boarding house. She's taken in several lads like you and has a way about her that is perfect for the job."

They jumped out of Carole and started walking up the sidewalk. Tony paused under a street lamp, so unsure of himself he was nearly trembling. He wrapped his arms around himself, covering his forearms.

RJ laid a gentle hand on his arm, smiling softly. "What did you do before, Tony?"

"I was a mechanic at Jiffy Lube."

"And was that what you wanted to do?"

"Hardly," he snorted.

"Then what's your heart's desire?"

Tony kicked at a pebble. "Who the fuck cares?"

RJ burst out laughing. "Why, I do, of course. What is it then? A musician? A soldier?"

Tony shook his head. "A sculptor," he mumbled.

"What was that?"

"I like to work with clay." He frowned. "I learned in juevy. We had art class once a month, and sometimes we got to work with clay."

"An artist it is, then."

Tony's brow furrowed. "What do you mean?"

"It's my job to find you a job, and you just told me your heart's desire." RJ scratched her jaw speculatively. "I don't think we've any other sculptors in Glory, but I'm sure we can find a kiln someplace. Now, let's get inside. Mrs. Amos will be expecting us."

"My jacket. It—"

RJ gently tugged one of Tony's arms from around his torso. The street lamp easily illuminated the long line of lurid track marks that scarred his flesh. She laid a warm palm on the scars. "Nobody will be judging you here, Tony." She grinned, and with a swipe of her hand, the marks on his arm disappeared. "But, just to make you feel a little better."

Tony's eyes widened and he stared at RJ in awe.

The woman laughed. "C'mon now. If I'm late with you, Mrs. Amos will be telling my mother I'm not doing my job, and there'll be hell to pay." RJ made quick work of the side-walk...with Tony scrambling after her.

The squirrels jumped out of the truck. A town! A park! This was feeling much more like home.

"Where are we?" asked the male.

"I have no idea. Wait." She scampered over to a tree at the edge of the park. A sign written in squirrel, far too small to be noticed by human eyes, was carved into the trunk of a large tree.

It said:

Welcome to Glory.   Your asses are dead.   Bummer.
Have a Nice Day!

Wide eyed and in shock, the squirrels looked at each other and screamed in unison, "Ahhhhhhhh!!"

Chapter
5

RJ rubbed the hood of her truck with a soft cloth, the pickup's shiny black paint job reflecting the morning sun. She bent over slightly and lifted her sunglasses as she peered at what she thought was a smudge. "Antique, indeed," she snorted as she wiped away the spot.

"It is an antique, RJ. It's almost sixty years old."

She stood up and turned to face Pete. "Now don't you be starting on my favorite girl, too. It's bad enough that Leigh thinks of her as a rust bucket."

"That's just the way she sees—"

RJ raised a hand to forestall the cook's words. "Yeah, yeah, yeah, I know. But look how beautiful she *really* is." She gazed at the truck woefully. "It's not fair that Leigh can't see her beauty as well."

Pete had to admit that RJ was right. The dark-haired woman had treated the truck with tender love and care for a very long time. He blew out a deep breath and handed RJ the cup of coffee he'd brought her. He'd been doing it since the late '40s, and it had become a comforting ritual for them both. A cup of coffee in the small downtown park before their day began, just so they could talk about everything that was going on at the diner or in Glory, or how their community's latest addition was fitting in.

RJ tossed the rag into the front seat of the truck, then followed Pete to a bench under the tall oak tree across from Mrs. Amos' house. As she took her seat, she noticed Flea sitting at the base of the tree, her eyes narrowed in concentration as she stared up into the branches. *Leigh's right. She gets stranger every day.*

She sipped her coffee, then glanced across the lawn at the store where her mother was shopping. RJ pulled her cigarettes out of her pocket, hoping she'd be able to finish one before her mother was done shopping and she would need to drive her back home.

"So," Pete sniffed his coffee appreciatively, "how's Tony doing?"

RJ thought about that for a moment before she answered. "He's gonna be just fine. He's already making new friends and is adjusting to all this very well." The way that young folks fit into Glory always surprised RJ. Had she not been doing this for a lifetime, she would have guessed that the older people would be more prepared for death and what lay beyond. They'd lived longer, known it was coming, had time to plan and prepare. But that usually wasn't the case. The young folks, so often stunned to be here at all, tended to take things in stride, adjusting to death the way they'd adjusted to life—with a blind acceptance. To them, forever was just a word, and tomorrow was greeted with more enthusiasm than fear.

In Glory, a person's outer form was a combination of how they saw themselves and how others saw them. And Glory had its share of old codgers. She laughed to herself, admitting that most of them were lovable souls that somehow still managed to be thorns in her butt.

She turned to Pete. "He asked for something called a CD player. I don't have a clue."

Pete nodded. "I'll take care of it. Don't worry about it."

"I need to try and catch up a little." RJ scowled unbecomingly. "Seems that a lot of things have gotten past me. I'm starting to feel a little out of touch again."

"Speaking of that," Pete bumped shoulders with his friend, "we think you should take a little vacation."

"Oh, 'we' do, do 'we'? And where would I be going? My options are pretty limited."

Pete scratched his jaw, wishing he hadn't forgotten to shave this morning. He hated stubble. "That's not completely true, RJ. Arrangements can be made, you know. And I can think of one cute, fair-haired trucker who'd probably be pretty happy if you wanted to spend some time on the road with her."

RJ rolled her eyes, her head dropping forward. These people wouldn't give up until she was barefoot and pregnant. Not that Leigh would be much help in that department.

"Pete," her tone was serious, "I don't know about that. Not that it wouldn't be a lot of fun." She groaned inwardly, her mind flashing to the soft lips pressed against her throat. "But I'm not so sure that'd be a good idea. Not to mention the fact that you'd best be minding your own business."

"She makes you happy, Fitz. Any fool can see that."

"Especially if that old fool happened to be sitting just outside the bathroom in the garage the other night, eh?"

Surprisingly, Pete blushed to the roots of his hair. "Let me amend my former statement. She makes you *really* happy."

"Smart ass," she murmured. Not that Pete was wrong. She just didn't like the fact that he was rubbing her nose in it.

RJ crossed her arms over her chest. "But it's not like we can really be together, is it?" Sure, the sex had been great. Better than great. But she was already feeling a little guilty about the time they'd spent together. *Damn Catholic upbringing.* "She's a beautiful woman, who should be spending her time with someone...with someone..."

"Like you?"

"I wasn't going to say that!"

"Of course not." He looked smug. "You're not as smart as me."

RJ's eyebrow quirked but she said nothing, burying her nose in her coffee cup instead.

Pete pressed on. "We've been talking about all this, RJ. You've worked hard. And we love you. But let's face it, you've never been a hundred percent happy here. Getting out for a while, spending some time with Leigh, it would be fun, wouldn't it?"

"Pete..."

"What's your heart's desire, RJ Fitzgerald?" Pete's eyes twinkled.

RJ shook her head, laughing softly. "Very funny."

She sighed and nodded. "Yeah, yeah, I admit it, it would fun." *The way I feel with her... Jesus.* "I'm a little ashamed to admit it, but being with her was the best time I've had in years."

Of course it was. "You should go for a few days. It's not

impossible, Fitz. You know that."

"It may not be impossible, but it's still not likely. And Leigh might not want to be traipsing around with someone who is nearly a stranger."

"You didn't seem like strangers to me. Especially considering what you two were doing."

RJ narrowed her eyes. "You know what I mean, Peter, the troublemaker."

Pete tossed his cup into a trash bin alongside the bench. He stood and pulled up the pants that had dropped just a little below his ample belly. "If nothing else, it would be an opportunity to 'catch up' with the world a little, so you won't feel so out of touch when someone like Tony comes along."

She nodded reluctantly. That much was true. Based on the folks coming into Glory and that radio in the diner that only got that hideous A.M. station, things had changed since WWII in ways she couldn't even imagine. RJ focused on Flea as she circled the base of the tree. "What makes you think that Leigh would be wanting me to tag along with her to begin with? We were only having a bit of fun, Pete."

"Oh, puhleeeze!" Pete tried not to roll his eyes. RJ was certainly a stubborn one. But after talking to Leigh only a few times, he suspected that she was exactly the same way. He was hedging his bets. "Let's just say that someone who is very persuasive is planting a tiny seed in your friend's brain."

"Would that friend be the lady trucker?"

RJ jumped to her feet at the sound of the familiar voice. She spun around to face her mother, who was holding an overflowing bag of groceries.

Katherine passed the bag to her daughter and looked at her disapprovingly, clucking her tongue against her cheek as she waited for an answer.

RJ began poking around the sack so she wouldn't have to meet her mother's inquiring stare. "Uh...well..."

"Ruth Jean, I don't like that girl."

RJ's eyes darted helplessly to Pete, then back to the forceful older woman. "Mother, you don't even know her."

"What do I need to know about her other than the fact that she's alive? I think even you'd have the good sense to know that tiny detail is going to keep you apart from her. Assuming you ever get past just wanting to take her to bed."

RJ's mouth dropped open. "Mother!"

Pete tried to intervene and save his rapidly sinking assistant. "Now, Katie—"

"Don't you 'Now Katie' me, Pete. You, more than anyone, should know it's not possible for them to be together, and you shouldn't be encouraging Ruth Jean to go and be with that girl. In the long run, it'll only hurt them both. That is, if they ever get past just wanting to—"

"I know. I know," RJ said quickly. "For the love of Mike, you don't have to say it again."

Pete sighed heavily. "But they seem to make each other happy."

"All right, so they make each other happy. Eating ten pounds of chocolate in one sitting would make me as happy as a lark, but that doesn't mean it's what I should do, now does it?"

"Bu—"

"Are you gonna let Ruth Jean out then? Are you gonna let her leave Glory permanently? Are you gonna let them be together, should they want that?"

"Be together?" RJ tried to throw her hands in the air, which was a terrible mistake considering she was still holding her mother's groceries. She fumbled with the bag. "Is it necessary to marry me off just because I took notice of a pretty woman?"

Katherine ignored her daughter's comment and continued to focus on Pete. "Or are you gonna let them be happy for a short time, and then make her come back so she can be more miserable than before. She—"

"I'm not miserable!"

Pete and Katherine both shot RJ a stern look and barked, "Don't interrupt."

"Stop!" RJ moved between Pete and Katherine. "Just stop."

The anger and hint of defeat in RJ's voice made Pete's chest tighten.

"I won't be pushed into doing," she glared at Pete, "or not doing," the glare shifted to her mother, "something to please either one of you. It's my eternity, and I'll spend it the way I see fit!"

RJ was breathing hard and both Pete and Katie could hear the tears in her voice. In all the time Pete had known her, he'd never heard her raise her voice to Katherine. And by the look on the older woman's face, she realized she'd pushed RJ too far.

RJ cleared her throat and took firm hold of her emotions.

"Come now, Mother. I'll take you home." She strode over to the truck, not bothering to say goodbye to Pete or wait for her mother to join her.

Pete's voice dropped to whisper. "You should be ashamed, Katie. RJ deserves a chance to be happy just like everyone else here. And she never will be if you keep acting like this."

"If you can figure out a way for her to be happy with this girl, I'll gladly accept it. Otherwise, don't be filling her head with such foolishness. You know better than anyone that almost nobody leaves Glory." She spoke faster when it appeared that Pete was going to break in. "If you can arrange for RJ to go be with this girl, I would never stand in her way. I'm not a fool, Peter."

Pete's shoulders sagged.

"I can see the connection between them, same as you. And despite the teachings of my generation, I'd gladly welcome the trucker—"

"Leigh," he supplied.

Katherine nodded. "Leigh...into my family." She paused and searched Pete's face, her eyes widening with realization. "Ruth Jean's already been given permission to go?"

"Almost."

Katherine pursed her lips. "When 'almost' becomes 'yes,' you won't hear another word from me. Until then, don't be getting her hopes up."

With that, Katherine marched over to Carole, waiting patiently as RJ opened the passenger door. Before she got in, Katherine looked up at her daughter and smiled reassuringly. She kissed her on the cheek and got into the truck.

Pete frowned, his heavy brow furrowing as the truck drove out of sight. Flea, who was apparently satisfied that there was nothing up the tree that she couldn't live without, jumped up on the husky man's shoulder and nuzzled his neck. Pete absently stroked her soft, coal-black fur. "What do you think, Flea?"

The cat meowed loudly and batted at Pete's face with her paw. "Yeah. I know," he grumbled. "I need a shave."

"You take these with you, Ruth Jean!" Katherine tossed her daughter two Golden Delicious apples as the young woman hurried down the back porch steps.

RJ pulled them out of the air and tossed them through the open passenger window of her truck. "Thank you, Mother. But I'll be taking Tony down to the diner. Don't know why you're throwing fruit at me. We can eat there."

"Because the fruit is good for you. That greasy food they serve at the diner, 'tis not fit for man nor beast. Even Flea won't eat everything there. And she's not exactly discriminating."

"Not like it's gonna kill me or anything," RJ mumbled. She pulled her sunglasses from her pocket and slid them on as she started up the truck and pulled out of the driveway. Despite herself, she reached over and grabbed one of the apples, taking a large bite. It was cool and juicy. "Perfect."

Flea crawled out from under the seat and jumped up onto the wide dashboard, stretching out her long silky body. She gave a long yawn and licked a paw before scrubbing behind an ear.

"Well, there you are. Did you hear what my mother said about you?"

The cat yawned again. She only occasionally paid attention to humans. They were a tad tedious for her tastes.

"I thought you'd be going to the diner with Pete, the troublemaker, today."

Bored, she flicked her tail in an irritable manner and turned away from RJ to soak in the sun at a better angle.

"Uh huh. Maybe I like talking to myself. Ever think of that?" RJ stuck her tongue out at Flea, then took another bite of the apple. "You know, you should be grateful there aren't any dogs in Glory."

After a brief stop at her brother Patrick's shop to pick up a surprise, RJ continued on to Mrs. Amos' boarding house. She pulled up out front and climbed out of Carole, but reached through the window and gave the horn a couple of quick blasts. "Tony Hampton, get your backside down here, boy! The day is a'wastin'."

A window flew up on the second floor, and Tony's smiling face appeared in the space.

Huh. He got a haircut. She chuckled. *I'll bet Mrs. Amos insisted.*

"I'll be right down, RJ, just let me grab my jacket and—"

"It's warm as can be! You don't need your jacket. Come on!"

Mrs. Amos opened the front door. She stepped out on the porch and shook her dishtowel at RJ. "You don't need to be coming by here making all that racket, RJ Fitzgerald! You can come up to the door and knock like a respectable human being. How am I supposed to teach these boys some manners with you acting like that? Hmmm?"

Before she could reply, the screen door opened and Tony darted past Mrs. Amos, running for RJ.

"Ahem."

Tony cringed and skidded to a halt just before reaching the short set of steps off the front porch. He turned and walked calmly back to Mrs. Amos, planting a gentle kiss on the old woman's cheek. "I'll be home in time for dinner."

Mrs. Amos smiled. Tony was one of the sweetest and easiest boys she'd boarded in a long while. He was eager to please and had a tender heart. Tony just didn't know it yet. "You do that. And don't you be eating any of that food that Pete is fixing at that diner." She swatted at the young man's bottom with her towel as he once again darted for RJ. "And don't you be giving that boy any cigarettes, Ruth Jean."

"Yes, ma'am." RJ mumbled a few grumpy words to herself and climbed back into the truck as Tony jumped in the passenger side.

RJ waited until they were out of sight of Mrs. Amos' house before she offered Tony a cigarette.

He looked pathetically gratefully. "Thanks." He lit the tip, then rested his elbow out the window as he took a deep drag. Tony exhaled with a happy sigh, his expression turning thoughtful. "How come we can go down to the diner?"

"Huh?" RJ's eyes slid sideways.

"The diner?" Mrs. Amos had tried to explain this all, but it still didn't make any sense to Tony. "How is it we can go back and forth to the diner, which is outside Glory, and we're dead. And some folks who are alive can go to the diner, but not Glory. Like the blonde."

"Excuse me?"

Tony shrugged. "Everyone knows you're banging her like a screen door in a hurricane."

The tall woman began to choke on the smoke from her cigarette. Coughing, she glared at Tony with astonished eyes.

"Well, you are, aren't you? Either that, or someone in that bathroom was in some serious pain and found religion, all at the same time." Tony's eyes glazed over. "Nothing wrong with it, you know. She's damn cute. And what a great ass! If I thought she'd let me—"

"Don't even think about it," RJ warned, her eyes watering from her hacking. She shook her head fiercely. The back of her throat stung and she coughed again, using the time to collect her scattered thoughts. The boy's bluntness had thrown her for a loop.

RJ tossed her cigarette out the window. "One: I'll thank you not to be saying things like that about Ms. Matthews. She's a very nice woman."

Tony grinned. "What I saw was very nice."

RJ smacked him on the back of the head. "Two: Wipe away that thought right now, Romeo."

"Hey!" Tony rubbed the spot.

"She's too old for you by ten years." RJ smirked. "Though your lack of facial hair would probably work in your favor."

Tony scowled and self-consciously rubbed his baby-smooth cheeks. "Some women appreciate a clean-shaven face," he muttered defensively.

"Assuming you actually need to shave."

"I shave!" *Okay, once a month. But that counts!*

Not believing Tony's protest for a second, RJ continued by saying, "Three: there's no need for you to be so...so...vivid with your language. Especially about something that is none of your business."

Tony looked to his sneakers and then to RJ, giving her his best puppy dog face. "I'm sorry."

RJ lifted an eyebrow at the teen.

"Okay, I'm *sort of* sorry."

"Better."

"I didn't mean to upset you, RJ." He stuffed his cigarette in the truck's ashtray, searching for the words it would take to get himself out of hot water. "It's just that you're so laid back, it didn't seem serious between you and—" He paused. He was beginning to stumble over the words and feel stupid, which he hated. "I'm sorry."

RJ exhaled slowly. "Look, lad, we can talk about anything. But you need to show a little respect, especially when it comes to Ms. Matthews." She reached out and massaged the spot on the back of his head where she'd smacked him. "Lucky for me you finally decided to wash that hair. Or my hand would be slipping right off your head."

"Ha, ha. Very funny." He crossed his arms over his chest,

but couldn't help cracking a smile. RJ was pretty cool.

"Just watch what you say from now on."

"Yes, ma'am." The last word was an effort, but not as much as he thought it would be.

"Now, in answer to your original question. The diner is sort of...well..." She scratched her chin. Even after all these years, she had never really come up with a good answer to this question. "It's a place that exists between the two realms—life, and life after life. Think of it as a spiritual bus station. Only with onion rings." She chuckled at her own joke, vowing to use that again with the next person who asked her. "It was your last stop. For the living folks, well, their journey goes on. It's where the living and dead mingle without the living knowing it, but they both enjoy a good cup of coffee."

"Or a little more." Tony grinned wickedly.

She raised a hand in warning, and Tony playfully ducked out of the way.

"So, is Glory heaven?" His face went serious as he mumbled, "No way in hell I'd end up in heaven."

RJ let out a heartfelt sigh. "Not in the way you're thinking of it, no. It's another stage of existence. You might say we're 'ghosts.' But as you know, our bodies are still real, even if things don't work quite the same. A caterpillar turns into a butterfly, but it will still go splat against your windshield when you hit it."

"Huh?"

For emphasis she reached over and pinched Tony on the thigh, earning a loud yelp.

He rubbed his leg. "I see what you mean." Tony thought for moment. "So I can die again?" He shivered a little at the last thoughts of his lifetime: paramedics shoving tubes down his throat, needles poking his arms, a burning sensation traveling through his veins.

"No. You won't age physically, and if you get hurt," RJ steered around a large pothole, "you'll feel something very similar to pain, but your body will heal and you'll go on."

"Like a fuckin' superhero!"

"Hardly," she laughed. "Something else that's important, Tony, is to understand that just because you've left one stage of existence and moved into another doesn't mean you're not real. You are. You're just different than you were before." RJ's smile grew broader. "Why, some of those children running around

Glory didn't die young. They were born right here to parents who had come here from the living."

Tony's eyes widened. "Oh, man! Condoms here, too?"

RJ snorted. *Is he ever going to be surprised!* "There are more possibilities in Glory than you've even imagined."

They were silent for several moments, the cool breeze blowing gently against their faces as they drove along.

"You do know the stuff I did when I was alive?" the young man asked hesitantly, still unable to leave behind the concept of heaven and hell that had been drilled into his head as a small child.

RJ nodded. "I know. But Glory isn't about punishment or reward, any more than the caterpillar is being punished or rewarded by turning into a butterfly."

Tony still looked confused, and she cursed herself for repeating a lame analogy that hadn't worked the first time. She sighed, wondering when this had gotten so difficult to explain. "Glory just 'is.'" One of RJ's hands dropped from the steering wheel, and she motioned out in front her. "There are no flying angels with white wings and harps. Things aren't perfect; and it sure as hell isn't Utopia." Her tone softened. "But Glory is a very good place, Tony. And how content you are in your after-life is going to be up to you." *There. That sounded easy, didn't it?*

"But you're happy here, right?"

RJ blinked. No one had ever asked her that so directly before, though in fairness, Pete had been hinting around it for the last forty years or so. She found herself unwilling to examine the question too closely and roughly pushed it from her mind.

When the silence in the truck grew, Tony made a face, causing RJ to roll her eyes. "Don't worry so much. You have all the time in the world to figure things out."

Tony clapped his hands together eagerly. "An eternity at the diner picking up chicks just like you doesn't seem so bad to me."

"Behave yourself, or you'll be chopping the wood today instead of fixing up that kiln we've got back there." RJ gestured over her shoulder to the crate in the back of the pickup.

"Cool!" But Tony's excitement disappeared almost as quickly as it came. "Um...RJ, I might not have mentioned this, but—just because I like making things with clay, doesn't mean

I'm any good at it."

RJ couldn't help but laugh at the boy's woebegone expression. "Tony, I wouldn't be worrying if I were you. You've got a *really* long time to practice."

Leigh pushed open the door to the diner. It had been nearly a week since she'd been by on her last route. One more delivery on each end, and she was due her week break. She couldn't wait. Weary blue eyes flicked around the diner, looking for RJ.

"She's not here yet," Mavis said from behind the counter, not looking up from the silverware she was sorting and placing in trays.

"Oh." Leigh tried not sound disappointed. "I wasn't—" She suddenly closed her mouth. Even to herself, Leigh couldn't make it believable. She wasn't even going to try to lie to Mavis. She coughed awkwardly, then rolled her tongue over her teeth as she walked to the counter.

The waitress looked up after she put away the last of the spoons. "Have a seat." She lifted a carafe in Leigh's direction. "Coffee?"

Leigh slid onto the stool and nodded. "Sure." She plucked a sugar packet from a bowl on the table and restlessly picked at the paper. "Do umm...do you know if she's going to stop in today?"

Mavis smothered a grin. "Soon, I expect. You're here a little early today." She turned over a coffee cup, which was waiting upside down, and poured in the fresh brew, placing a clean spoon next to it.

Leigh nodded again. "Got in last night late and slept in the truck."

"You look tired."

Leigh frowned. She knew she did. Most folks, however, never said anything about it. Even Rooster and her other trucker friends seemed to overlook what had become nearly permanent shadows under her eyes. "I know," she admitted quietly.

Mavis leaned forward, her elbows on the countertop. "You've got some time off coming up, right?"

"One more week, and I'll get a week off." *I can't wait.*

"What are your plans?" Mavis asked nonchalantly, absently straightening the salt and pepper shakers.

Leigh shrugged. "Sleep. Sleep. Fun. And no driving."

"Alone?"

Leigh's eyebrows jumped. "Contrary to the evil reputation I have with some folks, Mavis, I do usually sleep alone."

Mavis tsked Leigh. "That's not what I meant. Did you know that RJ has a little time off coming up?"

"No." Leigh drew out the word.

"She doesn't get out too much. And I happen to know she's got a...friend in Seattle she'd love to meet. That's where you live, right?"

"Sort of." Leigh looked at Mavis knowingly. "Are you suggesting that I should invite RJ to come with me on my week off?" *Like I haven't already thought of doing that very thing.*

"Of course not. You don't even know each other, right?"

"Right." But Leigh's answer was reluctant.

"I can tell...you girls are just out for a little fun, and spending a week together would probably be awkward." Mavis pinned Leigh with her eyes. "Right?"

Leigh blinked. "Well, I don't—"

Mavis turned her back to Leigh and reached for a plate. She smiled. "I mean, just because you've laughed and enjoyed each other whenever you've stopped by the diner over these past few weeks, doesn't mean it would be like that away from here."

Leigh swallowed but didn't answer. *Would it?* "I'm..." She pushed away from the counter, suddenly feeling very confused. *I'm lonely?* "I'm not ready to eat just yet, Mavis," she said quickly. "I'm going to grab a fast shower next door, and then I'll be back."

Leigh grabbed her backpack and hustled out the back door just as Pete walked through the front door.

"How'd it go," Pete whispered conspiratorially to Mavis as she pulled an apron over his head and tied it.

Mavis winked, then kissed the cook on the cheek. "Mission accomplished."

RJ moved her ladder over another few feet and climbed it, getting off carefully and trudging across the roof of the garage. The spring storms had been especially hard on the old building, and it was in need of a few basic repairs. Setting her hammer down, she pulled a small crowbar from her belt and began to peel back the shingles that covered the roof, then the roofing paper.

The male and female squirrels, who had hitched a ride back from Glory with Pete, sat in a tree outside the garage, watching RJ.

"I can't believe you killed me," the female whined. "And on your first try, too." She herself had used poison on her mate. Not to mention all the blunt trauma episodes in their past. The smaller squirrel had seemed indestructible, nearly mystical in his ability to avoid actual death. Figured that, in the end, only he could end his miserable little life.

The male puffed out his chest. "And you said I could never do anything right."

"What a time to be wrong."

"Exactly."

"What are we going to do? We're in Glory—squirrel purgatory! We're being punished!"

"I know." He began to sob. "We'll never see our park again." His cries grew louder. "Never spend the day with our seventeen baby squirrels."

You mean my seventeen babies and your three. Heh. The female's ears perked up and her eyes went unfocused. "No more gathering food for everyone, preparing it for everyone, and cleaning it up," she whispered.

"No entertaining our friends."

"I will miss that delicious beaver, though."

The male's head jerked sideways.

"In a purely platonic way, of course," she said insincerely.

"Oh. Right." He snuggled closer to her, seeking her comfort in this, his hour of need. "We'll never entertain at our nest."

"No more taking those same five feathers that line our nest and rearranging them so the neighbors will think we have new wallpaper." Her eyes widened a little with realization.

"I know," the male anguished. "No more spending every Saturday with my mother."

The female knocked her mate down in her enthusiasm. She began kissing him wildly. "Thank you, thank you!"

RJ stared down at the roof. She thought she heard something. When she peeled away the next two shingles and paper, the noise grew louder. One more shingle and she could tell that it was water running. Pulling away a bit more paper, she gasped. She could see directly down into the shower, where Leigh was currently soaping her feet. Sure, she had to crane her head around a beam and lean wayyyyy into the hole. But she could see her.

The male squirrel glanced curiously at RJ. "The human is a peeping Tom."

"This is news?" his mate answered. "They're all perverts."

Leigh's soapy hands worked up one leg, and RJ bit her lip, stifling a groan. She pulled her head out of the hole and shook it a few times to clear it of the vision. "I will not look," she told herself firmly. "That's a disgusting thin' to do."

She wiped off her brow. Despite the fact that it was a relatively cool spring morning, RJ was feeling a little flushed. *But I have to clear away that bit of insulation. It's my job. I'll be nothing but professional and avert my eyes.* She snorted. *Yeah, right.* But still, RJ hesitated.

"The human is having an attack of conscience. I can tell," the male declared.

His wife made a face. "How would you know?"

"Not by watching you, that's for damn sure."

Losing the battle with herself, RJ peered back into the garage, easily getting a luscious eyeful of Leigh's slick, naked body through the gentle cloud of steam. She was careful not to make any noise as she pulled away a piece of insulation that was obstructing her view.

Leigh soaped a large blue washcloth, running it slowly across her stomach.

RJ swallowed convulsively and whimpered just a tiny bit.

The hot water felt wonderful against Leigh's skin. The shower in the garage was blessed with fabulous water pressure, and her skin tingled where the water stuck her. She moaned with pleasure, and RJ nearly lost her footing.

Swearing quietly, RJ backed up out of the hole and looked around self-consciously. This was like some demented test. And she was failing. Miserably. Giving up any pretense of restraint, she tossed the hammer and crowbar on the ground so she wouldn't risk dropping them into the shower, and stuck her head back down inside. Her hair was now damp from the escaping steam, and her forehead and upper lip were beaded with perspiration.

Leigh soaped her washcloth again and tilted her head back. Eyes closed, she ran it languidly up her neck, then back down to circle both her breasts.

This time RJ couldn't stop the escape of a low groan of

pleasure as she watched Leigh's nipples tighten.

But Leigh didn't seem to hear it above the spray of the water.

The blonde lifted one arm, trailing the cloth from her underarms to the tips of her fingers. Then switched hands and repeated the procedure. Her skin was pink and flushed, and RJ could feel an increase in the rising and falling of her own chest.

"Lord, ha' mercy," RJ moaned, her eyes riveted on her lover, a throbbing in her lower belly making itself painfully known.

Leigh stuck her head directly under the spray, washing out the shampoo. Bubbles cascaded down her body over slippery firm breasts and disappeared over her thighs and between her legs. She picked up the washcloth and followed the bubble trail as she began to slowly drag the cloth between her legs.

RJ gasped. Her feet lost their purchase on the sloped roof, and her arms began to flail wildly in an attempt to keep her balance. Her head popped out of the hole.

Leigh looked up into the empty hole. She cocked her head to the side and waited a few seconds before hearing a few loud thumps, what sounded like frantic clawing, and a high-pitched yelp. There was an even louder thudding sound, immediately followed by, "Son of a bitch!"

Leigh laughed and turned on the cold water. If RJ could swear, then she was still alive. And Leigh needed to cool down. RJ wasn't the only one affected by her little show.

The male and female looked down at RJ, who was laughing and coughing weakly, sprawled out in the dirt alongside her hammer and crowbar.

The male scowled and put his acorn into his mate's waiting, outstretched hand. "I'll have to owe you the rest," he mumbled grumpily.

"Are you good for it?"

"No."

"That's what I thought."

"Will you accept payment in sexual favors?" he asked hopefully.

The female thought about that for a moment. One acorn would last her the afternoon. She shrugged. "What the heck, I could stand a quickie."

"Is there another kind?"

"Not for squirrels."

Chapter
6

RJ sat on the front porch of the diner, sipping coffee, intently watching the road from behind her sunglasses. She was bound and determined not to look as excited as she felt. She groaned inwardly, deciding not to think about the ways Leigh excited her. At least, not until they were alone. She cleared her throat and shifted a little in her chair.

After Leigh's little "show" in the shower the other morning, she'd been left so frustrated and horny that she couldn't even begin to say no when the smirking trucker invited her to come along for a "little adventure." As a matter of fact, she'd answered yes just a little louder and more quickly than she meant to.

Pete bit back a grin as he sat down in the chair next to RJ. It had taken a little work, but he'd finally gotten permission for his friend to leave Glory and the diner for a time. Which was lucky, considering RJ had already accepted Leigh's invitation. In his heart, Pete really believed RJ deserved, and needed, this time off. "So, you ready to go? Got everything you need?"

RJ gave the half-full duffel bag at her foot a nudge. "Yeah, I think I'm about as ready as I can be."

Pete tugged an envelope from his hip pocket and pressed it into RJ's hand. "You'll need this."

The tall woman cracked it open and stared at the thick pile

of bills. "Oh, Pete. I've got my own savings." *Though why I've bothered to tuck it away for all these years, I'm not really sure.* "I can't be taking your money. There's—"

"There's no sense in arguing about it." He wrapped RJ's fingers around the envelope and held them there. "We all decided you should have it. You're going to need it out there." He grinned knowingly. "Besides, if you want to have a good time with Miss Leigh Matthews, part of that will mean being able to treat her properly."

RJ nodded reluctantly, touched by her friend's generosity. She tucked the money into her bag and swallowed. "Thank you, Peter. I'll make sure it goes to good use."

"Your good time is a good use. Enjoy it, Fitz. It's not everyone that gets a second chance to go back. Even for just a while."

"Now that's the truth." RJ ducked her head and smiled. She knew that Pete and several others had petitioned like hell on her behalf. She wasn't about to waste this opportunity. RJ had something special she was burning to do...now if she could only figure out a way to have Leigh take her there without being too suspicious.

"Leigh'll be here in about twenty minutes." Pete stood up.

"Smart ass," RJ mumbled, tossing the cold coffee into the parking lot. "You might have mentioned that a half an hour ago."

"And kill all that wonderful anticipation?" Pete pushed open the diner door, smiling broadly. "Nah."

RJ followed Pete inside so she could get a quick bite to eat. It was, she had to admit, very early; the sun had only just begun to peek over the horizon, invading the shadows with splashes of gold. She hoped Leigh would slow down long enough to enjoy some breakfast before they started out on the road.

The dark-haired woman settled down at the counter and looked to Mavis. "Don't suppose I could get a little breakfast before I go?"

Mavis rolled her eyes as if RJ's request was a huge imposition. "If you *insist*. Usual?"

"If you don't mind."

Mavis simply called RJ's name back to the kitchen. "So how does it feel to be famous?"

RJ scowled. She knew what Mavis meant. Glory was buzzing over her receiving permission to spend some time in the outside world.

"I didn't ask to be famous."

"Sometimes things happen without you asking for them, RJ. Even a pilot, gone handyman, gone two-bit tour guide like yourself should know that by now."

"Two-bit!"

"If the crooked halo fits."

RJ's eyes narrowed. "It's no wonder Pete married you. You're *both* troublemakers."

Mavis just laughed and scooted her scrawny ass behind the counter. "And here I thought it was for my body."

"It was!" Pete exclaimed happily, smacking Mavis on her bony rump as he passed by.

RJ made a face at the couple. "I'm going to be sick."

"Before you've eaten Pete's eggs?"

Even RJ laughed at the indignant look on her friend's face. Pete took his cooking abilities very seriously.

"You both eat hash browns with onion, peppers and ketchup," Mavis told RJ casually, as she laid silverware down at the spot next to RJ.

"Me and Pete?"

"You and Leigh."

"Really?" RJ smiled. "I suppose next you'll be telling me that we're soulmates or some other such silly nonsense, just because we eat our hash browns the same way. If she likes her eggs scrambled, I suppose you'll be thinking she's obligated to have my baby."

Mavis turned her back on RJ and reached through the service hole to pick up a plate. "I was just making an observation, you grumpy thing. I for one will be glad to be rid of you for a few days. A little peace and quiet couldn't be a bad thing."

"I love you too, Mavis."

The waitress placed a heavy dish on the counter in front of RJ and smiled. "Don't forget, when you get out there, you're going to need to eat and sleep and do all the things you did when you were alive."

RJ shot her an annoyed look and opened her mouth.

"I know. I know. You do those things now. But doing them because you need to is a lot different than doing them out of habit." Her expression softened, "And for heaven's sake, RJ, be careful. Things are a lot different now than you remember them."

"I will, Mavis." She gave the older woman's hand a little squeeze. "Thank you."

Pete looked up just a second before the diner door opened and Leigh walked in. She was wearing jeans, a soft teal-colored t-shirt that brought out the color of her eyes, and a happy smile. She stopped alongside RJ and placed her hand on the taller woman's shoulder, giving it an affectionate squeeze. "I'm back," she said needlessly.

RJ didn't even try to hide the grin on her face when she turned her head around to see Leigh. "Yes, you are. Can I interest you in a little breakfast?" *Lord, did she look so pretty the last time she was here?*

"Depends."

"Pete made extra greasy bacon, extra crunchy hash browns and extra runny eggs. Mavis burnt the toast." She laughed and took Leigh's hand. Without thinking, she lifted it to her mouth and softly kissed the fingers.

Leigh's eyes twinkled at the unexpectedly affectionate gesture. "It sounds wonderful. And for once I won't be in too much of a hurry to enjoy it."

The trucker sat down on the stool next to RJ's, picking up a few grumbles from a couple of men who were eating at the nearest table. She pushed their comments out of her mind until one particularly loud one caused a flush to rise to Mavis' cheeks. Leigh jumped to her feet and was ready to stalk over there, when RJ's hand on her arm stopped her dead in her tracks.

"Don't, Leigh, it's not worth it. Just settle down and eat your breakfast." Her voice went a little cold. "I'll take care of it." She waited until her friend was settled next to her, then she stood and crossed the room with a purposeful gait. RJ placed two fists on the table and leaned over as she spoke quietly to the men.

Leigh watched nervously, ready to jump up and help RJ should the need arise.

When RJ was finished, both men laid down money for their bill and got up from the table. They walked slowly and carefully over to Leigh, frequently glancing back at RJ, who was standing tall, her arms crossed over her chest with one auburn eyebrow perched high on her forehead. The younger of the two cleared his throat awkwardly and faced Leigh. "We're sorry, miss. We didn't mean to offend you or your friend."

Leigh blinked. "Okay," she said slowly, her questioning

gaze shifting to RJ. She refocused on the men. "What you said was wrong." Leigh stared pointedly at the older man's crotch, making him squirm. "We really don't need or want one of *those*, you know."

Both men blushed.

"Though I'm sure it comes in handy on camping trips or for writing your name in snow."

"Unless your name is Bartholomew," one of the men mumbled unhappily.

Leigh winced. Even after a six-pack, that name would be a real bitch.

RJ cleared her throat from behind them, and the men nearly bolted from the diner. She tried her best not to smile as she approached Leigh. "And here I was telling *them* to be nice."

"What?" Leigh affected an innocent face.

"They're entitled to their opinion, but they don't need to be voicing it in such a manner." RJ sat back down next to Leigh. "There's no need to be rude."

"What did you—"

"It's not important." RJ winked at Leigh and picked up a fork, poking her hash browns. "If you'd put a little ketchup on those, they'd be ready to eat."

Leigh glanced down at the hash browns Mavis had slid in front of her when she wasn't paying attention. They were gently steaming and smelled like bacon grease. She groaned with pleasure. *RJ's right. It's not important. Besides, I can always torture it out of her later.*

Leigh wanted to start her week off on a good foot, and she was bound and determined not to let a couple of assholes spoil her plans. She smiled brightly at RJ. "Ketchup it is."

RJ shouldered her bag as they walked hand in hand toward Leigh's truck. She wasn't expecting to see the trailer attached. "Has something changed?" Mildly alarmed green eyes shifted to Leigh. "I thought you had the week off."

Leigh tugged on RJ's hand. "Hush. Nothing has changed. We're headed to Seattle. I own the trailer," she pointed toward the back of the truck, "and the tractor," her finger shifted to the cab. "And right now, the trailer is sitting empty."

She stopped and turned to RJ, running the tip of that same

finger up the centerline of her chest, to her shoulder, then down her arm. "We're going to have a great week together." *At least I hope we are.* Leigh was a little nervous. She'd never driven with anyone but her dad, and she'd certainly never traveled or spent more than a few hours at a time with any woman. *I am pitiful,* she admitted to herself.

RJ smiled fondly at Leigh. "I'm sure we will." Her attention turned back to the bright red truck. "That's an awfully big rig for such a—"

Leigh turned and began walking backwards in front of RJ. She laughed and poked RJ in the chest playfully. "Don't say it! There are no short jokes allowed."

"Who'd be joking?"

"You're evil."

RJ quirked a brow. "You're just now noticing that?" They began to walk around to the passenger side when RJ's hand grazed the big machine. She let out an explosive breath. It suddenly felt like someone was standing squarely in the center of her chest. She gasped and squeezed her eyes shut, feeling dizzy and queasy at the same time. RJ barely heard Leigh asking her what was wrong over the buzzing in her ears. Then strong hands were holding her upright against the truck. She gasped again, taking in a deep breath and opening her eyes. RJ blinked, stunned. Colors and smells seemed just a shade dimmer, and as the buzzing receded, Leigh's words came into focus.

"Jesus Christ! Are you okay?" Leigh desperately searched RJ's face. *She's having a heart attack?*

"Yeah. Yeah." RJ swallowed and looked around her. The sensation was indescribable. She felt alive. *God! I didn't know this was going to happen!* RJ had simply assumed that for her little journey she would remain in the same form that she did at the diner: tangible to those living, but still existing in her own realm. Her eyes flickered from object to object, and her ears perked up at the faint sound of birds in the distance. Things weren't as vivid as they were normally were. This wasn't worse, just...her mind scrambled for the right description. *Just "different."*

"Are you sure? Maybe you should go to the—"

"I'm well and truly all right, Leigh." RJ was still a little dazed but did her best not to show it. She was scaring her companion. But how could she not react? It had been a lifetime since she'd felt this way. With every breath, her lungs tingled in a way that was as familiar as it was new. RJ took Leigh's hands in her own. They were trembling slightly. "I was just light-headed for a moment. Musta been my amazing speed as I rounded that corner." Her gaze softened. "Truly."

Leigh studied her carefully. As though nothing had happened, RJ looked like the very picture of health. "You're sure?" she finally asked.

"I'm very sure."

Leigh narrowed her eyes. "It's probably those disgusting cigarettes you smoke."

"Oh Lord. Not another one." RJ threw her hands in the air. "There are worse habits, you know. It's not like I'm a killer of small animals or defiler of virgins."

At the teasing note in RJ's voice, Leigh instantly relaxed. *I guess she is okay.*

When they rounded the corner of the truck to the passenger's side, RJ's feet froze mid-step. "My, my." She pointed at the rig. "Is there a reason you've got a naked woman painted on the side of your truck?" RJ laughed throatily. "A very buxom, naked woman, I should say."

"She's not naked," Leigh protested. "She's wearing panties." The blonde woman groaned and let her head sag forward a little. God, she hated that picture. Not that the woman wasn't pretty. She was. She just also happened to be a picture of Leigh's mother, who had died when the trucker was still in diapers. The fact that she was plastered naked on the side of Leigh's truck for all the world to see was not something she appreciated. She had loved her father with all her heart; but the man was tacky as hell.

RJ's eyes widened a little as she examined the picture in detail. "It's you with long hair!" Her eyes shot from Leigh to the picture and back again. She smiled delightedly. *Watch yourself, RJ. This lass is a wild one.*

Leigh ground her teeth together. "It's *not* me," she insisted petulantly. "I'm not that...that...you know." She pointed to the picture's ample breasts. There was no way she was going to say who it really was.

RJ snorted appreciatively. "Damn near."

"It's not me."

"Sure it's not." RJ's tone made it clear she didn't believe a word of what Leigh was saying. She gestured toward the center of the painting. "And what happened here?" She scowled like a child denied one of her favorite toys. Or in this case, an adult denied one of her favorite toys. "You're covering the best part!"

A black strip had been painted over the woman's chest, mostly hiding her more spectacular assets.

Leigh put her hands on her hips. "I 'fixed' it, if you must know." In actuality, the week before, after enjoying her fifth tequila shooter and enduring yet another comment about the picture, Leigh had had a full-blown hissy fit and taken a can of spray paint to the truck. She'd been meaning to get the whole thing repainted ever since, but she hadn't had a day off yet. Her favorite body shop was going to be her first stop when she got back to Seattle.

RJ scratched her jaw, not willing to peel her eyes away from the picture. "Why would you need to *fix* your own truck?"

"It was my father's rig. I sort of inherited it." *Along with its $2,000.00 a month payment,* she thought wryly.

Even though the tall woman was clearly absorbed in the picture, Leigh refused to look at it. There were some things a daughter didn't really want to know about her mother. How she looked in a purple, polka-dotted thong was one of them. "It was his paint job. Not mine."

RJ groaned enthusiastically, examining the picture with a critical eye. "It's a lovely picture."

"Pervert!" Leigh barked irrationally. This was her mother, for God's sake! She dug into her pocket and pulled out her keys, wordlessly deactivating the alarm and opening RJ's door before stalking around to the other side of the cab.

RJ blinked. "What did I say?"

RJ felt a certain amount of apprehension about leaving. *This is a once in a lifetime...err...after lifetime chance. Don't blow it.* Taking a deep breath, she tossed in her duffel and grabbed the door handles, pulling herself up into the passenger seat. Once she'd stowed her bag at her feet, she pulled the door shut and took a good look around. "Jesus, Mary and Joseph!"

Leigh jumped a little bit at RJ's loud exclamation. "What? What's wrong?" She stood up and began looking around the cab. She'd seen two rather odd-looking squirrels puttering around her truck the last time she was at the diner. Could they have gotten inside?

"Where the hell do you hide Buck Rogers in this thing?" RJ's eyes were as wide as saucers as they took in the truck's high tech console.

Leigh flushed with pleasure at RJ's reaction to her baby.

"Does he live in the closet?" RJ pointed back into the sleeping area, then jumped to her feet and began to explore the space. "Holy hell! It's larger than my room at my mother's."

Leigh snickered.

"What?"

She sat back in her seat and buckled her seatbelt, sliding her sunglasses on with one hand as she started the truck with the other. "Do you really live with your mother?"

RJ sat back in the seat and reluctantly tore her eyes from the dashboard to focus on Leigh. "Yes, I really live with my mother," she informed her bluntly. "Is there something wrong with that?"

"You don't attend Star Trek and Xena conventions wearing silly costumes and stalking the actors, do you?"

RJ looked totally confused. "I have no idea what on this earth you're talking about."

"Good." Leigh nodded. A girl couldn't be too careful. Serial killers were one thing, but those weirdo convention-goers were something else entirely.

"Why shouldn't I live with my mother?" RJ pressed. *Maybe folks don't do that anymore.*

"No reason." Leigh shrugged one shoulder. She hadn't meant to insult RJ. "It's sweet. Old-fashioned as hell, but sweet."

RJ relaxed a little. She'd been right. Things were just different now. This adjusting to things in the twenty-first century wouldn't be so bad. She would just have to be savvy about things. "Maybe I'm just a sweet, old-fashioned kind of woman."

"Yeah, right," Leigh snorted as she put the truck into gear and pulled away from the diner.

"And what's that supposed to mean?" RJ crossed her arms over her chest as she sank into the soft leather of the seat. She gripped her biceps in an effort to keep from reaching out and playing with the buttons on the console in front of her. Her fingers literally itched.

"Sweet, old-fashioned women *do not,* I repeat *do not,* know how to do the things with their tongues that you do."

RJ bit the inside of her cheek, fighting not to smile stupidly. The level of appreciation in Leigh's voice had her ego purring nicely, but it wouldn't do to come off like an arrogant s.o.b. "I aim to please," she finally chuckled, feeling the heat in her cheeks.

"Your aim is dead on." Leigh's gaze slid sideways. "Don't forget to buckle up."

RJ hesitated. "Ummm...buckle..."

"Your seatbelt."

"No, thank you," RJ muttered uneasily. "I'm sure I'll be fine." Her pulse began to pound, and her mind flashed on a scene of the ocean coming closer and closer, before a stunning impact. Then, there was no air as she weakly, helplessly, tried to unhook herself from her plane as it sank.

"Hey," Leigh slowed the truck, "are you okay?" *What the hell is going on?*

"I...um..." RJ licked her lips, tasting the sudden saltiness of her own sweat.

"It's against the law not to wear your belt. You know that."

"Of course," RJ said quickly. *A law?* "It's just...just..."

Leigh pulled over on the shoulder and stopped the truck. She quickly unbuckled herself and knelt in the space between her and RJ's seat. "Tell me what's the matter?" she asked earnestly, slipping off her sunglasses to get a better look at RJ.

RJ felt a little cornered, but Leigh's voice was reassuring. "I had an accident when I was younger. And now I get..." she licked her lips, "I get a little claustrophobic. If wearing the belt is a requirement, then you'd best turn around and—"

"Hold on." Leigh cupped RJ's cheek and frowned. Her skin felt cool and clammy, and her eyes held a hint of panic. *That must be what happened back in the parking lot. Some sort of panic attack.* "You don't have to buckle up if you don't want to." *I'd pay twice the ticket to keep you from being upset.* "I just don't want something to happen to you."

RJ let out a shuddering breath. "It won't." She pinned Leigh with her eyes. "I mean, you'll be careful driving, right?"

"Cross my heart."

"Okay, then, Leigh Matthews," RJ smiled tentatively, "time to get this show on the road."

The day had gone better than either woman had dared hope. RJ and Leigh had laughed, talked, and sung along with the radio. Neither woman was even remotely shy, which helped...since RJ didn't know a single word to any of the songs she was singing along to.

"Margaritaville" would have kicked arse in the 1930s, RJ mused.

Over the past day, RJ had learned more than one truly interesting fact about her new friend. But at the moment, it wasn't Leigh who was occupying her mind.

RJ had to pee. God, she had to pee! Her back was aching from sitting all day, and she sat up a little straighter, stretching her sore, tired muscles. She wiggled her toes in her shoes, which felt tight and constricting. *My feet must be swollen.* Next, her stomach growled, and she laid her hand across it, feeling a little lightheaded. Had she skipped lunch? She couldn't remember. *How could I forget that being alive totally sucked?*

To top it off, Leigh had seemed a little jumpy for the past hour or so, casting the cab in an uneasy silence. She fidgeted constantly, her eyes straying to her odometer every few moments.

"Leigh, we need to stop."

No, no, no, no. God is not this cruel. They were about three miles outside of Rosie's Diner, which happened to be located smack dab in the middle of nowhere. "Why do we need to stop?" she challenged desperately. "We stopped only five and half hours ago!"

"Are you listening to yourself, Leigh?" RJ's eyebrows shot skyward. "We just do."

"Why?"

RJ looked at Leigh like she was insane. "Because I didn't pack any diapers, and I've got to go!"

"It's only forty-five more miles until we reach a Burger King. How about we stop there for dinner?" She gave RJ her best wishing look.

"Forty-five more miles," RJ groaned. "Perhaps I didn't make myself clear. We *need* to stop. Besides, only a moment or two ago, I saw a sign for a diner that said it was five more miles. What's wrong with stopping there?"

"It's closed."

"At six o'clock on a Monday night?"

"Yes. It burned down last summer."

"Really?"

"Absolutely."

RJ squirmed in the seat, bemoaning her rotten luck. Then she noticed Leigh wouldn't meet her eyes. "What aren't you telling me, Ms. Matthews? I smell a rat."

Before Leigh could answer, a small building appeared on the horizon. The lot in front of it was filled with cars and trucks.

"Shit," Leigh mumbled.

"Look. It's not burned down or closed."

"I must have been thinking of someplace else," Leigh lied unconvincingly. "But that place is disgusting. There aren't even any roaches there. They're all gone, striking for better conditions."

"I don't care. I'm not going to lick the floor; I just need to use the bathroom."

"But Burger King's bathroom is reeeeeally clean. And they have these little sanitary paper seat covers. And—"

RJ cocked her head to the side. Leigh was a beauty and all, but a bit odd at times. "Lemme put it this way. How attached are you to these nice leather seats? 'Cause if I have to wait more than a few minutes, I'm thinking you'll be needing to re-cover them."

Leigh pointed out her side window. "There's a perfectly good ditch right there. Whaddya say? I have paper towels in the back." *Oh, God, she's going to think I'm demented.*

She's demented!

Leigh started to ease her foot off the accelerator, hoping RJ wouldn't notice the subtle change in speeds.

"Don't even think about it." RJ's eyes flashed. "You might be used to relieving yourself on the side of the road, but I certainly am not. Not when I can see a perfectly good restaurant up ahead," she complained bitterly. *My mother was right. The world has gone to hell in a hand basket.*

"Fine. Fine." Leigh gunned the engine, causing RJ to flop back in her seat.

"Sudden movement is bad," she growled. "Very bad."

"Sorry."

Leigh pulled into the diner's parking lot, driving at a snail's pace as she scanned the lot. Using her CB while RJ napped, she'd made it a point to call a couple of the truckers she knew who hung out at the diner. One of them had known what type of car Judith drove. And when it came to women you could never be too careful. *Her car isn't here. Thank you, thank you, thank you!* Leigh didn't handle "unhappy women scenes" very well. *This must be her day off.*

RJ stood up in the truck and began to bang on her door with

her fist. Was Leigh some sort of sadist? What had she gotten herself into all in the name of great sex? "Do you just want to see me wet my pants?"

Leigh grimaced. "Not particularly." She pulled into an extra-long space that was designated for trucks only. Unfortunately, they were now at the far end of a very long parking lot.

The trucker chewed her bottom lip, feeling a little guilty over RJ's suffering. "Do you want me to drop you—"

The tuck hadn't even stopped completely before RJ was halfway out the door.

"Or we can walk," Leigh commented drolly as she shut off the ignition.

Both women jumped out of the truck, and RJ landed right in the center of a deep, very cold, mud puddle, sending a wave of frigid water over her feet and onto her calves. "Sweet Jesus." She shivered, gritting her teeth at the sensation of the water and the immediate signal it sent to her protesting bladder.

Leigh bit back a laugh. Now that she wasn't freaked out about them running into Judith, she was starting to see the humor in this situation. Mainly because she wasn't the one suffering. Which wasn't very nice, but it was still funny.

They walked quickly across the lot, and with every step, the impulse for Leigh to come clean with RJ grew. *Especially since you never know who you could run into.* Leigh didn't want Judith to think she was callous. Even as casual as they were with each other, some things were just plain rude. She tilted her head down, focusing her eyes on her shoes, and she walked along, studiously avoiding the bigger puddles. "RJ?"

"Yes?" Her voice was tight.

"Umm...you see, there...there's this woman that I'm sort of personal friends with—"

"How nice for you."

Leigh groaned inwardly. She really couldn't blame RJ for being sore at her for wanting her to pee in the ditch for no apparent reason—but she didn't have to be snippy about it, did she?

Leigh quickly apologized and received only a miserable grunt as a reply. *I'll make it up to you, RJ. I promise.*

"Anyway," the trucker continued in a rush, "about this woman. She umm...well, we've been friends for a couple of years now. Good friends." Leigh held up her palms. "Now, before you ask, it's not like she's a girlfriend or anything." She shook her head emphatically. "Absolutely not. Our relationship isn't like that." A deep breath as she gestured wildly. "I've been totally up front with her from the very beginning. We're only friends. Good friends. Did I mention that?"

Leigh decided to leave out the fact that Judith had actually had a couple of serious relationships since she'd known her. Last summer, when the waitress got engaged to the guy who delivered the hamburger buns to the diner, Leigh assumed their "good friendship" would be over. But Judith had convinced her otherwise. In the broom closet near the diner's exit. Twice. Which was more than enough to ease the teensy weensy, nearly non-existent amount of guilt Leigh had felt over their relationship.

"I just don't want things to be awkward if we happen to see her. Which we won't," Leigh continued. God, this being honest was a pain in the ass. She'd always suspected that it would be. "Judith works here." Leigh's brows knit. "And for some reason I get the feeling that she's sort of the possessive —"

RJ had been so quiet during Leigh's confession that the blonde woman paused and glanced up to gauge her reaction, wondering if RJ thought she was a huge slut. *Not like she's in a position to judge, though,* Leigh considered testily. She suddenly stopped walking.

"What in the..." Leigh spun around in a circle. Not only wasn't RJ next to her, she was nowhere near her. She looked toward the diner and caught a flash of her new lover as she opened the door and ran in. Which meant that RJ hadn't heard most of Leigh's one-sided conversation. She sighed heavily. "Thanks so much, RJ. I knew you'd understand. Pouring out this incredibly awkward story was much easier than I anticipated."

"Talking to yourself is the first sign you're cracking, Tom Cat."

Leigh turned around to see her old family friend. "Hello, Rooster. And if you ever call me Tom Cat again, I'm going to kick your tubby ass from here to the Pacific Ocean."

"Last time it was just to the state line." Rooster grinned unrepentantly. "I must be getting more annoying in my old age."

"I can vouch for that," Leigh said against his bristly cheek, as she pulled the man into a warm hug.

Rooster tried several times to coax Leigh inside. But for some reason she seemed reluctant, so they talked in the parking lot about trucking and sports, the only two topics Rooster had

much interest in. Other than sex. And ever since the time Leigh
cold-cocked him for going into too much detail about his best
weekend ever, he'd at least tried to avoid that subject.

When Leigh glanced down at her watch, then up at the diner
door for tenth time, Rooster asked, "Gotta get back on the road?"

"No. It's my week off," she answered absently.

Rooster grinned. "Waiting for somebody?"

Leigh nodded.

"Me?"

"You wish."

"Who, then?"

"RJ." *Where in the hell is she? It's been nearly twenty minutes.*

"Holy shit! A man?" Rooster moved around in front of
Leigh to capture her attention.

"Get the fuck out of my way, Rooster," Leigh laughed, gently shoved the large man out of the way and continued eyeing the
door. "RJ is a woman. I met her in South Dakota."

"South Dakota!" He waggled a scolding finger at Leigh.
"Tell me you didn't pick up a hitchhiker. I've warned you about
that!"

Unaccountably, Leigh felt herself blushing. "She's not a
hitchhiker."

"And." He drew out the word.

"She's a friend I'm taking with me to Seattle." *And that's
all you're getting out of me, Mr. Gossip.*

Rooster put his hands on his hips. "And just what do you
know about her? Hmm?" he pressed. "She could be dangerous!"

Leigh lips formed a thin line. "Don't get in my business,
Rooster." But her eyes softened almost immediately. "I'm fine.
You don't need to worry about me."

Rooster straightened indignantly. "Who's worried?" He
pulled his belt up as far as his enormous belly would allow.

Leigh patted his arm. "Not you." *Is she going to make me
go in there after her? Uh oh. What if something's happened to
her?* The blonde woman's face clouded with worry. "I need to
go inside now." Without waiting for Rooster to answer, Leigh
resumed her trek. This time at a much faster pace.

"Is she good-lookin'?" Rooster struggled to catch up, his
ample girth making the task more difficult.

"Beautiful," Leigh answered without hesitation.

Rooster scowled and walked around two cars that Leigh

scooted between. "She's not all mannish, is she?" He shook his head, which caused the rolls of fat around his neck to wobble wildly. "I can't stand those types."

Leigh smirked. "Doesn't matter. You're going to think she's attractive, either way."

The red-haired man scrubbed his face. "That's what you think!"

Years before, Rooster and his buddies had complained bitterly about the "unfeminine" ways of a woman Leigh had taken an interest in. Problem was, the woman was undeniably attractive, and all the men knew it. Just to be a bitch, Leigh had informed them that the woman was so "unfeminine" that if any of them found her even remotely appealing, it meant that they were gay but in denial of their true feelings. Ever since, Rooster had been paranoid about any woman not in a dress.

Leigh threw open the diner door. She headed straight for the bathroom, but was sidetracked by a loud gasp. Spinning around, her eyes widened and she felt her heart drop to her knees. Judith was standing in front of RJ with a large knife in her hand, and RJ's white shirt was covered in blood.

The trucker bolted across the room, knocking down a chair in the process. "Goddamn it, you didn't have to stab her!" she yelled frantically, pawing at RJ's shirt to find the wound.

RJ looked down at Leigh in shock.

"Stab?" Judith whispered, looking at the knife in her hands as though she didn't know she was holding it. "What in the world are you talking about?"

RJ quickly grabbed Leigh's hands. "Whoa! Calm down. I'm not stabbed, lass."

Leigh's eyes darted back to Judith. "But the knife, the blood..."

RJ burst into laughter. "She was just bringing me a knife to cut my burger. And this ketchup bottle exploded on me when I opened it." She gestured toward the bottle that was still oozing. RJ casually reached down to her plate and picked up a french fry. Raising a sassy eyebrow, she dipped the fry on her shirt and popped it into her mouth.

Leigh was so pale, she looked like she was about to pass out, so RJ quickly wrapped an arm around her, careful not to stain Leigh's shirt with any errant ketchup. "Hang on," she told her worriedly.

Judith's hackles immediately rose at the interaction between

Leigh and RJ. Leigh was still touching the woman as though she was worried about her, and RJ's voice, while amused, held an undeniable hint of affection. "You two know each other?" Judith asked curiously, hoping she didn't sound as anxious about the answer as she suddenly was.

Leigh swallowed. The fact that RJ wasn't stabbed and that she was talking to Judith was just now starting to sink in. "Hello, Judith. I didn't see your car out front." *Oh, that was brilliant.*

"Ken has it in the garage tonight. He's putting new brakes on it for me, so I got a ride in with Buck this afternoon." She glanced at RJ, who was looking between her and Leigh with bemused detachment, happily munching away at her fries. The smug look annoyed Judith, and she took a step closer to Leigh, who was now standing without any help. "You take on a new co-driver?"

"Yeah, right," Leigh snorted. Like she'd actually let someone else drive her truck. What was Judith thinking? "Well, nice seeing you. Bye." Leigh tugged RJ's hand to leave, but the tall woman's feet were rooted firmly to the ground. She tugged again. But RJ refused to move. Leigh closed her eyes. *C'mon, RJ. It's time to go, before there's a scene!*

"Leigh, could you relax just a bit? We've been in that truck for hours now. We're supposed to be on vacation." A little defiantly, she paused and took a long, slow sip of her Coke. "We've got nowhere to be, and I'm hungry and a little tired. Can't we just take a short break?"

Oooo...not the right thing to say, Irish, Rooster thought as he sank heavily into a booth where he'd have a ringside seat for all the action. He felt in his pocket for a quarter in case he needed to call the cops.

Leigh spoke without moving her mouth. "I don't wanna stay. I wanna go right this very minute."

"Well," RJ looked confused. But her friend seemed so stressed that she decided to give in, just so she wouldn't make things worse. "I suppose we can—"

"Yeah, you want to go! You always want to go." Judith's head bobbed curtly. "And now I know why." She blinked, disgusted by how jealous and just plain pissed off she felt.

"Now, Judith—"

"Don't you 'now Judith' me! You, you ..." Judith's head looked like it was going to explode as she fought for words.

Unexpectedly, she whirled around and snatched up a towel from the counter for RJ. "Here." She thrust it forward. "You'll need this to keep from dripping."

RJ took the towel, muttering a quiet "Thanks" as she sat down. *Oh, boy.* She sensed that things between Leigh and the waitress were about to get very ugly.

"No problem." Judith stared at the trucker, "I mean, we wouldn't want you to make a mess in Leigh's precious truck, right? She's probably got to get back on the road this very god-damned instant!"

Leigh winced and braced herself. At this point, it had been her experience that women either began to cry or hit. She silently prayed she could avoid a black eye. That had looked ridiculous. "Maybe you should go out to the truck, RJ. Judith and I need to have a personal discussion. Alone," she emphasized.

"No, we don't," Judith snapped. "I'll be right back with your order." The waitress stormed away.

"But I didn't order anything," Leigh muttered in frustration.

RJ winced. "I ordered for you. I figured you'd be hungry."

Leigh smiled insincerely. "Thanks."

"Umm, Leigh, I didn't mean to cause you any trouble with that woman." RJ tilted her head toward the kitchen. "I didn't know you had a regular thing with anyone. I thought, well, I just figured—"

"We're not a 'regular' anything, honest."

But you're sure something to her. That much is crystal clear. RJ handed Leigh her towel. The shirt she was wearing was a lost cause now anyway.

Leigh leaned against the table and began wiping the globs of sticky ketchup from her fingers. Nervously, she glanced back to the kitchen. "Let's go before she comes back." *I'm such a chickenshit.*

"If you're not a 'regular anything' with that woman, then don't be afraid to face her. We're not doing anything but eating here." She gestured longingly toward her food. "Come on, Leigh, I'm starved, and the food here is so much different than it is at Fitz's." These fries were shaped in curlicues with Cajun salt!

"Look, RJ, I'm not sure if you understand." *I don't even understand it.* "Judith and I—"

Just then, Judith emerged from the kitchen with a plate in

her hand. She slammed it down in front of Leigh. "Eat!" she commanded.

Leigh gulped and looked down into the plate of food she wouldn't dare eat even if she were starving to death. "That was fast."

"Of course it was. I know how you hate to wait for anything!"

"Christ." Leigh rolled her eyes. This was going to turn into a catfight. She just knew it.

RJ thrust out her hand to the waitress. "I'm RJ Fitzgerald. And you are?"

"Oh, I'm no one important. I'm just a stop along the route. One of many, no doubt."

Leigh narrowed her eyes.

Judith took the time to shake RJ's hand. "My name's Judith." She flicked an icy glare at Leigh, even though she continued to talk to RJ. "It's nice to meet you, though, Ms. Fitzgerald. You known Tom Cat long?"

RJ eyebrows crawled up her forehead. "Tom Cat?"

Leigh's face took on an angry flush. "You know I hate to be called that, Judith," she ground out forcefully. She was losing patience fast. Leigh hadn't wanted to stop at Rosie's and would have preferred to avoid the diner and Judith altogether. But they were here now, and Judith had no cause to be bent out of shape. "I've known RJ for a little over a month," she answered coolly for RJ, knowing it would annoy the waitress.

"Well, then, I'm sure you're *intimately* acquainted by now. How long did we know each other first?" She laughed without a trace of humor. "The first time I saw you, you asked me out. Then it was your very next time through that you—"

"That's enough." Leigh's voice went cold. "There's no reason to act this way, Judith. We're not a couple, and we never have been."

Judith lifted her chin at Leigh's pronouncement. But she couldn't deny it.

Leigh lowered her voice. "I've been completely honest in all my relationships."

Judith's eyes snapped angrily at the dig about her former fiancé. "You're right. And you're never gonna let me live it down. I guess I'm just not as perfect as you are...Tom Cat," she added acidly. Judith took a cleansing breath and turned her attention to RJ. "I'm sorry, Ms. Fitzgerald."

"Call me RJ."

She nodded. "RJ. I'm sure you'll find Tom Cat is an enjoyable ride, just not much for commitment."

RJ cleared her throat. She could feel Leigh's body stiffen next to hers, and a surge of anger welled up within her. RJ reached out and took Leigh's hand, giving it a firm squeeze. "I don't think you need to concern yourself about the commitment between Leigh and me. I'm *very* clear on the boundaries of our relationship, and am more than happy to enjoy the time we have together without pressing for what'll never be. And so far," her lips curved into an unexpected, devastatingly sexy smile, "I've not a single complaint." She gazed fondly at her companion, giving her a ghost of a wink. *That'll show Ms. Attitude a thing or two.*

Leigh smiled gratefully at RJ. In a couple of sentences she'd managed to completely shut Judith up. The blonde woman blocked out Judith's presence altogether and quietly asked RJ, "Can we leave now. Please?"

"You betcha, beautiful. It's my plan to take you somewhere wonderful tonight and show you what it means to love the Irish." The look on RJ's face clearly told Judith that the conversation was over.

The waitress actually found herself taking a step backwards.

RJ bent down and kissed Leigh on the cheek, allowing her lips to linger until Leigh's face broke out into a full-fledged smile. "I'm going to go and change my shirt and muddy pants."

Leigh reached into her pocket and tossed a couple of bills on the table as RJ headed for the door. "I'm sorry, Judith." Even after this little scene, she couldn't bring herself to be anything more than mildly angry. Judith was the kind of woman who'd always needed more than Leigh was willing to give. She smiled weakly. "At least you didn't punch me in the nose."

Unable to stop herself, Judith smiled back. "It's not like I didn't think of it." She sighed sadly, knowing she was going to miss this particular trucker, and quite sure she'd never lay eyes on her again. "Good bye, Leigh." Judith turned on her heels and disappeared into the kitchen.

Leigh shook her head. "See ya around, Rooster," she said softly as she walked passed the man and toward what she just knew was going to be a fabulous week.

"See ya 'round, Leigh," he replied brightly, waving.

When Leigh had exited the diner, he jumped up from the

booth and shuffled over to her table, plopping down to enjoy her uneaten meal. He'd been scoping it for the past ten minutes like a vulture waiting for its prey to finally croak.

Judith strode out of the kitchen and stopped at the table. "What do you think you're doing?"

Rooster unrolled the large paper napkin, spilling a knife and fork out into his hand. "What's it look like? I'm going to eat her dinner. She didn't even touch it!" He complained, jealously guarding the plate with a beefy arm.

"Trust me, Rooster." Judith couldn't help but snigger. "Unless you don't want to leave the throne for the next couple days, you do *not* want to eat that food."

Rooster yanked his hands off the plate as though he'd been burned. Damn, women were vicious. Tears welled in his eyes. How could she ruin a perfectly innocent burger? Was nothing sacred?

Chapter
7

RJ settled back into her seat, glancing sideways as her friend took her seat behind the steering wheel and buckled her seat belt. The tall woman looked over at the shoulder strap to her right and sighed. *It couldn't possibly happen twice. And if it'll keep Leigh from getting into trouble...* Taking a deep breath, she reached over and pulled the belt across her chest. Her eyes fluttered shut as she clicked it into place just as she had seen Leigh do to hers.

RJ exhaled slowly, trying to push past her current anxiety. "So, I hope you're not too mad at me for that little stunt back there. Your friend was getting on my nerves with the way she was treating you."

Leigh smiled wryly. "Mad?" She laughed. "I don't think so. Though the look Judith gave you when you said you wouldn't 'press' for what could never be was pure evil. I was surprised you didn't disintegrate on the spot." Leigh had noticed that RJ had slipped her seat belt on, but didn't want to draw attention to the fact that she'd noticed.

"Yeah, it did get a bit chilly in there." RJ smirked. "Now, I don't mean any disrespect to you, Leigh Matthews, but I'd really like to know—are there gonna be a lot of women who will hate me and want to slap you when they see us together?"

"Are you asking if I have a girl in every city?" Leigh wiggled pale eyebrows at RJ.

"Girl in every city, dame in every port." RJ gestured aimlessly. "You know what I mean," she retorted, wiggling her brows right back. "I just want to know if we're gonna be in constant danger."

"Nah," Leigh scoffed. "We should be safe." Then she bit her lip. "Mostly."

"Mostly?" RJ thought about that for a second and decided she could live with it. "All right, then; I can accept that. You are a beautiful woman; I totally understand why so many women would be after you. But next time, could you just warn me ahead of time?"

"No need," Leigh assured her, still grinning at RJ's compliment. "There's just a few places in Seattle that we won't be going. It won't be a loss, trust me."

There were a few moments of comfortable silence in the cab before Leigh's brows drew together and she wondered aloud, "Did you mean what you said to Judith? Or was that all just to get her?"

Deciding to invite RJ to spend a week with her had been a spur of the moment decision. When she'd come out of the garage after her shower and found RJ still sitting in the dirt with a sheepish look on her face that Leigh found totally irresistible, the trucker heard the invitation tumble from her lips before she had time to think about it. RJ had said yes so quickly that they really hadn't discussed it again.

"I meant it." RJ shrugged one shoulder. "I really enjoy your company, Leigh. And I umm...am willing to take anything you're willing to give, but I won't be pressuring for more."

Leigh didn't know what to say. No woman had ever been so gracious or aboveboard in seeking a week of uncomplicated companionship and mind-blowing sex. "Wow." It was exactly the way she felt about RJ. Wasn't it? "That's...a relief, RJ."

Eager to change the subject, Leigh brought up their plans for the upcoming week. Or their lack of plans, as happened to be the case. "So tell me, what would you like to do and see in Seattle?" Leigh passed a slow moving car. "I'm assuming you've never visited there before?"

"No. I've never been there. I'm at your mercy." She gave the blonde an ornery grin. "Do with me what you will."

"Oh, RJ." Leigh burst out laughing. "You do like to live dangerously, don't you?"

"Is there any other way? In case you haven't noticed, I'm Irish. Have I mentioned that?" Her smile broadened. "I work hard, I drink hard, if need be, I even fight hard. I'm a lover of beautiful women. Living dangerously is the only way to do it. It comes as naturally as breathing." *Though I haven't done that in a while, and I was a tad woozy at first.*

"And that's when I finally knew I wanted to try the open road for myself. I mean...I think it was the right thing to do, even though I've sort of outgrown the reasons why I did it in the first place." *And talking with you is making me realize just how much I've missed that. The CB is nice, but it's just not the same. You're such a good listener.* Leigh glanced over at RJ, who had been quietly listening to her talk for the last few minutes.

The woman's mouth was hanging open, and she was sound asleep.

Leigh rolled her eyes. "Why is it that our best conversations take place when you're paying no attention whatsoever?"

"I'm listening!" RJ suddenly jumped up, her eyes popping wide open. She looked around in utter confusion and began tugging wildly at her seat belt.

"Hey. It's okay! Shit," Leigh mumbled as she crossed two lanes of traffic and pushed down hard on the brakes, barely resisting the urge to slam the pedal to the floor. Still, she brought the truck to a screeching halt just as RJ began to thrash wildly in her seat. "Calm down! It's just me! It's just your seat belt."

RJ turned wild eyes on Leigh. Her heart was thudding painfully in her chest, threatening to burst free. She was trapped, and panic overwhelmed her. "Get...me...get me—" She sucked in a ragged breath. "Help me." Tears welled in her eyes and instantly spilled over. "Please."

Leigh felt like she'd been hit in the gut and swallowed hard, redoubling her efforts. "Stop moving..." She continued to wrestle with the belt. "I...can't." *Click.* And the seat belt came free.

RJ jumped to her feet, then faltered. Before Leigh could say or do anything, she wrenched the handle on the door and half-jumped, half-fell out of the cab.

"RJ!" Leigh scrambled over her seat and jumped out after RJ.

Leigh lost sight of the auburn-haired woman for a moment in the dusky twilight. But she heard retching into the ditch, which drew her eyes to RJ's kneeling form. Leigh shoved her hands into her pockets, at a total loss as to what to do. She turned her head to the sound of a car whizzing past them. "Are..." Leigh licked her lips nervously, taking a few steps closer to RJ and brushing away a butterfly that seemed to want to light in her hair. "Are you okay?"

"I'm, I'm sorry." RJ took a slow calming breath as the wild rush of adrenaline began to wane. She realized that she was shaking, and she wrapped her arms around her stomach. "I didn't mean to doze off on you like that." *God.*

"I don't care about that." Leigh took a hesitant step closer. "Wasn't such a great idea to buckle up, huh?" The question was obviously rhetorical, but the empathy in her voice was unmistakable. Her father had been a Vietnam vet, and she remembered vividly the nightmares he'd had that broke her heart when she was a child.

RJ shook her head and eyed the truck. "Probably not, but I didn't want you to get into trouble with the law." She cleared her throat and spat hard into the weeds. "If you'll just give me a minute, we can get going again." She took a deep breath and wiped tears from her eyes. "I really am sorry. I feel very silly."

"It's okay." Leigh took the final step to RJ and put a hand on her shoulder, squeezing gently. "Just 'cause we've had a bumpy start doesn't mean things are ruined. Heck, my whole life has been a bumpy start." She shrugged self-deprecatingly. "But things still seem to work out in the end, somehow." Leigh's hand drifted to RJ's hair, and she gently combed her fingers through it. "Don't feel bad, okay?"

She smiled at her friend, finding the feeling of the fingers in her hair extremely comforting. "Is that an order, Leigh Matthews?"

"If I say yes, will you obey it?"

"For you, lass?" RJ gave the back of Leigh's hand a gentle kiss. "I'll most certainly obey it."

Leigh looked at her hand and fought the urge to wipe it on her jeans. The gesture was romantic as hell. But the fact that RJ had just finished puking did manage to keep her from swooning. "I've got a bottle of water in the truck. Why don't you lie down? We're only about thirty minutes outside of Jackson."

"Are you sure? I don't know why I'm so tired." *I know*

perfectly well why I'm so tired. *Being alive takes a HUGE amount of energy.* "But I don't want to leave you all alone."

"I won't be alone," Leigh said easily. She smiled and offered RJ a hand up. "You'll be right behind me, and I'll wake you up when I find us a motel."

"You know, I really like smart, sexy women who baby me like this. You keep this up, and I'll just follow you around for-ever," RJ teased as she pulled herself into the cab.

"Watch out, RJ," Leigh warned in a semi-serious voice as she climbed back into her seat. "I had a cute puppy once who followed me around." She turned the key. "He got hit by a bus."

The male squirrel sighed dejectedly. The female humans were gone. "Who will we spy on now? Our entire recreation schedule revolves around watching humans and making snarky comments about their pathetic lives."

His mate could only nod. Purgatory was really starting to suck. "We could wreak havoc on that diner. It's full of unsus-pecting humans. And it really wouldn't take too much to knock over those flimsy garbage cans out back."

"Or," the male's face brightened, "we could get in touch with ourselves, embrace our inner, spiritual, squirrel children, and make the world a better place through our own journey of self-discovery, acceptance, and love!"

His mate glared at him. "You've been peeping in on Oprah again, haven't you?"

The male looked ashamed.

"I miss her old shows about shopoholic, hypochondriac, spouse-cheating, kinky-sex-addicted, cross-dressing, born-again, nipple-pierced, infertile, crack-using suburban housewives."

"That guy was great!" A nostalgic look flickered across his fuzzy face. "Those were the days." Why couldn't people leave well enough alone? But damn if they didn't know how to pro-duce a theme song! *I'm ev-errrry squirr-ellll*, he mentally sang.

The female shivered as she saw a black, vicious figure slink into the shadows created by the garage. It was a cat. The one the humans called "Flea." The one who had nearly murdered her beloved squirrel soulmate. There was something she didn't like about that particular feline. Sure, the fact that the cat would tear off her head and gorge herself on the mangled flesh if she could didn't help. But there was something else. Something she couldn't quit put her finger on...

The male snuggled up to the female for his nap. She was soft and warm, and he fell asleep immediately as his mate watched Flea with narrowed, wary eyes.

It was 9:30 p.m. when Leigh pulled around the back of the Sleepy Night Inn, located just on the outskirts of Jackson, Wyoming. The building looked like a small ski chalet, and she'd stayed there many times on her route when she couldn't stand to be cooped up in her truck for another second. She smiled inwardly. The rooms in this particular motel were beautiful, each holding one or two king-sized beds, a hot tub, and a private balcony that allowed you to gaze out at the stars and enjoy the peace of your surroundings.

Yawning, Leigh unbuckled her seat belt and pulled open the curtain to the sleeping area of the cab. RJ was curled up on the bed, sound asleep. She wore only a soft, pale yellow t-shirt and white cotton underpants. The rest of her clothes, ruined by mud, grease, and ketchup, lay pooled on the floor.

The trucker grinned and perched on the small bed next to RJ. She ran her fingers gently through the reddish-brown locks, now in total disarray. *I didn't know she snored.* But the sound was light and rhythmic and, at least for the moment, Leigh found it more endearing than annoying.

"RJ," she said softly, very aware of how RJ had woken up in a sheer panic earlier that day. She was bound and determined to have things go a little more smoothly this time. "Time to wake up."

RJ stirred but didn't wake.

"We're here," Leigh coaxed, giving RJ's shoulder a gentle rub. Then, purely on impulse she bent down and softly kissed the slightly parted lips. It only took a second for RJ to respond by kissing Leigh back and wrapping her arm around the shorter woman's waist to hold her in place. The kisses were more tender and friendly than sexual, and Leigh hummed with pleasure at feeling something she had rarely known—contentment.

RJ pulled back slightly, her emerald eyes picking up the reflection of the streetlights outside the truck. "Hi," she said softly.

Leigh swallowed, feeling the intensity of the moment and RJ's gaze washing over her like a warm bath. She licked her suddenly dry lips. "Hi."

They froze, not even breathing for long seconds, hearing only the pounding of their hearts.

"We're at the hotel?" RJ finally asked, her voice still a little hoarse from sleep and the unexpected intimacy of Leigh's stare.

The blonde woman sucked in a breath. "We sure are." She stood up, suddenly feeling very awkward as she broke off eye contact and glanced down at RJ's clothes. "I...I hope those aren't all you brought."

RJ's brows furrowed at Leigh's hasty escape from the bed. "I'll be fine. Got another pair of trousers and several more shirts in my duffel."

Leigh nodded, backing up a step. "I'll wait outside while you get dressed."

"You don't—"

But before she could finish her sentence, Leigh was out the door, slamming it firmly behind her.

RJ's mouth dropped open. "What in the hell was that?" She quickly slipped into a pair of loose-fitting cargo pants. "Leigh," she called as she scrambled over the seat and opened the door. "Leigh."

No answer.

It was dark, except for the twinkling lights from the motel and the muted glow of a few street lamps and stars. "Leigh!" RJ spun in a circle. She winced and pulled her feet up a bit as the small rocks in the parking lot dug into her bare feet as she walked around, looking for her companion. "Leigh?"

Still no answer.

She began to curse under her breath, then out loud. "Bloody hell! Leigh!"

A truck to the side of RJ pulled away, bringing Leigh into view. "Over here," came Leigh's somewhat sheepish reply.

RJ let out a deep breath as she stalked over to Leigh, who was standing with her hands shoved deeply into her pockets, leaning against a light post. Its yellow light cast her in a soft, golden aura.

A small, slightly embarrassed smile curled Leigh's lips. "You sure got dressed fast. But you could have finished." She stared pointedly at RJ's feet. "It wasn't like I was going to leave my," she grinned unrepentantly, "truck."

RJ arched a slender eyebrow. "Very funny. I'm not used to women running away from me as though I was a leper."

"That's not—"

"That's exactly what you did, Leigh Matthews." Inexplicably, RJ's temper flared. Why had Leigh jumped out of the cab that way? And more annoying still, why hadn't she answered her? "So don't bother denying it!"

Pale eyes narrowed dangerously. "Don't yell at me, RJ."

"I'm not yelling!"

"Oh yes, you are!" Leigh shouted back, marching up to RJ and standing toe to toe with her.

RJ bristled at the challenge in Leigh's voice and at the top of her lungs cried out, "*This is yelling*!"

Several women who were walking out to their cars turned to stare at RJ and Leigh. The oldest in the group put her hands on her hips and pointed directly at RJ while she spoke to Leigh. "You don't have to take that crap. You're not going to let her bellow at you like that, are you?"

Leigh glared back and wrapped her arm around RJ's waist. "Yes! And mind your own damn business!"

RJ lowered her voice and smiled, bending her head until her lips brushed Leigh's ear. "You are?"

"Hell no!" Leigh ground out quietly. She turned and smacked RJ's arm hard, causing the taller woman to slap her hand over her stinging skin and scowl.

The group of woman launched into a round of applause and began moving away once again.

"Be nice." Leigh's voice was reprimanding, but considering she was now gently rubbing the spot on RJ's arm where she just had smacked her, RJ wasn't inclined to complain.

"I am nice," RJ insisted, all the while shooting an evil look at the group of women as they disappeared into their cars.

Leigh bit her lip. She didn't want to smile, but it was nearly impossible not to. "I really shouldn't find someone who loses their temper and yells at me for no reason whatsoever so utterly attractive."

"Only a brat hides when someone is looking for them," RJ informed her blithely.

"I wasn't hiding. You just hadn't seen me yet."

RJ rolled her eyes. This conversation wasn't getting them anywhere. Something had spooked Leigh. But whatever it was, it was obvious that she wouldn't find out more about it until later. "Can we go inside at least? I'm dead on my feet."

Leigh jumped back a step when, for some unknown reason, RJ burst out laughing so hard her entire body was shaking. "What?" She looked down at her friend, whose arms were wrapped around her stomach as she howled. "What?"

"Inside..." RJ snorted loudly, "inside joke."

Leigh regarded RJ carefully. Was the woman insane as Rooster had hinted? She thought for a moment. If she was, did it really matter now?

"Well, lass, are we going in or not?" RJ stepped forward, a large but tired smile spread across her face, and drew her fingertips down Leigh's bare arms. "Please?"

Leigh nodded, any lingering doubts about RJ vanishing in the wake of the tiny tingles rushing down her arms at the taller woman's tender touch. *Being such a ho is going to be the death of me yet.* "C'mon." She reached for RJ's hand, deciding to go back to the truck for her overnight bag later. "Let's see if I can make you scream for a completely different reason."

"I don't scream," RJ complained, giving Leigh a mock-aggrieved look. "Yelling and screaming are two very different things."

The trucker laughed, recognizing the gauntlet when it was tossed at her feet. "We'll see, Irish. We'll see."

RJ slowly rolled over from her back to her right side. She inhaled deeply and smiled. Eyes closed, her other senses sharpened and took over. She heard the water dripping in the bathroom, felt the slightly rough sheets against her skin. Her nostrils flared in delight. Leigh had used a lilac-scented shampoo recently, and maybe just a drop of perfume. *So sweet,* she mentally purred. The fragrance was light and citrusy, and you had to be very close to notice it at all.

It wouldn't do for "Tom Cat" Matthews to be smellin' nice in front of the boys, now would it? RJ snuggled closer to her companion. But as much as her arms ached to reach out and draw Leigh close, she didn't make any attempt to touch Leigh in a restrictive way. A British nurse in '43 had taught her the hard way that some women don't like waking up that way. It took RJ a week to convince her commander that two broken fingers shouldn't keep her from flying. And the truth was, they hadn't.

RJ sniggered privately. It had kept her from doing a lot of other things she loved, but flying wasn't one of them.

But just because she didn't feel quite comfortable in wrapping Leigh up in a bear hug, didn't mean she wasn't going to stop just short of that. Despite the early hour, she felt alert and focused. Unlike the night before.

Much to both women's chagrin, the motel had been booked solid. With a quick glance at the clock, the clerk told them that a room reservation had been made without a credit card, and if the guest didn't show up within the next hour, he'd cancel the reservation and give them the room. Leigh had been ready to simply drive into Jackson and find another motel, but RJ convinced her that an hour wasn't too long to wait. They made their way to a smoke-filled bar and enjoyed several drinks before the hotel clerk kindly sought them out and told them they could have the room.

RJ had quickly jumped to her feet, only to have the world begin to spin. Leigh had laughed and made a comment about how such a tall girl really should be able to hold her liquor better. *It wasn't the liquor*, the pilot had groused to herself. *It was this being alive crap.* The liquid sat warm in her belly, making her feel sluggish and even more tired. By the time they got to their room, she was so tired that she lay face down on the bed and instantly fell asleep. She didn't even remember undressing or getting under the covers.

RJ made a face. Leigh had mostly undressed her, and she had missed it all.

But now...now she wasn't missing a thing. For weeks, she'd wanted this woman in a nice soft bed. She snuggled close to Leigh, her body barely touching the smaller woman's, as she drew a deep satisfied breath, the smell of Leigh's shampoo and perfume now mixing with the scent of the trucker's skin. *How wonderful is this? My God, if I were a man, you'd be awake by now. Good thing for us both I have such fantastic self-control and restraint.* She clamped her hand over her mouth to smother a snort. *Yeah, right. Who in the hell am I trying to kid?*

Her hand slid up onto Leigh's outer thigh, just above her knee. Very, very slowly, she let it travel up the firm leg. *Damn, woman. How does a trucker get muscles like this in her thighs?* Then her mind flashed back to the bathroom at the diner; they were leaning against the wall with those legs wrapped around her waist. *Oh, yeah. That's one way.*

RJ shivered with pleasure as she recalled their encounter in the garage and the feeling of small fingers digging into her upper arms—Leigh's hips thrusting into her, and then her body stiffening slightly as she leaned forward and bit down on RJ's shoulder to keep from crying out. She closed her eyes as she remembered the deep, tortured groan of pleasure torn from Leigh's throat as she came hard...again. Their time together had been so intense, so...breathtaking, that it was all RJ could do to hold on for the ride. *Thank God my mother didn't see that bruise. I'd still be saying Hail Marys.*

RJ's fingertips drifted up from Leigh's thigh to her hipbone. A low hum from the trucker drew her back to the present.

Leigh stretched, the shift causing RJ's hand to travel a bit south of its last destination. Her fingers skimmed lightly across baby soft skin. She smiled when she heard, then felt, the quiet gasp as Leigh's body shifted back, melding itself to RJ.

"Nice," Leigh mumbled. Reaching down and back she twined her fingers with RJ's and slowly guided the warm hand to her breast. She carefully released her hold on RJ's hand when she felt a thumb gently brush across her sensitive nipple, which had begun to tighten the moment she felt RJ roll over, her warm breath caressing Leigh's ear. It was all she could do to keep from moaning then. She bit her lip and closed her eyes, unsure that she could stop herself now.

Leigh was amazed at how soft RJ's hands were. She should have calluses from the hard work she seemed to enjoy so much, shouldn't she? But they were smooth and soft and very warm. The blonde let her hand travel across the back of RJ's, and she swallowed hard at the thought of those long, skilled fingers and what they could do for her later.

The trucker cleared her throat and opened one eye, giving her bedmate a tiny smile. "Hiya, beautiful," she muttered softly.

RJ leaned in a little closer, her breasts pressing softly into Leigh's back. She placed a gentle kiss on Leigh's cheek. "Same to you. Sorry about last night. I didn't realize I'd fall asleep like that." She smiled at her friend, never faltering in her soft caress of the blonde's breast, which had now become open-handed massage.

"Ooo," Leigh sighed. *God, that feels so good.* "That's okay. Riding in a rig can take its toll if you're not used to it. But I've seen you drink more at the diner than you did yesterday."

"Must be the travel." *Or having to deal with a body again.* She kissed Leigh for a second time, her lips lingering as she said against the downy soft skin, "It may take a day or two for me to get used to it. You'll need to be patient." RJ smirked. "If that is even possible."

"I can be patient," Leigh protested, knowing she was lying through her teeth. "Very patient. So long as I don't have to wait, there's never a problem," she said innocently.

A soft chuckle. "Somehow I knew that."

The tall woman placed a tender kiss on Leigh's shoulder. "Hmm...don't know how you drive around all the time. Don't you get tired of moving in a big circle?" RJ's hand shifted slowly to Leigh's other breast. Her thumb played idly over the nipple, hardening it to the same state of painful arousal as its twin.

Leigh arched slightly into the touch, craving more contact, but not wanting to leave the warm nest of RJ's body. "It's..." A tiny gasp. "It's not easy but, I...I manage pretty well. Grew up around trucks. Traveled with my..." Her words trailed off. She really didn't want to think about her rig or her dad or anything else right now.

Leigh rolled over to face RJ and let her hands caress RJ's bare shoulder. "This is a very nice shoulder, Ms. Fitzgerald." She traced a slow path down the shoulder until her fingers glanced over a particularly sensitive patch of skin, earning a slight jerk from RJ, who grinned at her friend. "I have fond memories of this shoulder."

"Evil," RJ whispered.

"Nope." Leigh nodded, kissing just slightly to the left of RJ's pulse point. Her lips curled into a sexy grin when she saw her companion swallow hard. She could feel the gradual but steady increase in the beat of RJ's heart.

"Me and naughty," she whispered.

"Intimately acquainted. I remember." RJ moaned when Leigh reached down and pulled the tall woman's leg over her own legs and hip, bringing their bodies together. "Ohhh, yeah...that's good..." RJ's eyes closed as she felt a spark travel through her body, igniting her blood.

"You like this, do you, Irish?" The blonde pushed closer to RJ until the tall woman had no choice but to roll onto her back, finding herself covered in feisty blonde. "Because if you like this—" She gave her thigh, which was now nestled securely between RJ's legs, a hard flex and a slight upward thrust, sending RJ's head back and drawing a muffled groan from her chest. "—then you're gonna love what I come back and do to you after I brush my teeth."

RJ grabbed for her lover as Leigh jumped off the bed and dashed into the bathroom, giving RJ a very nice peek at her luscious body. "Oh, you are a wench!" She fell back onto the bed with a groan, hearing Leigh laugh just as the water came on in the bathroom. "And what would be so funny, Leigh Matthews?"

"Sometimes your—" She paused to spit into the sink, losing sight of RJ as the brunette climbed out of bed. "Sometimes your accent adds a surreal quality to all this, and then—" She stopped again, taking time to quickly but thoroughly brush and rinse. Laying her toothbrush on the sink, she said, "When you say something like 'wench,'" Leigh shrugged one shoulder, "I dunno. It kinda adds a kinky quality to the encounter." She wiggled pale eyebrows.

"Kinky?" RJ's eyebrows disappeared behind disheveled bangs. "My accent is kinky? And here all this time I thought that ropes and whips were kinky." RJ put the canister of baking soda back in her duffel and gave her own teeth a quick brushing in the tiny kitchen area of the room. She returned to the bed, straightened the covers, and fluffed the pillows, placing two under her head and then resting with her hands laced behind her head.

Leigh peeked out from around the corner of the bathroom with a silly grin on her face. "You know the difference between erotic and kinky, don't you?"

"What?" RJ was already smiling.

"Erotic is using the feather." She waited a beat. "Kinky is using the whole bird."

"Oh, Lord!" RJ rolled her eyes and laughed. "All right then." She sat up in the bed, allowing the covers to fall to her waist as she extended her hand. "You've been on the road for far too long, lass. It's time to come and have your oil changed."

"You should know that truck talk drives me wild." The blonde slid out of the bathroom and clicked off the light. She closed the door behind her and then leaned back against the wood. Its cool surface felt good against her overheated skin. She rubbed her back against the door wantonly, an innocent, youthful smile contrasting sharply with the vision of her writhing, naked body.

RJ's nostrils flared.

"Would you be interested in rotating anything while I'm here?"

RJ crooked her finger and spoke in a husky voice. "Come here and we'll give you a complete once over." She grinned. "Twice."

"Now how can I refuse that offer?" Leigh replied seriously. She moved slowly to the bed, squaring her shoulders and walking with confidence toward her lover. She could feel her pulse quicken with every step, and she purposely slid back on top of RJ, resuming her former position with her thigh planted firmly between RJ's legs. A hot coating of moisture met her thigh, searing her to the bone. Her jaw clenched, and her eyes darkened with desire.

RJ cleared her throat. It had been a long time since a woman had managed to captivate her body so completely. She actually worried that if Leigh became any more purposeful, she'd completely lose control of her body and come on the spot.

Her hands rested on Leigh's hips, and she looked up into playful, but undeniably aroused, blue eyes. "You are truly adorable, Leigh Matthews," she began sincerely. "And one of the most beautiful and sexy women I've had the pleasure to meet. Thank you for letting me have this time with you." She slid her hand up Leigh's back, pulling her forward a little so she could tuck an errant lock of fiery blonde hair back behind Leigh's ear.

Their gazes never left each other, and the same silly little smiles they'd shared earlier broke out on each of their faces.

Leigh's voice was warm and sure. "I feel the same way about you, RJ. Thank you right back."

RJ brought her head up slowly to meet Leigh's gaze, and they fell into a deep, passionate kiss. Each of them moaned softly. The moment was sweet and tender, each opening up to the other in a way they hadn't experienced before. Their encounters at the diner were generally fast and furious, if for no other reason than they were taking place in a garage—not the most romantic or private spot on the planet.

Now they were well rested, in a soft, warm bed, and already thoroughly enjoying each other. Their kisses were painfully slow, deeply erotic and on the verge of sending them both into the type of sensual haze that, once entered, left a woman utterly helpless until a final spasm of pleasure uncoiled from her body— releasing her from its spell.

Leigh's lips strayed from RJ's mouth to her jaw, then neck, where she nipped and nibbled on skin that had gone damp and carried with it a faint taste of salt.

RJ groaned loudly and began to massage Leigh's bottom. Losing all patience, she used her grip on Leigh to pull her closer and find a gentle rhythm between them.

"Your skin tastes salty sweet, RJ." Leigh sighed contentedly as she traveled down RJ's long firm body with her hands and mouth. "Very sweet." The blonde rubbed her cheek against the silky skin of RJ's upper breast, then in a quick move, licked a broad stroke over RJ's nipple. She took it into her mouth, sucking gently at first, savoring it. Then she suckled with more vigor, earning a loud groan from RJ and a renewed flood of heat against her thigh.

RJ's heart thudded wildly.

Leigh smiled and continued her quest down the body of the beautiful woman beneath her. She'd wanted RJ like this since the very first moment she saw her. Now she was going to have her. She felt the heat building between them as their bodies continued to rock and slide against each other. Leigh pressed her palms into the mattress on either side of RJ's shoulders. She pushed up and away from her lover and closed her eyes as she concentrated on the rhythm of her thigh between RJ's legs. The intimate contact sent a wild thrill through her own body as she felt RJ press against her...all but coming off the bed to meet her.

The trucker loved the fact that she was eliciting the most sensual sounds and erotic scents from her lover. The temperature in the room continued to rise, and it took on the aroma of passion and sex.

Leigh whispered brokenly, "I need to—" She suddenly stopped and shook her head, deciding to let her actions speak for her. She slid farther down RJ's body and stopped just below her belly button, kissing the spot tenderly.

The pilot was dizzy with pleasure and anticipation. Leigh was most certainly a talented woman. She kept her eyes closed in an effort to stay grounded, because when she opened them, the room would start to spin a little. She clutched at the sheets helplessly, twisting them and balling them into her fists. Every cell in her body cried out for her to lift her hips from the bed and demand attention from her companion. She was trying to be patient and allow Leigh to proceed at her own pace, but she was rapidly disintegrating under the insistent, maddening, sensual onslaught of Leigh's lips and fingers. *Get on with it, woman! Before I die—again!*

Leigh slowly extended her tongue and took a small taste, dipping down into dark, soft curls that tickled her nose and sent her senses into overdrive. She kissed RJ's flesh tenderly, moving reverently lower and lower, making sure RJ knew how much she enjoyed loving her like this. Her hands traveled up until she felt the white-knuckled death grip that RJ had on the sheets. She gently caressed the tall woman's hands until they released the bedding.

Their fingers wove together naturally, and Leigh turned her head and began a serious exploration of her lover, her own center pulsing in time with RJ's.

"Ah, God!" RJ's eyes snapped shut as she threw her head back, hissing loudly. She tried not to hurt Leigh with the grip on her hands. RJ opened herself further, shifting to give the blonde more room.

"Hmmm, yes." Leigh moaned softly against the slick, sensitive flesh, as she gladly took what was being offered. "So good," she whispered. Her mouth watered as she took a second taste of the essence that was completely RJ, losing herself in the task.

RJ was helpless to stop or even slow her body's reaction to Leigh. She felt the muscles expand and contract all over her frame. Her heartbeat was so loud and furious that she feared it would never return to normal. RJ's enjoyment began to spiral upward as she listened to Leigh moan and groan while performing for her pleasure. She had truly forgotten that some women found a great deal of gratification in this, the most intense and intimate of acts. She thanked God that Leigh was among them.

"Oh, Leigh..." RJ breathed. Her stomach muscles contracted, sending her hips upward. She felt the trucker release her hands and then wrap both hands around her thighs as Leigh continued to take total command of her body, pleasuring her. With a mind of their own, RJ hips began to rock with Leigh.

"Please...don't...stop." The pilot pushed the words from her throat even as it closed and her orgasm began to take hold of her body. She dug her heels into the bed, bending her legs and trying not to push away from the ecstasy she was experiencing. The sensations were overwhelming, and she felt as though she wanted to cry out in utter delight and burst into tears at the same time. Before she realized it, her hands had slipped into Leigh's hair, tangling there and holding her exactly where she wanted her most.

Leigh gently nipped at tender, swollen flesh, feeling RJ's fingers slide tentatively over the back of her head and into her hair. She didn't mind that in the least, admitting privately that she would have done the same thing. Only much sooner. The sound of RJ begging her not to stop and whimpering for her to take her "faster" and "harder," nearly sent her over the edge herself. But it was the quaking in RJ's thighs and the long, languid moan as she finally succumbed to her lips and tongue that sent the trucker over as well.

Leigh closed her eyes and pressed her cheek against RJ's damp, musky, inner thigh as she dug her fingers into RJ's hips, her own release causing her to shake from the inside out. *Damn. That's never happened before. Not from just...* Unwilling to leave this haven too soon, she continued to gently kiss RJ intimately for a few moments as their bodies relaxed and their heartbeats began to approach normal. Then she crawled up to her lover's side, a little shaken by the intensity of the exchange.

RJ was quick to pull the sheet across them and take Leigh into her arms. The sun was just peeking through the curtains, but she couldn't think of a single reason to move from this very spot. "I need to hold you, Leigh," she gasped, first kissing the top of Leigh's head, then her forehead, and finally capturing her lips.

"You're amazing, woman." RJ gently touched Leigh's cheek and looked deeply into her eyes. She could see fear and affection warring against each other, and she gently kissed Leigh on the cheek. When she pulled away, she was greeted with a tentative but genuine smile. "That was incredible." RJ sucked in another deep breath and let it out slowly as Leigh settled against her. She could feel the smaller woman's heartbeat against her chest and allowed her eyelids to flutter closed at the sweet sensation. "As soon as I summon the strength to move," she mumbled, "you're all mine, Leigh Matthews."

A soft laugh that tickled the damp skin of her throat was her only answer.

Chapter
8

Leigh let her foot off the brake and turned right at the stop-light. She was driving her Jeep, having dropped off her rig at a body shop on the outskirts of Seattle. From there, a taxi took them to the storage unit where she kept her beloved first automobile and a few odds and ends that she'd saved.

They'd spent all yesterday on the road from Jackson, and stayed the night just a few miles outside the city. Leigh was having a wonderful time, and by the nearly permanent smile affixed on RJ's face, she was fairly certain her undeniably sweet companion felt the same way.

She parked the Jeep as close to the mall entrance as she could. As usual, it was just far enough away to be annoying, but just close enough so that she really couldn't bitch. At least, not too much.

RJ considered her pants, which had been turned into a pair of shorts. "Two pairs of trousers. It's hard to believe that I ruined two pairs in less than a day."

Leigh bit the inside of her cheek to keep from laughing. It really wasn't funny, and she did feel somewhat responsible for RJ ripping her second pair. If they hadn't been roughhousing in the motel room before they left this morning, RJ wouldn't have gotten them caught on the metal bed frame. "You're just lucky, I guess."

RJ lifted a brow and shook her finger in Leigh's direction.
"It's all your fault, you evil little minx. If you hadn't been teasing me so, this never would have happened."

Leigh raised her own eyebrow in response. "You're lucky I
let you get dressed at all," she said flatly, eyes twinkling. "This
morning...and the morning before..." She sighed, letting the
words trail off. RJ didn't need to be reminded of the special
time that they'd spent holed up in their motel rooms simply
indulging in each other.

"Were incredible," RJ murmured as she looked out at the
huge building, her bright green eyes widening just a bit. She
leaned forward in her seat, trying not to think about the belt
strapping her in. "What's this, then?"

Leigh looked at RJ as though she was an alien. "What do
you think it is? It's a mall, of course." She shut off the ignition.

RJ realized she was letting her lack of knowledge about the
outside world show entirely too much. She was just so comfortable with Leigh, that it was easy to forget she was supposed to
know these things and that she had to pretend. "Right." She
thought frantically. "We just don't have anything this," she
waved her hands aimlessly, "large in Glory." RJ cleared her
throat, her gaze sliding sideways as she watched Leigh from the
corner of her eye.

Leigh fumbled with the handle of the Jeep door, needing to
give it a firm push before it would open. RJ exited her side,
stretching her legs as they both stepped out into the cool spring
air.

RJ breathed a sigh of relief as the fresh breeze blew gently
across her skin, waking up her nerve endings. While her time
with Leigh had so far exceeded her fondest hopes, she wasn't
one to be cooped up for long periods of time, and she was looking forward to putting down stakes here in Seattle for a few
days.

Leigh eyed the building speculatively, considering RJ's earlier comment. It wasn't a very large mall. Then again, Glory
wasn't much of a town, from what she could gather. Poor RJ.
Everything they did seemed to be a new experience for her.
Well, not everything, she reminded herself with a mental
chuckle. *Thank goodness.*

"I'm sure we'll find something for you here, Irish. What's
your pleasure?" Leigh raked her appreciative gaze down RJ's
body. The long tear in RJ's pants had come at mid-calf, and

Leigh, with the help of a sharp pair of scissors, had turned the pants into a pair of shorts. Very short shorts. Her smile shifted into a slight leer. "Or...you could always stay in those for the week. I'm certainly not complaining."

"Umm...somehow I think that if I don't get me some new trousers, I won't be seeing much of the outside of our hotel room. Not that *I'm* complaining." RJ chuckled softly. "As a matter of fact, you look like you're ready to baste me in something and start nibbling right now."

Leigh burst into surprised laughter. *How can someone I barely know understand me so well?* "Okay." She nodded, a self-deprecating look stealing across her face. "You're right. Some new pants are in order." *Though I reserve the right to baste you in something and nibble it off later.* "I think we can manage that in a reasonable amount of time, too."

Leigh stepped aside as an exhausted man shuffled past her carrying an armload of packages. "Ooo...I know you butch types don't appreciate shopping." She herself didn't much care for it, unless, that is, she was buying for someone else. With that thought, her face broke into a broad, mischievous smile. "Let me buy you an outfit or two, RJ." It wasn't really a question. "I just got paid, and I know you couldn't have brought much with you in that tiny duffel bag." *I'm taking you out tonight, gorgeous. I can tell being in that truck was starting to make you a little twitchy.*

"Oh, no." RJ tried not to sound insulted. "I'm in fine shape for money, and this week I want you to relax and enjoy yourself," she insisted. "Let me take care of myself and you as well. I want to treat you this week, Leigh."

RJ reached over and took the trucker's hand in her own, not caring that they were in public. People were bound to be more accepting nowadays than they had been in her time. "I want you to remember our time together as being very special." She tilted her head toward the mall, causing dark, wavy bangs to fall down across her forehead and scatter into her eyes. "You can help me pick out the clothes. I've never been any good at that at all. Left to my own devices, I always look like a ragamuffin."

Leigh leaned forward and affectionately smoothed the hair away from RJ's face, letting her hand linger on RJ's cheek. "You look beautiful." RJ's face turned a lovely shade of rose, and Leigh felt a sudden rush of fondness for the lanky woman. It came on so quickly and fiercely, that it was actually unsettling.

Pulling her hand away slowly, she pushed those thoughts aside for later consideration. Much later.

The blonde woman pursed her lips. "Okay. How 'bout this? I'll let you buy me something, but only if I can buy you something in return." She squeezed RJ's hand. No woman had ever taken her hand in public before and, much to her surprise, she thoroughly loved it. She felt comforted and secure with RJ's strong fingers wrapped around hers. She sighed. The rest of the world could just drop dead. "Deal?"

"Sounds fair." RJ paused and considered the "mall" they were approaching, which she assumed housed the world's most enormous store. "So what do you think I'd look good in?" She stopped just long enough to make sure she could get the outer door open for Leigh, holding it with one foot as she reached for the second inner door. "I'm sure things have changed a bit since the last time I did any real shopping." *Now that's an understatement. What's it been? Fifty, nearly sixty years? And look at these funny clothes. It's more than a shame that women aren't wearing dresses anymore. I've seen nary a one since Glory!*

"RJ, you look fabulous in absolutely nothing." Leigh bumped hips with the brunette. "So I'm sure clothes won't be a problem." She glanced over at her friend, suddenly realizing that RJ was taking her seriously. *Does she think I'd dress her in a skintight mini-skirt? Oooo...a miniskirt...*

"Leigh?"

Nothing.

"Lass?" A little louder.

"Yeah?" Leigh jerked her head sideways. "Sorry." She shook her head a little as she stopped in front of a large rectangular sign that listed the different stores and showed their locations on a basically useless map. "Let's go with something similar to what got wrecked. I want you to be happy. And you looked good enough to eat." *Still do.* She groaned inwardly. *God, what is up with me?*

"As I seem to recall, you did just that. More than once." RJ held her tongue for a split second before bursting into laughter at the sight of Leigh's gaping mouth. *Oops. Weren't expecting that, I see.* But, to her credit, she had at least tried not to laugh outright at her friend. "So, yeah. Let's go with something similar."

This time it was Leigh's turn to blush. "And here I thought *I* was incorrigible."

RJ leaned toward the smaller woman to whisper in her ear, "You know damn good and well that I'm not one for holding back when it comes to what I'm thinking." Her voice went very serious. "Life's far too short for that, Leigh." She kissed a spot alongside Leigh's ear and made a conscious effort to lighten her tone. "And you're just so damned cute when you blush like that."

Leigh pulled away and stuck out her tongue at RJ, but didn't let go of her hand. "Just for that, we get to pick out your clothes first." She pointed to a store that the map showed was on the second floor in the middle of the mall. "This is where I want to start. They have a lot of great unisex clothes in colors I can actually stand." She appraised RJ with mock-seriousness. "You really don't look like a lime green, chartreuse, or tangerine sort of girl to me."

"That's good," RJ allowed hesitantly. *I think.*

"I just can't stand that horrible 70s retro-shit." Leigh gave an involuntary shiver as they made their way toward the escalators.

RJ's eyebrows drew tightly together as Leigh expertly guided them around the people, plants, and strollers. "Have you been here before?"

"Nope."

"How can that be? You walk around like you know exactly where you're going. And I know that pitiful excuse for a map isn't the reason."

Leigh shrugged. "Isn't one mall pretty much like another? Food court on the lower level, escalators and elevators in the middle, bathrooms at the ends?"

"If you say so." *There is more than one of these places?*

They passed store after store until RJ exclaimed in disbelief, "All these stores are in this one building."

"I should hope so," Leigh said, fully believing RJ was teasing her. "I'm not moving the Jeep unless I have to."

RJ looked a little dazed. *Who could have imagined that? Wait until I tell Mavis. She'll collapse on the spot!* "I'd lose my mother in this place, never to see her again."

Leigh laughed. "She wouldn't be the first person to succumb to mall madness, lemme tell you."

RJ followed her companion to the steps, but hesitated when she saw that they were moving. She paused for just a second, having only ridden on one once when she was a child. A few seconds later, when she looked up, she found herself watching Leigh growing smaller and smaller.

Leigh turned her head to open her mouth and say something to RJ when she noticed she was gone. She looked down past several people and spied RJ at the bottom of the steps, looking up at her in confusion. Leigh lifted her hands in question and silently mouthed, "What happened?"

"Right." RJ mumbled, waving at Leigh. *Get a grip, woman, or Leigh's gonna think you've gone 'round the bend.* She took the steps two at a time, politely making her way past the people between her and Leigh. She caught up with the trucker just as Leigh reached the second floor. "You know how sometimes you just get a little dizzy from looking at stairs?" RJ said offhandedly, shrugging and smiling, hoping Leigh wouldn't ask for more of an explanation.

"Not really," Leigh said slowly. Her eyes filled with concern, and she carefully examined RJ's face. "You're not going to be sick again, are you?"

"No!" *Sweet Jesus, I'm a pilot and now she thinks I'm going to puke on the escalators? Okay, I was the one who brought up being dizzy. But still,* she whined. "Well, I umm...never mind." She glanced around, her eyes drawn to the bright lights and all the stores and kiosks. RJ realized she had far more important things to worry about than looking bad on a moving stairway. "So, where are you taking me? Some place that fits with your naughty disposition, I'm betting."

Leigh let out a relieved breath. RJ seemed fine. Well, as weird as she usually seemed...but at least not about to barf. "Actually, I'm not." She stopped dead in her tracks and wrinkled her nose as she sniffed the air. "Yes!" Leigh suddenly veered to the left, pulling RJ right along with her as she trotted over to a pretzel stand and pulled a ten dollar bill from her jeans pocket. "Can I tempt you with one of these?" A batch of fresh pretzels had just been pulled from the oven, and the heavenly smell had Leigh's eyes rolling back in their sockets.

"You can tempt me with all kinds of things, and you know it." RJ looked at the girl behind the counter, who was staring openly at them. "What, haven't you ever seen two people shopping for clothes before?"

The young girl looked utterly bored as she pulled her chewing gum out of her mouth and then pushed it back in before resuming chewing. "Whatever, Granny. What kind do you and your girlfriend want?"

RJ laughed out loud, looking at Leigh. "Well, what do you know? You're my girlfriend. Did you know you had signed on for the long haul?"

"That's news to me. Pretzel girl here must be psychic."

The girl rolled her eyes. *Dykes were such bitches.* "Do you want a pretzel or not? I'm totally busy." Now she snapped her gum, glancing down at her fake black fingernails.

Leigh looked around her. They were the girl's only customers and another pimply-faced boy was making a fresh batch. She shook her head slowly. "I can see that you're swamped."

The girl narrowed her eyes, and Leigh got on with it. "I'd like a cinnamon and sugar pretzel, please." Leigh's gaze slid sideways. "And for you, honey buns?"

RJ shook her head. Leigh was nothing but trouble. But luckily, the pilot really enjoyed being in trouble. "When in Rome..." she shrugged, looking around a little more seriously now. "Whatever you choose is fine, or I could just eat yours."

Leigh blushed again, causing RJ to clamp her hand over her mouth and the teenaged cashier to snigger. The trucker giggled despite herself, and quickly handed over the ten dollar bill, getting back only a few ones for change. "You like doing that, don't you?" she accused RJ.

"I will admit to getting a certain," she paused and locked eyes with Leigh. Bringing the hand that held the pretzel to her mouth, she took a long slow bite, humming with pleasure before she even started to chew. "...amount of pleasure from it. Yes."

The girl at the counter said, "You two really need to get a room. And if you're into movies, like, I know this guy, Freddy, who wants to be a director some day, and he'd love to tape you two going at—"

"God." Leigh made a face and quickly began pushing RJ away from the counter.

RJ skidded her feet and turned so she was walking backward facing Leigh. "Wanna make a movie? That young lady seems to know someone who would—"

"Someone who would require us to get extra shots of antibiotics just to be around him." She leaned close to RJ and stood on her tiptoes so she could whisper in her ear. *I can't believe I'm about to say this.* "If you really want to make a movie, I'd prefer we do it alone."

RJ nodded before turning around and re-taking Leigh's

hand. "Alone would be good, too. I like being alone with you. You get all feisty and sweaty."

Leigh smiled, a little bewildered, suddenly wondering if she and RJ were talking about the same thing at all.

RJ began looking around. The sweet-tasting pretzel and Leigh's hand firmly placed in hers had given her spirits another boost upward, making her feel like a kid on Christmas morning. Full of excitement, her natural instinct to explore began to kick in. Then something caught her eye. She stopped and stared at the scantily clad mannequins in the store window. "Jesus, Mary and Joseph!"

Leigh turned to see what had RJ standing in the middle of the mall with her jaw on the floor. She followed her line of sight and began to cluck her approval. "Victoria's Secret." She bit her lip and let out a low groan. "If their catalog doesn't turn you on to women, check for a pulse." She giggled at RJ's continued open-mouthed stare and used her fingertip to close the now panting orifice. "I'd love to get you in, and then immediately out of, something from that store. But since I don't think that will happen, you can shop for me there instead."

RJ gripped Leigh's hand tighter and began pulling her in the direction of their goal. "Let's go then. I'll be happy to buy you anything you like from this place."

"No, no, no, no." Leigh shook her head. "You first. I have a feeling we'll be all day if we start in there. I guess they don't have one of those in Glory, either." Around a bit of pretzel, she said, "Are you sure that you're not really a prisoner who's been recently released on parole after a hundred-year sentence? You seem like a kid in a candy store," she teased.

RJ reluctantly tore her eyes from the storefront and followed Leigh past another shop, not bothering to respond to Leigh's comments. They hit a little too close for comfort, and with startling clarity RJ realized how lonely Glory had become for her. She stuffed the rest of the pretzel into her mouth and tossed the napkin in a trash bin.

The tall woman winced a bit at the volume of the music that was playing. But once she adjusted to it, she actually started to enjoy the beat a bit. *Glenn Miller, it isn't. But it's not bad.* But she couldn't get her mind off the store with all the pretty, girly nighties. "We could have had so much fun in the other place, Leigh. I noticed this little black number you would look just wonderful in...then out of." She leered just a little, hoping to earn another blush. She really did enjoy doing that, guessing that not too many people could get that sort of reaction out of Leigh.

Leigh smacked RJ in the belly as they walked. "Not this time, Stretch." She rolled her eyes playfully. "I'm long past blushing about scantily clad women." After passing another few stores, Leigh announced that they were "here," and dragged RJ inside. They hadn't gotten three paces into the store when a prissy sales clerk scampered over to them, appraising each of their outfits with what appeared to be genuine interest.

The tall, rail-thin man was wearing a pair of crisply pressed chinos, an obnoxious lavender-colored cotton shirt, and what RJ was sure were women's shoes. His head was covered with a sparse patch of white blonde hair. "Hello, ladies," he exclaimed excitedly in a featherlight voice. When he got a good look at RJ, he slapped his cheeks with both hands. "Look at those long legs. Aren't you simply divine."

"Watch it," RJ warned playfully. She hadn't seen a man so light in the loafers in years. He was Section Eight material if ever there was some. "My," she glanced at Leigh and grinned, "girlfriend, here, will kick your butt for talk such as that. I'll be needing a couple pairs of trousers."

"Ohhh," he squealed, happily playing along with RJ. "Whip me, beat me, teach me how to love. I am so all over that, girl-friend. Whatever it takes to make the little one happy." He winked at down at Leigh, his admiration clear.

RJ crossed her arms across her chest. "You keep that up, and I'll be the one kicking your butt. Just help me find a couple pairs of trousers. I have better things to be doing with my time than buying my own clothes. There's a shop back there," she jerked her thumb over her shoulder, "I need to get her into."

The clerk held up his hand to forestall any further comment. "Victoria's Secret." He crossed himself and reverently said, "Say no more. I shop there."

"For yourself," Leigh mumbled playfully.

"I'm Alan." The man shifted into professional mode. "I understand you would like some trousers?"

"That's what she said, Alan," Leigh supplied. "But we'll be needing just a few more things besides the pants. We're going out on the town tonight."

RJ looked a little surprised. Leigh hadn't mentioned this before. She had just assumed they'd go back to the motel, have tons of obnoxiously satisfying sex, and then go to bed.

Leigh gave the man a satisfied smirk. "And I want the entire city wishing they were me. Not that they won't be anyway."

They both turned and stared at RJ, who was standing there looking like a deer caught in headlights.

"Not a problem," Alan declared.

"And I want her to be completely comfortable in what she's wearing."

Alan scowled. "I sense a problem."

Pete ran a shaking hand through his thick white hair. "I know, Katherine. I'm not disagreeing with you."

"How could you do it?" Her gaze raked across the table of men and women, and not a single one of them would lift their eyes to meet hers. "She's falling in love with that girl, whether she knows it yet or not. And there is no way they can be together. You're going to let her get her heart broken." The middle-aged woman was nearly in tears.

"Katherine," Pete rumbled in a low voice, "we can't change what's destined to happen." He squared his shoulders, firming his resolve against the formidable woman. "You've been in Glory long enough to know that."

"Peter," she narrowed her eyes, "are you saying that me daughter is destined to have her heart torn from her chest and stomped on?"

"I'm not a fortune teller." Pete winced. "So I don't know."

"If you don't know, then why are you saying it's destined to happen?"

"Katherine," Pete's voice softened, "that they're right for each other is obvious. Any fool can see that." Before she could respond, he beat her to the punch by saying, "Yes, even a fool like me. RJ might get her heart broken." He looked directly into her eyes, an uncharacteristic helplessness overtaking his strong features. "There's nothing—"

"I refuse to accept that. Her life was short enough as it was. Now she's being shortchanged in her afterlife, too?" Katherine slammed her fist against the table. Her husband, Harris, who was sitting quietly at the other end of the table, nodded approvingly. A man who was married to a woman like Katherine didn't need to say much. Thank the Lord. And he could see she was on a roll. "I, for one, won't stand here idly while that happens. Ruth Jean deserves better."

Pete hung his head. "You're right, Katherine." When he looked up, he pinned every member of the Glory City Council with a withering gaze. "RJ has given us sixty years of dedicated service." He sat down in his chair, jumping back up when Flea hissed in outrage. "Sorry, Flea," Pete offered contritely, as he picked up the fat cat and set her on the table in front of him. "I think maybe we need to consider breaking the rules and letting RJ leave Glory permanently."

Katherine, along with everyone else in the room, gasped, a pang in her chest making it hard to breathe. Would they really let RJ leave? *Lord above, it would take a miracle.* But she nodded. Her daughter deserved her chance at happiness, and she would take her petition to the very top if she had to.

RJ didn't know where to start when they got back to the lingerie store. There were just so many options. She began counting on her fingers, her brows drawing together.

"What are you doing?" Leigh asked as she took notice of a nice little purple number that was a distinct possibility.

"Counting how many nights we have."

"Nuh uh, RJ." Leigh shook her head. "I only got to buy you one outfit. And you insisted on buying yourself those jeans." She smiled at RJ's new Levis. "That means you can only pick one thing for me." She smiled mischievously. "Fair is fair."

RJ growled deeply and loudly at her stubborn companion. She usually enjoyed the fire and the fight that Leigh so easily displayed, but couldn't she see reason just this once? There were so many...interesting outfits to be had here. All of which the blonde would look completely delightful in. "Fine," she muttered, only somewhat dejected. She was still buying one, by God. "Which one do you like, lass?"

"Doesn't matter." Leigh smiled coyly. "If I'm not mistaken," batting her eyelashes, she drew her fingertip from RJ's belly button all the way to collarbone where she let it rest, "this is really for you, right?" Her smile broadened when she heard RJ swallow. Hard. *God, I love flirting with her.*

RJ captured Leigh's hand and kissed the tip of her wandering but much appreciated finger. "Well, that's true, but I want you to feel good in whatever it is you wear. If you feel good, you'll enjoy it more. And if you enjoy it more, I'll enjoy it more." She gently bit the tip of Leigh's finger. "And if I enjoy it more, you'll enjoy it more." She gave the blonde a wicked little sneer as one eyebrow arched up and she said, "Don't you agree?"

This particular conversation was making Leigh dizzy, though the "feel good" theme was registering loud and clear. "How about this?" She walked over to a rack of short silk robes and watched as RJ's eyes lit up. *Hmm...nice reaction,* her ego purred happily. *But how about...* As an experiment, she walked over to another rack, this one containing lacy bras, and received an equally enthusiastic reaction. "Oh, boy." She laughed. "I think we're going to be here for a while."

Leigh crooked her finger at RJ, and the tall woman immediately complied by stepping over to her. "You know they have dressing rooms here, right?" she said with the innocence of an angel.

"You know, lass..." She shifted, just slightly. Suddenly her clothes were becoming very restrictive, and warm, very warm. "If you're suggesting what I think you're suggesting..." RJ whimpered at the thought.

Leigh's smile grew even larger. "Yes?"

"Well, then, that might be—" RJ was forced to stop and clear her throat. "That might be a mistake. Now mind you, I'm not certain, but I'm thinking even in the great state of Washington, you can get arrested for what would happen if we went into that dressing room together."

Leigh pouted just a little, and RJ tweaked her lower lip.

"It might be best if you find an outfit or three that you like, and then we take them to the hotel and try 'em out." RJ was quite certain there was nothing in this store that Leigh wouldn't make look even better.

"Tch," Leigh scoffed. "Such a dirty mind." What RJ had said was, however, right on target. The thoughts that were floating around in Leigh's brain and sending lovely signals to the rest of her anatomy would most certainly get them into deep trouble if they got caught. "I was just suggesting that you pick out a few of your favorites for me to try on." The trucker tried her best to look innocent, which even at the best of times was a bit of a stretch.

"Right." RJ eyed her companion, knowing better than to fall for that sweet, innocent look. Leigh Matthews was many things, but "sweet" and "innocent" were not among them. "All right, tell you what. Why don't you pick one you like and I'll pick one I like, and we'll go with those? We can surprise each other."

"Okay," Leigh agreed immediately. She spent a few moments perusing the racks, intentionally staying on the opposite side of the store from her lover. She began to gnaw on a fingernail as she scanned the garments.

She felt decidedly girly as she rolled the fabric of a silky pair of panties in her hand. It was nice to feel feminine. She spent most of her time in a man's world or completely alone. And while she clearly had a preference for strong women, she couldn't stand being dominated. *RJ is the perfect combination of feminine/masculine*, she mused. *Strong and self-assured, but still caring and funny. She doesn't dictate my every move. She just lets me be myself. Even her body is just right. Long and muscular, but still soft and inviting.*

Leigh quickly began fanning her flushed cheeks, turning her back to the part of the store she knew RJ was looking in. "Oh, boy." She laughed at the state she'd worked herself into. "Okay, time to focus." Pale brows creased. *What would she like that she might not pick out herself?* RJ was by no means shy; then again, some of the lingerie, especially the stuff in the very back of the store, was a little on the racy side. Tasteful. Hot as hell. But undeniably racy.

Something in the palest of greens caught her eye. She picked it up and held it in front of her body. Taking a chance, she nodded and folded it under her arm.

RJ tucked her thumbs in her pockets and wandered around the store. She tried to keep an eye on Leigh, but her attention couldn't help but drift to the clothing all around. She pictured the blonde in almost everything she laid eyes on. *If I keep this up, we won't make it back to the hotel. I can't take the stress of being with her. Why does she have to be so damn sexy and so willing to play with me? Wish I'd met her when we could have had a lifetime together.*

The thought shocked her, and she reached up to wipe away the moisture that had collected in the bottom of her eyes. She sucked in a deep breath and picked up a particularly attractive

black number that came with a pair of sheer black hose and gar-
ters to match. "Oh, yeah. Always had a thing for those."

A low voice burred directly into RJ's ear. "No man could
resist them. Those are very nice."

The pilot swallowed hard and nodded. "Yes. Yes they are."
RJ turned around to see a distinguished-looking woman in her
mid-fifties. She wore enormous glasses with red frames, and her
nose resembled a beak, accentuating her already owlish features.

"What size are you?" the decidedly cheerful woman
inquired.

RJ finally tore her eyes from the outfit and took in the clerk
who was offering her assistance. "Oh, no. It's...umm...not for
me."

"Oh." The clerk stiffened, her attitude immediately cooling
as she followed RJ's line of sight to Leigh, who was talking to
another clerk at the register. She stroked her perfectly pressed
sleeve. "For a friend's bachelorette party or wedding shower?"

RJ stood up to her full height and stared at the clerk, lifting
a single, defiant brow. "No. For a friend. But not for a party.
At least, not one that's going to have more than two partici-
pants."

"I see." The clerk's nose wrinkled ever so slightly. "You
don't look as though you need any help. I'll leave you to your
shopping." She'd turned to leave when she felt a tap on her
shoulder.

"No, actually," RJ made the clerk turn around to face her, "I
think I'd really like you to help my friend. She's right over
there." RJ pointed to the blonde. "Isn't she beautiful?"

The clerk's eyes widened. "She...I mean...of course—"

So much for people being more accepting in these times.
Dear Lord, what have people been doing for the last sixty years?
"And don't you think she deserves the most beautiful outfit that
you have in your stock?"

"Well, I mean," the woman began to sputter. "She's quite
attractive. But—"

"Oh, but nothing." She took the woman by the arm and
moved her across the store toward the blonde at a nearly frightening speed. "Leigh, sweetheart, this lady was just saying how
much she'd love to help you find something for us to enjoy this
week while we're together." RJ hoped her grin would convey to
her friend what was going on. If not, she was pretty sure the
trucker would figure it out as soon as the clerk opened her

mouth. She had to admit Leigh was damn quick on the uptake.

One look at the prudish clerk, and Leigh sighed. *Has Miss Straight and Narrow been giving you a hard time, RJ? Now, that's just not nice.* "Thank you, honey." She marched right up to RJ and placed a light, but decidedly not chaste kiss on her lips. "You're so thoughtful."

"Oh, that's me all right—thoughtful. I'm looking forward to being all kinds of 'thoughtful' with you later. So pick something very nice." RJ winked and took a step backwards, perfectly happy to watch the master go to work.

Already wearing a light coat of perspiration, the saleswoman looked like she was ready to bolt.

"You know..." Leigh tapped her chin, "this is what I think I'd like you to do." She paused. "It is your job to help two love birds like us find satisfaction with our lingerie choices," Leigh smiled sweetly, "isn't it?"

"I...I..."

"Of course it is." Leigh moved right up alongside the woman, invading her personal space and intentionally making her even more uncomfortable. "My lover, the beautiful brunette you've already met, would like to buy me something. I've already selected something for myself, which is waiting for me at the register. But I think I might need to be measured for what she'd like to buy me." She turned to RJ, the mischief fairly dancing in her sky blue eyes. "Isn't that right, baby?"

"Oh, absolutely. Have to make sure it fits properly, don't we, darlin'? Wouldn't want you getting pinched in a 'sensitive' spot. Unless of course I'm doing the pinching." RJ leaned over to the saleswoman. "She really likes it when I bite her on the—"

RJ couldn't finish her sentence before Leigh's lips crushed against hers in a passionate kiss.

The salesclerk gasped, then paled as the kiss continued and several large women in the front of the store began hooting and clapping.

"Mmmm..." Leigh pulled away from RJ, her eyes still closed. She opened them slowly and shrugged one shoulder, a small smile playing at her lips. "I was missing you," she said softly. Truly meaning it.

RJ wasn't sure if her friend was playing or serious, but she placed her hand on the blonde's cheek and replied sincerely, "I was missing you as well, Leigh Matthews." She stood up straight before the moment got too intense and turned back to the clerk, who looked as if she were going to pass out at any moment. "See how sweet she is? Now I'm sure you can find it in your heart to help her out."

The woman stood dumbfounded, simply staring at Leigh, who was staring at RJ, utterly charmed by RJ's response to her kiss. She started to slip away when Leigh's hand shot out and grabbed a tape measure that was barely sticking out of the saleswoman's pocket. "I believe the dressing rooms are this way. And I just know I'm going to need some help." *This woman is acting like my cooties will kill her. I love it!* Leigh turned on her heel and began marching toward her destination. When she was almost there, she stopped and looked over her shoulder.

The saleswoman was torn. She couldn't stand waiting on this kind, but she couldn't afford to lose this job either. The woman reluctantly scurried after Leigh, taking the tape measure from her outstretched hand and walking past her into the dressing rooms.

Leigh's eyes were riveted on RJ. "Wait for me?"

A nod. "For eternity, if I must," she said quietly.

"Where is she? What's she doing?" the female squirrel whispered loudly. Her mate was standing on her shoulders, peering inside Fitz's diner at the Glory Town Council meeting.

"She was ranting about broken hearts and her daughter. But now they're all just sitting around a table drinking iced tea."

The female rolled her eyes. "Not the humans, dipshit! The cat. Flea. What's she doing?"

The male stuck his face up to the glass, pressing his tiny, wet, squirrel nose against its dusty surface and fogging it up with his moist breath. "She's lying on the table while Elvis scratches her belly."

"Elvis! Really?"

"No," he admitted dejectedly. "But that would be cool, wouldn't it?"

The female jerked to the side, sending her mate tumbling to the ground at her feet. "This is not a joke. That cat is after us. She's toying with us, torturing us, watching us writhe and sweat just for sport."

"Females," the male snorted. "You're all alike."

"True."

"So what can we do?"

"We can fight back. I'm not going to spend the rest of eternity running from that nasty feline. Just look at this." She pointed to the scratches on her back. Apparently, being dead didn't make you immune to injury.

"The cat didn't give you those." He wriggled the skin above his eyes that would have been squirrel eyebrows had God not been preoccupied by Republicans—and other manner of hideous assaults upon nature—that day. "I did."

The female tackled her mate. She pressed into him, exciting him with her shapely squirrel form and her low, sexy, rodent voice. "Is that a grain of rice in your pocket, or are you just happy to see me?"

The male squirrel purred happily and slid his hand between their bodies. "It's rice!" He whipped out a single long grain and shoved it right in front of his mate's face, forcing her to cross her eyes to look at it. "I'm hoarding for the Apocalypse."

"But we're already dead."

"Oh, yeah." The male immediately popped the grain of rice into his mouth.

Chapter
9

RJ sank down on the bed, taking in her surroundings. "So this is where you stay when you're in Seattle?"

"This is it," Leigh confirmed as she tossed her bag onto her bed at the Piedmont Residential Suites Hotel. She had a standing reservation for the last week of every month. And this was "her" suite.

It was small, but well furnished, with one bedroom barely big enough to hold a dresser, standing mirror, and queen-sized bed. The kitchen was painted a stark white and filled with new, apartment-sized appliances. It connected to the living room, which had hardwood floors covered by soft, thick rugs and filled with comfortable furniture. The bathroom was tiny and completely dominated by its deep, sunken bathtub. The suite's long, narrow balcony had a view of the Puget Sound, and it housed two side-by-side chaise recliners, one of which had always remained empty.

The place suited her needs nicely. It was about the same price she'd pay for an apartment for the entire month; the view was costing her dearly and she knew it. But Leigh never had to do any cleaning, or pay utilities, or deal with a yard. And the management allowed her to use the laundry, pool, and gym whenever she was back in town, whether she was staying at the hotel or simply going to turn around the next day and drive in the opposite direction.

The location was perfect—within walking distance of East Pine Street, where a thriving gay community added color and life to an already eclectic metropolis. It all was convenient and utterly uncomplicated. Just the way Leigh tried to keep her life.

"It's very nice," RJ allowed, shifting her position to look out the window. Her eyes went a little round at the magnificent view. What seemed to be a legion of sailboats dotted the ocean with splashes of color.

Leigh nodded, parking herself next to RJ and peering out the window along with her. An unconscious smile crossed her face at the sight of a particularly quick boat skimming the water's sparkling surface along with the breeze. "They look free, don't they? They're floating," she remarked a little wistfully.

RJ frowned. "You're free, too."

Leigh's head jerked sideways, and she gave RJ an annoyed look. "What are you talking about? I know I'm free." She stood up abruptly and marched toward the door.

RJ followed Leigh out of the room. "You're not tied to the road, Leigh. You can float along too, if that's what you really want."

"Sure I can," Leigh snorted sarcastically. "I can't even swim."

"That's not what I meant, and you know it." RJ halted Leigh's motion by gently placing her hands on her shoulders. She spun her around. "What's your heart's desire, Leigh?" Without warning, RJ felt the breath rush from her body. Never before had she so badly wanted to make someone's dreams come true and yet been completely helpless to do so. It was a sickening feeling, and she laid her hand over her belly in stunned reaction.

"My heart's desire?" Leigh blinked. She was about to make an offhand comment that involved sex and a hammock in Jamaica, when she saw the look on RJ's face. "Was that a serious question?"

RJ didn't answer.

Their eyes met, and Leigh distantly chided herself for allowing that to happen way too often. It was too easy to lose herself in those soulful emerald depths. "I...I can see that it was," she said more to herself than RJ. Her head dropped, and she paused so long that RJ thought she wasn't going to answer at all.

The taller woman drew in a breath to change the subject when Leigh finally managed, softly, "I don't know." She looked back up at RJ with such a painfully open expression that the pilot felt her heartbeat increase in response. In an instant, the look was gone, replaced instead by a neutral smile.

"Let's get something to eat," RJ heard herself say, sorry she'd taken the conversation down this path to begin with. She reached down and took Leigh's hand.

"I could use a bite." Leigh's smile became a little more relaxed as she focused on the reassuring grip of RJ's warm hand. *God, I need this time off. When did I become such a fucking mess?* "I intend to keep you up way past your bedtime tonight, RJ, so we'll need to fortify our reserves." Now a real, full grin appeared.

"Oh, I imagine we do." RJ patted her flat stomach. "Especially me. I'm used to consuming all that grease at Fitz's. I'm starting to shake from withdrawal. Besides, you're not an easy woman to keep up with." *Though I'm getting stronger each day.*

"Seems to me that you're managing just fine." There was only a second's hesitation before Leigh blurted out, "I love it when you hold my hand," startling herself in the process.

RJ bent down and brushed her lips across Leigh's. "So do I, lass. So do I."

"Well?" There was a note of uncertainty in RJ's voice.

"Oh, my God."

RJ fidgeted a little with her collar. "Is that good blasphemy or bad blasphemy?"

"Oh, my God," Leigh mumbled again, her eyes going comically round.

"Leigh."

As though in a trance, Leigh stepped forward, her arms outstretched in a fair imitation of Frankenstein's monster as she approached RJ. She let her hands land first on the slightly rough linen shirt, then headed downward, skimming them over the smooth, supple leather that was stretched tightly over RJ's muscular thighs. She licked dry lips. "Have I said, 'Oh, my God'?"

RJ laughed, finally confident that Leigh's reaction was a good thing. "So the prissy sales clerk was right then?" *He said this would drive you wild.*

Leigh nodded furiously. "You look..." She bit her lower lip. Alan, the clerk, had taken RJ back into the dressing rooms with a few items that he'd insisted would be perfect. He'd insisted that the outfit would "work" better as a surprise to Leigh. He was right. "You...um...you look..." *Oh. My. God. I want her right this second.* "Let's stay here tonight," she said quickly, already in love with the idea.

"No." RJ crossed her arms over her chest defiantly, but the very corner of her mouth was already beginning to curl upward.

"Yes."

"No."

"Please," Leigh begged a little breathlessly.

RJ's stance instantly softened. "Well, maybe."

Leigh smiled.

Green eyes narrowed. "Oh, no. That's not going to work." RJ steeled her resolve, though the hands on her thighs were doing their best to undermine her intentions. "You bought me these lovely black leather pants and this nice shirt." RJ squared her shoulders in the pristine white, linen shirt that was cut in the style of a loose-fitting men's dress shirt. "We should at least take them out for a test drive."

"We could stay in and I could take you for a test drive," Leigh growled, allowing her hands to drift back up RJ's torso.

The darker woman grabbed Leigh's hands, catching a subtle whiff of perfume. "Your perfume," RJ inhaled again, "is lovely."

"What perfume?" Leigh asked with devastating innocence. *I'm so busted.*

"The perfume that you put here..." RJ swooped down and kissed behind Leigh's ear, laughing as the smaller woman began to squeal with laughter. *Ticklish? Oh, you're mine, now.* "And here." RJ's head shot lower, and she happily buried her face in Leigh's cleavage, licking as well as nipping, as the blonde squirmed, only half-heartedly trying to push RJ away.

Satisfied she'd made her point, RJ eventually relented, but only because she was getting so horny she started to seriously consider Leigh's idea of staying home. "Don't be thinking I don't notice that delicious scent, Ms. Macho Truck Driver. I'm quite aware that it's calculated to drive me mad. Your wicked, feminine wiles are working quite nicely, thank you very much."

Leigh looked up at RJ from behind fair lashes. "Is it really driving you mad?"

"Very." Taking Leigh's hand, she placed it over her heart. "Feel."

A charmed smile eased its way across Leigh's face as she pressed her hand to RJ's chest. The tall woman's intense body heat radiated through thin linen directly into Leigh's hand. She longed to repeat the process with her other hand, absorbing more of RJ's sensual warmth. So she did.

RJ felt her heart skip a beat and she knew that Leigh felt it, too.

"It's beating awfully fast," Leigh said, a touch of wonder coloring her voice.

"It always does when you're near."

Leigh sighed. "Keep up that sweet talk, RJ, and I won't be letting you go when this week is over." Her face scrunched up into a happy grin. "I'll be right back." She headed for the bedroom to pick up a light jacket. A faint drizzle had begun, and it looked like the night was going to be a little chilly.

RJ watched her companion retreat to the bedroom and whispered quietly, "I wish it were that easy, Leigh Matthews. I wouldn't go."

The women went to one of Leigh's favorite Seattle haunts, The Doll House, a women's club and definitely a local hotspot. Despite the predominantly lesbian clientele, nearly a quarter of the Doll House's patrons were straight couples, who came to enjoy the wonderful dance floor, or "girls' night out" groups, who used the club as a refuge from the intoxicated men who tended to intrude on their private gatherings.

RJ looked at another couple, openly kissing on the dance floor. *Good Lord!* "Interesting place you chose for us tonight." RJ held Leigh's hand just a little tighter. The last thing she wanted to do was lose her friend in the crowd. *That would be bad*, she decided, the moment she saw the woman dressed all in black with purple hair and things that looked very painful sticking out of her face. "You don't intend to try to talk me into anything like that, do you?"

"Not hardly," Leigh laughed. "Dance with me?"

"But—"

"I'll take that as a yes."

It was a relatively slow song, much to RJ's relief. But she soon realized she didn't need to worry about all this new music or how to dance to it. Leigh had wrapped her arms around her neck and was pressed tightly against her as they swayed to the beat of whatever played. The silk of Leigh's rust-colored blouse felt cool against RJ's hands.

"Not so bad, right?" Leigh whispered a few moments later, lacing her hands behind RJ's head. She had no intention of letting RJ flounder around on the dance floor, feeling uncomfortable. "Let me guess, they don't have clubs like these in Glory?"

RJ chuckled at the gentle tease. "No, they don't. But after being in this place, I think that's something we need to change."

"Good." Leigh leaned forward and kissed RJ's cheek and, growing slightly bolder, moved a bit away from RJ for the next, only slightly faster dance. She placed RJ's hands on her swaying hips, smiling when RJ's movements easily began to mirror her own.

It was nearly an hour later that they strolled off the dance floor, perspiring lightly and both in desperate need of drinks and a place to sit and rest for a few minutes.

"I'm really starting to feel the need to march across the room and poke her eyes out." Leigh fumed as she all but snarled at the tall, stacked blonde who seemed to be fixated on her dance partner. The woman had been staring at and drooling over RJ all night. Leigh had seen her in the Doll House before, and even those brief visual encounters from afar were enough to set off the warning bells in Leigh's head tonight. The woman was a predator. Not that Leigh or RJ were shy, but this woman was different.

RJ looked up from her companion for the first time that evening, trying to see who Leigh was glaring at. "Has she done something to you?"

"No." Leigh's jaw worked. "But she'd like to do something to you."

RJ's eyebrows popped up. "Who would like to do what to me?"

Leigh smiled as the woman headed toward the door. "Never mind, RJ." She patted the pilot's arm. "Thirsty?"

"In the worst way."

"Whew." She fanned herself. "Same here." Leigh pushed herself up on tiptoes and softly bussed RJ's chin. As the evening progressed, the club had grown more and more crowded. The temperature began to rise, and Leigh felt a trickle of perspiration disappear down the center of her back. A slow song began playing and she leaned close to RJ, feeling the heat of her skin through her clothes. "I'm going for more drinks." She pointed to the throng of women, with a few men interspersed, around the bar. "Beer?" she asked, already planning her strategic route through the crowd.

"Absolutely. Never turn down beer," RJ paused and winked, "or the beautiful woman you're with." She wiggled her brows and allowed a roguish grin to appear. "You get the drinks, and I'll try and find a seat." RJ gave Leigh a playful wink before turning and scanning the back of the room. It took a moment, but she finally spied two empty seats at a small table. "Don't be too long, love. You never know who might try to steal me away."

"God," Leigh laughed, rolling her eyes as she headed toward the bar. "There is no way I should find someone so obnoxious so completely attractive in every way." *But I don't think I have a choice.*

The woman near the door waited until Leigh disappeared from sight before making her way over to RJ, who was seated in the corner, but still watching the writhing bodies on the dance floor with interest. "Hello."

RJ looked up at the woman and quirked a brow. "Good evening to you." She tilted her head and gave her a friendly smile before going back to watching the dancing couples. *In my day, that would have gotten them arrested.*

"I'm Ali." She had to raise her voice above the pulsing music. "I haven't seen you here before."

"Never been here before." RJ tore her eyes from the dance floor and refocused on the tall, curly haired blonde, taking note for the first time of her considerable attributes. *How in the hell does a skinny woman like this get those?* "I'm RJ Fitzgerald. Nice to meet you."

"It's nice to meet you, too. May I sit down?" Not waiting for an answer, Ali slid into the chair next to RJ that was saved for Leigh. She scooted it so close to RJ that their arms touched. "I knew you hadn't been here before," Ali admitted. "I would have remembered a beautiful woman like you." *And you would have remembered me. I promise you that.*

RJ shifted her body to put as much space as possible between them, though she couldn't manage much. "Oh, I'm not that memorable, lass." She smiled politely, then glanced over Ali's head, trying to find Leigh in the crowd at the bar. But her much shorter companion had simply been swallowed up by the masses.

"Let me see your hand."

RJ looked blankly at Ali. "My hand? Why do you want to see my hand?"

"Your hand," Ali repeated impatiently, holding hers out so she could take RJ's. "I'm not going to hurt you." She made a show of assuring RJ her hand was empty.

RJ offered the woman her hand slowly, palm up. Her eyes glinted with curiosity. "Are you gonna tell my fortune?" *I can see it now. "You're already dead!" And my gypsy has a heart attack on the spot.*

"Not at all." Ali carefully turned RJ's hand over, gently trailing her fingertips across RJ's third finger. "No gold band in sight. So you really don't need to feel guilty and can stop looking toward the bar for the short blonde." Ali's voice was filled with confidence. "Would you like to dance?"

The pilot pulled her hand back. "I'm flattered. I really am. But you see, I'm here with someone very special, and I wouldn't want to be doing something that might upset her." RJ held her left hand in front of Ali's face and wiggled her fingers. "Golden band or no, makes no difference."

Ali gently ran her palm over the butter-soft leather of RJ's pants. "I don't think that's true." She gestured lightly with her chin toward the dance floor. "When you look out there, that's lust I see on your face, not domestic bliss." She leaned close, catching a whiff of RJ's perspiration and shampoo despite the cloud of thick cloud of smoke that hovered in the room like a heavy fog. "Dance with me. You won't be sorry."

RJ felt her heart rate increase. She really wished Leigh would come back. She briefly considered going to look for her, but quickly dismissed that thought, knowing she'd just get lost and then they'd be separated for even longer. "Like I said, lass, I'm flattered, but I'm here tonight with someone I'm very fond of."

"I heard you the first time, RJ Fitzgerald." Ali placed her other hand on RJ's leg, alongside her first. "You're beautiful." She looked genuinely curious. "You don't find me attractive?"

"Now, I never said that," RJ corrected gently, again wishing that Leigh was back. "You're very attractive. And I can see that you know it. You could have nearly any woman in here; you don't need me." She grinned tentatively, hoping that the woman would take the hint.

"You're right." Ali leaned forward, her long, curly blonde hair brushing across RJ's forearm like a whisper. "It's not a matter of needing, it's a matter of wanting. I want you," she said bluntly, her blood red fingernails tracing a swirling pattern on RJ's leg. "And I think you want me." Ever so slowly, her hands inched upward, pausing when she heard RJ's sharp intake of breath.

RJ jumped a bit, quickly grasping the wandering hands. "Now, play nice. I don't remember inviting you to touch me like that." She cleared her throat and let out a long slow breath. *You're outclassed tonight. Move on, girl.* "I'm pretty sure that my friend wouldn't find this conversation we're having the least bit amusing. I have a feeling she's a bit overprotective."

Ali didn't move a muscle.

RJ was beginning to wonder if this Ali person understood what the word "no" meant. The club was too crowded, and with Ali's close presence she felt like the place was closing in on her, growing louder and louder with each moment. "You're a very attractive woman, and if I weren't with someone, I'd be more than happy to spend some time with you; but I don't play games with the feelings of the person I'm with."

"But with games, there's always a winner." Ali shamelessly thrust her best assets forward. "Think of all you could win, RJ," she purred.

Licking her lips, RJ tried hard not to notice the spectacular cleavage being presented for her inspection. "Actually, I'm thinking about what I might lose, and that's far more important than what I might win. My answer, once again, has to be no."

"Good answer, RJ." Leigh slammed two sweating mugs of beer on the table, causing the foamy contents to slosh over the sides and onto the floor. Blue eyes flashed angrily, boring into Ali's hands, which were once again resting comfortably, intimately, on RJ's leg. Had she herself not heard her lover trying to ditch Ali, the woman's current positioning so close to RJ, and her hands moving sensually over the lanky form would have convinced her they were lovers. As it was, she was an annoyance. "Who the hell are you, and how many times does someone have to say 'no' before you catch a clue?" Leigh reached down and unceremoniously yanked Ali's hands off RJ's leg.

"This is Ali," RJ said, answering for Ali who was wearing a smug grin that she could tell Leigh was about ready to wipe away. Forcefully.

Ali pushed her chair back and stood. She towered over the trucker, and it was clear by the irritated, challenging look on her face that she wasn't used to being turned down. By anyone. "Beat it, short stuff."

The nerve. "I'll beat—"

"Now wait just a minute." RJ stood and wrapped her arms around Leigh's waist from behind, resting her chin on her shoulder. "There's no need for a problem." She gave Leigh a little kiss on the ear. Feeling the blonde's muscles tighten and her hands ball into fists, she whispered, "I'm not going anywhere, lass. Let it go."

RJ's senses were on overload. Leigh's body was pressed tightly against hers, people were squeezing by each other just to move, just to breath, and she could sense the energy in the place increasing and expanding as the alcohol flowed and the women danced. The entire club felt like a powder keg in search of a spark.

Leigh spun around in RJ's arms, temporarily tuning out the scrawny slut behind her. Her eyes burned two holes into RJ with the precision and intensity of a laser. She'd seen the blonde coming on to RJ from across the room, but had had to wade through the hideous crowd to make it back to their table. Why hadn't she noticed how impossible this place was before? "I don't recall asking—" She stopped and let out a shuddering breath. With effort, she rephrased what she was going to say. "I'm handling this, RJ."

The pilot nodded and raised her hands, acknowledging what Leigh was saying. She understood better than anyone the right to be upset and the need to deal with it in your own way. "All right, love, all right. I trust you." She winked, but her voice was serious. "I'm here if you need me."

Love? "You'd better be." The heat behind Leigh's words, at least the ones directed at RJ, however, had gone from scalding to merely hot. Ali, however, wasn't so lucky. Leigh turned around and did her best to look bored. "Are you still here?"

"You asked who the hell I was," Ali reminded Leigh tartly. "And since I have no intention of going anyplace...alone," she emphasized her last word and winked at RJ, "I thought I'd at least stay to tell you."

"Jesus!" Leigh threw her hands in the air. "You're the type of woman who gives blondes a bad name." Her eyes flicked upwards, and she wrinkled her nose. "Well, tacky, bleached blondes, that is."

RJ snorted and reached for her beer. It looked as though Leigh had things well in hand for the moment. She had discovered a lifetime ago that busted lips and bruises hurt a hell of a lot less when you had a few beers in you first. She had a feeling if Ali didn't back off, and fast, they were going to be nursing a few of each later. Leigh's voice was calm, but her flushed cheeks and trembling body convinced RJ that she was about to blow like a hand grenade.

Ali looked over Leigh's head at RJ and licked her full lips provocatively. "Given any more thought to that dance?"

"Yeah." The pilot straightened and pulled Leigh closer to her. "Actually, I have. Leigh, would you like to dance with me?"

Leigh reached behind her without looking at RJ. "In a minute, hon," she murmured distractedly. "Did you just proposition her in front of me?" Leigh asked incredulously. "In case you're actually mentally handicapped and not just stupid, I should remind you that she's here with me tonight, and that she's said *several* times that she's not interested."

Ali was growing weary of the chatterbox between her and the brunette she sought. She had hoped that when RJ saw how determined she was to have her, it would tip the scales in her favor. But she was finally starting to think that RJ might actually have been sincere when she said she wouldn't dance with her, though the prospect seemed highly unlikely to Ali.

Ali finally glanced down at Leigh. "It's not who she's with *now* that matters. It's who she goes home with at the end of the evening."

Leigh's face went deadly serious. "That person would be me. Now, and for the very last time, please leave us alone." *I won't ask again.*

As she watched the tall blonde stare at Leigh, RJ wondered why Ali didn't seem to understand that she wasn't interested in being with her. Had things changed that much? She remembered briefly their encounter with the waitress at the truck stop. Apparently it wasn't uncommon to have more than one partner these days. *It wasn't uncommon in my day either, just a hell of a lot harder.* She put a little space between her and Leigh, crossing her arms and waiting to see what Ali was going to do.

Ali didn't say a word. Instead, she started to move...

Leigh began to gladly step aside, breathing a sigh of relief that this little incident was over. She froze, however, when she caught Ali eyeing her RJ like she was a piece of meat and some- one had just rung the dinner bell. The light bulb popped on in Leigh's head, and her voice cracked with agitation. "You're moving past me to get to her?" *I cannot believe this woman. I should have known those leather pants on RJ would send these women into a feeding frenzy.*

"For all your talk, RJ is still standing here," Ali smiled, showing off two neat rows of pearly whites, "looking at *me*. Step aside, *Tom Cat*." *Oh, yes, I know who you are. I know all the regulars in my playground. Even if they don't know me. Yet.*

Leigh's eyes widened at the use of her much-despised nick- name, and her brain officially began to short-circuit.

Uh oh. The pilot stiffened and put her hands on Leigh's shoulders. "Come on, lass, let's go have that dance," she said a trifle urgently. "By the time we're done, she will have moved on to the next person who's breathing."

Every muscle in Leigh's body twitched with anticipation as adrenaline sang through her blood. RJ was right, of course. But it felt utterly wrong to leave any doubt as to who would be tak- ing her home tonight. *She's mine, bitch. At least for now,* Leigh's mind begrudgingly amended.

Ali had moved around the table, effectively doing an end run around Leigh without the trucker being able to stop her. This put her directly in behind RJ, who automatically turned around at Ali's advance. She leaned forward and whispered something that made RJ blush furiously. "No answer for that, I see," Ali said smugly.

Leigh grabbed hold of the table between them and violently shoved it out of her way, knocking over a chair in the process. Then she simply launched herself at Ali, taking RJ down in the process.

Ali screamed and knocked into the woman behind her, who landed on the feet of the next woman over, and so on.

"Fuck. Watch it!" someone in the crowd shouted.

"You watch it, cow," was the disembodied shout heard over the loud music.

Then all hell broke loose.

RJ did her best to stop the barrage of hands that were flying around her head. With a loud grunt, she managed to get herself turned around to make a grab for Leigh's fists. This only served to piss off her companion even more, and she heard a loud growl as Leigh jerked her hands away and made another lunge for Ali, catching the screaming woman right in the nose.

Ali tried to scramble out from under RJ, digging her high heels into RJ's legs in the process and going a long way toward making her deaf from the screams leveled right into her ear. "Wait," RJ barked. She turned again, facing Ali and knocking away several of her flailing punches. In a quick change of tactics, Ali decided to use RJ as a human shield.

"Jesus," RJ mumbled, wide eyed, as the blows came even closer to her head. "Leigh—" She turned as she said the word, stopping Leigh's flying fist. With her eye.

"Oh, God." Leigh stared at RJ in horror and scrambled off her friend.

Ali used the momentary distraction to push her way out from under RJ and vanish among the fighting, yelling, cursing women.

Sirens sounded in the distance.

Leigh's hands moved shakily to RJ's face. She cupped her cheeks gently and began examining RJ's tightly shut eye. "I am so sorry." Her voice cracked a little as she spoke, all thoughts of Ali forgotten. "I didn't mean to do that."

A beer mug crashed against the wall behind RJ, sending shards of glass and droplets of brew showering down on them.

Leigh closed her eyes as the warm liquid splashed against her back.

RJ tried to shake her head a little to clear the stars. "Damn, lass. That's a hell of a right hook you've got there. You should be a boxer." She tried to grin, but it hurt to move her face at all. And she couldn't keep stop her eye from tearing up.

Leigh's heart clenched painfully. *She's crying? Aww, shit.* "Please don't cry." Tears welled in Leigh's own eyes as she peppered RJ's face with soft kisses. "I'm so, so sorry."

"Ahh, come on, darlin'." RJ gave her friend a quick peck on the cheek. "I'm not crying; I'm tougher than that. It's just watering." She leaned up, feeling decidedly lightheaded. The air was knocked from her lungs when Leigh crashed into her as they both ducked a flying chair. Instinctively, her arms tightened around Leigh as she tried to protect her from flying furniture and bits of wood. "I think we need to get the hell out of here. It's like London during the Blitz!"

"But I hit you." Leigh continued kissing her face. "I swear, I'll never touch you again."

RJ pushed them to their feet, looking for the exit. She kissed Leigh back soundly, right in the middle of the melee. "Don't be saying things like that, Leigh Matthews. I intend to take you home right now and let you touch me all you want." She tugged on Leigh's arm. "C'mon."

"Hold still."

"Ouch."

"God, RJ, if you don't hold still, I can't look at it!"

RJ continued to flinch away from Leigh's fingers. Her touch wasn't as gentle as it had been before the fight in the bar. The taller woman could tell Leigh was angry, though she couldn't tell if it was with her. "You don't need to look at it. It's just my eye."

"I know that," Leigh ground out, trying her best to be patient, especially since she was the one who'd hit RJ. That thought froze her hands in mid-motion.

RJ stopped squirming. "What's the matter?"

Leigh shook her head sharply and bolted from the room.

RJ blinked. "Why does this keep happening?"

A loud crash sounded from the kitchen, causing RJ to jump at the sound. Then there was another and another. *Oh, Lord. There won't be a glass left in the house by morning. The lass has to be Irish! Mother has a standing order of replacement glasses every month at Bedford's Hardware store.* She rose to go to Leigh, then abruptly sat back down. *Better those glasses than me.*

A few moments later, Leigh barreled back into the living room, holding two tumblers filled generously with ice and an amber-colored liquid. "Well...that was fast," RJ teased gently.

Leigh closed her eyes and held her bruised knuckles against the cold glass, sighing in relief as the dull throb eased. She drained half her glass, then passed a heavy tumbler to JR. "My emergency ice pack is in my truck," she informed her bluntly. "I'll have to go out to the store and buy another one."

"I'm fine."

"Your eye is swollen completely shut."

RJ shrugged. "I'm not surprised." She hissed a little as the whiskey slid down her throat, burning a hot trail to her belly. "You have a wicked right hook."

Though Leigh tried to stop it, RJ's praise caused a small smile to appear. "Is that supposed to be a compliment?"

"From an Irishman, love, that's a tremendous compliment." RJ picked up Leigh's hand and gave the back of it a little kiss, the wet, cool skin chilling her lips. "You should be proud of that punch."

"Well, I'm not," Leigh countered harshly. "Not at all." She roughly pulled her hand away. "And I'm mad at you." The pent-up anger and frustration at RJ that had been banked since leaving the bar came roaring back to life.

"Me?" RJ's eyes widened. "What did I do?"

"What do you mean, 'what did I do'?" Leigh poked RJ's chest just as she stood up, placing them toe to toe. "You grabbed my hands. Not once, but...well...more than once!"

"Yeah?" RJ still wasn't clear on what the problem was, but was already getting annoyed. "So?"

Leigh nodded her head furiously. "So, I'm mad!"

RJ wanted to stick her hands into her pockets, but the leather fit too snugly to make it comfortable. She frowned irritably. "And what was so bad about that, lass? I only wanted to get us out of there without either of us getting hurt."

"Arghh. Are you being all calm and reasonable just to piss me off?"

RJ straightened and rested her fists on her hips. "No. I'm staying calm and reasonable because it's my nature." The angry undertone of her voice contradicted her words and she knew it, which made her even more agitated. "But if you want me to get mad, I can."

Leigh threw back the last of her drink and snorted. "That I'd like to see."

"All right, fine." RJ's voice was hard and loud as she nearly let the frustration of the moment overtake her. She tried to step back, grinding her teeth together for what had to be a full minute before she shook an angry finger at Leigh. "Now you're trying to piss me off. What is it that you want, Leigh Matthews? Do you want me to get mad enough so that I'll hit you back? Is that what you're after?" RJ challenged, her words somewhere between a yell and a dull roar. "Because if it is, you're not gonna get it." She downed the rest of her drink in one quick swallow, then threw the glass hard against the wall, shattering it and denting the wallpapered plaster. "There! Are you happy?"

Leigh looked at the stain on the wall and wordlessly handed RJ her own glass, lifting a pale eyebrow in challenge.

Without thinking, the pilot slammed Leigh's glass against the wall, throwing it even harder than she'd thrown hers and placing another small dent in the wall. RJ exhaled shakily and sank to the couch, running a hand through her hair. "Are you happy now? Now that I've made an ass of myself?"

"Actually," Leigh dropped down onto the sofa next to RJ, "I do feel a little better, mainly because of the 'ass' part."

"Well, good." RJ sighed sarcastically, glancing sideways at her friend. "Are you still mad at me?"

Leigh mulled that over.

"I wouldn't have done it, except I didn't want to see you hurt. I swear. Oops...and I'm sorry."

Apparently, those were the magic words because Leigh's face seemed to lighten. "Thanks for looking out for me. It wasn't necessary; but I guess it was sort of nice...in a weird, annoying, if-you-ever-do-it-again-I'll-murder-you sort of way."

The one of RJ's eyes that could narrow, did. "Are you sure there's no Irish in your blood?"

Leigh exhaled slowly. "Nope. None that I'm aware of." She nudged RJ's shoulder with her own. "C'mon, admit it. It felt good to blow off a little steam. I mean, I'm sure the quilting bees in Glory are great venting spots, but this was the best we had available at the moment."

"I don't attend those particular social events, thank you very much. I prefer to drink good whiskey with my brother and talk about women, if you must know." RJ gave Leigh a little smirk.

"Thank God. If you'd said you were a member of a quilting bee, I don't know what I would have done." Leigh turned sideways and crossed her legs under herself. "I'm sorry about your eye," she whispered. "I would never hurt you on purpose."

RJ sighed. "Don't take it so hard, Leigh. I know it was an accident, and I'm truly fine."

Leigh fiddled with the throw pillow, using any excuse not to look up at RJ's bruised face. "That's easy for you to say. How would you feel if you'd punched me, hurt me?"

RJ dropped her head and nodded. "I see what you mean. I'd feel awful if I hurt you. I'd never want to see you hurt, either." RJ shuddered inwardly, thankful that the situation wasn't reversed. And as Tony would say, that would truly suck. She smiled a little, trying to lighten her friend's mood. "But, umm, according to the women in the bar tonight—I talked to a couple in the bathroom—I think I'm supposed to be the 'butch' one in this relationship, right? So it's okay for me to get a shiner." RJ tugged on Leigh's hand, trying to play with her a little, but it wasn't working.

Leigh's face remained impassive, so RJ tried again. "It could be worse." She made a show of opening her mouth as wide as humanly possible, making it nearly impossible to speak. "You could have knocked out one of my good chewing teeth."

Leigh chuckled and grabbed for RJ's tongue. "There's always tomorrow, RJ."

Chapter
10

RJ opened her eyes slowly. They both worked, and the left one didn't even feel nearly as badly swollen this morning. She smiled at Leigh, who was still sound asleep, lying on her stomach with one arm dangling off the bed.

Propping herself up on her elbow, the pilot tenderly ran a gentle hand through Leigh's coarse, fair hair, tucking it behind a pink ear so that she could watch her sleep without anything blocking the lovely view. Leigh looked young and happy while slumbering. Her face, now slack in sleep, contrasted sharply with the woman who—even while trying to relax—seemed to hold RJ just a little further away than she wanted to be. RJ sighed, understanding exactly why Leigh was keeping her distance. When this week was over, their "lives" would go back to normal...and for both of them, that mainly meant being alone.

These past few days had been some of the most interesting RJ had ever experienced, and she would be forever grateful for the time that she and Leigh had been given together. She wished there was more she could do to make the young woman happy; but this wasn't Glory, and there just wasn't time. A firestorm of resentment built up inside her when she realized she only had a few days—time was slipping away like sand between her fingers...*I just need to stop feeling sorry for myself and make every moment count. And dammit, I will.*

RJ leaned over and gave the smaller woman a tender kiss on the cheek, getting swatted by a grumpy bedmate. She jerked her head back just in time to keep from getting smacked again by her growling companion. Drawing in a deep breath, RJ rolled out of bed, doing her best to ignore the kink that her neck had developed during the night. Not surprisingly, being dead was much more conducive to a good night's sleep. Moving quickly and quietly to the bathroom, she spent a few moments indulging in her morning ritual.

She inspected her eye, wincing at the lurid purple bruise that extended halfway down her cheek. "What's this?" She spied a small bottle of hand cream on the shelf above the sink. *Oh, yeah, this is good.* Cool and soothing, the cream caused RJ to sigh happily as she carefully rubbed it into the puffy skin around her eye. "Much better."

Leigh was still asleep when RJ clicked off the light and returned to the bed, sliding beneath the covers with the bottle of lotion still in hand. A light rain was tapping against the window, and the room was still steeped in early morning shadows.

RJ slowly pushed the covers down, exposing Leigh's bare back. She squeezed a bit of the cream into her hands and rubbed them together, warming it before beginning a gentle massage of Leigh's shoulders. She kept her touch light, waiting to see how Leigh would react to being awakened this way.

"Now that's the way I like to wake up," Leigh mumbled sleepily, still not opening her eyes.

RJ breathed an inner sigh of relief. "Well, good." *Because it would be one of my favorite ways to wake you up. I'd do it every morning if I could.* "Would you like a little more pressure?" RJ subtly dug into Leigh's muscles with her thumbs.

Leigh moaned. "Don't you dare change a thing." Her eyes rolled back in her head. "It's perfect."

A grin lit RJ's face as she continued to run her hands over soft, warm skin. Leigh's back was already relaxed from sleep, and her palms and fingers easily pressed into the muscles, drawing frequent, nearly sub-vocal sounds of praise from the trucker. More than once, Leigh drifted back to sleep.

RJ chewed her lip as she regarded Leigh, who at this very moment was mumbling happily. "Would you like to go back to sleep?" she whispered. "I can stop if you like." RJ was half teasing. She knew what she wanted to do, but if Leigh were more interested in sleep...well, that would be fine, too.

RJ glanced out the window. It was gray and drippy, a perfect day for lounging in bed. Or at least until they both got so antsy they couldn't stand it. Which, she suspected, would be early afternoon at the soonest. "You know, lass," she squeezed another dollop of lotion into her palm, "it's not really a nice day out. I could go out and find a market and pick us up a few things, and we could just stay in today. Would you like that?" She tilted her head in question. "Or did you have plans?"

"I could say I had plans," Leigh admitted, sighing as strong thumbs worked down the length of her spine, finding sensitive spots along the way. "Driving gets the muscles really tense there." *What was she asking me? Oh, right.* "Considering that this is way better than anything I had planned, I'd love to spend the day in bed. With you."

RJ's eyebrows jumped. "Well, I would hope it'd be with me. Seeing as how I'm the one who's gonna go out and get everything we need to have a lovely day together while you go back to sleep. How does that sound?"

Leigh mewed her agreement with the idea, gently patted RJ's leg, and promptly fell back to sleep.

With the help of the hotel clerk and a hand-drawn map, RJ found her way to a strip mall not too far from the hotel. It had several interesting stores full of electronic equipment that RJ couldn't imagine people really needed, and a decent-sized grocery store. She liked the fact that it was within walking distance. It gave her a chance to stretch her legs, and if she were lucky, she'd get back to Leigh's suite before it began raining any harder. Her jeans and light sweatshirt were already soaked but, oddly, she was enjoying every minute of it. While she had gotten used to her physical sensations being slightly dulled, she hadn't grown blasé about seeing this new and exciting world around her that was the same and yet so different.

The comfortable clothes that she had loved—and that had driven her mother and teachers to near fits—had become commonplace for woman. Hairstyles were a wild mix for both sexes; and from behind, RJ couldn't tell one from the other. The people even looked bigger than in her day. RJ's five feet eleven inches had made her taller than most of the men, and nearly freakishly tall for a woman. Nobody stared at her height in this time...and she walked the streets with a delicious sense of anonymity.

By the time she'd finished her shopping and returned home, she was wet to the bone, but in a cheerful mood. It wasn't until she made it back to the hotel that an actual storm cut loose, sending bolts of jagged lightning through the gray sky.

She fumbled for a moment as she tried to get the "key" to their room from her pocket without dropping anything. *What happened to real keys? These flimsy plastic cards don't work for shit.* On the fourth try, a tiny green light appeared on a box above the door handle and her timing was right. RJ breathed a sigh of relief when she could actually open the door. She wondered if all the noise she'd made rattling the door in frustration had sent the people next door calling for the police.

RJ set the wet sacks onto the counter, glad that she'd selected plastic and not paper. *Is everything plastic nowadays?* She thought of some of the horrible little cars she'd seen up close on her trek to the store, and decided that plastic had, indeed, taken over the world.

She peeled off her sweatshirt and padded out of the kitchen to hang it on the metal hook sticking out of the front door. RJ had turned for the kitchen when another loud clap of thunder shook the building. She looked up, annoyed, and sucked a puff of air through her teeth. "You could tone that down a bit, You know." Her hands moved to her hips. "Leigh's still sleeping."

She waited a moment, listening, as it seemed to move off into the distance. RJ grinned toothily and headed back to the kitchen. "Thank You." It didn't really matter if the storm had moved along due to her complaint or not. If RJ had learned one thing since dying, it was that it never hurt to be polite.

Hair still dripping rainwater into her face, she put away the groceries and took twenty minutes to figure out how to start the coffee pot. The one at the diner was a new-fangled model from the 1960s that Mavis had ordered from a catalog when the old one had officially died, but this little *plastic* one was all electronic. Luckily, her intellect prevailed. Eventually. Not only did she figure it out, but she was almost certain that she'd fixed it to where it would come on for the next morning while they slept. *Truly amazing.* The things in the electronic shops were fascinating and not terribly expensive, considering the fantastic technology that made her head spin. But milk was nearly three dollars a gallon, and gasoline almost two. This world made no sense.

RJ was in the process of scrambling eggs when she heard the bedroom door open, followed by the pattering of Leigh's soft footsteps. Leigh pushed open the swinging door to the small kitchen. Judging by her erratic movements, she was obviously still partially asleep. Her eyes were half closed and her hair was a mess, sticking up in several directions. She was also as naked as the day she was born.

To RJ's eyes, she looked lovely.

Leigh stumbled past RJ, completely oblivious to her presence, and opened the door to the fridge. Removing the carton of orange juice that RJ had put in there, she took a long drink.

RJ leaned against the counter, watching Leigh in amusement. Once Leigh was finished, she put the juice back and moved to RJ, giving her a soft kiss on the cheek as she reached around her and into the cupboard for a coffee cup.

I guess the lass did notice me after all. "You mean you're not gonna drink it straight from the pot?" She gestured toward the percolating coffee maker with her spatula.

One eyeball rolled in RJ's direction and fixed on her spectacular shiner. "Who kicked your ass last night, Irish?"

"I said it was a good punch; I never said it wasn't a lucky one to boot." She winked her good eye. "Umm...tell me, did someone break in here in the middle of the night and steal your clothes? And isn't the cold floor making you chilly?"

Leigh's gaze drifted down her own body, but she couldn't dredge up even the slightest bit of embarrassment. They'd had sex in a dozen different locations since they'd met; it seemed sort of silly to start worrying about modesty now. Her brow creased. "It appears that *you* need to be reminded to actually remove your clothes before you take a shower. You're all wet."

"Groceries."

"Oh, right." Leigh yawned, remnants of their earlier conversation and a wonderful massage floating back to her. "Does me being naked bother you?"

"Depends on how you define 'bother.'" The pilot wiggled her eyebrows. She set the skillet off the burner and wrapped long arms around Leigh's waist. "If you're thinking it bothers me in a 'my-goodness-she's-runnin'-around-naked' way, then you'd be wrong. If you think it bothers me in a 'she's-naked-and-we're-wastin'-time-talkin'-about-it-in-the-kitchen' sort of way, then you'd be right." Her hands drifted down to the trucker's backside and she gave a little squeeze, her own body reacting fiercely to Leigh's presence. "How bad do you need that coffee, Leigh Matthews?" she whispered throatily.

"Bad." Leigh closed her eyes and let her lips brush against

RJ's damp collarbone, feeling the slight shock of cool wetness against her warm skin. "But not that bad."

RJ kissed her soundly, removing the coffee cup from Leigh's hand and placing it haphazardly on the counter behind her. She lifted the blonde and felt strong legs curl around her as she deepened the kiss, tasting the sweet tang of orange juice and Leigh's tongue. RJ slowly walked them to the bedroom and stopped at the foot of the bed, where Leigh's legs dropped.

Disencumbered, she began peeling off her undershirt. The thin white material had been rendered see-through by the rain, and Leigh growled impatiently at the sight. Reaching out with slightly trembling hands, she tugged at the buttons on RJ's jeans. "How can I want you so badly already today?" she breathed, popping the last button and quickly working the material over RJ's hips.

"I dunno, lass." RJ kicked out of her pants and underwear and pushed Leigh back into the cool, tangled sheets as their bodies met and their breasts pressed firmly together. *Sweet Jesus.* "But I feel the same way."

Leigh slowly opened her eyes, surprised to find RJ's arms and legs intimately wound around her like a snake. This was new. With most women, she was already gone by this point; and even with RJ, she woke up firmly on her own side of the bed.

Now, however, they were so close together—not in sex, but in mutual comfort and genuine affection—that it was hard to tell where RJ began and where she ended. It was what she'd always avoided. And she couldn't decide which was more cause for alarm: the fact that she immediately loved it so and that she didn't intend to move a single inch; or that she knew in her heart this was a very dangerous idea, but she couldn't dredge up an ounce of willpower against it. In the end, her body defied her brain and snuggled a little closer, sighing when she felt RJ's lips brush across the top of her head. "Hmm...nice." *So nice. God, too nice.*

"Yes, it is." The pilot pulled Leigh closer, feeling the hot tickle of her breath against her neck. "Is this all right?"

"I...I...I think so," Leigh said quietly, hearing the uncertainty in her own voice.

RJ's forehead creased, and she loosened her hold a little as she cleared her throat. "Can I ask you a question, Leigh?"

Leigh's body stiffened at the solemn note in RJ's voice. "You're not going to propose, are you? I'd hate to turn you down and ruin your morning," she teased feebly.

RJ chuckled and softly kissed her friend on the forehead. "Nah, I wouldn't do that. My mother would never forgive me for proposing to a woman who's not Irish or Catholic." *Though for you, Leigh, I think I could live with my mother's wrath.* "I was just wondering why you bolted from the truck the other night."

Leigh had been giggling along with RJ, but froze at her last words. "What did you say?" *Oh, that's brilliant. Maybe she'll think you're deaf and not just pathetic.*

"I was just wondering why you ran away from me the other night in front of that motel in Wyoming." RJ shifted a little so she could have eye contact, but still maintained a gentle hold on Leigh. The blue-eyed gaze that met her own was tinged with fear. *You're not getting out of this, Leigh Matthews. I want an answer.*

Leigh swallowed, her throat suddenly dry. "You want the truth?"

"That would be nice."

Leigh licked her lips. "Okay. I...Well...I'm not exactly sure why I did it." *Liar. Shit.*

RJ released Leigh and worked herself free from the woman, a little sick to her stomach and more than a little frustrated. She sat up on the edge of the bed and dropped her head forward, taking a few deep, calming breaths. "If you don't want to talk about it, just say that, but don't insult my intelligence by lying to me. I'm Irish; I'm not stupid." The pilot stood and pulled on her underwear and undershirt.

Leigh cursed herself. "RJ, wait." She scrambled off the bed, not bothering with the sheet. "I never said you were stupid."

"Yeah, I know." She looked for her socks for a second, and then decided she didn't need them. "Are you hungry? I can go fix breakfast now."

Guilt warring with resentment, Leigh watched as RJ shrugged into her clothes. *I don't owe you an explanation. Right?* "Please, RJ." She stepped forward, grabbing a handful of the tall woman's cotton undershirt to prevent her from leaving the room. "I'm not hungry, and I don't want breakfast."

The pilot nodded and gently pulled away. "Suit yourself.

I'll go make some fresh coffee, then. Seems we could both use it."

Leigh sighed. "I'm not going to beg you to stay and talk to me, RJ. I don't know what I can say anyway." She turned and stalked back to the bed, yanking up the covers. "Go make coffee." She made an irritated flicking gesture toward the door. "I'm not stopping you."

RJ just shook her head and left the bedroom, muttering, "Women."

Leigh jumped at the sound of the slamming door. "Fine," she mumbled. "I won't beg you to stay and talk to me," she repeated to herself. Leigh punched her pillow, moving her head back and forth against it in a vain attempt to get comfortable. "I don't even want to talk!" She lasted all of three seconds before jumping out of bed and heading for the door.

RJ looked up from the sink where she was refilling the coffee pot, just for something to do. She didn't say anything to Leigh as she set the pot to brew. She could tell that the blonde woman was mad, and she didn't want to annoy her any further. This was supposed to be a vacation; they were supposed to be having fun. Things weren't supposed to be getting complicated. "I'm sorry. I didn't mean to upset you. Let's forget it and start over. I'll fix some more eggs," she glanced at the clock, "for lunch. Then we can figure out how we want to spend the rest of the day."

Leigh crossed her arms over her chest, tapping her foot. *God, I hate this emotional shit.* She could see RJ wanted an explanation, and yet the dark-haired woman was going to make her chase her in order to give it. "I'm not—" Leigh paused. *No lies.* "Okay, I'm a little upset," she admitted, "but mostly not with you."

RJ watched the dark liquid streaming into the pot, her empty cup in hand. She grinned at the blonde woman standing there in the kitchen naked as a lark and looking like she was going to start spitting nails at any second. "Lass, I really didn't mean to upset you. I'd just been wondering why you jumped out of the truck the way you did that evening." *And holding you so close, I couldn't stand the thought of you running away from me.*

Leigh leaned against the counter. "I left because I was starting to feel...uncomfortable," she said seriously. "I needed some fresh air so I could think."

RJ cocked her head. "Was I making you uncomfortable?

And would you like a robe or a blanket or something? I have to admit having your chest out there like that is making concentrating very difficult." She grinned, hoping to lighten the mood a little.

"I don't want a robe." She plucked RJ's cup out of her hands and slammed it on the counter. "It wasn't entirely you that was making me uncomfortable, it was the situation. And you're making me insane. You act angry, but smile, then makes jokes about my chest." She crossed her arms over her breasts. "For once I'm not thinking about sex!"

For a moment RJ was speechless.

"Did that answer all your questions?" Without waiting for RJ to respond, Leigh turned on her heel, marched to the fridge, pulled out a Pepsi and cracked the top. She took a long, satisfying drink, looking at RJ over the top of the can. "Are we done?"

RJ nodded. Biting back a grin and trying not to laugh, she let her head sway slightly. "If you say so. You're so cute when you're grouchy."

"Argh." Leigh set her can on the counter and ran over to RJ. She held her hands up in front of the pilot's neck, shaking them wildly as though she was choking her. "You're trying to make me go nuts. I just know it." When RJ only winked back, Leigh dropped her hands in exasperation. She picked up the Pepsi can and stomped toward the bathroom, loudly calling out the same thing RJ had only mumbled before. "Women."

RJ puttered around the kitchen for a bit, hearing the shower go on in the bathroom. Then she remembered the cure for her black eye was in the fridge. She touched the tender skin as she pulled the steak from its wrapping, rinsed it in the sink, and then poured herself a cup of coffee. Hopping up on the counter, she placed the steak on her swollen eye and began sipping the dark liquid, wishing she'd thought to bring her cigarettes with her.

Leigh emerged from the bedroom a few minutes later. Her shower had been a quick one, and she hadn't bothered to blow-dry her hair. She was wearing a thin pair of gray sweats and a mint green t-shirt that somehow managed to make her eyes look even more sky blue.

RJ jumped off the counter and followed Leigh into the living room. "Feel better?"

"Jesus Christ!" Leigh's stomach churned queasily when RJ lifted the steak from her eye, leaving a pink, bloody ring around the discolored flesh. "God, RJ, that's disgusting."

"It's the perfect cure for a black eye, lass. But I'm guessing from that response, you won't be joining me for steak and eggs for lunch, then?"

Leigh shook her head and laughed. She gestured toward the steak, now resting comfortably back on RJ's eye. "What is this obsession with food? Over the last few days, you haven't had much appetite at all." She sat down on the sofa and curled one leg under her.

"I'm not obsessed with food." RJ went back into the kitchen and re-wrapped the steak, placing it back in the refrigerator. She then washed her hands and her face before joining Leigh, who was watching the rain through the glass door that led to the balcony. She gave the young woman's foot a little tickle. "I have much better things than food to be obsessed with."

Leigh feigned surprised. "Feet?" She made a face. "Ewww...I can barely stand to look at my own feet, much less anyone else's."

"No," RJ said in exasperation as she tickled her foot again. "Not feet. You. All of you."

"Oh." Leigh's ego hummed happily. "That's a plan I can get behind. So—" she paused and jerked her chin at the rainy gloom they were watching from the couch, "what do you want to do today? I know I want to go and see how the body shop is doing on my truck." *Those fuckers had better not be ogling Mom as they paint over her.*

"Well," RJ began a gentle massage of the foot she still held onto, "actually, there is someone here in Seattle I'd like to try and see." *Here goes.* "It's the woman who was my grandmother's co-pilot."

"You're going to wash that hand before touching me again, right?" Leigh pulled her foot from RJ's grasp and leaned forward, interested. "She was the one who tried to save your grandmother, right? Wow, she must be pretty old."

RJ looked at her hands. She shrugged and dropped them in her lap. "That'd be the one. She's probably in her mid-eighties by now. It's been sixty years since the end of the war." *Jesus, Mary and Joseph.* It had never seemed like that long ago until RJ actually said the words. *I can't even imagine that sweet, red-haired lass, Lucy, that old. Does this mean I'm robbing the cradle with Leigh?* "I just hoped maybe she'd be able to tell me something I didn't know about my grandmother. My mother suggested that I look her up if I was going to be in Seattle. *And I need to try and thank her for what she did for me.*

"Do you know where she lives? Seattle isn't a small place."

"She's in a nursing home. I have the address in my duffel bag. If you don't want to go, I'll understand. I could call a cab or something. Lots of folks can think of better ways to spend part of their day than visiting an old woman."

Leigh's gaze softened. "It's important to you, right?"

The pilot nodded, trying not to release the tears that threatened to spill. There was no way she could explain this type of emotion to Leigh, considering she supposedly hadn't even met the old woman yet. She swallowed hard. "It is, very, Leigh. She's the last one...who really knew my grandmother; and even though I didn't know her, she's important to my family."

"Hey." Leigh patted RJ's leg worriedly, feeling a pang in her guts over the sad look on RJ's face. "Don't worry. I'll take you. We didn't have any special plans for the day, and if it's something you want to do," she shrugged, "that's more than good enough for me."

RJ leaned over and gave Leigh a gentle kiss on the cheek. "Has anyone ever told you how special you are, Leigh Matthews?" *If I didn't know better, I'd say you are my guardian angel.*

"Only my junior high school guidance counselor. But that was just because I was tardy for 86 days in a row." Leigh quirked a grin and received a wry one in return. "I believe you have a hand to wash before we go?"

"Bait?" The male squirrel stood slack-jawed, his chin wobbling in disbelief.

The female nodded and shrugged. It had to be.

"I don't want to be bait." He began to tremble and blurted out in a panic, "Bait is bad. Bait is dangerous. Bait gets eaten! And I just know it would hurt."

"Don't make me alter my plan and remove the small contingency I've incorporated so that you have at least a minute chance of surviving," the female warned reasonably. "All missions have a certain level of acceptable losses for the greater good."

"Acceptable losses?"

She rolled her eyes. "That would be you, dear."

"Greater good?"

"That would be me."

"But I don't want to be bait," he whined, digging his little toe into the soil.

"Let me put it this way: one of us has to execute the plan with extreme precision, skill, brains, and cunning."

"I could do that part!"

The female simply stared at him until he cracked under her knowing gaze.

"I'm the bait," he sighed.

"Of course you are." She patted his shoulder comfortingly, thinking that she would always remember him. Then for the first time that afternoon she got a good look at his attire. "Why are you wearing that hideous outfit?"

He puffed up his chest. "I'm a warrior. Brave and strong. Ready to fight to save the squirrel I love most." *That would be me.*

"Uh huh."

The male was wearing an oak leaf twisted into a ridiculous hat, a dented beer bottle cap serving as a chest plate.

"I'm emulating my favorite warrior I saw on TV. No woman could resist him."

"The imbecilic moron?" The female's face twisted in disgust. Humans were such perverse animals.

The male looked aghast. "But kids love him, and he's the cornerstone of all the comedies."

"I am not having this discussion with you again." The female sat down on a large stick she'd dragged into their nest while her mate went in search of weapons to use in their battle against Flea, the bane of their eternity. He'd excitedly returned with rusty nails, bits of glass, a half-eaten Ho Ho which he'd refused to share, and an issue of *Play Squirrel.* He'd cried for hours when he discovered that the best parts had already been torn out, confirming once again that they were, in fact, in squirrel hell.

"What did you collect for our attack against the evil one?"

"I didn't collect anything. I made something. Just as a backup to my brilliant plan."

"What?"

"This." She reached behind the stick and thrust a large, furry thing in her mate's face.

"Ahhh!" he screamed, throwing himself under their bed. "Take it away. Take it away!"

"What? You don't like my voodoo doll?" She laughed wickedly, stroking her cat-like creation, which was complete with brown fur. She'd wanted black, but her choices had been woefully limited.

"No. I hate it. It's grotesque." He peeked his head out from under the bed. "But I see you managed to get lots of brown hair to glue onto the doll. Finally decide to shave your upper lip?" He burst out laughing at his own joke, his stubby arms wrapped around his shaking sides.

The female narrowed her eyes. "Yes, dear. That's exactly what I did." Her gaze flicked to his now bald back and ass, thinking it much improved over normal.

"You know," he paused and scratched an itch on his back that had been bothering him all day, "I had the weirdest dream last night."

Patrick and Liam just rolled their eyes as their mother continued to place dishes on the table in what they generously thought of as a less-than-loving manner. They both looked at their father, who simply shrugged and tried to remain inconspicuous.

The younger Fitzgeralds, ages 8 and 14, watched their mother with slightly widened eyes. She was in a rare temper. And for Katherine Fitzgerald that was saying a lot. Dinner hadn't even started yet and it was already a quiet affair—always a bad sign in the usually boisterous household.

Finally, Patrick couldn't stand it any longer. "Mother, you don't know what the Council's answer is going to be," he commented, reaching for the rolls.

"'Tis not a matter for the Council," she snapped, giving the red-haired man an annoyed look. "They already said no." She slammed down the gravy boat, biting her tongue when the brown sauce sloshed over the sides and onto her lace tablecloth. "'Tis up to a higher power now."

"Katherine, having a fit about it certainly isn't going to help." Harris' voice was calm as he tried to clean up a bit of the gravy.

"Harris, 'tis not a fit I'm throwin'." Katherine sat down, literally wringing her hands. "I'm the one who made the petition today. I'm the one who stood there and said that Ruth Jean deserves this chance. I'm only fretting because I can't decide what breaks me heart more: the idea of her leaving us for years on end, or the idea of her staying when her heart is driving around in a big red truck."

Liam leaned over and placed a serving of vegetables onto his sister Mary's plate. "Mother, RJ is a big girl. She knew what she was getting into when she went off with Leigh." He nodded to the younger children to eat, which they both began doing with varying degrees of enthusiasm. They were far more interested in finding out whether RJ would be leaving Glory.

Katherine tossed her napkin onto the table. "You shut your mouth, Liam. RJ had no idea this would happen when she left. Even now she might not be sure of her feelings for the truck driver. And she certainly didn't ask to be allowed to leave Glory for another lifetime."

The oldest of the children, Liam, who had died in a crop dusting accident in the late 1960s, always seemed to be the one who clashed with his mother. And he was as accustomed to his lot in the afterlife as he had been in life. "No, you're right, Mother, she didn't. You took that crusade upon yourself. How do you know Ruth Jean will even want to leave? Maybe when the week is over it's her intention to just come home where she belongs."

Katherine looked pointedly over at her husband, Harris, her gaze softening almost imperceptibly. "Tch. I know what I would do, and Ruth Jean is ten times as stubborn as I could ever hope to be."

The table burst out laughing.

"What?" Katherine demanded, looking at each face with accusing eyes.

"Mother," Patrick nearly choked on his coffee, "we love you. You know we do. But when it comes to stubborn, you've written the book."

Patrick's wife, Betsy, rolled her eyes. *When would the man learn to shut up?*

Katherine reached over and smacked Patrick in the back of head, earning a broad smile from Liam, who was the one who usually got smacked. "You just volunteered to say grace. Get to it, boy. Our dinner is gettin' cold."

Patrick scowled, but began reciting a commonly used blessing.

Under the table Harris reached over and squeezed his wife's

hand. Katherine gratefully squeezed back. This was where she found her strength. She wondered briefly where Ruth Jean found hers.

Chapter
11

Leigh and RJ made their way up the walkway that lead to the reception area of the Golden Link Retirement Center. As the sign proudly stated, it was an "assisted" living facility.

Stepping inside, RJ shook out the umbrella they'd both huddled under on their way from Leigh's Jeep.

Critical green eyes surveyed their surroundings. "You think this is the place?" It wasn't nearly as sterile as RJ had feared, but was filled with warm-colored furnishings and carpet, with cheerful Big Band-era tunes playing softly in the background.

"The address and name match," Leigh commented as she took off her jacket and tucked it under her arm. She began tugging RJ to the receptionist. "Are you sure we shouldn't have called first?" Leigh asked quietly, feeling like she was in a library and would be scolded for being too boisterous. Or for having sex in the bathroom. That was even worse than an overdue book. *Unless, of course, it was the actual librarian you were having sex with,* Leigh sniggered to herself.

"No. I'm not sure." RJ's voice was tight, and she felt Leigh pull her to a stop.

The blonde woman squeezed RJ's hand reassuringly, surprised to feel a slight chill. "Are you okay?"

"I'm a..." RJ licked her lips nervously, intentionally not looking at the curious receptionist who was watching them both.

"I'm a little nervous, I suppose. I've never been in one of these aged homes before."

Ah. Now that made sense. Even the nice ones could be a little unsettling, Leigh knew. "I visited my grandpa in a place sort of like this, only it looked a little more like a hospital than an apartment complex." She wrinkled her nose. "It smelled funny."

RJ nodded. "But this place isn't too bad."

Leigh smiled softly. "No. It's a very nice place." She allowed RJ a few more minutes to look around before gently prodding her with her elbow. "Ready? That receptionist is about ready to die from curiosity about the two woman standing in the middle of the room and not moving."

RJ shot Leigh a mild look. "I'm ready, lass. You're coming with me, right?"

"Do you want me to?" Leigh had figured on waiting in the visitor's lounge and reading two-year-old copies of *People Magazine* while RJ met with her granny's friend.

"I...I want—" RJ abruptly halted her speech and bent down to whisper in Leigh's ear. "I want you to come, Leigh. If only for a few moments."

Leigh's heart broke at the abject fear in RJ's voice. "Of course, I'll come."

RJ exhaled explosively and bravely headed for the reception desk. "Good." *I knew I could count on you, darlin'.*

"I don't have her listed as a resident or you as a visitor," the man said politely, rechecking his log one more time to be sure. "We have several Lucys. What was the resident's last name again?"

"Slocombe."

"I'm sorry."

"Was that her married name, RJ?" Leigh leaned forward over the desk, trying to get a peek at the ledger.

"No. She was single when...err...I don't know if she ever married."

The man closed his book. "Can you describe her?"

RJ's eyes went a little round. She had no idea what Lucy would look like now. "Short." She wrapped her arm around Leigh and pulled her directly in front of the man's face.

"Shorter than her even."

"Hey," Leigh squawked.

The man laughed and waited for more. When RJ remained silent he said, "Sorry. That doesn't help me much. This is a retirement community. All our Lucys are short. Anything else?" he prodded carefully.

"When she was young, her hair was flaming red and her face was covered with freck—"

"Oh, *that* Lucy. Lucy Gelland. The one who curses like a sailor when something happens that she doesn't like."

"Yes." RJ grinned broadly.

"When her TV blew during the World Series last year, I could hear her all the way in the parking lot."

RJ laughed. That *had* to be her Lucy Slocombe, who usually lost a full third of her paycheck in fines for cursing over their plane's radio. "That would be her."

"She's in room forty-two." He reopened the book, immediately turning to "G." "In fact, her granddaughter and her three devil children are due for a visit in just a while. I'll show you to her room and make sure that she's awake."

Leigh blinked in surprise.

"This is a residence for the elderly, not a prison," he assured her knowingly. So many people had the wrong idea about this type of facility. "The only folks who have restrictions on visitors are ones who place them there themselves. And Mrs. Gelland has never done that. So—"

"So, why are we still here?" RJ asked, smiling.

"Good point," the man agreed. "C'mon."

"Mrs. Gelland?" The receptionist knocked gently on her door. "Are you up for some visitors?"

"Are they Jehovah Witnesses? If they are, they can just go the hell away. The last thing I need at this point in my life is to be saved. Anyone else can come in. I don't bite. Especially when I forget to put in my damn teeth. God..." The rest of the sentence trailed off.

Leigh's hand flew to her mouth where she clamped down on a burst of laughter.

RJ smiled wistfully at the sound of her co-pilot's voice, which, even though it was a little scratchier than she remembered it, was still recognizable after all these years.

"They're not here to solicit you," the receptionist called to Lucy. One little mistake six years ago, and the residents never let him live it down. He turned to RJ. "You're not, right?"

"No worries." She patted him on the back. "We'll take it from here. Thank you."

He nodded and lowered his voice. "Just one thing. Mrs. Gelland suffers from Alzheimer's disease."

"A disease?" RJ hissed quietly.

"I'm afraid so. It's not terribly advanced, but she does tend to be a little forgetful at times." His face flushed. "You'll probably see for yourself, and I really shouldn't have said anything. I mean, I could lose my job and—"

Leigh quickly shook her head. "We didn't hear anything from you."

He exhaled in relief. "Thanks. I just didn't want you to be surprised or upset. Some people get that way and, well...it can be a little hard on the residents. And Mrs. Gelland isn't nearly as bad off as some."

"Thank you for warning us," RJ said sincerely. *She's senile is what he's sayin'. Not that I should be surprised.*

"I'm leaving you to your guests, Mrs. Gelland," he said loudly and turned to go.

"Yeah, yeah, go back to your desk, Leo," came the grumpy response from behind the door.

Leo laughed and began walking down the hall.

RJ reached for the door handle. Her hand was shaking so badly that Leigh closed her own over it, steadying it.

"Ready, sweetheart?" The endearment slipped out without Leigh even knowing it as she felt a surge of protectiveness for RJ, who suddenly looked a little pale.

RJ smiled and nodded, turning the handle. *Forgive me for all the lying I'm about to do to you, Leigh. It is, sadly, the only way, other than not having you with me at all. And right now, that's not an acceptable choice.*

Lucy Gelland was sitting in a recliner near the window. She was dressed in a long nightgown covered by a pink terrycloth robe. She appeared to be engrossed in a novel.

Then several things happened at once. Leo, the receptionist, remembered he had RJ and Leigh's visitors passes still in his hand, and he shouted to RJ who was standing in the doorway.

RJ stepped away from the door toward Leo, while Leigh

walked into the room.

Lucy turned toward the young blonde. "Helen?"

Leigh shifted uncomfortably, looking over her shoulder for RJ, who was nowhere in sight. "Sorry. But my name is—"

"I know good and goddamn well what your name is, young lady."

"But I'm not—"

"Come and give your great auntie a kiss on the cheek."

Leigh groaned inwardly and inched toward Lucy the way a kid makes a forced march to the principal's office.

"Jesus, girl. I'll be dead before you reach me at this rate. March like you've got a purpose in life. Move. Move. Move!"

Leigh bolted across the room. When she stopped in front of her chair, she fought the urge to salute Lucy. Bending, she reluctantly placed a gentle kiss on Lucy's cheek, her skin feeling soft, warm, and paper-thin. "Hello," she said softly.

"Hello, child. You look a little different than the last time you came to visit. Did you cut your hair?"

Leigh looked into Lucy's soft brown eyes and realized that she didn't want to upset or disappoint her. So she dutifully nodded.

Lucy smiled and Leigh smiled back, taking a good look at the woman. Her dark eyes smiled along with her lips, and the tiny freckles of Lucy's youth, though faded with time, still spattered her cheeks. *She's still beautiful.*

RJ walked into the room and closed the door gently behind her. Leigh and Lucy both turned their heads toward the sound.

Lucy's novel clattered to the floor.

"RJ Fi..." Lucy had to swallow and start again. "RJ?"

Leigh quickly moved back to RJ and whispered in her ear. "She thinks I'm someone else, too. Do you look like your grandmother?"

RJ's heart was thundering in her ears when she whispered back, "The spitting image. But—"

"I don't think we should upset her, RJ."

RJ nodded and said a small prayer of thanks. She'd wondered if Lucy would recognize her and how, exactly, she would explain it to Leigh. Things had just gotten a whole lot easier.

RJ quickly squeezed Leigh's shoulder and moved past her to greet her dear friend. "Hello, Lucy."

Lucy's round, tear-filled eyes grew even wider. "It is you." Then they narrowed quickly. "Isn't it?"

"Of course," RJ snorted through her own tears. "I look just the same, and you look older than Methuselah and twice as wrinkled." She winced inwardly at what Leigh would think of the seemingly rude words, but got the reaction from Lucy that she knew she would.

"RJ!" Lucy opened her arms wide and accepted an enthusiastic hug from the pilot.

Leigh shook her head, somewhat amazed at the scene before her. *You should get an Academy Award for this one, RJ.*

"Don't tell me I've finally died and you're here to take me to hell?" But Lucy's voice didn't sound the least bit fearful.

RJ laughed and shook her head. She knelt down in front of the big blue recliner that seemed to swallow her friend. "No, lass, you're alive and kicking, just like always. Besides, and I hate to break this to you, my friend, but, hell doesn't want you. They're afraid you'll take over the joint."

Lucy smiled a smile so incredibly wicked that Leigh actually gulped out loud. "I wouldn't want to take over, RJ. Only have a little fun." She and RJ burst out laughing at what seemed to be an old joke. Though Leigh knew that was impossible.

Then, as though Lucy had just realized something, and despite the fact that she seemed to know it only seconds before, the look on her face shifted to one of abject grief. Fat and hot, tears rolled down her cheeks, and she reached out and took RJ's hand, squeezing it with startling strength. "You died," she said fervently.

RJ's heart clenched as she slowly nodded.

Leigh moved forward, fascinated by the exchange. She allowed her hands to rest softly on RJ's shoulders.

RJ sighed silently at the touch that unknowingly comforted her.

"I've missed you, Ruth Jean. I'm so sorry I couldn't save you." Lucy's bottom lip began to quiver. "I tried. I—"

RJ was quick to calm her by gently wiping dry Lucy's wet cheeks.

Unexpected tears pricked Leigh's eyes. But she remained silent.

RJ sniffed. "I know. And I know you did everything you could. You kept me from drowning and being lost to the sea forever. The crash was just too much." She paused and wiped her own eyes after she finished with Lucy's cheeks. Flashes of her crash came rushing back, bold and vivid; and she could almost feel the water trying to reach up and claim her. She swallowed painfully and pushed those thoughts aside. Now was not the time to relive that particular memory. There were others—far sweeter—to be discussed in this place. "I didn't come here to talk about that." Her smile was bittersweet. "I came to talk to my co-pilot, and I see you're just as much trouble as always."

Weakly, Lucy slumped back in her chair. Her eyes flicked to Leigh, and a thought crossed her mind. "Why are you here with my niece, Helen? If you're sleeping with her, RJ, I swear I'll kick your ass. I've done it before." But the hacking cough at the end of her words did make them somewhat less threatening.

RJ snorted. "No, Luce, this isn't your niece, Helen. It's my very dear friend, Leigh Matthews." She rolled her eyes and nodded before Lucy could even ask. "Yes, if you must know, we're sleeping together."

Lucy looked at Leigh, who was fidgeting uncomfortably and trying to wrap her mind around the fact that RJ's grandmother was a lesbian. And one who really slept around to boot. She wondered idly, if that were the case, how RJ's mom ever came into being.

The old woman cocked her head to the side and examined Leigh's face. "You're not Helen, are you?"

"No, ma'am."

"Why didn't you just say so? I get confused sometimes, but I'm not deaf."

"I tried, but—"

"Young people and your lame-ass excuses."

RJ jumped in to tease her beloved copilot. It was one of the simple joys of life that she'd missed most. "She didn't say anything, you grumpy goat, because you didn't give her a damn chance. Just like always."

"Defending her, are you?" Lucy leaned forward and nudged RJ with a bony elbow. "And sweet on her, too, I'll bet. Course, when you've slept with the entire Army Nursing Corps, I suppose you'll eventually get so tired you've got no choice but to settle down or succumb from pure exhaustion." She glanced back up at Leigh. "And she's a pretty one, too. Not that I would expect anything less."

Leigh began to choke as she tried to stifle a laugh. By the sounds of things, RJ's grandmother had been as big a handful as the tiny Lucy Gelland. She could only imagine the pair they must have made.

"I didn't sleep with all of them," RJ protested half-heartedly. "Just the ones who wanted a *really* good time."

It was Lucy's turn to roll her eyes and snort.

"And Leigh and I aren't settling down, so don't be planning
the wedding just yet. Leigh doesn't like me that much. She just
wants me for my body." RJ turned her head and winked at the
trucker. "She rented it for a week or so."

"I take it you got out of hand, RJ, and she gave that shiner?
Damn, I haven't seen one that sweet in years." Lucy winced at
the lurid purple bruise.

Leigh blushed and gave the woman a small, slightly embarrassed nod. "But I swear it was an accident." She found herself
also wanting to say that RJ meant more to her than a week of
whoring fun. But the surprise words caught in her throat.

Thinking Leigh was upset about the comment about RJ's
eye, Lucy said, "Don't worry, girl. Ol' RJ's had much worse and
recovered nicely. Consider this accidental one a down payment
for the next time when she really deserves a bop in the eye."

"Hey!"

Lucy slapped her knee and laughed long and hard. By the
time she finished, however, she had something else entirely on
her mind. "RJ," Lucy said quietly, "I need to thank you for
something, and let you in on a tiny secret I've been keeping forever."

RJ's brows knit. "What secret could you possible have from
me?" They had told each other everything. Or so she'd thought.

Lucy drew her fingertips across RJ's cheeks, then reached
back and tugged on her auburn hair. "You're wearing it shorter
nowadays."

"That's the big secret?"

"Impatient as ever." Lucy sighed. "I've always been just a
little bit in love with you, RJ. Then, and every day since then."
She shrugged and smiled, her eyes twinkling softly. "Maybe it
wasn't such a big secret after all."

Leigh held her breath, waiting to hear how RJ would answer
for her long dead ancestor, already feeling the slight churning of
what she fully knew was an irrational jealously.

The tips of RJ's ears turned red. "Ah, lass, you know I've
always felt the same way." She smiled gently at Lucy, whose
bright grin answered her back. "Though we surely were never
meant to be together in that way."

Leigh blinked. *This is amazing. RJ's one hell of an actress. I keep forgetting she's not really her grandmother.*

"No," Lucy intoned seriously. "We weren't. But it didn't stop me from loving you just the same."

"And that goes double for me." RJ rubbed her eyes with the back of her hands. Just when she felt like she was about to unravel, she felt the gentle squeeze of Leigh's fingers again, telling her everything was okay. She reached up and absently patted one of the small hands. "You needed to come home and marry that flat-footed accountant you were always nattering on about. And by the looks of this room," RJ made a sweeping motion with both hands, indicating the dozens of photographs of happy people, "I'd guess that you did that very thing."

"As usual, RJ, you'd be wrong." Lucy's voice grew stronger. "No, I didn't marry Harold; and that's what I have to thank you for." The old woman reached over to the stand next to her chair and picked up a small picture in a heart-shaped, pewter frame. She brought it to her lips and kissed it reverently before setting it in her lap and beginning a short tale.

"I don't know how much you remember about us being fished out of the ocean when our plane went down." Lucy's face turned a little ashen, but she pressed on. "You weren't doing so good."

A grim look swept across RJ's features, but when she noticed how intently Lucy was watching her face, she replaced it with a more mild one, even managing to smile reassuringly. "Go on, lass. It's all in the past and can't hurt us now."

Lucy asked Leigh to fetch her Kleenex from the nightstand, which the trucker did, waiting patiently while trembling fingers pulled out exactly four tissues to blow her nose. "We were both Medevac'd to the island hospital. Me with a broken knee and foot and you...well...you." She sighed in bitter resignation and wiped the corner of her eyes with her Kleenex. Then, unexpectedly, a heart-stopping smile creased her still damp cheeks. "Your doctor was fresh out of his surgical residency, and you were his first patient. He was a beautiful blond man from Chicago, my Max. He was gentle and wild, and his eyes were bluer than a summer sky, just like your friend's here." Lucy's gnarled finger pointed over RJ's shoulder to Leigh.

"Anyway, after you...went and croaked...God dammit, RJ, I'm still pissed about that, you know!"

RJ crossed her arms over her chest and barked out, "It's not like it was on the top of my list of things to do that day, Lucy."

Leigh wondered if things might turn into an argument until Lucy continued speaking as though the outburst had never even happened.

"After you died, Max and I got so rip-roaring drunk that they locked us up in the stockade, in side-by-side cells. For a week! At first I was worried we'd kill each other. By the time the week was over, I was more concerned about getting pregnant." She laughed softly, lost in her own well-savored memories.

RJ's eyebrows crawled up into her hairline. "You both were in different cells, but you were still worried about getting pregnant?"

"Where there's a will there's way, Ruth Jean. As if I have to tell you that."

Leigh burst out laughing.

Lucy gave the young blonde a ghost of a wink. "Anyway, things on the island were crazy, and then quiet, and I guess they forgot about us there. Can you believe that?" She dropped her tissues into a wastebasket that sat alongside her chair. "Max and I were never were really apart after that, at least not in our hearts. He passed on two years and two months ago." She picked up the photo in her lap and proudly showed it to RJ.

It had clearly started as a black and white, with the color added later. Lucy's red hair was flaming, and her dark eyes fairly danced with merriment. Snuggled up to her cheek was a toothy, tow-headed man with a burr haircut and thin mustache. He was grinning like he'd won the lottery. As far as RJ was concerned, he had. "We have three children, six grandchildren, and eleven great-grandchildren. *That's* what I wanted to thank you for. My whole life."

Tears slipped down RJ's cheeks and she smiled through them, laughing softly as she spoke. She felt a tiny piece of resentment she'd always harbored deep in her heart shrivel up and blow away at Lucy's words. "Ah, lass, I'm glad some good came out of it, then. It sounds as though you have a wonderful life, and that's really what matters most. I always wanted that for you. Max was a lucky fella to have someone like you loving him for so many years."

"Fifty-six years," Lucy clarified, her pride evident. "Fifty-six wonderful years of marriage." She handed the picture to Leigh, who resettled it on the table next to the bed. Then she looked to RJ and gave another wicked little grin. "You still a hard drinker?"

The pilot nodded. "Is there any other way?"

Lucy gestured with her chin, to the dresser across the room. "Leigh, in the bottom drawer there, there's a bottle of good Irish whiskey. Get it for me, will you?"

It was all Leigh could do to keep from laughing out loud at these two. RJ played her grandmother's part perfectly, and Lucy seemed to come to life as she talked about the old days. Leigh was glad she'd come with RJ. Lucy was nothing short of an endearing character, and the trucker realized that without women like RJ's grandmother and Lucy, she certainly wouldn't be doing what she did for a living. Some women simply could not be made to fit into a mold, and they changed things for those who came after them, whether they'd intended to or not.

Leigh retrieved the bottle and found a couple of glasses, which she handed to RJ.

RJ glanced at the bottle and gave a low, appreciative whistle. "Whoa, lass. This is good stuff. How in the hell did you get this?"

Lucy smirked. "Leo's a good boy."

RJ cracked the seal on the bottle and drew in a good whiff of the strong liquor. "Hmm, now that's lovely." She poured a little into the glasses, handing one to Leigh and the other to Lucy. She winked. "I'll take mine straight from the bottle, if you don't mind."

"Yup," Lucy raised her glass in toast, "that's my RJ."

The trio brought their glasses together before throwing back their drinks.

Leigh hissed as it burned a path down her throat.

RJ hummed her pleasure, while Lucy licked her lips and shakily set her glass off to the side. RJ started to offer Lucy another, but the old woman shook her head.

"I'd better not, RJ. My granddaughter is due this afternoon, and she'll have a fit." She rolled her eyes in irritation. "But you and your lady friend can indulge as much as you like. I've been saving it for a special occasion, and this is the most wonderful surprise."

RJ tipped the bottle toward Leigh, who shook her head. She was driving, after all, and the last thing she need was to get stopped for DUI. The pilot, however, could think of no earthly reason not to indulge. She never could resist the call of a good bottle of Irish whiskey, and unrepentantly swallowed down another healthy swig.

"Leigh, has RJ ever bothered to tell you about the time she actually shot down two Jap fighters?"

Leigh smiled at RJ, wondering how she was going to get out of this one. She pasted on her most innocent look. "Why, no. RJ somehow failed to mention that to me."

"Well," RJ coughed as her mind raced to find a way to toss the ball back into Lucy's court. Finally, she shrugged and did her best to look humble. "That's because I'm so modest, you see."

"Oh, bullshit!" Lucy and Leigh exploded at the same time.

Leigh bit her lip, realizing once again she was supposed to be talking to RJ's long dead grandmother. Then again, it seemed like the women were an awful lot alike, and she privately figured that RJ would probably end up a lot like Lucy. The old woman had a fire in her that was still burning nice and hot despite her years.

"RJ Fitzgerald, you lying sack of—"

"Lucy! Now be nice."

The old woman shook a finger at her friend. "You know as well as I do that you were so proud of yourself for that, you nearly popped the buttons off your uniform."

Lucy's gaze swung to Leigh. "You see, what happened was this—we ran into a couple of Jap fighters while delivering a plane. But that particular plane had a Tucker gunner's turret, complete with a fully loaded antiaircraft gun. So, Lieutenant Fitzgerald here decided to turn the plane over to me while she slipped down below and shot those Jap planes right out of the air. I could scarcely believe my eyes. As far as I know, RJ is the only woman in history to have shot down two fighters."

The look of open admiration on Lucy's face turned into a scowl. "Course no one ever gave her the credit she deserved for doing it. Stupid, no good bastards," she grumbled, then slapped her knee. "But damned if she didn't! We weren't even supposed to be on that mission or a half dozen others that scared the livin' daylights out of us. But in times of need, Uncle Sam called on women more times than anyone dares admit." Lucy sat up a little straighter in her chair. "And by golly, we didn't disappoint!"

RJ scratched her cheek and tried not to blush at the story. She looked at Leigh and shrugged.

Leigh smiled indulgently at Lucy, suddenly glad that the old woman had told the story herself and that her RJ hadn't disappointed her by not knowing the details. *My RJ? Oh, boy.*

"That reminds me." Lucy brought her hand to her lips, a look of concentration sweeping over her face as she thought. "In the closet, there's a gray metal box. Could one of you get it for me?" She knew she sounded like a lazy old thing, but she figured the last thing RJ needed was to see her limp across the room. Her knee had never healed completely, and it had only gotten worse as she grew older. Some days it was all she could do to get out of bed and make it to her recliner.

Leigh quickly volunteered and was moving toward the closet before RJ could say a word. She found the box on a middle shelf and returned to the old woman, setting it gently in her lap.

Lucy opened the box and pulled out an old, faded photograph. She smiled and handed it up to Leigh, who leaned forward to take it. It was of RJ and her copilot in their heyday. They had their arms thrown over each other's shoulders and were standing in front of one of the bombers they flew, with grins a mile wide.

"That's us in forty-three, I think."

Leigh glanced down at the photograph. Her jaw dropped. "Holy shit." Her eyes flicked wildly between RJ and the picture and her jaw dropped a little further. "Bu...bu...bu..."

RJ snatched the picture from Leigh's fingertips. She looked at it for a long moment before holding it next to her face, "It's an old photo, lass, but you have to admit it's a good one." *How in the hell am I gonna get out of this one? Please, just buy it, Leigh.*

The look on Leigh's face shifted from amazement to something slightly more complicated. Her brow furrowed, and for a moment RJ thought she was going to let the cat out of the bag. But soon a small, if slightly confused, smile was tugging at Leigh's lips. When she looked up from the photo, she exhaled slowly, finding RJ's eyes with her own and holding the stare. "Yeah." Her voice softened, and her gaze turned fond. "It's an amazing picture."

Lucy broke the tension between the women with a loud exclamation as she pulled a small velvet box out of the gray metal one. "Here it is." She placed the box in RJ's hand. "I always wanted to give these to someone, but I wanted to do it in person and...well...it never happened. Now I guess I can just let you have them back—it's where they belong."

RJ cracked the lid to find her pilot's wings. That's when the dam broke and all the emotions that she had tried so hard to hold back began spill over. She sniffed loudly, unable to stop a scattering of tears from rolling down her cheeks. RJ nearly choked on the words when she softly said, "Thank you."

Just then a loud knock shook the door. "Granny. We're here!"

Lucy's eyes went a little round. "Good Lord, it's the devil children. Hide me."

Leigh tugged on RJ's limp hand until the woman stood. Her friend looked as though she was ready to burst into more tears, and for a second, Leigh had a hard time reconciling this person with the "cocky pilot" persona she'd seen only moments before.

Leigh bent down and hugged Lucy, who remained firmly seated in her recliner. "We need to go now, Lucy. It's been a pleasure meeting you."

RJ pocketed her wings and leaned over, kissing Lucy on the cheek. "God bless you, Lucy."

"Wait." Lucy cupped RJ's cheeks and confusion colored her words. "You're not a ghost?"

RJ shot Leigh an anxious look.

Leigh smiled sadly and went to wait in the hall, giving the two women a moment of privacy. *How am I going to stall the devil children? I don't know anything about children.* She reached for the whiskey bottle on her way out, only to change her mind at the last second. It wasn't like she had enough glasses to go around.

RJ turned back to her co-pilot, covering the wrinkled hands with her own. "No, lass. I'm not a ghost." She grinned broadly. "At least not today."

Lucy looked RJ dead in the eye. "I knew it."

"You were always too smart for your own good." RJ hugged her and leaned close so she could whisper directly into Lucy's ear. "Max will be waiting for you, but there's no need to hurry. Your family loves you too much for you to leave them anytime soon." She pulled back and winked, not caring when her lower lip began to quiver. "Be good."

The female squirrel shook her head in amazement. "I can't

believe you survived." The twitching of the body was a sure sign.

The male was sprawled out on his belly, his furry face caked with mud. He shook his head to try and dislodge a particular troublesome chunk of dirt from one of his nose holes. "What do you mean survived?" he gasped. "I was *already* dead before I stupidly agreed to be bait."

"True," she agreed happily, tossing her head back and laughing in that devil-may-care way that her mate usually loved. It was strongly reminiscent of Miss Piggy. Without hair. Or lipstick. Or pork.

The male sneered.

"But," she continued cheerfully, reaching down and boxing his ears.

"Ouch!"

"You can still feel pain."

He rubbed his ears.

"So it could have been worse. You could have been Flea's afternoon snack."

"Snack?" The male puffed up his chest indignantly. Unfortunately, the action only caused him to cough and wheeze. "I'm more than a snack, baby, and don't you forget it," he spouted cockily.

Out of pity, the female remained silent. Her husband's skinny-ass legs spoke for themselves.

"Did you see me? Did you? Huh? Huh? Did you?" he exploded, suddenly reliving what he was certain would be the second bravest and most triumphant moment of his squirrel afterlife. Someday he just *knew* he would drink an entire can of beer without belching even once. But for now, he couldn't have hoped for more.

"I saw." Her eyes misted over. "You were...it was just..."

"Magnificent," he breathed reverently.

The female had to agree. Even though her plan had failed, it had been a valiant effort. And one she would never forget...

"Okay, here's what you do...Nothing."

"What do you mean, nothing?"

"Nothing," she repeated impatiently. *"Flea is going to see you and come after you."* She finished tying a long length of twine around her mate's bushy tail. *"You are simply going to lure her."*

"Huh?"

"Like cheese in a mousetrap." She made a face. *"Only more stinky."*

"Hey," he snorted. *"I've been working here."*

His protest was ignored. *"Anyway, just when Flea is about ready to eat you, I'll pull you out of the way with this rope. She'll lunge for you and fall into the pit. And presto—"* The female snapped her fingers. Well, she would have snapped them, had squirrels been able to do such a thing. Spiteful God!

"Wait. Stop. Backup." He put his hands on his hips. *"Why does it have to be 'just' before Flea eats me. Why can't it be a reeeeeeeally long time before she eats me? Just to be on the safe side."*

The female rolled her eyes. *"DUH! If I pull you away too early, she won't lunge for you and fall into the pit."*

"But—"

"Cheese is braver than you."

The male gasped. *"It is not."*

"Is so."

"Is not!"

"Prove it!"

"I will! Let's go. I'm ready for that cat."

Males, *she snorted inwardly, nearly pitying her intellectually inferior husband.* Can't live with them. But they make great bait. Once.

The female squirrel put the twine between her teeth and scurried up the tree. She found the perfect branch and looped the twine over it, hiding herself in a handy hollow. When Flea showed up and tried to eat her mate, all she had to do was tug and he would be snatched from the jaws of death. So to speak.

Now they waited.

And waited.

And waited.

The male looked up. *"I'm wishing Flea would come and eat me and put me out of my misery,"* he barked, knowing his mate would hear him, even high up in the branches.

A large acorn mysteriously came flying out of the tree and hit him directly between the eyes.

"Ouch." He began to stagger. *"Of all the rotten luck."*

Just then Flea padded slowly out of the diner. She was a little depressed. RJ was one of her favorite humans, and she found herself surprised to be missing her. Wait, what was that? Flea's golden eyes narrowed as she spied her squirrel friends. Oh, *they'd been great fun. She hadn't indulged her dark side like this in years. She wondered briefly what it would take to import more rodents into Glory for entertainment purposes. Sure, she could always pester the humans...but generally, their dull wits bored her.*

Flea blinked. Was that a trap they had laid for her? Her day just kept getting better and better.

"That's her," the female hissed to her mate, giving the twine a little jerk just to make sure he was paying attention. She hated how he tended to tune out at the most inopportune times.

The female smiled. She should have put her mate on a leash years— Her joyful thoughts were interrupted by the rapid shaking movement of the rope in her paws. She looked down to see that Flea had her mate's entire head in her mouth. The cat was shaking him wildly, his bushy tail waving frantically in the breeze. "Oops."

The larger squirrel pulled hard on the string, and the male suddenly popped out of Flea's mouth.

"Ahhhhh!" he screamed. Then he went silent. What had Flea had for breakfast? *He licked the fur around his mouth.* Ummm...liver.

Flea stopped and cocked her head to the side as she stared at the squirrel, who was now hanging about a foot and a half off the ground by his tail. A piñata? How wonderful. *She hadn't been to a fiesta in weeks!*

"Higher. Higher!" the male hollered as Flea happily batted him about the head and shoulders, all the while deftly avoiding the branch-covered pit only inches from her paws.

Fearful that her mate wouldn't last too much longer—it wasn't like she had another immediate source of bait—the female pulled the string again, this time hauling her mate just out of Flea's immediate reach.

Flea hissed, unhappy at the temporary interruption in her play, and simply jumped up and grabbed onto the squirrel's body, swinging them both back and forth as the two animals shook and twisted wildly.

The female glanced down. They were both swinging directly over the pit now. If she cut the twine at precisely the right moment... No. That would be too cruel. Too hideous. But your mate is already dead, *her mind tempted.* And remember the time he got you a tiny squirrel vacuum for your anniversary? *She began to chew her squirrel nails as the anxiety welled up within her. Trying to push the consequences out of her mind, she brought her razor-sharp teeth to the twine, opened her mouth, and—*

"Flea," Mavis called. *"What are you doing to that poor animal?"*

Flea immediately let go of the male squirrel, dropping down to the ground just in front of the pit. She pointed at herself as if to ask, "Who, me?"

Mavis frowned. "If you want a ride back to Glory, then you'd better come on."

Flea was torn. Then again, she could always come back to the diner tomorrow and visit her new friends. It wasn't like they were going anywhere. Without wasting another second, the cat dashed away from the tree and the squirrels, and jumped into Mavis' waiting truck.

The male whimpered. Most of his body was numb.

The female whimpered. They had been so close! Gently, she lowered her mate to the ground, making sure he cleared the pit. She scrambled down the tree, unable to believe he was still in one piece. Who knew squirrel skin stretched like that?

"I was the best darn bait that ever was," the male said, shaken out of his reverie by the sound of a horn honking in the parking lot in front of the diner.

"You put earthworms and leeches to shame," his wife agreed.

"Damn straight." He stood up and dusted himself off, allowing his mate to untie his tail.

"We need a new plan."

"No shit."

"C'mon. I think better at home."

The male took one step, tripped on the acorn that had hit him in the head earlier, and fell backwards into the pit, crashing through the thin branches that covered it.

The female's beady black eyes widened as her mate plunged over the edge and she heard a splash. What had her mate put in the pit? She had assumed it was full of razor-sharp spikes, or broken glass, or something equally horrendous. What could have made a splash? She inched closer to the edge, not wanting to look inside, afraid she'd see her mate's bleached skeleton. What if he'd filled the pit with acid?

Then she heard a faint. "Mmmmmm." Overcome with curiosity she peeked inside the hole.

The male squirrel was floating happily in a pool of blue liquid.

"What is that?"

"Wow. This tastes really good." His butt and back stung a little, but he ignored it. He took another drink. "It's almost as good as beer!" *I wonder what kind of buzz I could get? And does it have as many calories? A squirrel's got to eat!*

"Ahem."

Lazily, he looked up. "It's antifreeze."

"Antifreeze?"

"Yeah. I've always heard it kills cats."

The female exhaled wearily as the male took another sip. "And just how do you think it kills cats, dear?"

The male swallowed his next drink loudly, gargling it a little as he did the backstroke. He looked up again, blue liquid oozing from the corners of his mouth. "Huh? I dunno." Suddenly he gasped and twisted. Grabbing for his throat, he fell face down in the pool.

"Huh." She scratched and flicked a tiny flea from her fur. "I wonder if he'll ever figure it out."

From the kitchen, Leigh watched RJ sit down on the couch. The tall woman was looking at the pilot's wings and wiping silent tears from her cheeks.

Nononnnonnonononononono! Please don't let her cry. I can't handle crying women. Her mind raced for a way out. *I could run out and buy Kleenex, and by the time I came back she'd be done crying.* Leigh heard another sniff, and her heart sank. She wouldn't do that. Again. The last time she'd run out on a crying woman, the evil bitch had smashed the motel television set to bits and disappeared into the night, leaving Leigh with the bill.

Even though she didn't want to go into the living room, she felt the urge, no, the demand, her heart was making on her to comfort RJ. For that one moment, however, her brain was still in charge of her. And Leigh's brain told her to stay in the kitchen and fix them tequila. And to make them doubles. And to drink a shot right from the bottle.

Her eyes, however, seemed to be ruled by her heart; and her gaze was drawn once again to the profoundly sad look on her friend's face. *Shit.* Leigh had no choice. Her muscles allied with her heart, and the resulting coup caused her to walk out of the kitchen and kneel down in front of RJ.

The blonde let her hand slowly move up RJ's leg, then up her arm, until it found her cheek. She tenderly caressed damp skin with her thumb. "Hey," she whispered, ducking her head, trying to get forced eye contact with her friend. "You okay?"

RJ tried to smile, and gave a little nod. "Yeah, I'm fine." She held up her wings for Leigh to see. "Impressive, aren't they?" She was thinking of the proud men and woman who'd worn them—their names were jumbled, but their faces were bright and clear, and forever young.

"They are." Leigh's eyes never left RJ's face. She wanted to make RJ feel better, but didn't have the slightest clue as to how. "It was nice of Lucy to give you those," she began nervously. Why had this visit affected RJ so? Ultimately, it wasn't sad at all. Lucy was alive and seemingly well, and they'd both heard several tales about RJ's grandmother, which had been the point, after all.

"I'm sorry about letting this get to me. I didn't mean for this to ruin our day. I'm not sure why—"

Leigh pressed her fingers to RJ's lips. "S'okay. We all have things that affect us in ways we don't expect." *Like the way you affect me for instance.* "But...um..." She licked her lips nervously. "You will be all right, right?"

RJ smiled and kissed Leigh's fingers. Then she reached out and brushed her own fingers through the smaller woman's thick hair. Feeling Leigh lean into her touch, she brought up her other hand and placed it on the other side of Leigh's head, pulling her closer. "I never expected this, Leigh Matthews," she whispered, staring intently into the trucker's eyes. Both women were surprised by the words, and RJ leaned forward and gently brushed her lips against Leigh's, sighing at their softness. *I never expected you to be like this.*

Startled by the outpouring of emotion in RJ's simple kiss, Leigh pulled back a little. "That's..." She paused and gathered her thoughts. "That's a good thing, though, isn't it?"

A brilliant smile was her answer. Then RJ yawned.

"C'mon." Leigh stood up and offered her hand to RJ. "Let's go to bed."

"It's only—"

"Who cares what time it is? I can see you're exhausted."

RJ let out a grumpy breath. She was exhausted. The mental drain of seeing Lucy had been more than she'd bargained for, though a big part of her knew she simply wasn't adjusted to being alive again or to the seemingly endless demands of her body.

Leigh led RJ into the bedroom. Not bothering with the light, she quietly stripped her companion out of her clothes, making a special effort to keep her hands to herself. RJ was exhausted, and although Leigh suspected that with even the slightest of overtures she could have her, it somehow didn't seem right this time.

RJ lifted her eyebrows when the last of her clothes hit the floor. "You're comin' too, right?"

"Uhhh..." Leigh heard the slight pleading in RJ's voice. "Sure," she heard herself say.

RJ slipped into bed, her eyes drooping before Leigh could even crawl beneath the covers.

The blonde lay facing RJ, feeling awkward as she gazed into heavy green eyes. Leigh blinked. *I've never done this before. Well, not since elementary school...* And she didn't really think you could count the time when she was seven years old. *There's always been sex.*

"Aren't you tired?" RJ yawned, fighting hard to stay awake. "I can get up. You must be—" The mumbled words drifted off as RJ's eyes slid shut.

Leigh rolled over and stared out the window into the just darkening sky.

She opened her eyes, not knowing how much time had passed. The room was draped in shadows when, over her shoulder, she heard a whispered voice, hoarse with sleep, float through the stillness.

"I love you, Leigh Matthews."

RJ's warm breath tickled Leigh's neck, but she remained still, wondering when she forgot how to breathe.

"God, forgive me, but I do." RJ exhaled wearily, and Leigh could easily visualize the worried, pensive look that held her face for just a second before dropping away.

Leigh's heart started beating again.

Chapter
12

Leigh rolled over in RJ's warm embrace, allowing her eyes to sweep over her lover's face. She looked different, Leigh decided, when she was asleep. Those beautiful, alert, emerald eyes always seemed so at odds with RJ's easy-going personality. Their gaze flicking impatiently from thing to thing, taking in the world as though she was seeing it for the first time. *So pretty.* The look on Leigh's face softened further. *So young, even though you sometimes act like a weird old soul.*

RJ threw her arm across her companion's waist, shifting a little and pulling her closer. She sighed happily, comforted even in sleep by Leigh's solid presence.

They couldn't have been asleep for more than a few hours. The room was still cast in deep, silvery shadows, the scent of warm skin and fresh sheets hanging heavily in the air.

RJ's breathing was slow and steady, and Leigh could see the faint movement of her eyes under closed lids. The corners of RJ's lips held just the barest hint of a smile. *I wonder what she's dreaming about.*

Leigh reached out to push away a dark tangle of hair that had fallen across RJ's forehead. She stopped mid-motion and stared at her hand, which was shaking. Everything about this was so frightening, so foreign; it felt like a fist closing over her heart.

She swallowed hard. *C'mon, Leigh, you chickenshit.* Stubbornly, she steadied her hand, determined to finish the simple act she'd started and push back that lock of disobedient hair. Once she had, she drew her fingertips lightly over RJ's face, barely tracing the soft, swollen skin around RJ's black eye before trailing down her cheek.

The tall woman twitched slightly at the featherlight touch.

Leigh smiled tensely, her brow furrowing. *God, what am I doing? I don't want this,* her mind hissed. *I don't want to fall in love with her. I can't fall in love with anyone and make it work. I won't.* But even as she thought them, Leigh couldn't make herself believe the words. She had lied shamelessly many times her life. But even when it threatened to turn her world upside down, and several times it had, she tried to never lie to herself. Until this week.

Tonight, even through the haze of her sleep-fogged brain, she'd heard RJ's sweet words, felt their quiet whisper against her skin and the corresponding tug on her heart. And in that place between sleep and wakefulness, they'd caused only a moment of unease, of raw fear, before she was able to push the words away and allow her eyes to drift shut. But now that she was awake, they seemed all too real. It was too much to handle.

Leigh carefully slid out from under the bedding. Tenderly, she pulled the sheet up over RJ's shoulders, watching the even rise and fall of her chest for several long moments as she tried desperately to fight off the anxiety welling in her chest. She couldn't do it. And she moved to the foot of the bed where she retrieved a rumpled blanket that had fallen to the floor.

Her thoughts began to pile on top of each other, filling her head with things she didn't want, visions she'd never allow herself to have. A panic began to build within her, and she shivered as she wrapped the blanket tightly around herself, barely registering its slight roughness against her naked skin. She fled the room without shutting the door, quickly padding to the balcony, her feet moving faster with every step. When she reached the sliding glass door, she threw it open, sucking in a huge lungful of cool night air like a drowning woman just breaking through the surface, her fear so real she could taste it in the back of her throat.

Leigh closed her eyes as she exhaled slowly, letting the chilly wind that rolled in off the sea beat against her, sending her already sleep-tousled hair into further disarray. She stepped all the way outside, ignoring the sudden shock of the cold concrete against her bare feet. She let out a sigh of utter relief; the room inside had started to close in on her. Now she could breathe.

Her gaze turned out toward Puget Sound and the twinkling harbor lights. "It's just sex," she told herself firmly as she began to pace.

"Okay, so it's *great* sex. And fun. More fun than I've ever had with anybody else. Even when we're just shopping or not doing anything at all. But that's it. There's nothing more to it. But when she looks at me, my knees go weak; and I have to keep from swooning like a pathetic teenager. And when she cries, it rips my heart out. Shit. Shit. Shit!" She closed her eyes in frustration. "Okay, so there is a little more than sex."

Leigh continued to babble to herself. "So what if she loves me?" She shrugged ruthlessly, as though that didn't matter at all. As though *she* didn't matter at all. "That happens sometimes. It's not my fault." Her eyes welled with unexpected tears. "I didn't encourage it." She swallowed hard, her throat closing.

She swung back around and looked through the darkened hotel suite toward the kitchen. "Dammit! I don't even have any more glasses to break." Leigh's mood vacillated wildly between anger and panic. "I'm down to coffee mugs, and I hate cleaning up ceramic!" She gave a passing thought to trying dishes, but decided her bill this month was already going to be ridiculous. *Maybe they won't notice the dents in the living room wall. Maybe she'll forget about what she said. Maybe I will. And about how I feel when I'm with her. Argh!*

Dejected, Leigh turned back around and leaned against the railing. *What am I going to do? What do I want to do?* Her mind mocked her with the answer. She wanted to pack her bags and slink out into the night like the skunk that she really was. Jump in her red truck, even if her mother was still plastered naked on its side, and drive east just as fast as those eighteen wheels could take her. But just the thought caused her stomach to flip flop.

Her hand snaked out from beneath the blanket, and she wiped her eyes, the cold spring breeze already drying her cheeks. "Or, I could not run away, march back into the suite, and take things one day at a time with RJ. I could have a relationship like a normal person. So what if I've never been able to do it before?" Leigh scowled. *Everything doesn't have to be neat and easy.* "I could be a real girlfriend." There was a long pause, where all she heard was the sound of her own heart and the whistling of the wind. Her shoulders sagged and her eyes turned downward. "Yeah," she snorted. "Like the odds of me not screwing *that* up aren't a gazillion to one."

"Screwing what up?"

Leigh whirled around to find RJ standing in the doorway, her body silhouetted by soft moonlight. She was wrapped in a thin sheet and already shivering. "What are you doing out here?" Leigh asked, her voice tight with emotion.

RJ put one hand on her hip and spoke in a motherly tone. "The real question is, why are you standing out in this wind? You're going to catch your death." But despite her words, and without the smallest bit of hesitation, she stepped out onto the porch to join her friend.

"I'm just thinking out loud," Leigh announced quietly, looking down at her toes. "I spend a lot of time alone in the truck, and unless I want to get on the radio, it's just me for company."

A pained expression worked its way onto RJ's face.

Leigh shrugged. "So, I talk to myself. It's nothing to worry about. I'm not cracked or anything." Flustered, she peeked up at RJ from behind pale lashes. "It's not so strange." *At least not to me.* Her eyes darted away again as she fumbled for a quick change of subject. "Did I wake you? I...ah...I didn't think I was mumbling that loud."

"You didn't wake me." It was mostly true. The cool, empty space next to her in bed was what woke her. RJ had discovered over the past few days that she liked having a bedmate; it struck a chord somewhere deep inside her, soothing a place she hadn't even known existed. At night, she was already reaching out for Leigh's presence. And that was a dangerous thing. But her mind simply refused to go there. Not tonight. Not yet.

"You're cold?" Leigh asked. Without thought, she opened her blanket, inviting RJ to step forward into its comfort and warmth.

The chilly sheet that was wrapped around RJ tickled the blonde's chest for just a second before RJ let it fall to the ground and returned Leigh's tender embrace. Blue eyes fluttered shut as their bodies came together in an explosion of sensation. *God, I don't think I can stop myself with you, RJ. I think it's too late to even try.*

The taller woman sighed, and her voice dropped. "Leigh,"

she growled, loving the feeling of their bodies nestled tightly together. She pressed her face against Leigh's head, her breath lightly scattering the tousled golden locks resting against her lips. "This is so nice."

Leigh nodded, helpless to do anything but agree. "It is." She leaned forward a little and kissed the lightly freckled skin on RJ's throat, feeling the wildly fluttering pulse against her mouth. "Mmm..." Greedily, Leigh drew in a deep breath, burying her nose in the crook of RJ's neck. "You smell so damn good." *How can I want you this badly? I shouldn't need you like this.* But Leigh pushed away any thought that didn't revolve around the here and now, wanting to drown in the sensation of RJ melting into her arms. Of holding and being held, needing and being needed.

RJ sucked in a quick breath at the feeling of soft lips against her cool skin. She reached up and threaded her fingers in Leigh's thick golden hair, tilting the smaller woman's head way back, bracing her with her other arm. She peered into Leigh's eyes and saw her own rising passion mirrored back at her.

The world around them began to fade away.

RJ ducked her head, and their lips meet in a deep, languid kiss that stole her breath away.

Leigh groaned softly as she felt her position adjusted by RJ so that she was leaning against the balcony railing. She was still holding the blanket around herself and her lover, her breasts nestled firmly beneath RJ's. Their lips were barely separated. "Do you want this?" For a moment Leigh wasn't sure whether she'd asked the question out loud or merely thought the words, or whether she meant much more than necking on the balcony.

The taller woman's hands slid down Leigh's back to capture firm buttocks. She drew their bodies closer together, and her lips slid to Leigh's ear where she gently traced its wind-chilled edge with her tongue. Fire raced through her veins as the weight of her own arousal came crashing in on her. "Yes," she whispered harshly, drawing the delicate earlobe into her mouth and sucking, earning a tiny gasp. Dropping her head further, she indulged in her lover's tender throat, unable to stop her teeth from closing gently around a sensitive fold of skin. "Yes, I want this."

Leigh moaned, very aware of the increasing moisture between her legs and the firm nipples that slid lightly across her chest every time RJ took a breath. Her skin tingled in the wake of RJ's touch, and her heart began beating faster. She wanted to bring RJ's lips back to hers, but she couldn't move her hands without exposing RJ's naked body to the cold night air. It took her several seconds of mounting frustration before she realized she could simply ask. Her tongue appeared and moistened her lips. "Kiss me on the mouth, RJ."

Responding instantly to the desire and desperation in the plea, RJ's head snapped up and she crushed her mouth against Leigh's. Hot and wet, their tongues swirled around each other, warring for dominance in a demanding, primal kiss.

Panting, RJ sank to her knees, allowing them to rest on the sheet still pooled beneath her. There was a shifting of movement and shadows before her world went black and she was completely engulfed by the blanket as Leigh's arms moved with her, covering her, though she was far from cold. The fragrance of Leigh's skin and sweat and arousal was stronger here, and she moaned as it washed over her senses. "Leigh," she breathed thickly. She had been so wrong before, for all these years.

This was heaven.

She kissed the soft underside of a breast, barely touching the skin, its salty dampness sending a flood of heated blood low in her belly. Nipping and licking, she drew a stream of incomprehensible sounds from Leigh's throat.

Leigh closed her eyes as the sensation sent a shot of pure, pulsing desire to her groin. She felt as though she was being devoured. When lips closed around her nipple and bit softly, giving it a firm tug, she groaned loudly, and eyes dilated by arousal snapped wide open. "God, yes," she hissed, giving in to the urge to pull RJ's head closer, feeling silky, thick hair tangle with her fingers as she tried to maintain her grip on the blanket. She was already feeling the first stirrings of climax, and they had barely begun. *What is she doing to me?*

Deciding she would die if she had to go another second without touching RJ, Leigh grasped both ends of the blanket in one hand. Its edges were barely hanging on her shoulders as she raked her fingers through RJ's silken tresses, caressing her scalp.

The gentle movement caused RJ to stop what she was doing and look up just as Leigh lowered the blanket, dropping it from her shoulders to her biceps and shifting so that RJ's head was once again exposed to the night's breeze. Their gazes locked, and Leigh could read every emotion on RJ's startlingly open face, every thought and desire. It was love, staring unflinchingly up at her, begging her to respond in kind and tugging at her spirit. Leigh's heart clenched painfully, and she found herself helpless under its spell. Her spell. She opened her mouth to say something, but no words would come. She blinked, and was suddenly looking at RJ through a haze of shimmering tears.

Leigh gently cupped RJ's chin and, with a tiny tug, sent her rising to her feet. The blanket nearly slipped from her grasp, but she caught it just as they moved back into a loose embrace.

"What?" RJ whispered.

Leigh shook her head, unable to answer. She looked away.

RJ frowned a little and drew a single finger up between Leigh's breasts, along the side of her throat, and behind her earlobe where she paused and gave it a gentle tug. "Do you want me to stop?" she asked raggedly, consciously tamping down the excitement that was making her body hum and her heart thunder. "Because I will, lass." A tiny but serious smile worked its way across her face. "But I'd rather you let me have you completely."

There was a white flash of teeth as a smile edged with affection, desire and a raw wanting made Leigh gasp with fear and need. She felt the low-husked words rumble right through her, and she managed her own tiny smile in return, wondering if the soul-deep fear she felt shone clearly in her eyes. She swallowed and let herself fall a little further and impossibly deeper.

RJ's warm palm cupped the side of her face, and her thumb slid lightly over her cheekbone in a gentle, affectionate move that stole Leigh's very heart.

The blonde woman abandoned herself to the touch and to RJ, offering herself up completely in every way she had to give. It was time. "I don't want you to stop. I don't want to stop," she said heavily as her blue eyes slid shut and she surged upward to capture RJ's lips in a wet, hungry kiss.

RJ growled deep in her chest, reacting unconsciously to Leigh's surrendering of her heart and body. Their kisses went from fiery to frantic as their excitement reached a fever pitch and the blanket fell away from RJ's back. They surged together, groping and needy. This time when RJ dropped to her knees, she didn't stop her progression down Leigh's body until her nose then tongue was brushing through damp, fragrant curls. She groaned loudly and her hands convulsively clenched Leigh's hips, roughly pulling her closer.

"Jesus!" Leigh threw her head back, and wide eyes gazed

unseeing into a million bright stars. Her thighs began to tremble and the blanket fell away from both their bodies, though it remained clenched in one fist. Cool air swept across hot skin, heightening every sensation. Leigh was truly surprised when steam didn't rise from their bodies. Another surge of RJ's tongue, and her knees nearly gave out.

RJ lifted one of Leigh's legs over her shoulder and pushed her back harder against the balcony railing as she supported most of her weight. She gave in to her every impulse to possess and consume and love completely as she feasted on Leigh.

"God," Leigh hissed as her painfully coiled body released with so much force she was completely swept away. Her drawn out, rapturous climax was howled into the cool spring night.

RJ carefully lowered Leigh's leg from her shoulder, making sure her arms were still wrapped tightly around the blonde, who was already swaying.

Leigh had just enough presence of mind to weakly swing the blanket around RJ's shoulders. She still felt like she was on fire and didn't even spare a thought for covering herself.

The auburn-haired woman rested her cheek against Leigh's heaving chest. She tilted her head upward when she thought she heard Leigh say her name.

Leigh's jaw worked, but she couldn't make the words come. They had time. *Later*, her mind whispered. *There'll be time later.* She let out a shuddering breath. "Never mind."

The clerk at the front desk of the Piedmont Suites Hotel hung up the phone and scratched his jaw, a puzzled look putting a deep crease in his forehead.

The night manager poked his head out of his office and, yawning, addressed the young man. "Another phone call?" They'd never had so many calls in the middle of the night.

"Yeah, it's weird. Half the rooms on the eighth floor, but only on the side with balconies facing the Puget Sound, just extended their stay for the rest of the week. One man started crying when I told him we'd already booked his room to some-one else for tomorrow night."

"Waaaahh!"

"It'll grow back," she muttered half-heartedly, for at least the hundredth time.

"When?" His lower lip poked out. "Can you tell me when?" The male squirrel burst into body-wracking sobs again. "Wahhh. Wahahahahaha!"

"Not soon enough for me. I'm never walking behind you," she grimaced, "or in front of you, again." She plopped down next to her bald mate, wondering if female humans understood that Nair was simply antifreeze in disguise. She cringed when her beady black gaze drifted upward toward his head. As white human males had discovered, you really had to have a good head to be completely bald. Otherwise, you just looked stupid.

He buried his face in his arms and continued to wail. "Eternity! I'm going to spend eternity looking like a naked mole rat." *Oh, the humiliation!*

"It could be worse," the female offered helpfully, kicking her feet out in front of her as she leaned back against their bed. They were safely in their nest, hidden away from Flea.

He sniffed pathetically. "How? How could it be worse?"

"I dunno." She shrugged and smiled toothily. "I was lying to try and make you feel better."

Whoever said that females were the more nurturing sex was clearly a whipped male squirrel trying to get laid. There could be no other explanation. "Waahahahahaahaha!"

"Oh, stop. At least you're alive, sort of. I thought you were a goner when you tipped over face first into the antifreeze. Your bottle cap chest plate made you sink right to the bottom."

He wiped his tears away on a leaf. "You saved me?" His eyes were round with wonderment. "You? You're nothing but a fat, lazy sloth. You wouldn't save me."

True, she conceded mentally, surprised by her mate's moment of insight. She had just let the antifreeze puddle soak into the ground before poking him awake with a stick.

"I'm the master of this couple from now on. All the future plans will be mine," he declared boldly.

The female just smiled placidly. She would tell him later that the leaf he'd just used to wipe his cheeks wasn't their normal toweling, but a poison oak leaf she'd collected for their war against Flea. Much later. Okay, never.

Just then the male grabbed the leaf and vigorously rubbed it against his butt. "Dang, being bald is itchy."

"I'm sure it is." She nodded gleefully. *Call me fat...* "In fact, I'd imagine that when the wind brushes against delicate body parts that have never really seen the light of day, it makes them tingle."

"Tingle?" Nothing was really tingling now that he'd relieved his itch, but he liked the idea of tingling. Unconsciously, he crossed his legs.

"Oh, yes." She nodded. "I'll bet delicate places not usually exposed to the elements would tingle as the cool air brushed over them, caressing them."

The male squirmed a little. "Del—" He paused and gulped, his mouth going a little dry. "Delicate places?" *Caressing?*

The female nodded again, her voice taking on that sensual squirrel quality that called to her mate on a subconscious, primal level. "Very delicate, highly sensitive places." She glanced around casually. "Can't you just feel the light breeze whistling through this place?"

The male instantly rubbed the leaf between his legs using quick, furious motions to relieve the insidious itch that came out of nowhere. "You're right. I can feel it!"

"No. But you will later."

"What?" Something was vaguely unsettling about seeing that sweet cherub-like smile on his wife's face.

"Oh, nothing important."

Leigh laughed, trying to hang on to all the little stuffed bears that threatened to tumble from her arms. "Good God, RJ, I can't hold them all." And true to her word, one of the bears plopped onto the cement beneath her sneakers.

The air was filled with the sound of laughing children, obnoxious teenagers, and game barkers. Better still was the delicious aroma of sugar, salt, and grease that could only be found at a carnival. RJ was hard-pressed to think of a better way to spend an afternoon.

"Hey, watch it." RJ shot a little boy a grumpy look as she bent to retrieve the bear he'd almost stepped on. "Well then, lass, let me see..." She looked around at the various booths and stands to see if any of the vendors might have a bag for the twenty or so small, bedraggled, brown teddy bears she'd won for Leigh while playing games on the fairway. One stand had neon pink bags covered with pictures of some boy band hanging from its canvas roof. RJ cringed; she *had* planned on offering to carry the bears for the rest of the day, but there was no way in hell she'd be caught dead carrying around one of those big, ugly, hot pink tote bags. *I have my pride,* she thought, a little indignantly. She was about to give up when she spied exactly what they needed. "C'mon, and we'll get a knapsack for all your furry little friends."

"Not all of them," Leigh chuckled softly, moving away from RJ's prodding hands. She placed a quick kiss on RJ's chin and allowed her gaze to slowly draw a line down the center of RJ's body. "My favorite furry friend is in your—"

"Leigh Matthews!"

"Hand," the blonde finished sweetly, snatching the lone black bear away. She winked at her companion.

"Watch your mouth, young lady," RJ warned playfully, "or I'll be forced to watch it for you."

Leigh looked to the bundle in her arms. "Can't we just pass them out to the people who were too pathetic to win them on their own?" *Except for the black one, he's all mine.* She made sure her voice was just loud enough for all the people standing around the game, where RJ had just cleaned house, to hear. Leigh smirked at several young men's petulant grumbles and curses.

"Wimps," she added for good measure.

"You're evil." RJ smiled, her grassy-green eyes shining in the afternoon sun. "You should be ashamed."

"Ashamed, that's me. I'm known far and wide for my hypersensitive conscience and over-developed sense of guilt."

"Uh huh. Sure." RJ maneuvered them alongside a platform with a padded metal block sitting squarely in its center. It was attached to a metal pole with a large silver bell on top.

"One swing, one ring, you get a prize. Only t-eeeew dollars," the barker sang out rhythmically as he swung the large wooden hammer.

RJ stripped off her jacket and, after a second's consideration, her short-sleeved denim shirt, leaving her clad in her usual undershirt.

Leigh blinked. "Uh...you are going to leave at least something on, aren't you? Not that I mind, but I didn't bring enough cash to bail you out of jail."

The barker gave a low, appreciative whistle at the sight of

RJ's underdressed body.

Leigh's head swung around and she practically snarled at the man, causing him to take a giant step backwards.

RJ rolled her eyes. "I'm gonna win a bag, and I need to be able to swing to do it." She scoffed at the puny hammer the man held out for her and marched behind him to a selection of slightly larger ones. She chose the biggest hammer they had.

Leigh laughed and gathered RJ's wrinkled clothes in her hands, still wrestling to keep the bears in her arms. "This is too butch, RJ, even for you." She quirked an eyebrow. "Is the spitting contest next?" But even as she continued to tease, her head was cocked slightly to the side as she openly admired RJ's broad shoulders and lean, muscular arms.

"I couldn't very well just let you fumble around with all those little beggars." RJ gestured to the stuffed animals, then rubbed her palms on her jeans as she prepared to heft the hammer for the first blow.

"We could just find a garbage sack," Leigh offered. She knew good and well RJ had already set her mind on another prize, but was enjoying needling her lover.

"Nah." RJ stood up straight and put one hand on her hip. She pinned Leigh with a glare more playful than withering. "Are you trying to spoil my fun?"

"Would I do that?"

RJ only snorted.

"Have at it then. But you promise you're going to pick the bag and not that enormous snake when you win, right?" It didn't even occur to the trucker to think that RJ wouldn't ring the bell.

"I think you'll look better toting around the knapsack." RJ lifted the hammer. She took two practice swings, exhaling slowly as she readied herself for the blow.

A small crowd had gathered. This game was strictly for the big boys, and no one believed the woman would be able to move the weight even halfway up the scale. Catcalls rang out, along with a few, mostly good-natured taunts.

"Ten bucks says the dyke can't do it," grumbled a scrawny young man, who looked like he needed a break from his job with the state roadside sanitation crew. Leigh wondered who was scraping up all the dead raccoons today.

"Make it twenty and you're on." His buddy spat in his hand and stuck it out for roadkill boy to shake, which he did after spitting in his own hand.

Leigh grimaced, not understanding why every woman on the planet wasn't a lesbian.

RJ rolled her shoulders one more time. Then, with a look of solid concentration, she swung the hammer, bringing it down with vicious force. The weight exploded up the pole as though a charge of gunpowder had gone off beneath it, causing a deafening ring of the bell before plunging back to the base.

Most of the crowd laughed and applauded when the pilot put the hammer down, gesturing to the bag that hung on the hook. The carny pulled down the large, navy, canvas bag and tossed it to the tall woman. RJ unzipped the bag and presented it to Leigh with a flourish, holding it open so she could deposit her booty inside.

Once Leigh had stuffed the bears in the bag, RJ zipped it up and handed it to the blonde. "There you go. One bag of bears." She wiggled her eyebrows, quite proud of herself.

Leigh smiled back; she couldn't help it. RJ's relaxed demeanor made this kind of thing more fun than she'd ever thought it could be. "You are disgustingly happy with yourself right now, aren't you?"

"Pretty much." RJ smirked.

Leigh was actually feeling like a woman who might be able to enjoy having a serious relationship. It still scared her, but the smile on RJ's face was relentlessly leading her places she'd never gone. At least successfully. "I think you deserve a kiss."

Without allowing her the chance to answer, Leigh dropped the bag to the ground at her feet and grabbed the front of RJ's undershirt in one hand to pull her down for a passionate kiss that left roadkill boy and his friend staring, wide-eyed. God, Leigh enjoyed torturing the straight people.

"Mmm." RJ licked her lips as they separated. "How about something to eat?"

Leigh bit her tongue to keep from saying the first thing that popped into her mind. "I dunno." She grinned wickedly. "What are you hungry for?"

After a lifetime of being the aggressor, RJ was still thrown off balance by Leigh's forwardness. She blushed, despite herself, easily reading the sudden fire that had erupted in those clear blue eyes. "I'm thinking maybe a steak sandwich or something. With a nice cold beer." *A really cold beer. And maybe a bucket of ice to dunk my head in, too.* She leaned in, whispering in her lover's ear, "But I'll have you for dessert later."

"Life is short, RJ." Leigh held up the soft denim shirt for her to slip into. "We could always start with dessert and end with the beef?" She produced her best wishing look as she draped RJ's jacket over her arm and retrieved the bag.

RJ growled inwardly. "We could at that, lass." She looked around for a moment then eyed the perfect spot. "How about the Ferris wheel? I'll pay the fella extra to leave us at the top for a few extra minutes," she tempted, mostly to see what would happen.

Leigh's gaze swung toward the big wheel. She didn't especially appreciate heights; on the other hand, she did appreciate the idea of getting a few moments in the sun with RJ in semi-privacy. "Okay. You're on."

The pilot lifted her brows, realizing it was a little late in the relationship to be surprised by something as tame as this. *Not after the balcony at the hotel...Lord, have mercy.* She grasped Leigh's hand and led her through the crowd. The line moved pretty quickly, and soon they were standing at the gate to the ride's entrance. RJ dug into her pocket, then slapped a bill in the attendant's hand while whispering in his ear.

He looked down at Leigh and grinned broadly. Shaking his head, he opened the gate and lifted the bar positioned over the seat for them.

Leigh gestured to the duffel bag full of stuffed toys. "Should we take these, too?"

"Sure. You might need something soft to hold onto. Or maybe even to bite down on."

"Promises, promises." Leigh sat down and tucked the large bag securely under her feet. "Have I mentioned that I really don't care for heights?"

"Then just close your eyes." RJ settled down next to the trucker. She put her arm around her shoulder and pulled her close.

Leigh smiled and snuggled closer, already feeling more comfortable with RJ's arm around her. "This is nice." She felt the ride start, taking them upward and had just started to relax when she felt RJ's thumb graze her nipple. "Behave."

RJ moved to pull her hand away, looking surprised.

Leigh grabbed it and winked. "Just until we get to the top."

Both women began to laugh.

Leigh flipped open the lid on the pizza box, humming to herself as the smell of pepperoni and extra cheese wafted upward. She began to salivate. "Oooo, this is going to be so good." She absently passed RJ a plate and a napkin with one hand, while she fixed hers with her other.

RJ scooted forward on the couch and eagerly took the plate. She glanced over at the trucker, who was tearing apart a gooey piece of pizza. "Did you have a good time today?"

"Absolutely," Leigh affirmed, closing her eyes and sinking her teeth into the pizza. She instantly burned the roof of her mouth. "Aww...shit." The blonde spat her bite out into her napkin.

RJ tried not to laugh too hard as she passed Leigh a bottle of cold beer. "Don't you hate it when that happens?" Green eyes twinkled. "You'd think that by now civilized man would have learned not to bite into hot cheese."

Leigh narrowed her watering eyes and took a deep swallow before saying, "No one, civilized or not, can resist the call of pizza." The air of authority in her voice made it clear that this was not merely opinion; this was fact. "It's positively primal." She took another bite and winced. "And far too good to wait for."

"That could be said for a lot of things in this room." RJ winked then plucked a piece of pizza from the box. *You'd be worth waiting for, lass. I wish we had a chance. I'm sorry that it has to end so soon.*

Leigh's brows drew together at the sudden look of worry that chased across RJ's face. "What's wrong? You're not going to be sick again, are you?" She leaned back out of the way. Just in case.

"No, lass, I'm fine," RJ grumbled. "Get sick once, and you're tagged for life." She sipped her beer. "I was just thinking about the fact that we'll be starting back soon." Try as she might, she couldn't quite stifle a heartfelt sigh. "Wishing we had a little more time, that's all."

"It has been fun, hasn't it?" Leigh questioned awkwardly, trying not to sound too eager for RJ's answer.

The pilot smiled at her friend. "It certainly has. I've had a wonderful time. You're a very special woman, Leigh Matthews."

"Thanks, RJ," Leigh answered softly. She closed her eyes and scrubbed at what she was certain was a light blush. "I um... You're great, too. And, well..."

Say it.

No! She hasn't said it again. What if she changed her mind?

So? You still know how you feel.

RJ waited patiently for Leigh continue. She tore at a piece of embedded pepperoni as she intently watched a myriad of emotions wash over Leigh's face.

"It's been nice and—" Leigh bit her lip, sorry she'd started down this path. *Candy-ass chicken. You've never had trouble talking to women before,* her inner voice mocked.

"Quiet," Leigh hissed tightly. *Oh, damn. By the way she's looking at me, I have a feeling I said that last part out loud.*

RJ pulled back a bit, her brows coming together tightly over the bridge of her nose. "I'm sorry." She shifted uncomfortably, thinking her wish for more time together had put Leigh on the spot. "I didn't mean to upset you."

"No, no, no." Leigh shook her head wildly. "Don't worry about it." When RJ's expression didn't change, she added, "You remember the cartoon where this kid had a good fairy on one shoulder and an evil fairy on the other, tempting him?"

RJ stared at her blankly.

"Figures." Leigh sighed. "Let's just say that one of the nasty fairies has been talking too much lately." *She thinks I'm insane. She'd be right. Very funny.* "I'm fine. Are you all packed?" Bright blue eyes begged RJ to allow the change in subjects.

RJ nodded slowly. *This was just a fling. Don't go blaming this woman because you let your foolish heart get the best of you and start craving something that'll never be yours.* "Yeah, I'm all set." She mustered a watery grin. She already knew it would break her heart to have Leigh confirm her words, yet she morbidly decided to probe the painful spot. "You'll probably be glad to be rid of me." The tease was weak at best.

"Yeah, you are so hard to live with," Leigh said dryly. "It's been real chore."

RJ actually chuckled before biting into her pizza. "Then maybe it's a good thing we're headed back. You've got such a high opinion of me right now, I'd hate to see it go up in a glorious puff of smoke when you find out what a pain I really am to be around on a full time basis. Just ask my mother, she'll tell you."

Leigh cringed at the mention of RJ's mother. She'd only seen her a couple of times, but that was more than enough for her get the idea that the strapping Irishwoman did not like her. "I think I'll avoid your mom, if it's all the same to you." *She looks at me as though I'm a walking advertisement for decadence and debauchery. God, how could she know me so well without even talking to me?*

RJ nodded and sipped her beer again. "My mother, God bless her, is a force to be reckoned with." She looked to Leigh and licked her lips. *It's time to figure out how you're going to end this when you get home, because you know good and well that to keep seeing her is only going to make the want deeper and the hurt worse.* "But just so there's no doubt in your mind, lass, I've had the best time of my life these past few days. Thank you for asking me along." She began picking relentlessly at her beer's label.

"My pleasure, RJ." Leigh pushed away her pizza. There was something else in the room whose call she found irresistible. She stood up and extended her hand to RJ.

RJ looked up in surprise. "Aren't you hungry, lass?"

"Yes."

RJ swallowed.

"You haven't seen what I bought at Victoria's Secret yet, RJ." A sexy grin twitched at the corners of Leigh's mouth. "Aren't you curious?"

RJ's eyes went a little wide. *Am I curious? What kind of stupid question is that?* She set her bottle down and took Leigh's hand as she got up from the couch. "Absolutely. I have a feeling this is going to be a night to remember for a long time."

"It should last you a lifetime," the trucker grinned mischievously as she led RJ to the bedroom.

Chapter
13

RJ leaned back in the seat of the truck. She kept her face firmly turned to the window as she chewed on the nail of her thumb. *I've got to make it clean. Do whatever it takes to make her leave and never come back. I can't go on like this.*

She glanced over at her companion, who at the moment was getting a report on the location of the nearest highway patrol over the CB. *I've just been alone too long. What if I fell for the first pretty woman to give me the time of day? Okay, maybe not the first...* She sighed. *Leigh is a special woman who deserves more than I can offer her. A once-a-week quickie in a garage is not a life. It's not what she needs. It's not even what I need.*

The pilot's foot began to bounce nervously as she continued to chew on her thumbnail. *Oh, I just had to go and fall in love with her, didn't I? Couldn't keep it to just sex. No. I had to go and get attached. Serves you right, you damn fool.*

Over the previous couple of days, RJ's mood had worsened with each passing mile. Leigh had hinted several times that she'd be by the diner to see RJ again very soon. And though her heart thrilled to hear the words, at the same time they made things a hundred times more complicated. That she was in love with the woman was one thing. But to have those feelings returned, knowing all the while she was only hours away from ending things outright, was nearly more than RJ could bear.

She'd had an upset stomach and headache for twenty-four hours straight and couldn't see things getting better anytime soon.

She glanced to the clock in the dashboard. Two more hours and she'd be home.

"You're awfully quiet today, RJ." Leigh peered into her side mirror before smoothly changing lanes. "Are you okay?" She'd asked that several times already, but couldn't help herself. Something wasn't right.

"Yeah, I'm fine, lass," RJ lied, not knowing how unconvincing she sounded. Every time she looked at Leigh, she felt her heart break again. She closed her eyes, forcing the tears away and trying to clear her mind. *God, I'm tired.*

"RJ," Leigh's soft voice coaxed from fitful sleep. "RJ, wake up."

RJ opened her eyes slowly, wishing that Leigh wasn't running her fingers through her hair. This was going to be hard enough without the sweet, lingering feeling of her touch.

"You have beautiful hair," Leigh whispered affectionately, still gently stroking the wavy auburn locks. "It would look even prettier longer, I'll bet."

"Yeah?"

Leigh grinned and nodded. "Yeah." She leaned forward and kissed RJ softly on the cheek. "We're back."

RJ slowly sat up in her seat. She took a deep breath, letting it out explosively when she saw the diner staring back at her through the front window of the truck. "So we are." She reached back and grabbed her travel bag, smiling sadly at the canvas duffel full of teddy bears that was tucked just behind the seats. Without looking back at Leigh, she opened the door and climbed down.

The air was warm and dry, and held the scent of tall grass, rich soil and home. Fitz's sign reflected the bright afternoon sun, and RJ could see that another bulb had blown out in her absence.

She was tempted to rush inside and not face Leigh, but couldn't force her feet to move in time. Leigh joined her in front of the truck and laid a warm hand on the small of her back, rubbing gently. The simple gesture nearly undid her. "Well," with a shaky hand RJ shifted her bag over one shoulder, "I guess this is where I get off."

Leigh shrugged half-heartedly. She ducked her head and kicked at a rock by her foot. "I wouldn't mind taking you home. To Glory, I mean." Truth be told, she was hoping for a few more moments together, admitting to herself for the first time that she didn't want to leave RJ at all. Besides, she'd been wondering about Glory for weeks.

RJ shook her head. "No, that's okay. My truck is right over there, and I should probably go inside and see if Fitz's is ready to fall down. With just Pete looking out for it, that's a definite possibility." She shifted uncomfortably, looking back and forth between Leigh and the diner.

Leigh frowned a little as a growing sense of apprehension blossomed in the pit of her stomach. "Okay." She drew out the word. "At least let me walk you to diner."

Do it, you damn coward. Do it now. "Okay," she heard herself say. They began a slow walk, with RJ detouring slightly to toss her bag into the bed of her pickup truck. She reached in through the open window, intent on snagging the open pack of cigarettes from the dashboard, but stopped herself. Instead, she fished a nearly empty pack from her pocket, quickly lighting a cigarette. RJ took a deep drag, holding her breath for a long satisfying moment before releasing the smoke into the afternoon breeze. "So," she cleared her throat and picked a tiny piece of tobacco from her tongue, "will you be going back to see Judith now?"

Leigh's blinked and her jaw sagged noticeably. "Wha...What?"

RJ tried for nonchalant. *I'm so sorry, lass. Please forgive me.* "I just figured that now that you're rid of me, you might try your hand at fixing things up with her. She was pretty enough. Nice hair and eyes. You could do worse." *Jesus, I'm dying all over again.*

During Leigh's long, stunned silence, RJ told herself that this was the best thing for both of them. That Leigh would be able to get back to her life, while she got back to her eternity. They could never really be together. This was the only way. *Say something, dammit. Anything.*

Leigh could tell by the look on RJ's face that she wasn't joking. She replayed what had just been said over and over in her mind, feeling the words as though each one were a 2x4 to her chest. "Why—" She stopped and swallowed back the acrid taste

that had built up in the back of her throat. *I will not puke.*
"Why would I go back to Judith?" *You can't want that, can you?*
I don't understand! her mind screamed.

"Just seems to me to be the logical thing for you to do." RJ
refused to look up from the toe of her boots. She took another
drag from her cigarette, releasing the thick white stream of
smoke through her nose. "I know I was a pleasant distraction for
you, but I think if you went back there, you could work things
out with her. She's had plenty of time to cool off."

"I don't want to work things out with her!" Leigh's hand
shot out and she snatched the cigarette out of RJ's mouth. She
flicked it to the ground and crushed it under her shoe. With the
palm of her hand, she grasped the taller woman's chin and forced
eye contact. "What in the hell are you talking about?" Her
voice was demanding and rough, and RJ couldn't help but hear
her rising panic.

She gulped hard and forced herself to directly meet Leigh's
confused but fiery glare. "Don't make this harder than it has to
be. Do I really have to explain things, lass?"

Leigh ran her hands through her hair. "I guess you do, RJ,
because I don't understand what the hell is happening."

"It's *over,* Leigh. The week is done. Now the best thing
you can do is climb in your truck and drive away." Every word
tasted foreign and bitter, and her heart cried out for her to stop.

But she didn't.

"We had fun." RJ shrugged again, pulling her chin from
Leigh's grasp and looking away. "But now the fun is over."

The fun is over? "You're dumping me?" Leigh whispered
incredulously, trying desperately to figure out what had happened. Things were wonderful between them. Better than wonderful. Sure, she hadn't said the words yet, but that didn't make
her feelings any less real.

RJ clenched her fists nervously. "C'mon, Leigh." The dull
ache in her chest intensified. "It was sex. A week of wonderful
sex, granted." She gave the trucker her best roguish look. "But
you've got to know I'm not exactly the type for anything long
term."

"I never asked for anything long term." But the protest
sounded hollow, even to Leigh's own ears. She hadn't asked for
it. But that's exactly what she found herself wanting.

RJ pointed at the truck. "Look, lass, I really think you need
to just climb back in your truck and head down the road. I'm

sure if you drive real fast, that pretty waitress will be more than happy to make you feel better." From the corner of her eye, she could see Pete and her mother standing in the door of the diner, waiting. RJ could sense their pity, and she would have none of it. She bit her lip and refocused on Leigh. She needed to end this now, before she changed her mind. "I'm sure she'll be more than happy to make a spot for you in her bed."

Leigh spun away from RJ and moaned out loud as though she was in physical pain. "I thought you loved me." She whirled back and glared. "You said that." She was yelling now. "I heard you."

The pilot clenched her teeth so hard it felt as though her jaw would break. *You heard that and you still stayed? This is not fair!* She gestured aimlessly. "Pillow talk."

"Why are you doing this?" Tears filled confused eyes. *This isn't how things are supposed to be. We're supposed to end up together. I know it.*

"Doing what, Leigh? Being true to my nature?" RJ forced out a cruel laugh. "Do I look like the type of person who wants to have someone attached to them?"

"I...I thought—"

"You thought wrong. Leigh, you don't really believe you're the only woman that I've had here, do you?" RJ closed her eyes briefly before forcing the next words from her lips. "You were my Tuesday afternoon distraction."

SMACK!

The sound of the loud slap rang out in the quiet parking lot. "You bitch." Leigh's face turned bright red. "That's a lie, and you know it."

RJ felt the slap deep into her soul and knew she deserved that and ten times worse. *Yes, it is, love.* She nearly faltered in her determination, but a deep breath allowed her to press on. "You give yourself a lot of credit, Leigh Matthews. That's one helluva ego you have." She pulled another cigarette from the pack, letting the empty wrapper fall to the ground. She lit it and tossed the match over her shoulder. "What's the matter? Don't like it when someone beats you at your own game? Don't care for it when someone uses *you* for a quick fuck?"

Through Leigh's astonishment and mounting anger, the truth in the words still tore at her. *Is that what this is? Some sort of cosmic revenge for enjoying women?* But she'd never led anyone on. Not like this. "Quick fuck," Leigh laughed humorlessly, saying it out loud to make it sound real. "Now, I see."

RJ let out a shaky breath. "Finally." She plucked her cigarette from her mouth and waved toward the rig again. "So why
don't you go ahead and head back to the waitress. Though I have
no doubt you've got one in every city between here and Seattle."

Leigh took a step closer to RJ, crossing the boundaries of
her personal space as though they didn't exist. "Smoking is a
nasty habit, RJ. It could kill you." She patted RJ's chest with
startling tenderness. "Enjoy your cigarette." With that, she
turned on her heel and began marching back to her truck. Tears
blurred her vision, and when she was far enough from RJ so that
she was certain that she couldn't hear, Leigh let out a gentle sob,
her shoulders shaking.

As she walked past RJ's rusted pickup, she kicked at one of
the tires, cursing at the instant pain it caused her foot. "Piece of
shit truck!" Fury and embarrassment washed over her, and when
she saw the crowbar lying in the pickup bed, she didn't hesitate
for even a second. She snatched it up and set out to demolish the
old machine.

"Jesus, Mary and Joseph!" RJ spun around when she heard
the first sounds of glass breaking. But Leigh managed to shatter
three windows, the front windshield, and put a huge hole in the
back glass before RJ could make it back to her. "Have you lost
your senses?" she yelled, as she tried to grab the crowbar away
from the furious blonde. "Christ, if you're mad at me, then hit
me! Don't take it out on my truck."

"Fine!" Leigh threw down the crowbar and took a swing at
RJ, barely missing her as the auburn-haired woman ducked out
of the way.

"Shit." The pilot continued to back up as Leigh kept swinging at her. "I hope this is making you feel better, because you
look like a lunatic."

The words only made Leigh madder, and she wailed out her
frustration at not being able to do any real damage as RJ ducked
and weaved out of her way.

"C'mon now and calm down. You give yourself a couple of
weeks, and you'll have forgotten I even exist."

Leigh swung again and again, grunting when she managed
to graze RJ's shoulder, the impact causing the taller woman to
wince. "I don't want to forget you!" she cried. Suddenly she
froze as the realization of what she was doing hit home. The
energy seemed to drain from her body and, like a rag doll, she

fell limply to her knees, panting. "That's not what I want." Her voice broke. *I want you.* She looked up at RJ hopefully, hot tears spilling over. "Please, RJ." Leigh stiffened when her lover didn't answer. "Is that really what you want? For me to forget everything?"

RJ felt her carefully measured control slipping. It wasn't supposed to be this horrible. This was too hard. She wanted nothing more than to pull Leigh into her arms, beg her forgiveness, and promise they would be together forever. But as sure as she was standing there, RJ knew one thing with soul-shattering certainty—her own heart's desire wasn't a possibility. Her hands shaped into white-knuckled fists. "Yes," she ground out harshly before turning and walking away.

She left Leigh on her knees in the dirt, crying. With her back to her lover, she allowed her own tears to fall. RJ could hear the love of her life—and afterlife—pick herself up, dust herself off, and stomp back toward her rig.

Leigh paused for a moment, wiping her cheeks on her shirtsleeve, embarrassed and angry over the tears. She turned slowly and watched RJ's retreating form move closer and closer to the diner. "You can go to hell, RJ," she called out.

RJ continued to walk, not even flinching at the words. Before stepping onto the porch, she warily peeked over her shoulder in time to see Leigh climb in the truck and start the engine. "I'm already there, Leigh Matthews." She continued to stare as Leigh slammed down hard on the accelerator, sending an enormous cloud of dust into the sky before she disappeared. "Take care of yourself, love. I'll miss you."

Sixty years of built-up resentment bubbled over, and RJ stomped her foot down hard on the porch steps, knowing what would happen. She felt her world spin and gasped as her chest tightened to an unbearable degree, just before everything went black.

She never felt Pete and her mother's loving hands lower her to the ground. They tried to ease her on her short journey back from life to what lay beyond. But, as always, this was one trip that could only be taken alone.

Katherine looked down at RJ's rumpled clothes, and then at the black pickup surrounded by shattered glass. At that very second, a large chunk of glass fell from the driver's side window into the dirt, breaking apart on impact. She cringed, the sound reminding her very much of what had just happened to her daughter's heart.

Pete looked bleakly down at RJ. "What have you done to her, Fitz?" he whispered. "What have you done to yourself?"

"Pay up, loser."

The male squirrel grumpily pulled his head back into their nest. "How?" He threw his paws into the air. "How could that have happened? The darker human has at least six inches and forty pounds on the smaller one." *Last time I ever bet on a human female fight.* "It was a sure thing. In the bar parking lot across from Potter Park, the fattest human female always wins," he bemoaned, slumping down on their bed. "Unless one has really big hair or is from New Jersey. But those are the only things that trump blubber. Everyone knows that."

"Wrong. Size doesn't necessarily matter."

He looked down at himself and then back up at her hopefully.

"Except there."

The male scowled and crossed his legs.

"Well?" She held out her paw. "You're not going to welch, are you?"

"Of course not!" he lied. The male pretended to look for an acorn in the soft grass that lined his bed. "You'll just have to take a rain check." His voice dropped to a mumble. "I don't happen to have payment at this very moment."

"What?" his mate roared.

"You heard me." He scratched his thigh. "It's not like I've been able to go out gathering for a few days, you know."

The female sucked on her incisors. This much was true. Her mate had spent the last three days in bed due to a mysteriously contracted itching illness. It had been pure hell. Her evil deceit had snared her like a spider caught in its own web. But she'd finally learned her lesson once and for all. Dammit. Never again. Next time she did it, she'd be sure to store up a good supply of food first.

"What are we going to do?"

She joined the male on the bed. Taking pity on him, she scratched his back, which was now covered with short, soft brown fur. "What do you mean?"

"I mean," he began to quake, "I can't take the pressure of

being in charge!" Tiny squirrel tears began to fall. "I know I said I was going to from now on. But...but, it's too much to handle. The pressure. The demands. The expectations. The sacrifice!"

"All you've done is lay in bed for seventy hours straight."

"I know," he cried miserably. "But I was thinking the whole time."

"Did it hurt?"

"You could tell?"

The female thought about that for a moment. She had assumed that the pained, nearly constipated look on his face was beer withdrawal. But thinking pains, so common in males, was another viable possibility.

"I'm not a modern squirrel. I'm not," he pressed.

She sighed. "Well, the truth is—"

"Please, please, can't we go back to our established familial roles? With me as the virile, squirrel-about-town, bread winner. The squirrel that makes your cold, black heart go pitter-patter. And with you as my loyal, scheming, and surprisingly organized housewife?"

"I do excel at scheming, and I am organized."

"And who are we to question the eternal wisdom of Meatloaf?" he crowed.

She had to admit, "Two outta three ain't bad."

"Exactly."

"But why should I?" She had never had any intention of losing the mantle of power. In fact, she'd forgotten he'd even said anything about it. But this was too fun to ignore.

"I'm losing my sense of self. I can't take it. I don't know *me* anymore. I'm adrift in a sea of confusion."

The female's eyes widened a little. Had he somehow gone from beer to crack without her knowing about it? How could he not offer to share?

He wiped away his tears, clearly sensing that she was weakening. "A switch in gender roles is not something that a squirrel can be expected to adapt to in a day or week. It takes years of inter-spousal communication and understanding. If done improperly, it could tear the very fabric of squirrel society, not to mention our marriage."

"You just couldn't think of a plan to save us from the cat," she said knowingly.

"Not a single one."

Pete watched as RJ propped a tall ladder against the frame of the sign. She hadn't said much since her return, and her mood was growing darker with each passing day. He knew she was hurt and upset, but he didn't have a clue as how to ease his friend's pain.

"Anything I can do to help?" he inquired as RJ started up the ladder, new bulbs in hand.

"No thanks."

Pete held the ladder steady as he watched her climb the steps. "Fitz, you can't keep doing this to yourself. You knew your time with Leigh was limited."

"I don't want to talk about it." She continued with her task, removing one of the burned out bulbs and laying it on the sign's ledge.

Pete called up, "Your mother is worried about you."

RJ scowled and touched a strand of blowing hair behind her ear. "My mother worries too much." She removed the next bad bulb and laughed without a trace of humor. "It's not like it can kill me."

"Stop saying that over and over. RJ, that's not even funny."

"Sure it is." She looked down at Pete. "Leigh will be fine."

"Will you? Eternity is a long time to have regrets."

One of the bulbs was rusted into place, and RJ cursed as it shattered in her hand and nicked her palm when she tried to remove it. "I'm sure I'll get used to it," she answered tersely. She quickly put the new bulbs into place and collected the old before starting down the ladder. At the bottom, she wiped her hands on a rag. "It's amazing the things you can get used to when necessary."

Before Pete could say another word, RJ collapsed the ladder and hoisted it onto her shoulder. She turned and walked toward the garage.

"What is it that you want, RJ?" Pete called after her retreating form. He hoped to get any reaction at all out of her. He figured that even anger was better than the listless and depressed woman who had taken the place of his friend.

RJ threw the ladder down with such force that it bounced once before settling on the ground. She spun around, causing dusty clouds to swirl in the dirt at her feet as she glared at Pete. "What I want? What I want is no doubt several hundred miles away by now!"

She stomped closer to him, her hands curled into tight fists. "Probably finding comfort in the arms of a woman who can't possibly love her as much as I do. The one I *want* thinks I'm a right bitch who used her and never cared for her, when in reality I've never loved anyone the way I love her!"

She was furious and shaking all over; tears leapt into her eyes, but she refused to let them fall.

"Is that what you wanted to hear, Peter? Did you want to hear that I'm miserable? That it hurts all the time? That I can't shake the feeling of her touch, that I hear her voice in my head every second. That when I close my eyes," she paused as the angry energy began to drain from her and the tears became nearly too much to fight, "I see her face."

He saw her shoulders slump as she turned and stalked over to her truck. She climbed in, sitting stock still for a moment before more anger erupted and she beat her fists against the steering wheel. Once the tide of fury had subsided, she started the truck and pulled out of the parking lot.

Pete watched her drive away, headed back to Glory. He sighed, then felt hands on his shoulders.

"She'll be all right. RJ's a strong woman," Mavis offered quietly.

"This is a hurt that's going to take a long time to heal."

"We'll help her." Mavis rested her cheek against Pete's shoulder.

"She doesn't want our help."

"In time, she'll realize she needs it."

"I hope so, but the one thing we know about RJ is—she's as stubborn as a two-dollar mule."

Highway patrolman Jerry Englund sat "meditating" in his patrol car in his hidden spot alongside the road. His eyes had just begun to droop and he'd let out a soft snore when a bright red semi-truck went barreling past him at what had to be over a hundred miles per hour.

Something crashing against his windshield and the loud dull thud sent him bolting upright. Confused, he rubbed his eyes and looked around, but the truck had already disappeared over the hill in front of him. "What the hell?" Had a bird hit his windshield while his car was standing still?

The patrolman exited the vehicle and walked around past the front bumper. His gaze dropped to the ground, and his deeply set, brown eyes widened. "I'll be good and god damned."

Over the past few months he'd found more than a dozen mutilated stuffed bears alongside the highway. They intrigued him to no end. *Who was this sicko?*

Patrolman Englund picked up the soft brown teddy bear and gasped. The head had very nearly been severed, remaining attached by only the barest of threads. Tire tracks were embedded in the fur, and there was a hole in the bear's chest where his heart should have been. If stuffed toys had hearts. Englund suspected they were dealing with an enraged sociopath. He grinned broadly and tossed the bear into his backseat as a souvenir. He was sure that someday it would fetch a handsome price on eBay. Maybe he could even sell the head separately.

RJ settled on her parents' front porch swing, watching the sun go down, sipping a beer. She looked at the sweating bottle, running her thumb through the condensation. She sniffed, then tipped the bottle to her lips, drinking deeply.

She glanced up when she heard the screen door creak open. Her brother Liam sat down next to her and took a deep breath as he contemplated very carefully what he wanted to say.

"I know," he finally started, "that this may not mean much right now, but it'll get better. It's only been a couple of months."

"Why did it happen, Liam? How could I let myself fall in love with her?"

The man scratched a stubbly jaw. "I suppose there's no good answer to that. I could say it's one of those lessons life is supposed to teach you that sometimes things don't work out like you want it to." He winced at how lame that sounded.

"I thought I learned that lesson when my plane crashed."

Liam nodded. "I suppose that's true, but that wasn't a lesson of the heart. Those are always the hardest lessons to learn."

The pilot grunted and rolled her eyes at her brother's attempt at waxing philosophical. She took another sip of beer. RJ was by no means drunk—yet. Right now she was feeling pleasantly numb. "I wonder if she misses me," she said softly, eyeing a rabbit that jumped happily through the yard.

Liam placed a gentle hand on his sister's knee. "I'm sure she does, RJ. But you know what you did was best for you both," he assured confidently.

Her auburn head bobbed weakly, and she became aware of the strands brushing the tops of her shoulders. She had started to go to Sammy's Barber Shop weeks ago, but couldn't bring herself to do it. She knew it was foolish, but every time she tried to get it cut, she kept hearing Leigh's comment about how good it would look longer. *Wish you could see it now, lass.*

"RJ, there's something I think you should know." Liam shifted uncomfortably on the swing. His sister deserved to know this, but he wasn't quite sure how she would take it. RJ was never one to appreciate meddling. "While you gone with Leigh, Mother tried to get the council to allow you to go permanently. So you could be together."

A single dark eyebrow shot upward.

"Her request was turned down."

RJ stared at her brother, her disbelief clear. "Really?" She blinked stupidly. "I thought Mother didn't care for Leigh."

Liam smiled sadly. "She wanted what she's always wanted, for you to be happy."

RJ sighed. "You know, brother, I'm starting to believe that I was never meant to be truly happy."

"Shut up, Rooster," Leigh said in warning. The man had been calling for her over the CB every day for the last few weeks. She'd listened to other truckers report they'd seen what they thought was her truck, but they couldn't be sure, since her mother's nude body no longer graced the side.

"C'mon, Leigh. I know you're out there somewhere. For Christ's sake, pick up the radio."

Leigh glared at the radio evilly. She was tempted to just shut the damn thing off, but she found the thundering silence too oppressive to bear.

"Tom Cat, I—"

Leigh snatched up he receiver. "You asshole, Rooster. I told you never to call me that." Her irritation was clear.

"Ah...I knew you were still alive."

"Of course I'm still alive. Why wouldn't I be?" She rubbed

her eyes tiredly, intentionally not thinking about the haunting, dark circles that now seemed a permanent fixture on her face.

"Well, I heard you picked up another route along with the already impossible one you drive."

Leigh didn't answer.

"Plus, I haven't seen you at Rosie's in forever."

"So?"

There was a longer silence this time.

"So the guys are worried about you," Rooster finally said.

"Bull shit. The *guys* don't even know me. And neither do you."

"Leigh—"

"Drive your truck and leave me alone, Rooster."

Rooster sighed, and Leigh could hear the enormous man shifting in his seat. The flat tone to her voice worried him, but he wasn't about to piss her off any further. She'd come around eventually. "If that's how you want it."

"That's exactly how I want it."

"Okay, but if—"

Leigh slammed the receiver back into its holder and clicked the radio off. The small teddy bear that was hanging by a home-made noose from her rear view mirror caught her attention, and for several moments she stared at it, her face a stone mask. Then she punched it and watched in satisfaction as it banged back and forth several times between her windshield and the roof. "I don't need you." Without warning, she felt tears sting her eyes for the first time in weeks. She would have sworn she was all cried out. "I don't need anybody," she whispered harshly as she punched the gas.

Three hours later, the road was blurring so badly she couldn't see it. Angry at her body's relentless demands, she jerked the wheel to the left and pulled off the road onto a wide shoulder. Fully dressed, she flopped gracelessly down on the small bed. After a brief war with herself, she reached out a hand slowly and rooted around in a pile of new towels she'd purchased the day before to avoid having to do laundry. Quickly, she found what she was looking for—a well worn, small black teddy bear, the last bear that remained, save the one hanging from her rear view mirror.

The bear's coal black eyes stared back at her, and she lightly fingered the soft black fur that stuck out in all directions. RJ had pinned the pilot wings Lucy had given her on the stuffed toy's chest. As furious and heart-broken as Leigh was, she didn't have the heart to remove them. She pulled the bear to her breast and curled up into the fetal position, trying not to feel the dull ache in her chest or think about anything at all as she let the infrequent hum of the late night traffic lull her into a fitful sleep.

RJ let the beer bottle drop carelessly to the floor of the truck as she drove toward the diner. She wiped the sweat from her face, wondering why it was so damn hot. Her vision was unfocused, and her head was spinning just a little.

The ache had only gotten worse ever since she'd parted with Leigh. For her, there simply was no peace. She continued with her duties as guide to Glory and handyman to the diner, even setting aside a portion of her day to remain utterly sober. What more did they want from her? *They have no right to ask for more. Why can't they just leave me the hell alone?*

Pulling her truck around behind the garage, she killed the engine and pushed the door open, stumbling out of the truck and nearly falling on her face in the dirt. At the last moment, she managed to retain a tiny bit of her balance and pull herself up by the door handle. She stared at the truck, which still had its broken windows, then she slammed the door and staggered toward the garage.

As she leaned drunkenly on the garage door, it fell open, sending her sprawling to the floor at the feet of a very surprised Tony.

"RJ? Are you okay?" He dropped to the floor near his friend.

She shook her head. "N...no." She burst out laughing. "I'm not even close to okay."

The smell of stale beer was overwhelming, and as much as Tony loved the beverage, when the odor came out of someone else's mouth, it was just plain putrid. He tried not to gag as he placed his hands under her and began to tug her to her feet.

"I think you need some coffee. C'mon, let's go to the diner."

"Don't want to go to the diner. Came to finish fixing the roof."

"No way, man. Just no way. I'm not going to let you up on the roof like this. You could kill yourself."

RJ laughed so hard, she started to cough. "You don't get it, do you, boy? We're dead. I *already* went splat. And from a lot higher than this roof. Trust me: I won't die again. If I could find a way, I would."

Tony went a little pale. "Stop talking like that." He pulled her up, wrapping his arm around her waist. "Let's get you sobered up."

"You know how?"

The young man nodded grimly, thinking of his own childhood.

RJ slapped him on the back. "Good lad."

He maneuvered them to the door, pulling her toward the diner. Just as they made it to the back door, they turned toward a crashing sound to see RJ's pickup truck rolling down a slight incline, tearing out small trees and bushes as it went. In stunned silence their eyes tracked the truck as it rolled right into the pond.

RJ pulled away from Tony, swaying and laughing as the black truck slowly began sinking into the murky water. "Guess I forgot to set the brake," she slurred before her eyes rolled back in her head and she passed out, falling face first to the ground.

Leigh switched off her ignition and stared at the diner. She knew it was a bad idea, coming back here, but she had no place else to go.

She yanked the hanging bear from her mirror and exited the truck. The sunset cast its orange and red rays across the plains, painting them in rich color. Leigh pulled off her sunglasses and drew in a deep breath of the fragrant late-summer air. Then she waited, knowing she was bound to see her soon. She swallowed nervously when the woman appeared out the front door of the diner and lit a cigarette. Leigh closed her eyes and steeled her resolve. With a negligent hand, she tossed the bear into the ditch alongside the parking lot. It was time to do something, and Leigh marched determinedly toward the front door.

"Leigh?" She quirked an eyebrow. "I didn't think I'd see you back here."

Leigh ducked her head. "Hello, Judith," she said quietly.

Judith took a step closer to her former lover, cringing visibly at Leigh's appearance. "Jesus Christ. What have you done to yourself?" She laid a comforting hand on Leigh's shoulder. "Have you given up sleep and food completely?" Her fingertips brushed across Leigh's arm. "You're all skin and bones."

Leigh sighed and closed her eyes at the comforting touch. "I'm okay," she assured softly.

"I can see that." But Judith's sarcasm held no real malice.

Leigh shook her head. "It's been a long time."

"Three months." Judith paused. "You're not really okay, are you?"

Leigh looked up with painfully honest eyes. "No," she admitted. "I guess I'm not."

"C'mere, honey." Judith opened her arms to her friend, and Leigh gratefully stepped into them.

Chapter
14

Judith climbed into bed alongside Leigh, who was curled up, facing away from her, wearing only an old t-shirt and her panties.

The bedroom was dark and quiet and held a note of familiarity that Leigh found soothing. Maybe here she'd find the restful sleep that had eluded her for so many weeks.

Judith kissed the back of Leigh's neck tenderly.

The blonde stiffened slightly in reaction, but didn't move to stop her.

"I like your hair like this." Leigh had cut it short the month prior. "It gives me easier access to your neck."

"Uh...thanks. It was...it was bothering me before, I guess."

"You can relax, Leigh," Judith whispered, spooning her body to Leigh's. She drew her hand down the soft skin of Leigh's thigh, her body easily remembering the many nights of unabashed pleasure they'd shared. She was hard pressed not to moan out loud. "I've missed you...missed this."

Leigh didn't know what to say. She closed her eyes when Judith's touch drifted across her belly and pushed up her shirt. She hesitated for a split second, then shifted slightly so her shirt could be pulled over her head. Leigh gasped a little when Judith's warm hands replaced the cotton and continued their lazy stroking.

"I'm not going to hurt you."

Leigh swallowed. "I know." But her taut muscles contradicted her words. With a light groan, Leigh turned over onto her back, allowing the sheet to pool around her waist.

Judith leaned forward and kissed Leigh lightly on the lips. The kiss was hesitantly returned and she deepened it, the taste of Leigh's mouth ringing familiar chords within her. But something felt different. She pulled back, nipping Leigh's lower lip as she moved away. Leigh's eyes met hers and, in an instant, a bone-deep understanding flashed between them.

Judith sighed. Her luck was never going to change when it came to this particular trucker. Leigh would never be hers, and Judith knew it. For a moment she gave serious consideration to kicking Leigh out of her bed, and life, for good. But this time, Judith didn't want to be left with nothing; she would live with just being friends. Beneath Tom Cat's persona was a woman she genuinely liked and wanted to get to know better. Tonight there were very specific parts of Leigh she wanted to get to know better. "Wanna tell me about it?"

"Tell you about what?"

"Don't screw with me, Leigh. I'm horny as hell, and that's just one step from homicidal. So I repeat, wanna tell me about it?"

Leigh sighed. "No."

"Liar."

Despite herself, Leigh chuckled. "How'd you get so smart all of a sudden?"

"All of a sudden?" Judith laid her head on her shoulder.

"Smartass."

Judith took Leigh's hands in hers, idly examining her fingers in the near darkness. "So tell me about the woman that finally broke your heart."

Leigh's pale blue eyes widened. "Damn. Could you always read minds, too?"

"Of course. I'm a fabulous catch. You were always just too busy leaving me to notice."

Judith felt Leigh draw in a deep breath, as it moved her body right along with it.

"Jesus, Judith. I'm so sorry," Leigh said honestly, her voice barely audible.

"Me, too. So talk." Judith's arms tightened around Leigh as the blonde began her story with that first night she'd accidentally stumbled upon a diner in the mist.

They talked until the moon hung low in the sky.

"Wow," was all Judith could think to say. Leigh had long since rolled over on her side, and the waitress hugged her tightly to her. She sniffed back her own tears. "That's the most horrible story I've ever heard."

Leigh nodded, the large lump in her throat making further speech impossible.

"When are you going back to her?" Judith asked, her warm breath tickling the back of Leigh's neck.

Leigh rolled her eyes. She hadn't made her final decision until that very moment. Judith knew her far too well. "Tomorrow."

"I can't believe I'm saying this, but, good luck."

Leigh took Judith's hand in hers and squeezed it gently. "Thank you."

The first rays of the morning sun and Leigh's nearly incoherent mumble finally broke the dark, silent moments that had stretched out between them. "Judith?"

Judith blinked dazedly. "Hmm?"

"Sometimes love..." A long pause. "Som...sometimes love...it fucking sucks."

Judith rolled her eyes, then gazed fondly at her already slumbering friend. She sighed. "Tell me about it, Leigh."

RJ stood back and appraised her truck. She sighed and shook her head when a large glop of mud fell off the mangled bumper. After she had sobered up, she, Liam, and Patrick had managed to tow it out of the pond. It was then that RJ realized that things had to change.

"It's not that bad." Patrick tried to sound optimistic as he peered into the water-damaged interior. He opened the door and a surge of water poured over his shoes. A hapless fish flopped out and dropped dead on his toe. "Eww." He kicked it away.

"Yeah. Yeah. It's going to take a long time to fix her back up." RJ dropped down onto the grass and pulled her cigarettes from her pocket. "I'm not sure I even want to."

"You have to. She was one of the sweetest trucks in Glory." Patrick joined his sister, taking one of her smokes for himself.

"*Was* being the operative word," RJ said glumly.

"What do you want, RJ?"

"I want Leigh."

"That's not what I meant."

RJ closed her eyes and leaned back, using her hand to brace her. "I know."

Patrick lit his own cigarette and turned his head to blow out the smoke. "It's bad to want something you can't have."

RJ exhaled calmly. "And Confucius say, kiss my arse! Since when are my brothers philosophers and head shrinkers? I'll go to Pete if I want a bunch of annoying advice."

Patrick furrowed his brow. "Confucius?"

RJ dropped onto her back, moaning. "Mary, sweet Mother of Jesus, please help me not to drown my brother in that lovely pond." She gestured over her shoulder.

"Hey," Patrick protested, "you brought it up."

RJ shook her head. "That I did." Her eyes took on a determined glint. "Besides, I'm not so sure I can't have what I want." She crossed her legs at the ankles. "I'm going to ask to leave Glory."

Patrick and Liam's jaws both dropped. "You're joking, right? You know Mother already tried—"

She waved him off. "That was Mother," her voice dropped to its lowest register, "not me. *I'm* going to ask." She plucked her cigarette from her lips and held it between two fingers. "I'm not happy here anymore, Patrick." Her eyes went a little unfocused. "I'm not sure I ever really was. My time with Leigh made me understand what I've been. There's no going back now. Not for me."

"RJ—"

"I know it sounds strange, but I really think that we were *meant* to be together. I'm going to find a way to make it happen."

The two men exchanged knowing looks. "You're going to get your heart broken all over again. What if you're told no again?"

"I won't be told no. I love her, and I'll follow her to the ends of the earth if I must." Her voice was growing stronger and more confident with every word. "I'm going to get out of Glory. I'm going to find her, drop to my knees and beg her forgiveness, and, God willing, I'm going to spend the rest of my days with her."

Patrick regarded his sister carefully for a moment. She'd

always had an eye for the ladies, but this was obviously different. "It's true love, is it." It wasn't a question.

"Absolutely." She nodded. "I've spent the last few months
trying to forget, and trying to convince myself otherwise, but it
can't be done. I've tried to play by the rules and forget what I
shouldn't crave. But I can't. She has my heart, boys. And it's
time she knew that."

"Then I wish you all the luck in the world," Patrick said
seriously.

"You're going to need it," Liam warned.

Patrick flicked his cigarette at his brother. "Be quiet, shit
for brains. She's made up her mind. Have you ever known her
not to eventually get her way once that's happened?"

Liam happily picked up the cigarette and took a long drag.
"No," he admitted finally. "I guess I haven't."

Patrick looked smug. "If she means that much to RJ, then
they should be together."

"And we will be," RJ said firmly. "We will."

The rain came down in steady, endless sheets as Leigh's
truck sped toward Fitz's diner. The rhythmic swaying of the
windshield wipers was only making it harder for Leigh to stay
awake.

After a few hours of the most restful sleep she'd had in
months, Leigh had kissed Judith on her cheek and said her good-
byes. Properly, this time. She'd said she'd stop by again some-
time, for a burger and some conversation. And Judith had
nodded; though in her heart she didn't think she'd be seeing this
particular woman again, she had long ago learned to never say
never.

That morning seemed far away to Leigh as she slowed her
rig for a slow-moving car. She felt drained, but hopeful. Hopeful that she could talk RJ into giving them another chance, hopeful that her destiny was in her own hands and not someone
else's.

Leigh had replayed their last moments together endlessly
since she'd driven away from the diner. At first, she couldn't
see beyond her own anger and pain. But last night, as she told
Judith what had happened, for the first time she could look
beyond her own emotions and focus on RJ. Not only on the

words that had broken her heart, but on the taller woman's face. On her eyes. On the slight quiver of her chin, and the way she ducked her head as she spoke. These were all clues that helped her wade through her confusion and resentment. She hadn't read RJ wrong. The woman was in love with her. Leigh could see it in those soulful green eyes, feel it whenever they touched. Now all she had to do was make RJ see it, too. Nothing was going to stop her.

In her lap sat the small black bear. She lifted it to her lips and kissed it softly as her eyes grew impossibly heavy. *The turnoff for the diner and Glory are around here somewhere.* She yawned. *I know it.* Her thoughts began to drift to RJ and finding her. And her eyelids fluttered shut.

Then she was floating and dreaming.

Leigh trudged up a small hill, running her palms along the tops of the tall, wet grass as she walked. The sun was shining and a cool breeze gently washed over her. Every step was hard, but she knew down deep inside that if she could just make it over the hill...

At the top, she shielded her eyes from the sun with the back of her hand and peered down the other side. It was the edge of a town, quaint and clean. "Glory," she said excitedly. "It has to be."

In a far-off way, she realized she was dreaming, that none of this was real. But she didn't care. It simply didn't matter as she ran as fast as she could down the long, gradually flattening terrain, teddy bear clutched tightly in her hand. The air smelled like summer blossoms, and the wind was at her back, pushing her toward her destination.

Finally, panting, she stepped onto the damp sidewalk and slowed her pace. Spinning in a circle she looked around at the neat rows of houses and lush trees that lined both sides of the street. She could hear the faint music of an ice cream truck and the sound of children laughing, and Leigh laughed. *It's a Stepford town*, she thought wryly, deciding instantly that she really didn't mind.

A tiny weathered-looking woman approached her, shuffling along in the opposite direction. "Well," Mrs. Amos stopped and smiled at Leigh, "it's about time you got here."

Leigh blinked. "What do you—"

"Never mind, dear." Mrs. Amos patted her arm gently. "You're here now, and that's all that matters."

Leigh shook her head a little. "Is...is this Glory?"

"Of course. And we had all our potholes filled last spring," she finished proudly. In her estimation it never hurt to show off that little fact.

Leigh stared at the woman. "Uh...okay. Glad to hear it. By any chance, you don't know a—"

"She'll be in the park about now. I'm certain." Mrs. Amos extended her arm and pointed a gnarled finger in the direction Leigh had been heading. "It's in the very center of town. You can't miss it. There's a lovely fountain right in the middle." She gave Leigh a little shove. "Go on now. I can't stand the thought of her moping another second. It's only a block or so away."

Leigh grinned and took off running. When she rounded the corner, she could see RJ and Pete sitting on a shaded bench, talking. She froze, suddenly unsure of what she was going to say. Thankfully, she was spared too long to worry over it, because as soon as she came into view, RJ's head snapped up and their eyes locked. RJ shot to her feet, and she could see her gesture wildly and say something nasty to Pete, who flinched.

"Okay." Leigh licked her lips nervously. "Now or never." As fast as her feet would carry her, she closed the remaining distance between them.

RJ opened her arms and Leigh flew into them, her impact knocking the taller woman back onto the damp grass. Each woman's lips frantically sought the other's, and they kissed deeply.

"Leigh," RJ breathed, backing away just enough to kiss the trucker's chin and cheeks. "What are you doing here, lass? God, you can't be here." She was shaking. "You can't."

Leigh kissed her again. "I am here. And I'm not going anywhere." The bear fell forgotten on the soft grass alongside RJ, and Leigh pinned the larger woman with strong arms. "Get used to it, RJ. You're stuck with me."

RJ shook her head wildly. "Dammit. No!" She pried Leigh's hands from her shirt and jumped to her feet to square off against Pete, who was trying his best to blend in with the background. "What the hell is this, Pete? She does not belong here." The words were nearly spat, and Pete couldn't help but back off a step.

"I belong with you," Leigh protested.

RJ grabbed Leigh's shoulders and gave them a desperate shake. "You don't understand. You don't know what you're saying."

Leigh's eyes flashed. "I do know."

"RJ," Pete held both hands up in surrender, "she does belong here. She's right. You're meant to be together."

RJ advanced a step, her eyes daring Pete to retreat another inch. "Not like this. She's got a lifetime to live. No, Peter. You can undo this. You fix this!" she shouted.

Leigh's head was snapping back and forth between them. *Why should Pete care one way or the other?*

"There's nothing to fix," Pete said firmly.

RJ closed her eyes and tilted her head back as she growled in frustration.

Leigh's gentle touch on her face drew her attention downward. "I don't understand," she said honestly. "I know you love me. Why won't you let us be together?"

RJ's heart clenched at the words. "You don't truly understand, Leigh. Or you wouldn't be here."

"But I want us to be together." Leigh stamped her foot furiously. "Why is that so hard to understand?"

RJ pulled her close. "You have to go back."

"She can't," Pete interrupted. His eyes softened as he spoke to his old friend. Flea, who had been watching the scene from her lounging spot under the large oak tree, jumped up onto Peter's shoulder and rubbed her face against his cheek. "She's been on the road to Glory for a while now, Fitz." He spread his hands out in entreaty. "Now is the right time, for you both. Accept it."

"I won't!"

"You don't have a choice."

RJ shot Pete an evil look and focused her attention on Leigh. "Lass, you need to listen to me, and listen good." She cupped her cheek, stroking Leigh's cheekbones with her thumbs. She looked tired and thin, and RJ ached for the pain they'd both already endured. "You can't be with me here. You'd have to give up too much."

"I'll give up anything," came the immediate answer.

"Your friends? Your job? Your whole life?"

"Yes." Her voice was resolute.

"You can't. We cannot be together." RJ felt tears well up in her eyes. "Not in this place. Not now."

Leigh's face showed all the bewilderment of a confused child. "But why?"

RJ pressed two fingers against Leigh's lips to quiet her. "Because it's not your time. This place is beyond the life you know. Beyond everything you know."

"I can do Mayberry," Leigh protested.

"Why does everyone keep calling it that?" Pete whispered to Flea.

The cat meowed grumpily.

RJ let out a frustrated breath, but when she opened her mouth to speak, it was Pete's stern words that broke the silence. "Ask her, RJ."

"Damn you, Peter. Don't you say that! I don't have to do that yet. She's not ready."

Pete smiled sadly. Why did Fitz always have to be such a pain in the ass? "Ask her," he repeated patiently.

"You don't need to ask me anything," Leigh broke in. "I need to stay here. I need to be with you. I don't have a life on the road. I want *you* to be my family. Families should be together."

Hot tears spilled down RJ's cheeks, and Leigh reached up and tenderly wiped them away. She bent over and retrieved the bear, pressing it into RJ's hands. "You're my heart's desire, RJ. I love you, and we were meant to be together. No matter what."

The words were still hanging when Leigh gasped and clutched her chest. Her legs felt wobbly, and it suddenly seemed as though she couldn't breathe.

RJ wrapped long arms tightly around Leigh, and the younger woman buried her face against RJ's chest.

"Hang on, lass." She squeezed Leigh as close to her as she could, melding their bodies together and feeling Leigh's pounding heartbeat begin to fade...

"C'mon! Hurry."

"Done." The fireman lifted his welder's mask as he moved out of the way and a young paramedic scooted around him, dropping herself into Leigh's partially crushed cab. The rain cooled his sweaty skin, and after a moment he called down to the woman, "Is she alive?" He glanced past the milling fire, police, and ambulance crew at the highway.

"Barely."

Tossing his wet mask aside, he peered down past the deflated airbag and the twisted pieces of metal. He spoke conversationally as the paramedic worked frantically. There was only room for one in the cab with Leigh, so there was nothing else he could do. "No skid marks. She didn't touch the brakes. Booze, do you think?"

"Doubtful," the woman answered as she fumbled for a chest tube in her bag. "Last trucker like this I worked on had me sitting on a mountain of beer cans in his cab. Nothing like that here. She probably just fell asleep."

"Little thing for such a big rig." He squinted and imagined her face without the blood. "Young, and pretty, too." He shook his head. "Damn shame." There was no answer, but he didn't take offense. The paramedic was focusing on her patient.

"Shit. She's coding." The woman reached around the mangled steering wheel and pressed harder into Leigh's throat, trying to find a pulse. "We've got to get her out of here now!"

Two other men joined the fireman at her words. "Paddles?"

"I can't." She tossed her bag straight up, and it was plucked out the air by one of the waiting fireman. "Can't get the right angle. Now, Steve." Her voice had a renewed urgency. "Or it's not going to matter."

"That's it." RJ continued to hang onto Leigh, supporting nearly all of her weight. "It's almost over, love."

Leigh suddenly gasped. Her eyes popped open as cool, clean air tinged with the scent of her lover's skin filled her senses and the pressure on her chest began to ease. "RJ?" she questioned weakly, trying to put some weight back on her own two feet.

"I'm here. Relax against me." A small smile touched her lips when Leigh instantly did just that.

"What—" She paused and swallowed, slowly pushing away from RJ's protective arms. Leigh looked around with wide eyes. "What happened?" Her senses all seemed intensified, and she could feel the breeze caress the downy hair that covered her skin. Then she glanced up into eyes that had always called to her, and fell all over again into their endless affection and warm devotion.

RJ thought for a moment about how to explain, and then decided to simply be blunt. If ever there was a woman who appreciated blunt, it was Leigh Matthews. "You died."

Leigh's eyes widened and her mouth formed a tiny "O."

RJ reached out to steady her, but she didn't falter.

Finally, Leigh muttered, "Wow!"

Leigh ran a hand through her hair. "Oh, man. Oh, man. Are you sure I'm not just insane? I'm not going to wake up hungover someplace?"

"No, darlin'. You're really here." RJ's gaze slid sideways to Pete. She saw the question in his eyes and nodded quietly. It wasn't what she wanted for Leigh, but there was no way on earth or in heaven that she was going to give her back now.

Pete smiled and reached up to pet Flea, grateful that he wasn't going to have to find a new place to live. RJ was not the sort of person you wanted pissed off at you for an eternity.

The pilot let Leigh have a moment to at least scratch the surface of a process that would take a while, knowing she'd have a million and one questions, but hoping to convey the most important stuff first. She had half-expected Leigh to freak out. That hadn't exactly happened yet, and somehow, RJ found that infinitely scarier. "Are you all right?"

"I...um..." Leigh took stock of her body. She felt lighter and stronger than ever, though a quick look at her body confirmed that she now had regained the weight she'd lost over the past three months. A bird flew overhead, and his call sounded sweet and pristine. It was as though she had been viewing the world through a light fog, and now the fog was simply gone. Every last bit of her, at least physically, felt fabulous. "Yeah. I don't know how that's possible." She pinched herself. "Ouch."

RJ laughed. Everyone did that.

"I feel great," Leigh said in amazement. She reached out and laid her palms against RJ's chest. She felt a heartbeat and the chest's steady rise and fall. Then she removed one hand and placed it against her own chest and frowned. "My heart is beating? But I'm still dead?"

"Yes. And you eat and sleep and do all those things you did before. Only you're not quite so ruled by your physical self. I'll explain it all."

"And you're dead, too?"

RJ nodded and let out a slow breath. "For sixty years now.

Though I was allowed a second chance at life with you when we went our trip. When you dropped me back at the diner, our time together was finished, Leigh. I swear, I didn't want to leave you, but I had no choice."

Leigh put her hands on her hips. "So that's why you dumped me like yesterday's trash? Because you were some sort of ghost?"

"I am no such thing." RJ looked aghast. "And just remember, whatever it is I am, you are too." Her face went serious. "I did what I thought would give you a life, Leigh. Because I love you, and for no other reason."

Leigh's eyes narrowed. She reached out and grabbed a handful of RJ's shirt, pulling them nose to nose. "We've got a lot to talk about; but this very second, there is only question I have."

"Yes?" RJ asked reluctantly.

"Are we in this..." she gestured broadly, "whatever you call it—life, or next life—together?"

"Forever."

"Promise?"

"That's two questions."

"Shut up."

"Gladly." RJ pulled Leigh into a crushing embrace and occupied her mouth with something far more pleasurable than talking.

Leigh moaned her approval at RJ's choice, and hoped it was one her lover would make for lifetimes to come.

Pete sighed. It wasn't unmanly to shed a tear for true love, was it?

Flea jumped off his shoulder, and they both began strolling toward Pete's car. Over their shoulders, they heard Leigh exclaim delightedly, "I knew I could never love anyone who owned a piece of shit!"

Pete laughed. "I guess she finally got a glimpse of RJ's truck in all its glory. Thank goodness RJ and her brothers spent all those nights working on it."

Flea padded along quietly, ignoring Pete and already thinking ahead to the next glorious time she could finagle two more squirrels into Glory.

"Maybe we should change the name." Pete opened the door and Flea jumped in, taking her customary spot on the dashboard.

She looked at Pete.

The big man rolled his eyes. "But everyone already calls it Mayberry. Why fight it? And no, I will not submit the request to you in triplicate. I don't care what you say."

Flea licked her paw with an air of boredom and superiority that could only be possessed by a cat.

"Fine," Pete huffed. "But don't blame me if you drown under a mound of paper work."

Flea closed her eyes for a short nap. They were serving liver at the diner tonight, and she wanted to be rested and ready when it came time to chow down. She had her priorities.

"And another thing..."

If Pete didn't stop droning on and on and on, Flea was going to be forced to do something drastic. The last time that had happened, the world had ended up with the platypus. And that was *before* she'd really gotten creative and learned what antifreeze could do.

"So this is your brilliant plan?"

"We're not currently being digested by Flea, are we?"

"No," the male groused. "I suppose not."

The male and female squirrels scampered across the hot roof of the garage that sat next to Fitz's diner, heading for the forgotten hammer they'd seen from their nest. "The human female should really be more careful. Leaving a heavy object on a slanted roof could be dangerous."

"For our sake, you'd better hope so." The female plopped herself down next to the hammer, breathing heavily. "Okay, do I need to repeat myself?"

"No. I started paying attention after the fourth time you went over your instructions." He puffed out his chest. "I can handle this. No problem."

The female's blood went cold at his words.

"Really," he insisted.

"Uh huh."

"Really!"

"Fine." She moved away from the hammer. "Hang your head over the edge, and see if she's still sleeping down there."

Her mate peered warily over the edge of the tall roof. "Yup. The fat cat is lying there, sound asleep." He laughed gleefully. She was about to meet her maker.

The female shrugged. "So, push the hammer over the edge and squish her."

"It's a brilliant plan."

She beamed. "I know." *I knew there was a reason I married him.*

The male spit on his hands and began to push.

The hammer didn't move.

He gave it a withering glare and then threw his scrawny back into it, grunting loudly. "I..." Grunt. "Can't...move..." Grunt. Grunt. "Move it."

"I can see that."

He stood up, sweat pouring off his furry brow. "Help me! I need your bulk."

"Ooooo, that sounds so sexy."

He winked charmingly. "Later. After the felinocide."

The female began to push on the hammer along with her mate and, little by little, the heavy tool moved closer to the edge. Where it stopped.

The male burst into tears. "Why can't any of our plans succeed? It's not fair."

The female uncharacteristically joined her mate and burst into tears, too. *How much could one rodent be expected to handle?* "I don't know!" she sobbed. "But let's try one more time."

They both began to push with all their might, and magically, somehow, the hammer began to move. Unfortunately, so did Flea. At the last second, the female tried to stop the hammer and change its trajectory. But she lost her balance and stood helplessly, teetering on the very edge of the roof.

"Help! Help!"

For a long moment, her mate was paralyzed by fear. Okay, he was really deciding whether or not to give her a good shove. But figuring that it wouldn't get rid of her permanently, he decided to save her. Sadly, he tripped along the way. The male fell straight forward and slammed into his mate, sending them both off of the roof and careening toward the ground at frightening speed.

"AHH!" the tangled Ball O'Squirrel screamed.

"AHH!" RJ sat bolt upright in bed, sweat dripping liberally from her face and neck. Panting and wide-eyed, she flicked her gaze around the shadow-filled bedroom.

Leigh threw her hand across RJ's lap. "Go back to sleep," she slurred tiredly, never bothering to open her eyes.

"I can't." Her chest was heaving. "God, I...it was the most fantastic dream."

"That's nice," Leigh answered into her pillow.

"You were in it, but your eyes were the wrong color, and your hair was a little different, and you were a truck driver with a naked woman on the side of your truck." RJ looked down at her naked lover. "She was hot, by the way."

Leigh only grunted.

"And I was a handyman in heaven or some other screwed up place where you go when you die." She made a face. That part had never been very clear. How pathetic. "And the squirrels from the park, the ones who spy on us, they were there, too."

Leigh lifted her head tiredly. Her hair was plastered to the side of her face, and she opened one eye to stare at RJ. "I told you to stop going to that park and talking to them. It's creepy. Okay, no more spicy burritos before bed for you."

"It is not the burritos."

A pale eyebrow lifted.

"Okay, maybe it is. But I swear they're talking about us. I just know it."

Leigh's head flopped back down. "They're rodents, RJ. They can't talk."

"That's what you think."

"Yes," Leigh pushed herself up again and kissed RJ gently on the lips, smiling at the sweet contact. "That's what I think. I also think that I'm going back to sleep, and that you should, too." She sighed. *Definitely, no more burritos before bed for her.*

RJ looked annoyed, but didn't have a real reason to argue. It was the middle of the night. "Okay. Good night," she paused, then added, "Tom Cat."

Leigh's forehead wrinkled as she tried half-heartedly to make sense of RJ's words. Finally she just mumbled sleepily, "I don't know why you're calling me that." She yawned. "But I don't like it."

RJ straightened their covers and glared at the fat, black cat with golden eyes that was lying at the foot of their bed. She sneered. "I hate you."

The cat purred happily.

"I don't care if Leigh did run you down with that god awful Jeep of hers," she grumbled petulantly. "You're going to the pound tomorrow."

"Stop lying to the cat," Leigh interrupted unexpectedly. "She knows it was you that hit her, not me. And she's staying until she's healed. Go to sleep."

"Fine." RJ lay back down and pulled the sheet up to her neck. She glared at the feline. "Stop mocking me!"

"RJ," Leigh warned.

"Okay. Okay. If she has to stay, at least we can give her a name."

"I already did that this afternoon while you were calling all the shelters and cursing them out for not taking injured cats."

"Well, what is it?"

Leigh rolled over and fluffed her pillow before closing her eyes again and groaning inwardly. She had to work the next morning. "Flea."

"AHH!!"

Unseen in the darkness, Flea just grinned.

Be sure to read these other RAP books by
Blayne Cooper and T. Novan:

Madam President

By Blayne Cooper and T. Novan

It's the year 2020 and history has been made by Devlyn Marlowe—the first woman to win the U.S. Presidency. When it comes time to select a biographer to chronicle her historic term in office, Devlyn breaks with tradition and choses a writer based on very personal reasons. She wants Lauren Strayer, a young author whose writing has always captivated her. There's only one problem—Lauren isn't interested in the job.

Despite Lauren's reservations, the persuasive Commander-in-Chief is able to sway the author's opinion with the promise of true editorial freedom—a biographer's dream come true. Realizing that the opportunity of a lifetime awaits her, Lauren reluctantly accepts the position and soon finds herself residing at 1600 Pennsylvania Avenue alongside the First Family.

Caught up in the frenzy of life at the White House, Lauren begins to unravel the complex woman that is the President and finds herself more intrigued by Devlyn with each passing day.

Painfully realistic at times, funny, romantic, and endearing, Madam President is a drama set against one of the most dynamic backdrops imaginable and follows two lives destined to be entwined.

ISBN: 1-930928-69-6

Available at booksellers everywhere.

Words Heard In Silence

By T. Novan and Taylor Rickard

In 1864, as the Civil War ground to an end, the people of Virginia were tired and worn down by the battles that had raged across their homes. Slowly, inexorably, the Union Army was enclosing the dwindling Confederate forces. Richmond and Petersburg lay under siege as Union troops settled into winter quarters throughout the state. The 13th Pennsylvania Cavalry, led by Colonel Charles Redmond, chose Gaines Cove, a once lovely horse farm outside of Culpeper Virginia, owned by the widow Rebecca Gaines.

Rebecca finds herself intrigued by this man who had seen so much violence and somehow retained his gentle soul. Yet, it is treason to the South and a discredit to her dead husband's memory that Rebecca should find an officer of the enemy attractive. Charlie is faced with his own problems, not the least of which is a deadly secret that, if discovered, would result in his being expelled from the Army. For Charlie was one of that handful of women who disguised their gender and served with honor and distinction on both sides of the war.

As the winter months pass, and Charlie and Rebecca come to know one another, a tender love grows between them. Against a backdrop of shattered refugees, displaced children, fearsome battles and the terrible tolls of war, they embark on a journey of discovery. They finally hear the words the other is speaking, words of discovery, love, and commitment that fall into the silence of their hearts and bring new hope and a future to both.

Available Winter 2003

Cobb Island

By Blayne Cooper

Cobb Island offers not one but three romances in this novel set off the coast of Virginia. Marcy and Doug have had only sporadic contact since Marcy's family moved away a year ago. Their older sisters agree to supervise the lovesick teens during a week-long stay in an eerie island house that has been in Marcy's family since the late 1600s. But who will chaperone the chaperones? Sparks fly between them almost from the beginning, growing into lightning-size bolts when Liv notices that Kayla is answering her questions before she has even voiced them. It is Liv's training in translating foreign languages, however that proves to be the key that unlocks the house's secret history—and the story of a tragic love begun and ended four centuries earlier.

Available Summer 2002

Echoes From the Mist

By Blayne Cooper

In this sequel to *Cobb Island*, paranormal researchers Kayla Redding and Olivia Hazelwood begin their professional and personal partnership as they tackle their first case together in the world's most haunted city—Edinburgh, Scotland. While in Edinburgh, the women visit the Cobb family ancestral home. The Cobb family historian takes the women on a journey back through time to 17th Century Colonial Virginia. He weaves the tale of Faylinn Cobb, explaining what happened to her and her family after her sister-in-law, Bridget Redding, was branded a witch.

Available Fall 2002.

Don't miss this exciting story - the first in a trilogy - from

Silver Dragon Books

The Claiming of Ford
By T. Novan

This piece is set in and unknown future of an alien world. The story follows Garron Ford Kurrathian as she deals with the military, political, religious and personal aspects of her role in her own society. With her on this journey, is a slave named Marra, who will be an important factor in all of the decisions Ford makes after she takes possession of the slave.

Together, they will bring about changes in the world that might just destroy it.

Royalty proceeds from the sale of The Claiming of Ford *series will go to the STARSHIP Foundation.*

Available at booksellers everywhere.
ISBN: 1-930928-63-7

Also Available
By Blayne Cooper

The Story of Me
(written under the pen name Advocate)

If you enjoyed the mad-cap antics of male and female squirrel in *The Road to Glory* then you'll want to read the crazy romantic-comedy that introduced the characters and started it all.

In *The Story of Me* Randi is just trying to make sense of it all as she sits in the park, pouring out her woes to a pair of squirrels. The first thing she determines is that she sucks at thinking up snappy titles. Hence, the prosaic name for this classic farce that is described as a free fall into insanity. In truth, it would be hard to find something better to call this screwball comedy, featuring the misadventures of a tall, dark driving instructor and the blonde nurse who is stalking her. Mac is intent on drawing Randi into a madcap plot to exact revenge upon a common enemy; the two-timing wench who dumped Mac for her brother, the doctor—and who, years earlier, deprived Randi of academic fame and a college scholarship. The ill-conceived plan takes them across America to Las Vegas. It's a 'road trip from Hell' that features a wild array of occurrences, ranging from mere mishap to outright disaster. Inexorably—delightfully—the women slide into an endearing, nutty relationship that was simply meant to be.

ISBN 059513744X

Other Books from
RAP

Darkness Before the Dawn
By Belle Reilly
ISBN 1-930928-06-8

Chasing Shadows
By C. Paradee
ISBN 0-9674196-8-9

Forces of Evil
By Trish Kocialski
ISBN 1-930928-07-6

Out of Darkness
By Mary D. Brooks
ISBN 1-930928-15-7

Glass Houses
By Ciarán Llachlan Leavitt
ISBN 1-930928-23-8

Storm Front
By Belle Reilly
ISBN 1-930928-19-X

Retribution
By Susanne Beck
ISBN 1-930928-24-6

Coming Home
By Lois Cloarec Hart
ISBN 1-930928-50-5

Printed in the United States
3578

9 781930 928275